MALL PRIEST

THE SECOND COMING

Heinicke & Reedwood

Mall Priest 2 – The Second Coming

Cover Design by Kate Reedwood, KC Stories www.LegacyHunter.space
Manuscript Services—Swish Design and Editing https://www.swishgrafix.com.au/

'Mall Priest 2' has been created in conjunction with Alexander Reed and is based on an original story concept by him.

This book is a work of fiction. The characters and events portrayed in this book are fictitious. Any similarity to real persons, living or dead, is coincidental and not intended by the author.

Both authors and editor have taken great effort in presenting a manuscript free of errors. However, editing errors are ultimately the responsibility of the authors. This book is written in US English, therefore, includes US diction.

No AI generated text or imagery has been used in the creation of this book.

E-book ISBN: 978-1-998194-00-1

Paperback ISBN: 978-1-998194-01-8

www.LegacyHunter.space

To Grandpa, Eric Claude Crocker

July 22, 1923-November 27, 2022

Gone, but never forgotten.

~Chris

And to my grandmother, Ena Elizabeth Chesworth (nee Jones)

1908-1961

I never got to meet you, but I have always felt your love.

~Kate

Buried within the lines of this tome is the number 32
Brought to you by Peep the Cat going zoom, zoom
We left it in as her own artistic contribution
If you can find it, congrats to you!

remnant 1 of 2 noun

rem·nant *'rem-nənt*

1 a: a usually small part, member, or trace remaining
  b: a small surviving group —often used in plural

2: an unsold or unused end of piece goods

remnant 2 of 2 adjective

rem·nant *'rem-nənt*
: still remaining

Ashes to Ashes...

December 2, 1986

"Loose Vegas," Warren Betts slurred as he stumbled out the back door of the nightclub and spied the neon sign, glowing blood red against the darkness of the night. "Loose Vegas," he repeated, chuckling as if the pun had only just sunk in, which it had. Maybe it took several shots of tequila chased by several pints of beer for things like the club's name to become funny. If so, he was right on track for experiencing the most hilarious night of his life.

He staggered into the parking lot, assisted by a hefty shove from one of the club's bouncers.

"Don't think about coming back here again, asshole," the broad-shouldered man yelled, pointing a beefy finger at Warren.

"Is this how you treat a 'Nam Vet?" Warren waved off the bouncer and managed to remain upright as he stepped away from the doorway. "Fuck this place," he mumbled. And fuck those lousy ingrates. He'd fought against better dickwads than these jerks. Okay, so that had been a while ago now, but still. *Bah, who needed a club like this anyway?*

Hell, the girl hadn't even been all that hot. Having shelled out a couple of hundred dollars for a private room and a lap dance, you'd think he'd have the right to grab that pair of double Ds jiggling within inches of his face. But nope. These dicks were all about cheating their customers. The first offense had earned him a slap to the face from the stripper, the second had earned him a heave-ho out of the premises—after they'd tried to break his face.

He rubbed his jaw where the bouncer had hit him and winced. "That was stupid, Warren." He smacked his forehead with his palm and then wished he hadn't, as it failed to knock any sense into him but did make the ache in his jaw spread through his skull. *Shit. Time to go home.* He pushed away from the brick wall he was leaning against and glanced around. "Where's my car?"

Apart from the white Mercedes parked within a few yards of the club, the parking lot was empty. A single light high atop a lamppost illuminated the shadowy paved area. A rat, or some other critter, scurried from the shadows to his left, heading for the dumpster to go diving.

He spat on the ground after it. "Fucking disgusting."

Vermin. The city was filled with them. Big ones, small ones. Thieving, asshole, bar—

A high-pitched explosion pierced the air as the streetlamp popped and burned out in a shower of sparks, plunging the parking lot into complete darkness if not for the neon bar sign.

Warren jumped, nearly losing his footing. Damn. It was definitely time to get the hell out of there and find a way back to his hotel. He staggered away from the neon sign and into the darkness. The air smelled heavy and faintly acrid like it might rain. His car? Where was his car? *Fuck.* How much had he had to drink? He'd lost count of the money he'd spent at the bar. After winning big at the Bellagio casino by betting on number six, he'd wandered the street, letting chance take him where it wanted, which apparently had been the strip club.

The casino. That's right. He'd left his car at the casino.

Now, if he could just remember where that was.

He turned in a circle, looking for clues, but his bleary vision couldn't penetrate the darkness. Where was the sidewalk? Or the road? Or anything? He tripped on an uneven bit of pavement and staggered, arms outstretched to keep his balance. "*Goddamn motherfucker.*"

"I thought I told you to get the hell out of here," the bouncer yelled.

"I'm trying, man," Warren muttered. As he turned back to the club, he realized he hadn't moved more than a few yards. *Damn my drunken head.*

He rubbed his eyes as he studied the parking lot. How could a city that never sleeps become so dark and quiet? Maybe he should call a cab. There was a phone inside the bar, but if he went back in there, the bald-headed, brick wall of a bouncer would tear him in half.

The cool night air blew across the open pavement and caressed his skin. He shivered involuntarily as he placed one foot in front of the other. There had to be an alleyway that led to the front of the building and probably a phone booth by the street.

He kept walking, following the edge of the building in as straight a line as he could manage. *Just keep going. And going.* But as the parking lot seemed to continue endlessly in the darkness, he stopped and squinted. He should have reached the alley by now.

Something heavy thumped onto the ground behind him.

Warren froze. Was it the bouncer? Had he gone in circles? Struggling to keep his balance, he turned toward the sound. "Listen, man, how 'bout callin' me a cab—"

Nothing was there.

No bouncer.

No anything.

Just the dark shadow of the wall to his left and the even darker pavement beneath his feet. The dank night air seemed to swirl around him. Had a mist rolled in? Did that happen in Vegas?

Warren shook his head. Something wasn't right. The sort of something that made the hairs on his arms stand straight up and his heart race. Maybe someone had slipped cocaine into his drink. Was that even how it worked? And where the fuck had the strip club gone? He couldn't have walked so far that the neon sign wouldn't be visible.

Unless... there was something wrong with his eyes.

He rubbed them, trying to clear his vision.

I swear I'll never drink again.

He sensed rather than heard movement in the nearby darkness. *Probably just a rat.* "Hey! Is anyone there?" he called out, just in case someone was there. Another soul lost in the darkness.

His last word echoed several times before fading away. *Okay. That was weird.* He rubbed his arms, trying to keep warm as his shivers increased. The temperature seemed to be dropping by the minute, and without a flashlight, he could barely see a thing in any direction. *Gotta be fog.* But what the fuck? This was Vegas. He should be able to see lights and hear the sounds of traffic and people, even in a mist or fog.

Maybe he was dreaming. *Yeah, that's it. I fell asleep at one of the bars.* He'd spoken to several women earlier, none of whom were interested in him. But why should they be? He was overweight, balding, and in his forties, and he wasn't the only man in Vegas flashing wads of cash. That was why he frequented strip clubs. Figures he'd dream about forgetting the *look don't touch* policy like some kind of desperate perve.

A gust of wind swept through the lot, swirling the dank air about him. He pulled his cheap plaid shirt as tight as he could around him and continued walking in what he hoped was a steady direction. The thin fabric did little to shield him, however, and his shivers increased as the chill crept right into his bones. Even his teeth were chattering. What the hell was this? He'd read somewhere that the desert got cold at night, and Vegas was in a desert, wasn't it? But why the hell would he dream about being half-frozen and blind drunk in a bar parking lot? He wouldn't be surprised if a blizzard showed up at any second. *Fuck this dream. I need to wake up.* He closed his eyes and squeezed them tight, making his aching head hurt even more. *Wake up, dammit!*

Opening his eyes again, he glanced around. Everything was the same. The darkness, the cold air. "*Fuck,*" he shouted.

"Tut-tut. Language, Warren," a deep voice growled nearby.

"Who's there?" Warren staggered as he spun on his heel but couldn't see anyone within the endless darkness. *This guy knows my name.* Was he a friend? An enemy? "What do you want?"

Silence. He looked up. The moon shone bright against a clear, dark sky. A full moon. But then... that would mean the parking lot should be bathed in moonlight? So why could he see the sky but not the world around him? Something was definitely not right.

This wasn't a dream.

It was a nightmare.

"Whoever you are, I don't believe in werewolves."

"I don't give a shit."

Warren froze as every hair on his body bristled. He didn't recognize the voice, but it sounded as if it came from all around him. At any moment, Warren would be grabbed and mugged, or worse, he was sure of it. He should move, but which direction was safe?

"Run, you dumb fuck," the deep voice rasped by his ear.

Run, yes! Warren wanted to run, but his knees seemed to be locked, and all he could do was stand there, trembling.

"This is your last chance, soldier. *Run,*" the voice commanded with the barking authority of a squad sergeant.

The stink of rotting, sour breath got Warren moving. One step, two. His unsteady gait caused his feet to slide in a shallow puddle, threatening to send him tumbling to the unforgiving pavement. Regaining his balance, he continued trying his best to run, each footstep echoing loudly in the parking lot. *Damn me for not keeping up with working out.*

Who the hell was chasing him? And why? That deep voice didn't sound like the bouncer, and it couldn't be the stripper, whatever her name was, unless she had incredible voice-changing skills. A veteran from his 'Nam days at the bar to have some fun?

Sickness roiled inside his stomach as he pushed on, trying to gain distance from whoever was after him. Was he following? Was he laughing as Warren stumbled blindly in the darkness? He wheezed, trying to catch his breath as his lungs protested at the pace he'd set.

As his legs gave out and he stopped in his tracks, the contents of his stomach rose. He squeezed his eyes shut and leaned forward, placing his hands on his knees. Vomit sprayed the ground as he heaved up what felt like everything he'd consumed in the past twenty-four hours. It burned like acid and tasted worse. He coughed, gagging as he tried to breathe.

"Finished?" The man growled behind him.

Warren turned around and shook his head. Whatever the guy wanted, he was done with this game. He wiped at his lips and sucked in air, but there was no calming his racing pulse. "I can't do this."

"What if your life depends on it?"

"Well, I guess I'm fucked then." Out of breath and unable to run, what was he supposed to do? He didn't have a gun. He hadn't touched one since 'Nam, but thinking about the situation he was in now, maybe that was a mistake.

"Look up at me when I speak to you."

Warren raised his head. The rancid smell of rotting flesh filled his nostrils, making him want to vomit again. A hooded figure stood a few feet before him, its face hidden in shadow. "What is it you want?"

The figure laughed in a deep, raspy tone that sent a new shiver through Warren. "Want?" the man questioned after a few seconds. "No, it's what I need."

The cloaked figure took a long, calculated step forward, gloved hands clenched at his sides as he quickly closed the gap between them.

Warren took a hasty step back, accidentally stepping in the puddle of vomit he'd created. As his feet skidded out from under him, he landed hard on his backside. Pain shot through his spine and hip. He winced, realizing the chill he'd experienced earlier was gone. The shivers wracking him now were from pure, unbridled fear. "Please don't kill me," he whimpered.

A glow flashed from the cloaked figure's face in the area where his eyes should be. "Pathetic. And you call yourself a soldier?"

Warren shook his head as he inched further backward, a feeble attempt to build some distance between him and the dark being. "Not for a long time."

He wasn't one to believe in werewolves or vampires, but he knew demons existed. Not just the stories in the papers about what had happened at that mall last Christmas, he'd seen the worst kinds of demons in person on the battlefield in 'Nam. There were soldiers who did their duty because it was their job, and then there were those whose eyes lit up when they made the kill and looked for any reason to do it again. This guy had that feeling about him. He stalked his prey and enjoyed it—and tonight, Warren was his prey.

Despite all he'd been through during the war, for the first time in his life, Warren feared he might not make it out of this situation alive.

Using one hand to push himself along the pavement, he used the other to dig his wallet from his pants pocket. He'd spent a lot of money but must have some of the twenty grand left. "Here, take it all. I don't need it." He threw the wallet at the man's feet in a last-ditch attempt to plead for mercy.

"Money? You think money is what I need? Do I look like I need money? *Do you think I chased you because I need money?*"

Fuck this. Warren wasn't going to die without a fight, not now, not ever. Ignoring the puddle of vomit he sat in, he put his hands on the ground and pushed himself to his feet. Facing the dark figure, he raised his fists. He hadn't fought anyone in a long time, but now seemed a good time to start again. "Come on then, asshole, let's do this."

He took a swing at the figure and staggered forward as his fist passed through a shower of glowing embers that filled the space where the cloaked man had stood. Warren might have fallen forward at the unexpected absence before him, except for the arm that curled around his waist from behind and the hand that grabbed his throat.

"Scream for me," the dark voice commanded by his ear.

Pinned backward against the man, the scent of rotting flesh mixed with the unmistakable odor of burning plastic and gasoline filled Warren's nostrils. It was a combination of smells that had been imprinted on his memory more than a decade ago. *Napalm. He smells like death and napalm.*

Heat passed from the dark figure into Warren, wiping away any remaining trace of the night chill. The warmth built quickly, changing from comfortable to uncomfortable in seconds.

Warren struggled and tried to break his captor's hold, but the more he fought, the more the scent of napalm increased, as did the heat that seared his blood. "Please... let me go." His words came out little more than a wheeze.

"No, Warren," the figure chastised. "I want you to scream for me. Like I screamed for you once."

What? Who was this guy? He wanted to spin around and look his captor in the eyes, but the hand on his throat was slowly crushing his windpipe in a pincer grip and holding him tight.

The demon chuckled his deep raspy laugh. "If you don't scream, you'll never find out."

Shit, he can hear me even when I don't speak. God almighty, maybe he is a real demon.

"Really, Warren? And I always thought you were so smart." The pressure searing Warren's nerves increased. "Now give me what I want and *scream.*"

As his skin caught fire, Warren opened his mouth, and an ear-piercing shriek whistled through his crushed windpipe. He caught sight of the full moon as his head tipped back, but a red misty spray hazed the view. He fell to his knees, realizing the red mist was his own blood, which caught fire as it fell to the ground. He was burning. All of him. His clothes, his insides, his bones. The scent of singed hair filled his nostrils a second before they ceased to exist. But his eyes... his eyes still functioned, as did his ears and his mind, which shrieked from the pain and terror of the flames.

A white toothy smile gave his enemy's position away, the hooded figure emerging from the darkness to laugh at Warren's demise. In a second of horror, Warren recognized him then. That smile. That icy glow in his eyes. The smell of death and napalm.

"That's right, Warren. It's me, your old pal Wrath." The devil's laughter filled the air in discordant tones as he stepped away and studied his victim. "And you, you pathetic sack of shit, are dead."

Warren stared at the figure, trying to comprehend. Corporal William Rathburn. The Denver Devil. How could he still be alive? *We burned him. We burned him and sent him to hell.* This had to be a trick. The conjuring of his dying mind. No one could survive being burned like that. But if this demon was real and Wrath had returned...

Warren had never been a praying man, but with the last of his strength, he pleaded one now, *Dear God, forgive me. Forgive us all.*

As strips of his charred skin slid off his hands, revealing the burned bones beneath, Warren slumped forward onto the ground. He did not feel the pavement. He did not feel anything as the heat inside him escalated, and his world turned black.

Chapter 1

December 20, 1986

NV 375 Highway, Nevada

Dust clouds billowed a winding path behind the car, heralding the station wagon's passage through hell. *If Hell is Nevada*, Samuel Morris thought, which he was starting to think it might be.

He checked the rearview mirror and saw the same view he'd seen for the past hour. The empty road carved a path through the dry Nevada desert.

A path to where? Salvation? Doom? The World's Biggest Cactus? They'd passed a few of those 'World's Biggest' attractions since leaving Springfield. His newly adopted daughter, Bella, had wanted to stop at them all, and he'd been more than happy to oblige. He'd do anything to see her smile more. There'd been too many frowns lately.

"Are you sure you took the right turn?" Sam's wife, Sarah, asked from beside him in that irritated tone that suggested she doubted his sanity.

That's okay. I'm beginning to doubt my sanity too.

Whatever idyllic notions he'd had about a family road trip being a fun adventure, this was not it.

"Yes." He nodded. "We're near Groom Lake. That's where they said to go."

"And who exactly are *they* again?" Sarah questioned in the same snappish tone. The large paper map in her hands rustled as she turned it and studied it closely, frowning.

Sam sighed, unable to suppress his impatience any longer. "You know who. The Church of the New World Order. Mother Agnes invited us. We've talked about this a hundred times." It was hot. Way too hot for this conversation, and the wind blowing through the windows wasn't doing anything to cool things down.

"Well, it's not like we really know anything about these people, do we? Other than what they've told *you* over the phone? But by all means, let's just pack up, hop in the car, and go live in the middle of nowhere in some weird religious commune that isn't even on the *damn map*." As she said map, a gust of wind blew in through the window and caught the large rectangle of paper, snatching it from her hands. "Shit," Sarah shouted as it sailed out the window, evading her hasty grab to snatch it back.

"Oops," Bella said from the back seat behind Sam.

"Great, just great," Sam muttered as he watched the map tumble and fly into the desert behind them.

"Well, it's not like it was all that helpful anyway," Sarah huffed, crossing her arms over her chest.

"Now, now, kids," Ena Ridley, Sarah's mother, piped up from beside Bella in the back seat. She leaned forward until her face appeared between Sam and Sarah's shoulders and patted them both on the arm. "Why don't we sing some more songs? It's a beautiful time of year with *so much* to be grateful for, don't you think?"

Grateful? Sam let out a long breath and flexed his fingers on the steering wheel, forcing himself to relax. Yes, he had to agree with Ena about that. There was a lot to be grateful for despite the stress of their current situation. And surely they would have a much happier Holiday season this year.

Sarah groaned and leaned her head back against the headrest of her seat. "Not 'Jingle Bells' again. *Please.*"

Bella giggled. "Yes! Jingle Bells," she shouted and launched into an energetic rendition of the song accompanied by Ena. The lyrics included Batman smelling and Robin laying an egg, and the song ended in peals of laughter.

Sam smiled and pressed play on the Chevy's tape deck, filling the car with a new Christmas tune for the 'Backseat Girls' to sing along with. As Bella and Ena started to cheerily accompany "Rudolph the Red-Nosed Reindeer," Sam reached over and entwined his fingers with Sarah's, giving her hand a reassuring squeeze.

She gave his hand a small squeeze back, and a fleeting smile touched her lips as she glanced down at her belly. Her free hand rested on her abdomen, massaging it in small circles. Seven months pregnant and due in February. She had every right to be a bit testy that he'd uprooted their growing family from Springfield, trusting God's will that a better life awaited them in the desert. Was he anxious about venturing into the unknown? Despite his faith in the Almighty, heck yeah. But what choice was there?

It had been almost a year since the demon attack at Springfield Mall and nearly six months since he'd relinquished his vows as a priest. Now he was no longer employed by the Catholic Church, and he needed a job. Despite the notoriety he'd received as the 'Mall Priest,' choices for employment had been surprisingly slim to none in Springfield, and with Sarah being unable to work due to complications with her pregnancy, the Church of the New World Order's offer of a trial residency as a pastor at the compound had seemed a blessing. With the added promises of schooling for Bella and a top medical facility for Sarah and the baby, how could he turn it down?

Besides, he still had Father Clint's cross in his possession, and this trip was an ideal opportunity to return it to the Church. Although he kept it safely on a chain around his neck, he'd be happy to be rid of it if he was honest. Seeing the cross brought back memories of the Mallzilla Massacre, where hundreds had perished, and many others had suffered permanent injuries, including varying degrees of psychological damage.

He didn't need to look far to see someone who fit into the last category.

"How you feeling, babe?" he asked Sarah quietly.

Another fleeting smile was her answer before she turned away to look out the window. She'd seemed distant and not herself for weeks, which worried Sam more than he let on. The nightmares she'd experienced since being possessed by Abaddon hadn't gone away over time like the psychologists said they would.

Ena seemed to think Sarah's moodiness was normal because of hormones and the baby, but Sam feared it was more than that. Then again, this whole pregnancy thing was new to him, so what did he know? He was probably overthinking everything.

Bella and Ena clapped as Rudolf ended and another song began. "It's beginning to look a lot like—"

"Crap-mas," Sarah finished in a louder singing voice than the backseat passengers. She pressed the middle button beneath the tape deck to cease playback and pushed the button again to eject the cassette. "How about you listen to it on your Walkman?" She tossed the cassette to the back seat, the object landing somewhere between the two passengers.

Silence filled the car. Sam caught Bella's gaze in the rearview mirror and flashed her a wistful smile. The past few weeks had been challenging in a year filled with all types of obstacles, including going through the adoption process with Bella, which had proven neither easy nor cheap. If it hadn't been for Ena's financial support, as well as her moving in with them to assist with caring for the orphaned child, the adoption might not have happened.

Bella grinned back at Sam. While the whole parenting thing was new to him, they'd developed a strong bond and shared a silent understanding. *Mommy loves us. She's just going through a lot and needs time.* But they were all victims of the trauma that had altered their lives forever, even Ena, who'd watched her daughter change from an organized, happy woman before the mall incident to the moody person she was now.

"Would you like a break, dear?" Ena asked Sarah, placing her hand on her daughter's shoulder. "We can pull over for a bit and stretch our legs, can't we, Sam?"

Sam nodded and prepared to move the car onto the side of the empty road, but Sarah shook her head. "No, it's okay." She glanced back at her mother. "It's just... Christmas music gives me a headache."

Sam exchanged a quick look with Ena. *Yeah, it was a good decision to leave town and avoid Springfield this Christmas.*

"How about we listen to something else?" Sarah opened the glove compartment and rustled through the contents. "Hall and Oates? John Cougar Mellencamp?"

Sam frowned. "I thought he was John Cougar?"

"He's changed to John Cougar Mellencamp for his last two or three albums."

Could Sarah really be annoyed at him for not knowing? "Maybe he'll call himself John Mellencamp next." He chuckled.

"Ricky Gibson?" Sarah said, sounding puzzled as she pulled another cassette from the compartment. "It's still in its wrapper." She glanced around the car at the others.

"Oh, I forgot. That arrived in the mail just before we left," Sam explained. "He sent a copy of his new album."

"Play it." Bella clapped excitedly. "I want to hear his voice again."

None of them had seen Ricky since the demon uprising, but they'd followed him in the news, and he'd occasionally sent a quick 'pen pal' letter to Bella. She often sent him a letter and, only two days ago, a postcard, hoping they would reach him. He'd skyrocketed to fame under a new manager who had taken full advantage of him being a celebrity survivor of the Mallzilla Massacre.

" 'Don't Free the Demon,' " Sarah said, reading the title out loud as she unwrapped the cassette case. "These record producers really don't give a damn, do they? They'll do anything for money. Poor Ricky." She placed the cassette in the deck, and the car filled with silence while they waited for the music to begin.

As the synthesizer introduction to track one, "Demon Lady," trailed off, Ricky's smooth voice sang about a dark-haired woman on the dancefloor, wearing red and looking like the devil.

"Wow, what a refreshing take on women." Sarah shook her head and passed the cassette case to Bella, who was reaching to see it. "Ricky, I love you, but you're just being a puppet."

"A puppet?" Bella asked, looking at the cassette case quizzically. "But he's a man."

"She's just saying that Ricky is doing what the bosses tell him and not doing what he wants to do himself. They just want him to make them lots of money," Sam explained. "But lucky for Ricky, he gets to make lots of money too." He slowed the car as they approached a road even less traveled than the one they were on. "Okay, we gotta turn here, I think."

Sarah frowned. "Are you sure?"

Sam shrugged. "Well, it's hard to say since we don't have a map..." He resisted tossing a sideways glance at Sarah and continued, "But Brother Trevor gave me directions on the phone, and this looks about right."

"You trust him?"

"I've never even met him." *You already know that,* he wanted to add, but it would only serve as more fuel for the fire. He hated arguing with Sarah.

"My point exactly."

The urge to pull over and stretch his legs for a while filled Sam. The car felt more confined by the second, and he needed space to clear his head. Sarah's constant questioning of his decisions was getting to him, but he knew it wouldn't end until they'd reached their destination, and she saw for herself that everything was okay.

He focused on navigating the dirt road, which wound through desert scrub and around rocky mounds before straightening again. The dust kicked up by their wheels billowed behind the car, obscuring everything behind them for a few seconds before it was swept away by the wind. What if he *had* taken the wrong turn? Would they end up lost in the wasteland, never to be seen alive again? Their bones bleached by the sun like the empty-eyed skulls of the long-horned cows they passed? Sam frowned. Why'd he have to think about that? He'd seen enough death to last a lifetime. But it was so dry here in the southwest. How did anything live in this place? And yet, someone clearly did as the first signs of habitation they'd seen for at least an hour lined the road at the next crossing.

"Fences," he announced, feeling relieved. "See? We must be getting close now." He turned off the dirt road and onto the fence-lined one.

"Big fences," Sarah said, looking out the car window. "They must be at least twenty feet high."

She was right. Apart from prison yards, Sam had never seen chain link fences so high, and, just like those around prison yards, these were topped with a row of barbed wire.

"Don't seem all that friendly," Sarah observed a moment later as they sped past a large white sign bolted to the fence with the words, 'No Trespassing,' written on it.

"Well, they are expert demon hunters," Sam said. "Maybe it's for protection."

"Seriously?" Sarah's frown was clear in her voice, as was Bella's loud gasp from the back seat.

Sam caught the little girl's wide-eyed stare in the rearview mirror.

"There's demons in the desert?" Bella's voice rose in pitch so high it squeaked with each word.

"No, I'm sure there isn't," Ena replied. She put her arm around the girl and gave her a reassuring hug. "Papa was just being silly to make some fun."

The look Ena gave Sam matched the scathing one from Sarah.

"Sorry," Sam said, wishing the trip would hurry up and end, or he'd get swallowed by his seat or both. "I wasn't thinking." He caught Bella's gaze again. He hadn't meant to frighten her. "Nana's right. I was being silly. Demons don't live in the desert." *Even if it is hotter than hell out here.*

"That's okay," Bella chirped, smiling again. "Demons aren't scary. I've got my necklace." She clutched the tourmaline shard that hung around her neck. It was a relic gifted to Bella by her real mother before she'd been killed by the demon that had nearly taken them all. The little girl never took it off except to sleep, and even then, she kept it within easy reach beneath her pillow. The image of Bella using it to stab Abaddon had been burned into Sam's memory forever.

"You are the bravest, little love," Ena said. She gave Bella a tight squeeze and kissed the top of her head. Of all the things Sam was most grateful for, it was how Ena had welcomed Bella. She accepted the girl as if she were her own flesh and blood granddaughter, taking the child under her wing almost immediately when she'd arrived in Sarah's care, needing a new home last Christmas.

Sarah opened her mouth as if to say something to Sam. Then she closed it again and turned to Bella instead, giving her a warm, loving smile as she reached back to grasp her hand. "She's a fighter, like her mama," Sarah said with pride.

"That she is," Sam agreed and smiled, watching the three girls. Bella might not be his and Sarah's birth daughter, but the fierce love and protectiveness they shared for her couldn't be any stronger. A wave of relief washed over Sam as a renewed feeling of love filled the car. This road trip had been a long, tense experience. Maybe the drama was nearing an end?

"Are we there yet?" Bella asked, looking out the window and giggling.

"Soon, I think. This road must lead somewhere, mustn't it?" Ena asked.

Sam frowned. As time passed, along with the miles, it all looked the same. A gravelly road with a high fence on one side and desert on the other. He feared Ena was way off the mark, and so was he. How big was this compound? Shouldn't they be there by now? As they passed the umpteenth 'No Trespassing' sign, he couldn't help wondering if he had messed up Brother Trevor's directions. Where the heck were they?

Sarah rubbed her stomach as if it pained her. It happened a lot—the stomach rubbing and the pain—way more than Sam or the others liked. It was the reason Sarah had not been able to work past her first trimester. According to their gynecologist in Springfield, the baby was growing faster than normal, putting stress on her body. Given her age and that this was her first pregnancy, she was at high risk of miscarriage. But here they were, seven months in, though Sarah looked more like nine, according to Ena, and the baby was still going strong.

Sarah let out a loud gasp and winced.

"What's wrong?" Sam glanced at her sharply. *Dear God, don't let her go into labor in the middle of the Nevada desert.*

"Little Monster has a mighty kick," she explained and let out an awkward laugh.

Sam shook his head and tried to focus on driving. Did Sarah have any idea that he had a minor heart attack every time she frowned and looked like she might pass out?

"It's a boy, I'm sure of it," Ena said. "Boys always carry lower and kick like that. He's going to be a quarterback."

"Well, this one can stop practicing field plays. He's giving me bruises."

It was true. Sam had seen them. Purple bruises marred her abdomen, spreading outward from the inside. Little Monster was a good nickname for the baby. He caught Bella's silent look of horror in the mirror. She was staring at Sarah as if she might be about to sprout horns.

"What kind of a song is 'Demon Licker'?" Ena asked, abruptly switching topics to the song playing over the car stereo. "It doesn't sound entirely appropriate for young ears."

Sam practically heard Sarah's eye roll. "Mom, Ricky's managed by his record label. They give him the songs to sing, and he does it."

"Well, give me some Neil Sedaka or Gene Pitney any day."

"Okay, Mother." Sarah ejected the cassette from the deck, tossed it to Bella to put in the case, and then selected something else from the compartment. "How about Metallica, Master of Puppets?" She inserted the tape into the player and pressed the play button.

Sam grinned, wondering if Ena had any idea what she was about to hear. "Looks like there's a different sign up there on the side of the road. Maybe it will tell us where we are."

"Ah-ha!" Sarah pointed a finger at him. "So, you admit we *are* lost?"

Sam shook his head. "I didn't say that."

"Uh-huh. Sure." Sarah grinned at him knowingly.

"Oh, this music sounds lovely." Ena smiled as the gentle acoustic guitar introduction on the opening track, "Battery," began to play. "I thought it was going to be loud and heavy and... Oh, and there it is."

Sam smirked as the drums, bass, and distorted electric guitar took over, and Sarah began to shake her head, her hair moving about in the wind. Bella did the same, grinning as she imitated her.

Since the demon invasion, Sarah had found solace in listening to loud music, quite often heavy metal. It was a genre he'd found hard to adjust to at first, given it was known as 'Devil's music' and was quite the opposite of the church choir hymns he'd spent his life internalizing. But after listening to the lyrics, he'd soon realized how few songs specifically mentioned the devil. And if music helped Sarah blow off steam and relax, it was a much better option than turning to alcohol or drugs. Plus, the music didn't bother him when it accompanied hot sex. But that was before she'd become pregnant and received doctor's orders to not do anything physical that might stress her or the baby.

Sarah stopped headbanging to the music and turned it off, her attention caught by the sign Sam had seen in the distance through the windshield. "Does that say, 'Restricted Access'?"

Sam peered at the sign as they drew nearer. "Yeah, I think it does." Along with a lot of other words he couldn't quite make out below the main heading. But the sign was red and clearly meant as a warning.

"I don't have a good feeling about this," Sarah said, rubbing her abdomen again. "Maybe we should turn around and head back to that town we passed. Rachel or whatever it was called."

"Yeah, I think you're right." Wherever they were, it had an odd military feel to it with the warning signs and fences and wasn't at all welcoming, as Sarah had pointed out earlier. "We can phone the compound from there and ask them where to go exactly." *And buy a new map,* he added silently.

"*Mommy,*" Bella suddenly shrieked.

"Jesus Christ!" Sarah shouted, turning sharply to face the child while placing her hand over her heart like it had tried to jump out of her body. "What's wrong?"

Considering his heart had done the same, Sam knew how she felt. He moved his foot from the gas pedal to the brake, ready to bring the car to a sudden stop.

He glanced at Bella in the rearview mirror. "Bells?" he asked, using her pet name. "You okay?"

Bella looked ashamed and leaned over to whisper something into Ena's ear.

The elderly woman pursed her lips knowingly at whatever Bella said and nodded. "Pull over, please, Sam." She raised her brows dramatically. "Us ladies need to make a pit stop."

"Oh, Lord," Sarah said with a sigh. "I thought you'd been bitten by a snake or something. Why didn't you just ask to go instead of scaring us half to death?"

"Sorry, Mama, I didn't mean to." Bella sounded forlorn and close to tears. "I don't wanna have to go. I tried to hold it."

"It's all right," Ena murmured in what Sam recognized as her 'Nana-to-the-rescue-voice.' "We'll find a nice rock or something you can go behind, and then we'll be back on the road in a jiffy."

Sam quickly pulled to the side of the road and stopped the car. From his experience with kids and bathroom breaks, Bella had probably been holding it in since the last rest stop, which meant they had less than half a minute before they'd have hysterical tears and a mess to clean up.

They all got out of the car. Sam helped Sarah walk a slow path beside the road, massaging the small of her back where it pained her. Ena, murmuring encouraging words too low for Sam to hear, led Bella away from the car and toward the fence. Sure enough, there was a large rock surrounded by a patch of scrub that could act as a private place for the little girl to relieve herself. Not that there was anyone around to notice.

Or was there?

Sam paused massaging Sarah's back, and peered down the road where a dust cloud billowed in the distance. "Is that a car?" He shielded his eyes against the sun.

"Yeah, I think it might be." Sarah raised one eyebrow at him. "Where did that suddenly come from?" A hot gust of wind blew her long hair about her face.

Good question. "Maybe someone from the compound is coming to meet us?"

As the sudden sound of approaching engines echoed in the sky, they looked up and shielded their eyes. They were hard to make out against the bright sunlight, but Sam swore a pair of dark shapes were flying toward them above the horizon.

"Do you see what I see?" He pointed to where he saw the dark shapes.

"Oh shit," she said, following his finger. "Great, now you got us lost, *and* we're going to be abducted by aliens."

"Calm down, they're not UFOs."

"We're in the middle of the Nevada desert. Anything's possible. Remember what that guy said at the Flying Saucer Restaurant?"

"He just wanted us to buy his overpriced alien souvenirs." Which they had. On top of an overpriced lunch, they'd walked away with a green alien stuffie for Bella.

"Okay, Mr. Non-believer… what is that then?"

"Military choppers, perhaps," Sam suggested. The shopkeeper had also talked about a secret government base hidden in the desert. While the idea made more sense than flying saucers, it didn't ease his anxiety. He'd thought the guy had been trying to sell them a story, but maybe the base did exist. Had they stumbled upon somewhere they shouldn't? It wasn't likely that the Church of the New World Order would send choppers to intercept them. It was a bit weird that the vehicles had appeared when they'd pulled over to make the pit stop, but that thought triggered another. Relieving oneself on a public roadway was illegal in some states, wasn't it? Was Nevada one of those places? Surely the desert was fair game, though. It wasn't like there was a restroom anywhere to go in. *Don't be an idiot,* he mentally slapped himself, *the Pee Police aren't a thing.*

So, what was happening then?

The dark shape barreling down the road toward them had now turned into several dark shapes, stirring up clouds of dust.

"Um… okay, everyone back in the car," Sarah called out. "We don't need to spend the day talking to the military. Or aliens. Or whoever they are."

"This is America. They won't do anything to us. We're Americans." Sam said, sounding more confident than he felt. "But yeah, I agree with you, babe. Time to go. Everyone get back in the car."

"*Mom,*" Sarah shouted when Ena and Bella didn't reappear from behind the rock. She reached for the passenger door and paused. "*Time to go.*"

"Honestly, Sarah," Ena snapped, sounding flustered. "What is the fuss about now?" She smoothed her graying hair with her free hand as she helped Bella make her way from behind the privacy of the rocky scrub. Dressed in her usual attire of a printed sundress and sensible flats, Ena would probably look prim and proper just about anywhere, even in the desert heat. But she paused mid-step and looked up as the sound of the choppers drew nearer.

"Attention, civilians," a commanding voice boomed through a megaphone from the lead chopper. "This is a restricted area. Unauthorized entry is strictly prohibited. Raise your hands and refrain from reentering your vehicle."

"Oh my God." Sarah's eyes were wide as she turned from the helicopters to Sam. "What have you gotten us into?" She quickly snatched her hand back from the door handle and raised both in the air as instructed.

"What's going on?" Ena asked, sounding breathless as she and Bella hurried to join them.

"I don't know. A misunderstanding. Just do what they say," Sam advised.

"Are you telling those words to us or yourself?" Sarah asked.

"Both."

The dark gray choppers buzzed above them in a circle, close enough that they saw men dressed in military fatigues positioned in the open side doors, weapons trained on Sam and his family.

"Papa?" Bella squeaked, the unmistakable sound of fear clear in her voice. Her tiny hand pulled at the bottom of his shirt as she tried to gain his attention. "It's the demons," the little girl whimpered, close to tears. "They've come to get us because we had to stop for me to pee."

"No, they're not, sweetheart." Sam lowered one of his hands and gave her a reassuring squeeze. "It's the Army or the Air Force. We just took a wrong turn. They'll understand once we explain." *I hope.* He pushed her behind him and moved to stand in front of her and the others, doing his best to shield them. "Stay with Mommy and Nana," he instructed. "It'll be okay."

Would it, though? There were no markings on the choppers. Whoever these people were, they had him and his family trapped between the fence and the car. What had they done to cause this kind of trouble? They hadn't crossed any boundaries or even a gate that he recalled. There was no change to indicate they had trespassed into a restricted area.

As the choppers tightened their circle above, the noise of the rotors and wind pushing downward were enough to keep those below frozen in place even without the guns pointed at them.

"Sam!" Sarah called out. "If this is a joke, it's not funny. They're scaring Bella."

Sam nodded. He knew that. Of course he knew that. He was scared too, if he was being honest. They all were. And he'd somehow gotten them into this situation, though he wasn't sure how. He'd followed Brother Trevor's directions. At least, he thought he had. But either way, he needed to find a way out of this and fast. The stress couldn't be good for Sarah and the baby, let alone the rest of them.

But what could they do except wait to find out what the squads of soldiers wanted?

Sweat trickled down Sam's back as the swirling dust kicked up by the choppers suddenly parted, and a black sedan screeched to a halt on the road, angling behind their station wagon. The car was followed by a black van that blocked their vehicle from the front. They were cut off from retreating, even if they could get in their car without getting shot.

"Well, here we go," Sam said as the sedan's doors opened and two men wearing black suits and sunglasses got out of the car.

He tried not to worry. God was on their side, and they'd faced worse situations and won. But a demon's motive was to either possess or kill. These military types were unknown. While the proud American inside him believed they'd come to no harm, he also didn't trust the men. One carload of people in the middle of the Mojave Desert could be made to disappear without a trace, and those responsible were unlikely to face any consequences.

The men in black suits moved toward them, followed by a squad of armed soldiers who exited the van hurriedly, guns pointed toward them at the ready.

"Uh, hi!" Sam said, trying to sound friendly while shouting to be heard above the choppers. "I think there's been a big misunderstanding."

"State your identity," one of the Black Suits instructed. They stood ahead of the soldiers. Perhaps they were in charge.

"I'm—"

"Excuse me," Ena interjected, moving forward to stand beside Sam as she cut him off and addressed the two men in black. "I don't know who you are or what you want, but this is completely unacceptable. My daughter is pregnant and needs rest, not to be scared half to death. Put your guns away this instant and show some respect."

The two black-clad men shared a look and turned back to Sam.

"State your identity," the one who had spoken earlier instructed again.

"*My granddaughter is crying,*" Ena shouted.

Sam had never seen her so furious before, and, based on the fierceness in her posture and tone, he was kinda glad it wasn't directed at him. He also realized now where Sarah got her temper from. He'd always thought her feistiness came through the Latino blood on her dad's side. But no, no, Ena was just as fierce as Sarah when pushed to her breaking point—a point the soldiers appeared to have found.

The men in black suits glanced at Bella, who had her face buried in Ena's side and arms wrapped tightly around her waist, sobbing.

God forgive me for whatever sin I committed that's brought us to this moment.

He'd thought he was doing God's will by heading to the Church of the New World Order. But now Sarah was stressed and upset, and so was her mother, and Bella... poor sweet Bella. Hadn't she been through enough trauma in her life?

"Please," he said to the two men, keeping his hands open and where they could see them. "Let my family go. We mean you no harm. We took a wrong turn somewhere, that's all."

He wasn't above begging, but he swore he heard Sarah snort behind him.

"I can prove we are innocent." Sam lowered one of his hands and placed it on Bella's head, doing his best to soothe his daughter. With the other, he reached inside his T-shirt.

The soldiers tightened their gun sights on Sam, causing him to pause.

"Sam," Sarah said from behind him as she leaned against his back. "I'm not feeling very good." Standing in the heat and beyond stressed out that they might be shot, it was no wonder. The wind from the choppers pulled at their clothes and hair as if they were being attacked by a hoard of unseen demons.

To hell with this shit. They can shoot me if they want.

"I'm not armed. It's just a cross." He quickly pulled the holy relic given to him by Father Clint from beneath his shirt and held it high, letting everyone see he told the truth. "My name is Samuel Morris." He kept his voice calm and steady despite the need to shout and the anger burning inside him. Sarah was pale and sweating. He wrapped his arm around her, helping her stand. "This is my family. We were invited here by the Church of the New World Order. If you tell us where to find their compound, we'll gladly be on our way."

As the two men studied the cross dangling from Sam's grasp, the silver glinted in the afternoon sunlight, giving it a soft glow.

The agent in charge pressed the headset he wore to his ear as if listening to instructions being relayed from afar. Were they being watched? With a nod, the agent waved the choppers away and ordered the soldiers to stand down.

Taking several steps away from Sam, the second agent pressed his own headset to his ear and spoke into it, too quiet for Sam to hear distinctly. But as the choppers moved off and the noise and wind lessened, he made out the words "Mall Priest" and "little girl." The agent glanced at Sarah. "Yes, pregnant." A pause filled the air, and then the man in black nodded and said, "I understand."

Done with the conversation, the agent turned to Sam and gestured at him and the others. "You will come with us." Not waiting for a reply, both agents headed to the black sedan and proceeded to get inside.

The soldiers, however, moved forward quickly and herded Sam and his family toward the van, where a third man in a black suit waited by the open back doors.

"Wait. What?" Sam balked, confused by the turn of events. "What is going on?" They weren't free to go?

A soldier grabbed him by the arm and nodded toward the van. "Let's go."

Sam shook his head. He let the softly glowing cross fall back against his chest and hang on the chain around his neck. "Where are you taking us?"

The soldier didn't answer. He was joined by another who twisted Sam's arm behind his back. Pain shot through his wrist and elbow, forcing him to obey before they were broken. They pushed him toward the van. He staggered, wanting to resist but unable to even make a sound.

"You can't do this to us. This is illegal," Sarah shouted as she was shoved at gunpoint toward the van with the rest of them.

Bella tried to make a run for it, but was caught easily and carried to the van, kicking and screaming.

"Leave my daughter alone!" Sarah shouted.

Bella shrieked as she was placed in the back of the van, where another soldier waited to make sure she sat down rather than escape.

"*Don't touch me*," Ena warned, pointing a finger at the soldier who tried to lift her into the van after Bella. "I can do it myself." She smoothed her dress and directed an angry glare at the soldiers. "You should all be ashamed of yourselves. Absolutely no manners. Harassing decent God-fearing folk like this," she said as she climbed into the back of the van unaided. She went to Bella immediately and hugged her closely. "Heathens, all of you. I'll write to Congress about this."

Sarah was next, cursing the whole time. She managed to get in a swipe at the agent standing guard at the back doors. Her palm connected with his cheek, creating a loud smacking sound as flesh met flesh.

"Sarah!" Sam called out, finding his voice as he feared for her life. He struggled to get away and run to her, but the two soldiers who held him pinned tightened their hold.

With sunglasses covering the agent's eyes, his expression was unreadable. He touched his cheek where Sarah had hit him and looked at his fingers as if expecting to see blood.

Sarah grinned. "Scared ya, did I? Good. You should be scared. We've fought worse than the likes of you and won."

"Serves you right for trying to kill innocent people," Ena chimed in with a nod.

"With all due respect, ma'am, you all need to calm the hell down," the agent said as Sam was forced into the back of the van with the others. "If we wanted you dead, you'd be dead already. The choppers could have obliterated your car with one missile. They never miss."

Sam rubbed his wrists and elbow as he was released and forced to sit. Out of the sunlight, the cross had lost its glow, but it felt warm against his chest, even through the fabric of his T-shirt. Made of Holy Silver, which had demon-killing properties, it hadn't acted like this since he'd battled Abaddon nearly a year ago. Maybe there was something to what Bella had said about the soldiers being demons. Who were these people?

The agent climbed into the back of the van with them and pulled the doors shut with help from soldiers outside. Sam wrapped his arm protectively around Sarah. Bella and Ena sat on the other side of the van, wedged between two bulky soldiers.

Dear God. Please protect my family from whatever evil seeks to harm us.

"It's so dark in here," Bella whimpered. She burrowed into Ena's side, hiding her face again. But at least she'd stopped screaming and crying.

She was right, though. Once the door was closed, the van's interior was cast into near darkness. There were no windows, and the cab was a separate compartment without even a glass partition to connect it to the back. This type of van was used for carrying cargo—and today, they were the cargo.

The agent banged on the side of the van.

As the vehicle began to move, panel lights flickered on along the sides, illuminating the interior. The Black Suit grabbed a flask from a backpack and handed the container to Sarah.

She stared at him and didn't move.

"Drink. It's water," he prompted.

She shook her head, refusing the offer.

"Okay." The agent shrugged and unscrewed the cap, then took a swig himself. "Desert gets dry." He swallowed again and gave an appreciative sigh.

"Where are you taking us?" Sam asked.

The agent shrugged. "To the boss, of course. Our ETA is fifteen minutes, so you might as well relax while you can."

While we can?

Sam glanced at Sarah and caught her look, which spoke her thoughts loud and clear without her needing to say anything, probably because he was thinking the same thing.

What have you gotten us into, Samuel Morris?

CHAPTER 2

For the umpteenth time, Ricky Gibson's gaze strayed from the television set blaring music videos in his suite at the Admiral Hotel to the deathly silent phone on the desk. It hadn't rung all day. Not that he expected it to.

Should I call her? he asked himself, starting the same old argument in his head.

Don't be stupid. She doesn't want to talk to you. The problem with old arguments, he realized, was that they had the same old answers.

I fucked it, didn't I?

Yeah, you did, just like you always do.

Except in this case, he hadn't actually fucked it, not literally anyway. But he couldn't fault Grace for not believing his denials or not wanting to see him again, let alone accept his calls.

Let's face it, Ricky, with a reputation like yours, would you believe you?

No, he admitted.

But that's why it hurt so bad. Grace had been different from the other women he'd dated. Since surviving the Springfield Mall demon attack together, they'd shared a real connection. She'd seemed to see past the drug-addicted, alcoholic, rock star persona that the media loved to pin on him. Everything had been going so well until a few months ago, when his new manager, Gerry Goader, had suggested he break off his relationship with Grace. No reason given, he'd just said, "Drop the girl."

Naturally, Ricky had told him to go stuff himself down a drainpipe. Who was Gerry to tell him what to do? He was no Simon Sponger, that was for certain. *May he rest in peace.* Ricky made the sign of the cross and frowned.

Gerry made Ricky's previous manager, Simon, look like a Sunday School teacher. Although Ricky couldn't prove it, he knew Gerry had concocted the events that had resulted in him getting caught naked in a hotel bed with two supposed groupies. Yes, he had been drinking heavily, but even now, he clearly remembered the events of the night up until Gerry had bought him a drink at the bar. He knew he'd been set up. And he'd never forget the look on Grace's face as she came bursting through the doors of his hotel bedroom in the early hours of the morning and paused at the foot of the bed, staring at him.

The betrayal and pain.

Holy God, it had pierced through his sleep-hazed hangover like a dagger thrown from her eyes and straight to his heart. He'd tried to sit up and go after her as she ran out of the room, but with a naked blonde draped across his body on either side of him, it wasn't a good look. It also wasn't easy to move. And by the time he'd caught up to Grace, she wasn't having any of his excuses.

He hadn't had sex with those two women. He was sure of it. Just like he was sure he couldn't break his present contract with Gerry and the record label, Red Leonard Records, not without getting sued into the ground so deep he might as well be buried six feet under. He'd had a lawyer look the contract over after the fact, and 'iron-clad' was the least of his problems. They owned him. It was like he'd signed a deal with the devil. Which, upon reflection, he had to admit Gerry might be. Ricky knew demons, and Gerry always wore too much cologne, like he was trying to cover something up. But he didn't have glowing red eyes, so there was that.

Fucking hell, why did I sign that contract? I had my chance to be a grown-up, but I fucking blew it.

They'd suckered him in with their assurances, that's why. *"We'll take care of you, Ricky. You won't have to worry about anything."*

Fuuck. How stupid could he be?

Now Grace was gone, and for all his skyrocketing fame, he was trapped in a life of endless hotels, non-stop performances, and lonely nights without a single soul he could call a friend. Well, except Father Sam, Sarah, and little Bella Morris. But he had to be careful, didn't he? Who he reached out to, and what he said? The letters to the Morris's had been sent, he was sure of it. He'd mailed them himself through various hotels he'd stayed at, along with replies to regular fan letters. But if Bella, Sam, or Sarah had ever written back, he'd never seen their replies.

Gerry and the company watched everything. What he did, who he spoke to, including his mother. What he ate and drank. Who he fucked. Probably how often he took a shit too. The jury was still out as to what had caused the recent car accident that had left his father dead and burned nearly beyond recognition. But after the Grace incident, he knew they didn't mess around when they said things like 'there will be consequences.'

Consequence be thy name. Ricky laughed grimly and flicked the lid off the bottle of Johnnie Walker, watching it fall to the glass table in front of him. Having remained drug-free for over eighteen months, he hated how Gerry deliberately left dime bags of cocaine where he could see them. The slimeball manager also did lines in front of him, often offering Ricky a turn. So far, he'd always turned him down. But as time passed and loneliness and isolation from the outside world increased, it was becoming harder and harder to resist.

Don't do it Ricky. It was as if an angel sat on his right shoulder repeating the same four words, while a demon sat on his left shoulder pointing at the dime bag while whispering in his ear how nice it would be to escape reality. *Remember how good it feels?*

"Fuck off, that's what Johnnie's here for." *Shit, now I'm talking out loud to myself.* He took a long swill from the bottle.

He closed his eyes as the scotch flowed down his throat, warming his body in the process, and his calmness grew. But as often happened when he closed his eyes, he saw Grace. Her long dark hair and a smile radiated from her eyes as well as her mouth.

Shit. He wiped his eyes, feeling unexpected moisture gathering there as he remembered her tender touch and the subtle way she moved beneath him in the throes of passion. With Grace, it had never just been sex but something truly divine. Had that been what love was like?

"Fuck you, Gerry!" he screamed. Twisting himself around, he threw the near-empty bottle of scotch at the telephone, missing it by a few inches so the bottle smashed against the wall. Sure, he could call her, but what good would that do? If, by some miracle, he convinced her to take him back and see him again, what would Gerry do? Have her killed this time? Gerry's eyes might not be red and glowing, but they were soulless.

Leave Grace alone. She's better off without you, he reminded himself. A fact that threatened to tear his soul apart because it was true.

He moved from the couch and looked out the window at the busy street below, filled with traffic, people, and glittering signs. Many buildings had Christmas lights, as if Vegas needed even more lighting. He hated Vegas, always had. And knowing this year he'd be without Grace, he was hating Christmas too. While many people were drawn to Las Vegas by the glamour they saw on television and in movies, Ricky was repulsed by the sleazy underbelly of it all. Hookers and gambling, taking advantage of the addicted and abused, and fleecing them for their very souls. *When did you become so worried about other people's souls? Shouldn't you be a little more worried about your own?* Damn. Now, he was starting to sound like Father Sam. *I'm thinking too much. I need a beer.*

He made his way to the kitchen. There was plenty of booze in the fridge. Gerry made sure of that, and he still had a few days until he had to perform. Lots of time to get so drunk he could forget he existed, or at least why he was here. A brand-new establishment, Great Rock of Vegas Casino and Hotel, had opened, and he was performing on the main stage at eleven on Christmas Eve. Remembering what had happened last year at the same time, he really didn't want to do it. But the owner was cashing in on the notoriety of the demon invasion that had happened in Springfield, and Gerry had agreed. So here he was, just like last year, poised to perform in less than a week on Christmas Eve, except this time it wasn't in a shopping mall. It was a Vegas casino where the only demons around were people.

As he walked back into the living room, beer in hand, he caught a few words from the television as it interrupted the music videos for a breaking news program, "... body was left behind a dumpster in the parking lot. This is the sixth incident in the past several weeks where a body has been found burned nearly beyond recognition. So far, the police haven't identified a connection between the victims, but they suspect the homicides may be linked. The police are requesting that citizens and visitors alike show caution when out at night. If anyone has any information regarding the murders, please contact the police directly or call T.I.P.S to leave an anonymous—"

Ricky turned off the television and sat on the couch with a heavy thump, making it squeak. He stared at the darkened screen. A serial killer? In Vegas? At Christmas? And he was playing a gig? His heart raced. The situation was eerily similar to how the demon invasion had started in Springfield.

It wasn't happening again, was it?

Don't be an idiot, Ricky. What are the chances?

He chose not to answer that thought, but the question whispered at the back of his mind, sending a chill down his spine.

His hand shook as he set the beer bottle down on the table and sucked in a deep breath. It was going to take something a lot stronger to get through this fucked up week. His gaze slid to the dime bag of coke on the coffee table.

Don't do it, Ricky.

"Why the fuck not?" he asked the empty room.

It was impossible not to think of the Springfield Mall and the several hundreds of people who were lost to the murderous demon army. Simon, the two models whose names he couldn't remember, and very nearly Sarah and little Bella. Part of him wanted to go back in time and wipe that experience from existence. He'd never have met Grace, but then again, he also wouldn't have to suffer the pain of her absence now.

The suite's main entrance door opened, and Gerry, his tall, balding manager, walked in, a smile beaming from one side of his face to another. As always, it didn't quite reach his soulless eyes. "Hey, guess what?" he hissed in his usual way. His voice always sounded slightly slurred, like he had a forked tongue. If Ricky didn't know any better, he'd swear Gerry really was an escaped demon sent up from the flames of Hell to torment him. His manager paused and gave him a bland look. "I see you're drinking."

"Fuck all else to do here," Ricky slurred in turn.

"There's a whole city full of bars, casinos, strip joints. You don't have to sit around here all day moping. I said I'd stick with you if we went out for the day since you don't like security tailing you all the time. But look at you. Sauced to the gills, staring at nothing." He turned the television back on with a flick of the knob on the set and shook his head as he turned back to Ricky. "Lucky you don't have to perform tonight."

Ricky sneered, itching to fight the lanky dickhead judging him. "What did you think would happen? You bought the shit for me." He pointed at the bottle on the table and shook his head. "Why are you here?"

"I've organized someone to keep you company for the rest of the day. I know you'll like her."

Ricky narrowed his eyes. "She better have dark hair and big tits, or else you can take her to your room."

Gerry smirked. "Oh, you'll love her. I'll be right back." His manager vanished out the door as rapidly as he'd appeared.

Wish he'd stay gone. Ricky leaned back against the couch and tried to get a grip on himself. Maybe some afternoon sex would make him feel better, at least for a while. If he could perform, given the quantity of booze he'd consumed. He sat bolt upright again, remembering the last time that had happened... *Shit.*

The dime of cocaine on the table caught his eye. While the word on the street suggested long-term cocaine use could lead to erectile dysfunction, as a user in the past, he remembered it helped prolong sexual enjoyment.

"*Fuck it,*" he said aloud. He opened the bag and emptied the contents onto the glass coffee table. Grabbing one of Gerry's business cards, he pushed the white powder into a clump and divided it into lines.

"Breaking news from Sunny Tacos Casino Eatery," the news reporter on the television announced, interrupting the program with a new update. "The body of a woman has been found in a dumpster, her remains appearing to have been burned from the inside out. The identity of the woman remains unknown. This is the third reported homicide this week in the city of Las Vegas, and the seventh in the past several weeks..."

The business card slipped from between Ricky's fingers. "Fuck. *Another one?*" Jesus Christ, what was going on?

Just a few nights ago, he'd sat down for a plate of tacos at the diner-like establishment. The reporter continued discussing the details of the horrific murders. *This is why I don't like listening to the news.* He curled his hands into fists to stop them from shaking.

"As the investigation continues, Las Vegas police are searching for any possible leads and are pleading to the public, should anyone have any information, to please step forward."

People burned from the inside out?

Ricky wrapped his arms around his body, feeling suddenly cold. The description reminded him a bit of his father, Air Force Captain Johnathan Gibson, retired, burned in the wreck of his precious sports car. That had been four months ago in sunny California. They hadn't been close for a long time, but at the funeral, it felt like he was back in the mall, surrounded by death and filled with sadness and impotent rage at being unable to stop the nightmare from being real.

Possessed people.

Burned people.

Shit. It *was* happening again, wasn't it? But what could he do?

Run, the command echoed through his mind, galvanizing him into action. He stood abruptly, almost losing his footing in the process as the room tilted around him. Okay, so maybe Gerry was right, and he'd drunk too much. *Come on, Ricky, get your shit together.*

He glanced around the suite, careful not to do it too quickly. Where the hell was his suitcase? Fuck it, he could afford a new one. Right now, he needed to get out of the room, the hotel, and Las Vegas. And while he was at it, Nevada, too. All he needed was his Mastercard, wherever he left it. He hoped Gerry hadn't taken it from him again.

As he started for the door, it suddenly burst open, revealing Gerry's lanky body almost filling the frame.

"Getting impatient, were you?" Gerry asked with a sneer at Ricky. He turned sideways, and a dark-haired woman wearing a clinging black dress pushed into the room from behind him.

"Ricky," she screamed upon seeing the rock star and rushed at him.

He squinted, trying to focus on the large-breasted woman's face. *Not Grace, but then, why would Gerry try and bring her here anyway?*

"Do I know you?" he slurred.

She smiled and paused before reaching him. The woman hopped up and down, shaking her hands like she was carrying pompoms, which did amazing things for her breasts. They really were large, and her dress was especially clingy. "It's me, Kylie." She did a kick with her leg and a flourish with her arms. "Gooo, Rangers!" She beamed with excitement as she shouted the old high school cheer.

Oh, Christ. Kylie Summers. Ricky suddenly realized he did know her, at least he had some time ago. But his high school crush, here? Back when they were in classes together, she barely said hi to him, and now here she was, ready to be his own personal cheer squad, apparently.

"I'll leave you two alone to get reacquainted." Gerry turned and exited once again.

And don't fucking come back, Ricky wanted to yell as his manager disappeared from view, and he heard the main entrance door shut.

"Well, here we are, Kylie." He grinned from ear to ear. "It's been a while."

She smiled back at him. "I think you should get on that bed." She pointed to the bedroom, then reached around her back and started to unzip her dress. "We have a lot of time to make up for," she added as she pulled the straps from her shoulders, and the dress slipped to the floor over her stiletto-heeled feet.

She was naked beneath the dress. No bra or even a pair of wispy lace panties. *So that's what Kylie looks like.* He'd wondered back in the day if her nipples were pale pink or dusky brown. They were perky and pink and erect. The perfect complement to her pale skin.

Ricky decided that he could wait until morning to leave Vegas. One more night here wouldn't hurt, would it? At least he wouldn't be spending it alone. He walked around the couch and headed for his bedroom, where the king-sized bed waited. As Kylie followed him, he turned to her suddenly and pulled her close, looking into her eyes.

"Good." He nodded, satisfied they weren't red or glowing.

She furrowed her brows, puzzled. "What's good?"

"Nothing. Just checking."

She laughed. "You're weirder than I remember you being. But I don't mind."

Kylie brought her lips to his, and for the next hour or so, demons and serial killers were the last things on Ricky's mind.

Kylie Summers smiled as she exited the hotel lobby after earning more in an hour than she would normally make in a week. When first contacted by the tall, skinny, sleazy, middle-aged client manager for Red Leonard Records, she'd thought he wanted to buy her time for himself. Upon finding out Ricky Gibson was the client, she'd maintained a poker face while stating her fee. Truth be told, she would have fucked the rock star for free. Who knew the skinny, pimple-faced nerd from high school would have made it so big in the music scene? She certainly hadn't, or she'd have banged him back then and gotten her hooks in early. Maybe her life would have turned out differently.

As the late afternoon sun hit her eyes, she pulled her sunglasses from her handbag and put them on. Cocaine and booze always made things seem a bit too bright. *Damn cheap asshole manager.* You'd think he'd arrange a ride home for her in Ricky's hired car or at least spring for a cab, but here she was, walking to the nearest bus stop.

Slam, bam, thank you, ma'am, and out the door you go.

People never changed. Assholes, all of them. So she might as well make the most she could off the desperate and lonely ones, and there sure as fuck were lots of those in Vegas. She looked at her watch. There was plenty of time to get back to her unit, shower, change, and have a couple of hours to herself before her evening gig at the Jugs-R-Us club.

A freckle-faced young man approached the bus stop, smiling as their eyes met before looking away quickly. He couldn't have been any older than his early twenties and dressed as though he was heading to a nerd convention, one of those dragon hunting, or whatever they called it, game nights.

"Do you know how long the next bus will take?" she asked him.

"Um, about a minute." He smiled nervously.

"Thanks, hon."

His cheeks turned lightly pink, making his freckles stand out. Shit, was he even eighteen? His shyness was cute. A far cry from the leers she got when she stripped down to her thong at the club for the perverts and creeps. But she made good cash off her long dark hair and big tits, so she couldn't complain.

"Hey, um, the bus is coming," the nerdy guy pointed out.

She smiled. "Thanks again, hon."

As she glanced in the direction he pointed, she noticed the sly grin that spread across his face. Okay, maybe he wasn't so cute or innocent. A shiver ran up her spine as the bus came to a stop, and, suddenly feeling self-conscious, she pulled her thin jacket closer around her. Not much she could do about covering her body because her dress was purposefully revealing. She made sure to sit as far away from the creepy nerd as possible, which was difficult given the number of people on board during the afternoon rush.

Squeezing into an open spot in the middle, she fished in her purse for the 'special medication' she kept on hand. Time for a pick-me-up before her next gig to get into the mood. She was debuting her new routine tonight, a song the manager thought suitable with her double-D breasts, "Shake You Down," by Gregory Abbott. To her, it sounded cringey, but it would be sure to bring in some huge tips. Slow and seductive with suggestive lyrics, all eyes would be on her as she did what she did best and slowly removed nearly every bit of clothing.

The bus came to a stop near hers. As she moved toward the door to get ready to disembark, a gruff voice made her pause. "Hey, miss. You look familiar."

She glanced around. Everyone was ignoring her, either staring at nothing, lost in their own world or reading a book. She couldn't see who was talking.

"Yeah, you. I'm talking to you!" the middle-aged male voice repeated.

She scanned the passengers nearby again. It wasn't the nerdy guy. It wasn't anyone she could see. Maybe the person meant someone else?

"You, with the big tits!" the man shouted.

Nope, he definitely meant her. A chill went up her spine again, and she pulled her jacket tighter across her chest. Was no one else hearing this? Everyone around her seemed oblivious, ignoring the situation. *Fucking people.* As the bus stopped and the doors opened, she decided to get off early and walk the rest of the way home. It wasn't far, and it wasn't dark. Not yet.

Without looking around again, she reached the door and raised a closed hand above her shoulder, extending her middle finger up. *Why do guys think I owe them a greeting, whether it be a hello or a smile? I owe them nothing.* Sure, on stage, she adored the attention and wolf whistles, especially when 'dead presidents' made their way inside the waistband of her G-string.

As she stepped onto the street, the man's voice boomed, calling out again from behind her. She continued to answer his call with her middle finger salute and clutched her handbag with her free hand, ready to reach inside and grab a makeshift weapon if needed. Keys on a keyring between her knuckles, her deodorant spray, or even her hairbrush with its thick plastic frame could hurt someone. And the small pistol her father had made her learn to carry. Not that she'd had reason to shoot it. Yet.

Walking briskly, she kept her eyes focused straight ahead and her chin raised. *Don't look back. Don't look scared.* Two blocks to go. Had anyone followed her off the bus? She couldn't hear footsteps following her. Being December, the twilight shadows lengthened early. They crept across the sidewalk, swallowing it further and further in darkness until the only thing keeping the shadows at bay was the streetlamps that flickered on like beacons lighting her path.

Both the nerd and the man with the gruff voice had scared her today. Which was unusual.

Wasn't she used to the creepers and perverts yet? The city was full of them.

But she couldn't help hoping neither had gotten off the bus with her. What was making her panic today? Was it being with Ricky? He'd been okay. Nothing great, but nothing bad either. He certainly hadn't threatened her in any way. Had that sleazebag manager of his put something extra in her drink? She'd signed the non-disclosure agreement in good faith, but assholes were called assholes for a reason.

Her heels clicked a steady tempo on the sidewalk, matching the quick rhythm of her heartbeat. Turning off the main street, she walked down a narrow alleyway where the tops of low-rise apartment buildings shielded her from what remained of the daylight.

Near dark and full of white noise, her usual route rarely worried her, as people often sat outside on their balconies, watching the city. But today, she couldn't see a single person. *Why was no one outside today? Fuck, I don't like this.*

"Hey Kylie, why won't you talk to me?"

The man's sudden words right behind her made her miss a step and nearly trip. She regained her pace immediately and hurried toward her apartment building, not looking back. She didn't recognize the voice. It sounded different to the nerd and the man who'd hassled her when she made her way off the bus. She used the stage name of Busty Belle at whichever club she worked, and the fact this latest guy had called her by her real name didn't do anything to calm the panic. Had Ricky blabbed about her to anyone? Or that manager of his?

She kept her eyes focused on what was in front of her and picked up the pace. Her stilettos echoed with each footfall on the concrete. *Just keep going, Kylie, you're nearly there.*

Yes, just a few more yards, and she would be at the lobby entrance. She couldn't run in her heels, but that didn't stop her from trying the closer she got to safety. Who the fuck was stalking her now, and why? *Was it the killer?* That new thought caused the chill that already prickled her skin to turn into a shiver. A serial killer was making the rounds. Some guy who liked to burn people. It was all over the news. *What if it was him?* Her pulse was beating so fast, and her chest ached like her heart would burst if she didn't slow down.

A few seconds later, she reached the door to her building and pulled out her key ring. Hands shaking, it took a moment to locate the key to the complex. As the seconds mounted, so did the feeling that someone was right behind her, breathing down her neck. *He's right here. Right here!* She fumbled with the key, trying to insert it in the lock, and darted a glance to her left.

No one was there.

What?

She turned and studied the street behind her, but all that greeted her was the deepening night shadows and streetlights. No cars. No people at all. It was as if the world had gone empty and silent. Heart racing, she turned back to the door and tried to push the key into the lock once more. The key scraped against the brick. The lock was gone, and so was the door. So was her apartment lobby. Everything that should have been there was gone. Replaced by a brick wall in front of her.

"*What the fuck?*" she shouted and took a quick step back.

The entrance door was now about twenty yards from her to the right. Either she'd somehow moved sideways in her panic, or the building had. She squeezed her eyes shut tight. What the fuck had that asshole Gerry Goader put in her drink? *This isn't happening, no fucking way it can be real.*

"That's no way for a lady to speak."

Kylie spun to her left. "Where the hell are you?"

She fumbled with her keys, guiding them between her fingers to use as a weapon. Her other hand reached into her purse for her gun.

"I like a girl who puts up a fight."

The voice was so close. *Where is he?* She turned in a small circle, searching the area around her. He must be in the shadows. Hiding like a coward. Everything about the situation was totally fucked up. The tiny hairs on the back of her neck tingled as a breeze wafted upon her. "Just show yourself."

The wind picked up, whistling as a gust rattled its way down the street. The darkness increased, seeming to suck the light shining from the streetlamps into it and dimming everything with a dank mist. Kylie coughed as her heart pounded. What should she do? *Turn and fight? Or run like hell?*

Choosing the latter—she couldn't shoot a person she couldn't see—Kylie kicked off her stilettos and sprinted into the night. If she couldn't get into her apartment, maybe she could reach another. Her bare feet slapped against the rough pavement. She wouldn't be able to keep it up for long before the pain searing through her soles and up her legs put an end to it.

Stealing a glance behind her, she almost fell as her mind balked at what her eyes registered. Through the growing darkness of the day's end, a darker, hazy silhouette of something vaguely person-shaped was levitating above the ground. Despite, or maybe because of, the terror making it hard to reason, she couldn't help thinking how the ability to float above the ground would come in handy for her right now.

"You can't get away, Kylie." The figure's voice was deep and slightly raspy.

Too breathless and sore to respond, she fought against the pain to pick up the pace. If nothing else, she could simply run all the way down this street to the next, where she knew there were plenty of cars and pedestrians. Someone would save her.

"Help!" she called out as she ran forward. "Help me." It was a vain attempt, but someone might be nearby even if she couldn't see them.

The air was already dank and cold, and a sudden icy wind rushed past and seemingly through her, threatening to freeze her on the spot. She stopped running mid-step, unable to do more than breathe. It was as if the cold had wrapped around her, paralyzing her. *How?* She wanted to scream. Her throat stung like she'd tried to swallow a handful of razor blades. She coughed, struggling against the paralysis, and managed a few more steps. The pain was agonizing. All she needed to do was make it a few more yards, and she'd reach the end of the street and be on the main one. Vehicles passed by—left to right and vice versa—in the street ahead. Impossible to move now, she stood still as she froze by the second. The silhouette of a man crossed the sidewalk ahead. If only she could call out to him. Would he see her standing there?

The man stopped when he reached the halfway point of the street crossing. Could she be sure it was a man, given all she could see was a hooded outline against the combination of darkness and movement of bright lights behind it? She opened her mouth. "A..." was all she could manage before coughing violently.

"Poor Kylie. Bit cold, are you? Would you like me to warm you up?"

The man coming toward her raised his arms. Pointing them straight out to each side, he slowly turned them upward so his fingers pointed at the sky.

A feeling of warmth grew in the pit of Kylie's stomach, a much-welcome relief against the icy stabbing pain throughout her body. Maybe this person in front of her was her savior. If she could reach him, touch him, maybe the warmth would grow upon making physical contact.

Please, save me…

Please, if you can hear me… somehow.

Stepping toward her, the dark figure lowered his arms as if he were about to embrace her. The heat coming off him was intense. It thawed her limbs, allowing her to move once again. She leaned toward him and fell to her knees, overcome with relief. "Sweet Jesus," she managed to whisper as tears trickled down her cheeks. "Thank you."

"Jesus? Do you think He cares about you?"

The indignant sound in the man's raspy voice drew her gaze to him. Dressed in black and hidden by shadows, all she could make out was his hooded shape. But behind him, the end of the street appeared to disappear. *No way.* Rather than seeing a gap between the buildings at the end of the alley, she saw a brick wall. The figure took a couple of steps to its left, and there it was, the entrance to the apartment building. But how? How could she have run along the sidewalk toward the end of the street and now see the wall in front of her?

"Do you think *anyone* cares about you, Kylie?"

What? I'm asleep, that must be why I'm seeing weird shit. If she could wake herself from this crazy dream, she'd be okay. *Maybe I'm sleeping next to Ricky.* If so, she wanted to wake up even more and treat him to another round of reverse cowgirl, the position the pop singer loved most.

"Ricky doesn't care about you." The imperceptible sound of rustling filled the air as if the figure shook his head. "No one does. Not even you," the baritone voice boomed at her.

Was he reading her thoughts? She tried to stand, needing to run again, but the soothing heat that originated in her stomach was making its way down her legs, increasing in intensity. By the time it reached her feet, she screamed out as loud as she could ever recall. "Please… someone…" she sobbed.

"They. Can't. Hear. You," he sang.

An acrid, burning scent filled the air, twisting Kylie's stomach as she realized it might be coming from her. She wanted to vomit but fell face-first to the ground instead. Her entire body quickly heated to an unbearable temperature, and she rolled around on the ground as if on fire. The movement served zero purpose unless grazing her skin and failing to gain any distance from the menace leaning down above her counted as purposes, in which case they weren't helpful.

What the fuck are you?

"I'm just a guy doing his job. This isn't personal, you understand. A message needs to be sent. No one cared when you were alive, Kylie. But they will now you are dead."

As the fire burned, spreading through her bones and outward to her flesh, the agony of being seared was more than Kylie could take. She lost consciousness quickly, and her world turned mercifully black.

Chapter 3

"If we're being detained for something, I'd really like to talk to my lawyer," Sam said as he studied the two well-armed soldiers who stood by the closed door.

The van had stopped in an underground parking garage, and, following an escorted walk through a dimly lit hallway, he and the others had been left in what appeared to be some kind of holding room. From the cream-colored walls and fluorescent lighting to the metal chairs and rectangular table that occupied the center of the room, everything was utilitarian and gave little clue as to where they were. Additionally, other than a pitcher of water and a bowl of cellophane-wrapped packets that reminded Sam of airplane snacks, the room was bare.

"I'd like to talk to a lawyer regardless," Sarah muttered. She shifted in her seat beside Sam, not taking her eyes off the two agents who stood adjacent to a second closed door on the opposite side of the small room.

Bella sat beside her in silence, swinging her feet and looking both frightened and bored as she ate a chocolate chip cookie, but at least she was no longer crying.

Ena rhythmically tapped her nails against the glass of water in her hands, giving the two agents a glare that could have frozen the Abominable Snowman.

Sam leaned forward and pressed his hands flat on the table. "Can you at least tell us who you are if you can't tell us why we're here?"

The two agents exchanged a glance. They were not the men who had accompanied them in the van but wore the same dark suits, sunglasses, and communication devices in their right ears. They also hadn't said a word since Sam and the others had arrived.

"I'm Agent Jupiter, and this is Agent Saturn." The older agent gestured at the younger, bald-headed man next to him. "You are here for your own safety."

"It speaks!" Ena crowed. She placed the glass on the table and lifted her hands into the air in a 'hallelujah' gesture.

"Safety?" Sam asked the agents, ignoring Ena's antics. Safety wasn't a word he liked unless they were talking about seatbelts, stop signs, or condoms. He glanced at Bella and back at Agent Jupiter. "Are we in some kind of danger?"

The two agents shared another glance, and Saturn shook his head. Jupiter turned back to Sam. "This facility houses sensitive information that is restricted. Until you've received proper clearance, you all need to stay here with us."

"Oh, I get it now. You're on babysitting duty." Sarah let out a short laugh. "Gee, you really pulled the short straw when you picked assignments today, didn't you?"

"Proper clearance?" Sam asked. *Where the hell are we?*

The door behind the agents suddenly burst open, and an older woman entered wearing a simple black calf-length dress. Her silver-gray hair was coiled into a braid, and a silver cross hung on a chain about her neck. She paused for a second as she surveyed the occupants of the room, her sharp gaze falling on the agents.

"What are you two doing? These people are our invited guests. I told you to bring them through."

"Observing protocol, ma'am," Jupiter replied. "They haven't been cleared yet by command."

"Yes, they have," the elderly woman replied in a voice surprisingly clear and sharp, given her appearance. "I cleared them myself before they even got here." She shook her head and turned to Sam and the others, pressing her palms together in an apologetic gesture. "I am so sorry about all this, folks. The goon squad can get a bit overzealous with security protocols at times." She frowned at the agents, disapproval clear in her tone and posture. She was thin and wiry, reminding Sam of a sparrow with its feathers ruffled. "They were supposed to greet you at the gate and bring you right in." She nodded at

Sam and the others. "Let's start again, this time with a proper introduction. I'm Mother Agnes. We met briefly during the aftermath of the Springfield incident. Welcome to the Church of the New World Order." Her smile was as wide as her spread arms, indicating the room and the facility beyond.

Sam glanced at Sarah. She appeared as confused as he felt. While he remembered Mother Agnes, whom he'd spoken to several times on the phone since the 'Springfield incident' as she called it, this was not at all what he'd imagined when she'd brought up the location of the communal church.

"This... is the compound?" he asked, trying to figure out why it was in a top-secret facility and coming up blank.

Mother Agnes raised her brows. "Well, more like our base of operations, for lack of a better term. We share this facility... which some here call Area 51 due to the nature of the location... with several other organizations. Some of whom we work with closely despite their sometimes-inflexible attitudes." She glared at the agents. As they appeared unconcerned with her anger, she shook her head and turned back to Sam and the others. "Where are my manners? You must be excited to see everything yourself. Come on. Let me show you around." She turned toward the door she'd come through.

"Actually, we're a bit tired. My wife could use some rest," Sam said, glancing at Sarah, who hadn't regained her color since the overexertion in the desert.

"And food," Sarah added.

"And a better apology than that," Ena piped in. "We were kidnapped at gunpoint."

Mother Agnes turned back to them. She blinked and nodded, her smile never wavering. "Yes, of course. A quick check-in to get you settled at your quarters. We can do the proper tour later. I truly am sorry for everything that's happened here today. It's quite unacceptable."

"Quite," Ena agreed. She rose from her seat and held out her hand to Bella. "Shall we see what all the fuss is about then?"

Bella nodded and slid off her chair. The girl glanced at Sam as she took her grandmother's hand in her small one. Sam helped Sarah stand and kept his arm around her shoulders. He didn't like how tired she seemed. The sooner they got to a place where they could lie down and rest, the better.

"I'm so glad you could all come." Mother Agnes gave each of them a nod in turn as they moved toward the door together. "Sam. Sarah. And you must be Ena." She reached out a hand, which Ena accepted but shook somewhat guardedly. Dimples formed in Mother Agnes's cheeks as she took in Sarah's obviously pregnant belly. "My, you have been busy, haven't you?" She raised her brows at Sam, her smile never wavering, then focused on the smallest member of the group. "And Bella, you've grown another foot, I swear."

Bella giggled. She glanced at her feet and wiggled her toes in her sparkly purple jelly shoes. "No, I still only have two."

"She means you're taller, dear," Ena explained with a soft smile.

"I know." Bella giggled, seeming almost shy as she studied the elderly matriarch of the church. "Are there other kids here?"

"Why yes, there are." Mother Agnes put her hands on her knees and stooped to speak to Bella directly. "Quite a few boys and girls just like you. I bet you'll find a new friend to play with in no time."

Bella shrugged, seeming indifferent, but Sam knew she was hiding her anxiety at being in a new place. Her eyes kept darting around the room as if she expected something to jump out at them at any moment. He grasped her free hand and gave it a steadying squeeze.

"How about we see where we are before we decide anything permanent," Sarah interjected.

"Of course." Mother Agnes gave a quick nod.

She pushed the door open, and they passed into a hallway that reminded Sam of the accessways at the Springfield Mall, long, blank expanses of cream walls lit by fluorescent lights and interrupted by the occasional doorway. No windows. There hadn't been any in the holding room either. Or in the parking garage that he could recall.

"Are we underground?" he asked, turning to look back as the exit door closed behind them. The agents had followed the group into the hall, but the soldiers had stayed behind.

"For the most part, yes," Mother Agnes explained. "It's easier to maintain and safer from prying eyes. Though the base is a strict no-fly zone anyway."

"Is it a church or a military base?" Ena glanced at Sam and back at Mother Agnes. "This doesn't sound right."

"It does if you understand that our institution is founded on being more than a place of worship," the elderly woman explained as they continued down the hallway. "There's a reason we're the ones who get called when the outside world encounters a paranormal problem they can't handle."

"Oh my God," Sarah said, sounding like she'd suddenly had an epiphany. "You're the *Ghostbusters*."

She grinned cheekily, and Sam snickered at her reference to the hit movie that was one of her favorites.

"Not quite," Mother Agnes said, laughing. "It's not ghosts we're trained to fight here." As they paused before a set of double doors at the end of the hallway, she placed a wrinkled hand on Sam's shoulder and cocked a brow. "Though there's always a first time." She stepped in front of Sam and entered a seven-digit code into a keypad. A hiss emerged from the double doors. She pushed them open and stepped through. "Come on in, Father, don't be shy."

"Please, it's just Sam now," he corrected. Though he highly respected the elderly nun, he no longer felt comfortable being called the title he'd relinquished several months prior.

Mother Agnes peered at him, studying his face. "I wasn't always a nun, working for the church. I went to Harvard and studied science. And that's what I became... a scientist. I still am. Agnes Murray, BSc, MSc, PhD. Those credentials are still valid, as is my interest in both physics and parapsychology. A person can be many things, even if they don't call themselves all of them all the time. But so that you are aware, all our ordained men are called Fathers here, just as we also have Sisters and Brothers."

She turned away and walked forward into the room before Sam could reply. He exchanged a glance with Sarah. She raised her brows, seeming as amazed as he felt. Mother Agnes was a paranormal scientist? Who would have guessed? *That's the point, isn't it?* he realized. But she hadn't renounced science, unlike how he'd renounced his vows as a priest. *But you haven't renounced God, which is why you are here.* He shook his head to clear his spiraling thoughts, followed Mother Agnes into the room—and paused.

This... is a church? His jaw dropped as he surveyed the cavernous, brightly lit chamber. It was filled with glass-partitioned cubicles, where people sat at desks watching computer monitors. A dark-skinned woman sat behind a circular mahogany desk in the center of the room, several telephones and two monitors within arm's reach. On top of one of the screens, plastic figures of Jesus, Mary, and Jimi Hendrix greeted those who approached the desk.

"That's Sister Harriet, the receptionist," Mother Agnes said, exchanging a small wave with the dark-skinned woman. "The rest are analysts and researchers." She nodded in the direction of the people working in the glass cubicles.

"What do they research?" Sarah asked.

"Whatever we need. There's a vast library in this building. It houses many rare texts that aren't available anymore or anywhere else. Things like first-hand accounts passed down from the Demon Uprising of 1498, now safely preserved in microfilm."

"I thought that was kept at the Vatican," Sam said.

The Mother Superior shook her head. "A lot of people think a lot of things, but most are mistaken."

"Is there actually a church here?" Ena asked.

"Well, of course. Come on, let's keep going," Mother Agnes urged.

When they reached the far corner of the room, Mother Agnes pulled a heavy, metal-plated door inward and told them to go ahead. Doing as she requested, Sam stepped through into a short corridor that led into a room as cavernous as the previous one. The temperature in this room was cooler, and the air seemed fresher. Daylight streamed through a series of semi-opaque skylights in the roof, though wherever the sky was, they were too far underground to see it. Plants grew in container gardens beneath the skylights, including a large fir tree, the top of which nearly touched the ceiling. It was an unusual sight, if only because fir trees were not normally desert plants. However, within the controlled environment of the facility, it was quite possible for just about anything to grow.

Bella stopped and tugged Sam's hand. Her eyes were wide as she pointed at the tree. Sam nodded. It reminded him of the one at the Springfield Mall last Christmas, too, although this one wasn't decorated.

Mother Agnes smiled at Bella. "You like our tree? Well, you've come at a good time. The children are all busy making their paper cutouts and streamers. You can join them if you want. We decorate it on Christmas Eve. Oh, we also have big baubles the size of bowling balls, and a huge silver cross gets placed on top, but that's more a grown-up's job."

Bella shook her head and stepped closer to Sam as she wrapped her hand around her tourmaline shard necklace.

"We were attacked by the Christmas tree at the mall last year," Sam explained.

"Ah." Mother Agnes nodded. "I had forgotten. This tree isn't the possessed kind, dear," she assured Bella. "It's been blessed far too often for that nonsense. You are all safe here. Probably safer than anywhere else in the world."

Nevertheless, Bella kept her hand wrapped around her necklace and close to Sam as the elderly nun gestured at the room. "This courtyard is our training facility as well as the center of the commune."

Several men, women, and youths, some as young as Bella, were dressed in shorts and T-shirts and taking part in group exercises or sparring one-on-one in martial arts using practice weapons on the artificial turf of the courtyard lawn. The music in the background, full of frantic drums and guitar playing, appeared to spur everyone in the room to move quicker. Although it sounded familiar, Sam couldn't place the band. As they continued to practice, several trainees glanced curiously at the newcomers.

"Demon fighting requires not only knowing how to command a demon to leave someone's body, but physical fitness and strength. Even fully-fledged sisters and brothers of the church train regularly."

"Is Brother Trevor here?" Sam asked, thinking of the member of the church who had been his chief liaison in making the trip to the compound. He wanted to go over the directions he'd been given by the brother and figure out where he'd made the wrong turn.

"No. As my chief assistant, he can usually be found in my office. We'll pass by there on the way to the secular quarters."

"Is it much further?" Sarah asked. A faint sheen of sweat covered her brow. Sam tightened his arm around her shoulders. This trip had been about two days too long, and the part where they'd been held at gunpoint hadn't helped.

Mother Agnes shook her head. "The residence, church, and my office are just through here." She gestured to a path, one of several that branched off from the courtyard in different directions and led to arched hallways. "School and a medical clinic are through there. Kitchen and supplies are off this way." She indicated the various paths as they walked toward the first arch she'd pointed out. "We have a laundry, playground, whatever you think might be in a village, we have it here for the comfort of our members." Her smile was wistful as she slowed at the arched doorway. "We designed it like that."

"It's impressive," Sam agreed, nodding. He had to admit, he'd never seen anywhere quite like this place.

"I'm glad you like it." They stepped through the arch and stopped as the wide path branched off yet again. "Left is where the residences are. Church is to the right. And this is my office. I share it with Brother Trevor. There's a small office in here for you, too, Sam." She hesitated for a moment. "For when you are settled and ready to begin. No rush, of course. I want you to relax and get to know us first. I've had your car moved to the parking garage and your belongings brought to your quarters already, so you don't need to worry about that either."

"Thank you." Sam nodded.

She turned the doorknob and pushed the door open. The room beyond reminded Sam of a chapel with stained glass panels featuring the life of Christ set into the walls and lit from behind, giving the room a warm glow. A mahogany desk and matching velvet-covered chairs dominated the room. Dark mahogany trim accented two other doorways that led to smaller offices from the main area, one open and the other closed.

"Brother Trevor?" Mother Agnes called out, stepping into the room. "Our guests have arrived."

A rustling sound came from the open doorway, and a second later, a young man wearing plain brown pants and a cream button-up shirt wheeled into view. Catching sight of Brother Trevor in the flesh for the first time, Sam understood why he wasn't with the other members training in the courtyard. The round-faced monk's smile was wide as he angled his wheelchair through the doorway and into the room. "Well, now. I can hardly believe it. Here you all are. Father Sam and his family, in the flesh at last."

"It's good to meet you, Brother." Sam smiled and gave Trevor a nod, then looked at Sarah as she began to tremble. "Are you okay?"

"I... I don't know." Her eyes were wide as she stared at the young monk, then quickly squeezed them shut. "Urgh!" Sarah's agonized gasp as she grabbed her stomach with both hands caused Bella to back away even as Mother Agnes and Ena pressed forward.

"Mommy?" Bella's eyes were wide as she clutched the tourmaline shard and backed against the wall.

"What's wrong?" Mother Agnes asked, first looking at Sarah, then at Sam and Ena.

Sam shook his head. "I don't know."

"It's the baby," Ena said, her brow creased with a frown. "Hold on, sweetheart. Just try to breathe," she coached Sarah using soothing words.

Sarah moaned, seeming unable to speak. She kept her eyes shut tight and her jaw clenched. They helped her to the floor, Sam acting as a support for her to lean on.

"Is she going into labor?" he asked Ena as his heart skipped a beat and sped up. *Dear God, please, not now. Not yet.*

"She better not be," Ena snapped. She rounded on Mother Agnes and the agents. "This is what happens when you kidnap a seven-month pregnant woman and force her to stand in a hot desert at gunpoint."

"Call for backup," Mother Agnes instructed the agents. "We need a medical team here immediately."

"Already done," Agent Saturn replied. He had his fingers pressed to his earpiece.

Bella shook her head, eyes wide as she darted a quick glance around the room and focused on Sarah. If she could shrink into the wall and disappear, she probably would have. "Something's wrong." Her small voice was filled with dread, a sound Sam hadn't heard in nearly a year.

He shook his head, caught in the impossible situation of wanting to comfort and protect his wife and daughter at the same time but unable to move to reach Bella. "It's okay, Bells. Mommy will be okay."

"Your mom will be okay," Ena repeated, moving to comfort the child. She wrapped her in her arms and held her close. Once again, Sam was filled with gratitude for his mother-in-law's strength and presence in their lives.

"Just stick with Nana," he instructed Bella. "I promise you we'll be fine." *He hoped.* As Sarah continued holding her belly, screwing up her face, and grunting, he feared the worst. "Come on, babe, please be okay," he spoke softly and gripped one of her hands.

Her fingers tightened around his. "I'm... trying..." Her voice was a tense whisper.

"I feel so helpless," Brother Trevor said. He seemed stunned by the rapid turn of events, his face pale as he stared at Sarah. "My apologies if my appearance caused a shock."

"Don't be absurd, Trevor," Mother Agnes said. She knelt on the floor beside Sarah, checking her pulse. "This had nothing to do with you."

Sam frowned, confused by the discussion, and then shook his head as the realization struck that Trevor referred to his being in a wheelchair. "No, this is nothing like that," he assured the man. He had no idea why the brother used a wheelchair, but he was absolutely certain that whatever the cause, it wouldn't make Sarah panic and go into premature labor. If that's what was happening. *Dear God, don't let it be happening,* he asked again.

Surely, *He* still listens. After all, Sam had left the priesthood, not his faith, and he still maintained his relationship with God and trusted Him for guidance. While Bella had been brought up with different beliefs, and Sarah hadn't been a devout Catholic for many years, neither of them had an issue with his relationship with the Almighty.

Sarah squeezed his hand again, wincing as she looked at him.

"You're going to be okay, babe." Perhaps if he said the words aloud, they would be true. This was by far the worst episode of pain he'd witnessed her go through. If they'd been anywhere else, he'd have called an ambulance and rushed her to the hospital. But here... there was supposed to be a state-of-the-art medical facility somewhere within the complex. How long would it take for help to arrive?

The sound of the courtyard door opening was preceded by a group of four people dressed in white scrubs running in their direction, steering a stretcher their way.

"Hold on, Sarah, the medical team is here," Mother Agnes announced.

Sarah clutched at Sam's hand and opened her eyes, wincing as if the light in the room hurt. She tried to hang onto him as the medical team assisted her up and onto the stretcher, but it was impossible. In seconds, she was covered in a blanket and strapped down, her arms and legs restrained for easy transport.

One of the medical personnel, a tall, dark-haired woman, put a stethoscope on Sarah's wrist. She listened for a moment, looking at her watch, and frowned.

Sarah stared at her, eyes pinched and breaths unsteady. "What's happening?" The words came out as a gasp.

"I'm Doctor Katherine Stevens, or just Kat for short," the dark-haired woman explained as she placed a hand on Sarah's forehead. "We're going to take you to our clinic and run some tests."

"Is my baby going to be all right?" Sarah managed between agonizing breaths.

"Ma'am, that's what I intend to find out." She nodded at the rest of her team. "Let's go."

"*Sam,*" Sarah called, eyes frantic as she was wheeled toward the doorway.

"I'm coming," he reassured her. A lump was forming in his throat, making it hard to speak. "We're right behind you."

Sam caught sight of Bella's pale, frightened face, which mirrored Ena's expression and probably his as well. This was worse than when he'd faced Abaddon last year. A demon he could understand and master. The terror that consumed him at the thought of losing his wife, unborn child or both was nearly debilitating. If he hadn't already been up and moving, he'd be paralyzed by the pulse-pounding terror that chilled his soul.

"She'll be fine, Sam. They both will," Mother Agnes said as they followed the medical team and the stretcher back into the courtyard and headed toward the facility's clinic. The two agents brought up the rear of the group, leaving Brother Trevor alone in his office. "Doctor Stevens is the best there is. She's the chief physician here."

Sam nodded numbly. It had been a hellish day, in a hellish week, in a hellish year, and it wasn't over. It seemed like bad luck had followed them ever since the mall massacre. Joining the Church of the New World Order was supposed to be a fresh start. Were they cursed? Stalked by an invisible predator that fed off chaos?

Sarah is going to be all right, and so is the baby. He had to believe that.

But he was also starting to believe that he'd been woefully unprepared for the realities of secular life and that there were worse things in the world than demons.

Chapter 4

Ricky Gibson sat at the rectangular dining table in his suite at the Admiral Hotel between Gerry Goader and Evelyn Estrada, a lawyer provided by Red Leonard Records who had introduced herself as a recent Harvard graduate or some shit. He didn't care who she was or where she got her degree from as long as she could make this newest nightmare go away.

Still reeling from the news of Kylie's sudden death, Ricky studied the two detectives sitting across the table from him with disinterest. Everything seemed unreal like he was looking at it from a distance and not really there. Since she'd been found burned to a crisp mere hours after leaving his suite, the police had questions. Of course they did. They always had questions when things went to shit, like when his dad had died in a car accident.

"Do you have any reason to suspect your father might have been unhappy with his life?"

No, he'd answered at the time. But how would he know? He hadn't talked to the prick for years.

He hoped these two cops would be as quick in their investigation and fuck off. Because he really, *really*, couldn't handle any more bullshit.

When the news about Kylie had broken, the Red Leonard management team had immediately swung their legal department into action, hired more security, and kept the press away. But questions still needed to be answered to clear Ricky's and the company's names.

Evelyn leaned toward the pair of plain-clothed detectives and placed a cassette recorder on the table beside one belonging to the detectives. Switching it on, she said, "I'd like to reiterate for the record that my client, Mr. Gibson, has not been charged with any wrongdoing in the case of the deceased, Ms. Kylie Summers, and that this meeting today in no way represents any admission of wrongdoing by either my client or Red Leonard Records. Any information regarding the circumstance of the victim's last known whereabouts is offered strictly in good faith and does not in any way implicate my client, nor can it be used either in or out of a court of law to implicate him in any way."

That was a lot of words, Ricky thought as he stared at the lawyer. He hadn't touched a drop of booze in twenty-four hours, which was probably why he was in a shitty mood and had a screaming headache. He had no idea what Evelyn had just said, but apparently, the two investigators did.

"That is correct," the older of the two detectives, who had introduced himself as Detective Martin Briggs, agreed with a nod. "Mr. Gibson is not a suspect in the death of Ms. Summers. We wish to ask him a few questions we feel are pertinent to the case and appreciate his cooperation in answering them as truthfully as possible."

Evelyn studied Ricky. "Are you okay with this?"

Ricky shrugged. Did he have a choice? He scanned the table and found the pile of fan mail Gerry had allowed him to see in the hopes it might make him feel better. On the top was a postcard from Bella Morris, sent from somewhere in Nevada recently. He picked it up and read the brief message again, smiling as he thought of her and her family going on what sounded like a road trip from hell to some place near Groom Lake. Why the hell there? He'd never understand, but the fact his friends were nearby and in the same state was grounding.

"Ricky?" Evelyn prompted again. "Are you okay with the detectives asking you questions?"

He pushed the postcard aside and sucked in a deep breath. "Yeah, whatever. Let's just get it over with, please." He had a fresh bottle of Johnnie waiting for him once they were finished.

"Thank you. I know this must be a difficult time. Kylie was..." Detective Briggs flipped through the notebook he had on the table in front of him. "... a friend from high school. You knew each other well?"

"No. I hadn't seen her in years."

Briggs's brows flicked, and he nodded while he wrote in the notebook as if Ricky's statement corroborated what he already knew.

"What can you tell us of your interaction with the deceased?"

"She arrived at my room sometime in the afternoon. I had been drinking, so I'm not sure exactly what time she arrived. We talked briefly about old times, had a couple of drinks, and... engaged in sexual intercourse. I used condoms each time. After the third time, I must have fallen asleep, and when I woke up, she had left."

Again, the detective nodded. "Were you aware that she worked as an exotic dancer in various venues along the Strip?"

Ricky stared at both detectives and darted a quick glance at Gerry. "No, I had no idea. I mean, she had an amazing body and..." Shit, he'd guessed Gerry had paid her to spend the afternoon with him, but the stripping part, that was news. "She never mentioned anything about working as a stripper."

The detective studied him. "Did she talk about her personal life at all? Family, boyfriends, anything?"

Ricky shook his head. "No."

Detective Briggs wrote in his notebook for a long moment.

When the next question came, it was from the younger investigator, Detective Steven Bradley. "Did she ask you about the Springfield Mall incident at all? Maybe ask about the demon you encountered?"

Ricky furrowed his brow at the odd question. He shook his head. "No. We, ah... didn't do a lot of talking."

"So, she didn't show interest in the occult or supernatural." Detective Bradly seemed disappointed by that as he scribbled in his notebook and frowned.

"Not that I'm aware of, no." Ricky had to admit it did happen sometimes. A reporter would get past security, pretending to be a fan in order to get the inside scoop on what had happened at the mall. And sometimes the girls Gerry brought in would have weird fetishes, like the one who had been into biting and blood, which didn't do anything for Ricky except freak him the hell out. But Kylie hadn't been anything like that.

Evelyn intervened. "My client is talking to you of his own free will. Is this line of questioning relevant to this case?"

The two detectives exchanged glances, then Detective Briggs nodded. "We believe it is, yes."

Detective Bradley flipped through the folder of papers in front of him and looked at Ricky. "Your account of the Springfield incident is quite thorough, but is there anything more you can tell us about how the demon chose its victims?"

Ricky sucked in a sharp breath. He stared at the detectives, his pulse racing. *It's happening again.* He'd thought it might be the case when he had heard the news reports about the killings. And now the cops were here, asking him about demons.

"Mr. Gibson?" the detective prodded as the moment stretched and the silence built.

Ricky shook his head, unable to speak as the trembling began. It started in his hands, then went up his arms, and he had to wrap them around his chest to make it stop. *Fuck.*

Evelyn leaned forward and shook her head. "Excuse me, Detective. My client suffered severe trauma during the Springfield tragedy, and that topic is now off the table for discussion. If you have no further questions pertaining to Ms. Summers, I will kindly request you leave."

Detective Bradley raised his brows as he studied Ricky. Then he shrugged and started gathering his papers and folders. Both detectives rose.

"Thank you for your time," Detective Briggs said as he nodded at Ricky and the others in turn. "If you can think of anything that might be helpful, please call." He passed a business card across the table to Ricky. Then gave a polite smile and final nod. "We'll see ourselves out."

"Thank you," Evelyn said.

The feeling of being in a dream increased as Ricky watched the detectives head to the door. Except it wasn't a dream, it was a nightmare. One he knew he couldn't wake from. If the demon really was back or there was another one like it, a lot of people were going to die, and there wasn't anything the police or the army or anyone else could do to stop it. Well, except for one man, maybe. It wasn't Ricky the cops needed to talk to.

As Detective Briggs put his hand on the door handle, Ricky rose from the table.

"The Mall Priest," he called out. "You need to talk to Father Samuel Morris. He's the only one who can help."

Briggs gave him a slow nod. "You don't happen to know where he is, do you?"

Ricky picked Bella's postcard off the pile of fan mail on the table and read it again. "Groom Lake. He's somewhere near there with his family."

Chapter 5

Sam sat in a chair next to Sarah's bed in the compound's medical facility, holding her hand. The room itself was a comfortable size, large enough that it could probably fit two beds if needed. Ena sat on the other side of the bed, holding Sarah's other hand, with Bella snuggled on her knee.

Sarah's pain had mostly subsided. An intravenous drip had been connected to a port in her left arm. A fetal heart rate monitor was strapped around her abdomen. She rested calmly with her eyes closed as the various monitors in the room produced rhythmic sounds. The faster one was the baby's heart rate, the slower was Sarah's. Other than that, the room was quiet while they waited for answers.

Doctor Stevens nodded as she checked the latest readings on Sarah's chart. Then she placed the clipboard in the holder at the end of the bed, folded her arms across her chest, and looked at Sarah. "Dehydration and extreme exertion can cause muscle spasms. Did you know that?"

At the sound of the doctor's voice, Sarah's eyes slowly opened. She shook her head slightly.

"Well, it's nothing that the saline drip can't fix, so don't worry about that. You'll be feeling yourself again in no time. But it's imperative that you rest. I think it's best we keep you here for now, just in case."

Sam let out a pent-up breath in relief. He tried to think of the last time Sarah had drunk anything, probably at the rest stop during lunch. But she'd only picked at her food then, too, so he wasn't sure. He did know she had refused any water offered by the soldiers or agents since the kidnapping in the desert, claiming she didn't trust what was in it.

"My wife can be very stubborn," Sam admitted with a sigh as he cocked a brow at Sarah. Keeping her in bed at the clinic was probably a good thing, given how willful she was on a good day.

Sarah frowned at him and turned her attention back to the doctor. "The baby is okay?" Her voice was quiet and slightly hoarse, her face still paler than Sam liked.

Doctor Stephens nodded. "I'll say. He's a strong one. Listen to that beat." She tapped the baby's heart rate monitor, smiling. She let the steady rhythm run for a moment longer before turning it off. "He's big, though. You have a footballer growing in there, which is another reason I want you to keep off your feet. There are some risks involved with big babies that we need to talk about. We may want to consider inducing labor a bit earlier—"

"So it *is* a boy," Ena crowed, cutting the doctor off. "I thought so." She looked smugly at Sam and then Sarah, and gave Bella an excited hug. "Did you hear that? You're going to have a little brother."

Bella didn't say anything. Her face remained in the same closed-off expression she'd had since Sarah had started screaming in pain several hours earlier.

The doctor seemed taken aback. "Oh, I'm sorry. You didn't know?"

Sam caught Sarah's gaze and smiled. *They were having a boy.* She tightened her hold on his hand and gave it a squeeze as an answering smile touched her lips.

"We had thought to keep it a surprise until the birth," he explained to the doctor.

"Well, congratulations," Doctor Stephens said, sounding slightly awkward. "There are some other tests I'd like to run. More bloodwork, an ultrasound, amniocentesis, that kind of thing, though you might have had one already."

Sarah shared another glance with Sam and shook her head. "No needles."

The doctor seemed puzzled. "Do you mean the amnio?"

Sarah nodded. "No needles," she repeated. "Too risky."

Doctor Stephens paused. "Okay, well, we can discuss that later when you're feeling better. For now, you need sleep. And the rest of you, too." She pointed at Sam and the others. "You've had a busy day. There's probably some food in the mess hall still if you'd like some supper."

Sam shook his head. Food was the last thing on his mind. "Can another bed be brought in? I'd rather not leave my wife, and my daughter will sleep better if she's near Sarah."

The doctor let out a heavy sigh. "It can, yes, but other than needing rest, Sarah's fine and so is the baby. I'd advise that you all start getting settled in your new quarters. It's not far. Sarah can join you in a few days." When neither Sarah nor Sam answered, she added, "You'll sleep more comfortably in your own place without people walking in and out of the room all day and night checking on Sarah."

While Sam understood that what the doctor was saying made sense, he kept his eyes on Sarah. "What would you like, babe? Do you want us to stay?"

Sarah blinked and glanced around the room, her gaze landing on Bella. The little girl's blue eyes were watery, and she was starting to sniffle. Sarah immediately reached for her, struggling to sit up higher. "Oh, baby, what is it? What's wrong?"

"I thought you were going to die," Bella wailed. She launched at Sarah, climbing onto the bed to wrap her arms tightly around her neck.

"Oh, no, no, no," Sarah said, soothing the girl as best she could. She tried to comfort her by wrapping her in a hug, but the IV line made it awkward. "I'm not going to die, sweetheart," she insisted as Bella's sobs increased. "I promise."

Sam caught Sarah's worried gaze. *Oh shit.* He should have expected something like this. Having already lost her father in an accident years ago and her mother last year during the demon attack at the mall, Bella was especially sensitive to the fragility of life and the reality of death.

Sam reached across the bed. Putting his hand on the back of Bella's head, he gently stroked her hair. "Bells, hey," he said softly, trying to calm her down with his most soothing voice. "You heard the doctor. Mommy's fine, and so is the baby."

As the sniffles and sobs continued, Doctor Stephens moved forward, looking concerned. "That's right, Bella. Everything's okay," she reassured her. "Isn't it exciting? You're going to have a baby brother soon."

Still sobbing, Bella abruptly pushed away from Sarah and faced the doctor. Her face was blotchy and red, and her eyes swollen and watery with tears. "*He's not my baby brother*," she shouted.

Breaking away from the bed, she bolted for the door and ran from the room.

Stunned silence filled the room as everyone shared a horrified glance.

"Oh my God. Bella," Sarah whispered, struggling to throw off her sheets and get out of bed. Her face was a white mask of pain.

Sam shook his head and pressed her back against the pillows. "Don't you move," he ordered. He pointed at Ena next. "Make sure she stays here. I'll handle Bella."

Ena nodded numbly. Both she and Doctor Stevens seemed still in shock from Bella's sudden outburst.

"We'll sleep in here," Sam said to the doctor as he ran past her out the door after his daughter.

AFTER A FRANTIC HUNT that involved the help of several others, including agents Jupiter and Saturn, Sam finally found Bella sitting beneath the giant pine Christmas tree in the central courtyard, of all places.

She was huddled in a ball, her arms wrapped around her knees, seeming to stare at nothing.

Sam nodded sideways at Agent Jupiter as relief at seeing his daughter spread through him. "Thank you," he murmured. "I'll take it from here."

The agent nodded in return and pressed his fingers to his headset. He spoke into it in a voice too low for Sam to hear, but he picked up the word 'found.'

The agent moved off, motioning for the small crowd that had gathered to do the same.

Sam approached the tree cautiously as he studied Bella. The last thing he wanted was for her to run off and find somewhere else to hide. Neither his heart nor his body could take another round of 'Where's Bella?' The day had been beyond stressful enough.

She didn't look at him as he lifted the lowest branches and crawled into the dark space beneath the tree with her.

"Bells?" he called softly.

Her gaze flicked to him, but she otherwise didn't move or say anything.

Okay. "Nice place you've found here," he admitted as he glanced around at the tree.

The space they were in was just big enough for him to sit beside her comfortably, with his head brushing the lowest branches. The hard-packed dirt they sat on was cool but not damp and covered with a fine scattering of soft, dry pine needles. The air smelled like sap, and the tips of the branches dipped at the far edges to touch the ground in places, creating a shelter that was calm and peaceful. He could see why she had come here to escape for a bit and not gone to the chapel, which was where he'd looked first. Considering Bella had been raised pagan by her birth mother and still worshipped Gaia, he mentally kicked himself for not thinking she'd go where the plants were, even though she'd thought this tree scary earlier.

He rubbed his nose, trying not to sneeze from the strong pine scent, and wrapped his arm around her shoulders. She didn't move closer, but she didn't move away, which he took as a good start.

"What's going on, Bells? Why'd you run off like that?" he asked softly.

He felt rather than saw her thin shoulders shrug.

Okay. He sighed and tried a different tactic. "You know that Sarah and I both love you very much, right?"

She nodded.

"You are our daughter. Nothing can ever change that. Not even the baby. We won't ever love him more than we love you. It's not like that."

He glanced down and found her watching him. The look of mistrust in her eyes was hard to witness, but he didn't flinch or look away. "It's not," he insisted, willing her to believe him. A lump was forming in his throat that spread from the ache in his chest. He swallowed hard.

"I know," she whispered, turning her face away again. Her hands were wrapped in a death grip around her tourmaline shard necklace.

"Then why did you say that about the baby… about him not being your brother?"

"Because he isn't."

"Not by blood, no, but he's our child and part of our family, just like you, and that makes him your brother."

She didn't say anything. The silence built for a long moment.

"Don't you like the baby?" he asked.

Bella shook her head.

"Why not, love?"

"It's trying to kill Sarah," she whispered.

He stared at her. *Was that because of the pain Bella had witnessed Sarah going through earlier?*

He shook his head. "No, he's not."

She looked at him, her eyes wide and clear. "How do you know?"

He raised his brows. "Doctor Stevens said everything was fine. It's her job to know these things. Why would she lie?"

Bella fell into silence again and rolled the black shard attached to her necklace between her palms. After a long moment, she spoke in a voice so small he could barely hear it. "I don't like this place."

He gave her shoulders a small squeeze. "All new places seem strange at first. It'll be okay after a while." He gestured at the tree they were under. "You didn't like this tree when you first saw it, right? But now you know it better, it's a pretty good tree. It let you hide here, didn't it?" He grinned. "You know, I probably walked past this spot about seven times looking for you. But the tree wouldn't let me see you until you were ready to be found. I think you've made your first friend here."

Bella nodded, and this time, a faint smile flicked at the corners of her mouth. "It is a pretty good tree," she agreed. She patted the ground where the roots grew near the surface of the earth.

"I love you, Bells," Sam said. He wrapped her in a tight hug. Whether it was Gaia or God, or both who had brought them together, he'd always be grateful.

"I love you too, Sammy," she whispered. It was a funny thing with Bella. Most of the time, she called him Dad, Daddy, or Papa, depending on her mood and fancy, but when she was being really serious, she called him by his name, either Sam or Sammy.

As he pulled away, she reached up and tweaked the tip of his nose, pretending to hold it between her fingers by showing her thumb. "Got your nose." She grinned, and her teasing smile was the best thing Sam had seen all day.

"Come on, you monkey." Sam laughed and blinked away the tears that kept threatening to gather. Let's get back to Mom and Nana and tell them about the tree you've found."

"Okay," Bella agreed.

As they crawled toward the opening in the branches, she asked, "Do you think they have ice cream here?"

"Yes, we do," Mother Agnes answered. She was standing near the tree on the pathway, Brother Trevor beside her in his wheelchair, and Jupiter and Saturn stood like black-suited shadows behind.

The serious expression on their faces made Sam pause. What the hell was going on now? He slowly got to his feet and brushed pine needles off his legs, helping Bella do the same.

Mother Agnes held out her hand to Bella and smiled. "Why don't we find some ice cream for you to share with your nana and mom while I speak with your dad for a little while? I bet Mommy would like a treat after such a long and exciting day. What's her favorite flavor?"

"Chocolate," Bella answered. "Same as me. Daddy doesn't like ice cream, though."

"No?" Mother Agnes gave Sam a quick glance with raised brows.

"I know. He's weird," Bella said, taking the elderly woman's hand in hers. They looked at Sam together as if they were coconspirators.

"Hmm. What's his favorite food then?"

"Ham sandwiches."

"That's different." Mother Agnes gave Sam a smile.

"Mommy makes the best," Bella said as she set off toward the medical clinic with Mother Agnes. "That's what Daddy says, anyway.

Sam shook his head, feeling dizzy with whiplash from Bella's ever-changing moods. Seeing her chatting happily to Agnes now, it was as if nothing had even happened, and she hadn't just spent the better part of an hour hiding under a pine tree because she was afraid the baby was trying to kill Sarah.

God, give me strength. I am not cut out for this parenting thing.

At least Bella was happy again. He'd take that as a win.

After a short walk, they reached the medical clinic and Sarah's room. Mother Agnes and the others waited outside while Sam took Bella in to see Sarah. He was relieved to see a second bed had been added as well as a smaller cot, one on either side of Sarah's. Ena had apparently volunteered to sleep in their assigned quarters and begin unpacking their things, leaving Sam and Bella free to spend as much time as possible with Sarah.

The stuffed alien doll that they'd picked up at the rest stop in Rachel, as well as Bella's Walkman and headphones, had been neatly placed on the cot. Bella squealed when she saw them and darted forward, filled with renewed excitement.

"Thanks, Nana. I'm sorry for what I said." She gave Ena a kiss and a hug and moved to the bed to do the same with Sarah. "And for running off."

"It's okay, baby." Sarah gave Bella a soft smile and swept the girl's dark blonde hair back from her face with her fingers. "I understand. I'm just glad you're safe."

Bella climbed up onto the bed with Sarah and snuggled in beside her.

Sam stood off to the side, arms crossed, watching. Sarah caught his gaze. Her eyes were filled with warmth as she mouthed, "Thank you," at him over Bella's head.

"I made friends with a tree," Bella said, back to her normal chirpy self. "If you're well enough, I'll show it to you tomorrow."

Sarah's smile was tinged with tiredness. "I'd like that."

"I heard that someone in here likes ice cream," Mother Agnes interrupted, coming into the room with a nurse who pushed a cart holding a tray stacked with bowls, cups, cutlery, and a big tub of ice cream. There was even a sandwich wrapped on a plate that Sam assumed must be meant for him.

"Oh, my, look at that," Ena exclaimed. "Now, aren't you lucky, Bella?"

"It's chocolate," Bella said, grinning. "We can all have some. I already asked."

"Thank you," Sarah said to Agnes, who nodded in return.

The nun moved back into the hall, where she lingered outside the room with the others, watching everyone through the large observation window in the wall.

Sam followed her.

"Thanks for this." He nodded at the window, which showed Bella smiling and chatting to Sarah and Ena while they all sat together on Sarah's bed, eating ice cream. "For everything," he added.

"It's the least I can do," Agnes said. She sounded tired and seemed slightly sad as she watched the happy scene through the window.

Sam frowned. "You said earlier you wanted to speak to me?"

Mother Agnes raised her brows. She turned from the window to study Sam.

Brother Trevor opened his mouth as if to say something, but the elderly nun shook her head at him.

"It's nothing that can't wait until tomorrow." She patted Sam on the arm. "Go eat your sandwich and get some rest. We'll catch up in the morning."

Sam nodded. "Okay." He had to admit he was feeling tired. And a decent rest would do them all good.

But as he watched Mother Agnes set off down the hall with Brother Trevor and the two agents falling in behind, he couldn't shake the feeling that as chaotic as things had been today, something even worse was lurking on the horizon.

Chapter 6

The next morning, Sam woke stiff and sore from a restless sleep. His dreams had been filled with people with glowing red eyes and soldiers who forced him at gunpoint to walk to the steady beat of a heart rate monitor into the desert, where it was so hot that even the sand was on fire.

On the plus side, Sarah felt better and looked more like her usual self. As promised by Doctor Stevens, the IV treatment was doing the trick, but Sarah still needed more rest before she could be released. Bella was her usual bundle of energy and needed some exercise, so after a small breakfast of orange juice and pancakes in the mess hall, Ena took Bella to the playground to meet other children, and Sam made his way to the office to speak with Mother Agnes. The question of what she'd wanted to discuss was weighing in his mind, and if he was to take up the reins of his new position as pastor, he may as well get started.

Upon opening the door to Agnes's office, Sam found Brother Trevor sitting alone behind the main desk in the lobby area, and the doors to the two smaller offices closed.

The young clergyman glanced at his wristwatch. "Well, aren't you the perky one, showing up for work already, and it's not even nine." He raised his hands in the air as if he was making a benediction. "*Arise, shine, for your light has come, and the glory of the Lord rises upon you.*"

Sam wasn't in the mood for quotes from the Bible. He walked up to Trevor and shook his hand. "It's just me, not God himself, Brother Trevor."

The brother raised his brows. "Did you sleep well? And how is your lovely wife this morning? Feeling better, I trust."

"No, and yes."

"I see. You have the look of a man who could use a strong cup of coffee. I'll have some brought in." Trevor picked up the handpiece to the phone on his desk and pressed a button. "Brother Jim, can you bring a tray of refreshments to my office?" He paused for a response. "Thank you."

When he replaced the receiver, Sam asked. "Is Mother Agnes around? I'd like to speak with her if I may."

"She's taking a call but asked me to get you settled if you stopped in early." He smiled as he pushed back from the desk and wheeled his chair to the closed door on the right. "By the way, I owe her a bag of Reese's Pieces, thanks to you. I bet that you'd sleep until noon after all the commotion yesterday, but she pegged you as an early riser."

"Ah… sorry."

Brother Trevor laughed. "Don't worry about it, Sam. I'm just messing with you." He turned the handle on the mahogany door and pushed it open. "This is your office. It used to be Father Clint's, but… well, you know."

Sam studied the shelves of books that lined the walls and stacks of papers on the desk. Working in the same room Father Clint once occupied made him uncomfortable.

"I wasn't sure what you wanted to keep, so I left everything. Feel free to make it your own, though. Clint wasn't big on computers, but if you want one, we can get one set up. Whatever you need, just let us know."

Sam stayed where he was in the doorway. "I brought his cross with me. I thought it best to return it." He lifted the heavy silver cross from beneath his shirt and pulled it over his head. "I'm so sorry Father Clint passed away in battle. He was a great man, and one hell of a fighter." He offered the cross to Brother Trevor.

"Oh, no. That's not necessary. The cross is yours to keep," Mother Agnes said from behind Sam.

He turned around to face her. He hadn't heard her come in, but the door to the office on the opposite side of the room now stood open.

"Clint gave it to you, so it belongs to you," she added. She stood with her hands folded in front and wore her hair in a single braid over one shoulder and the same plain black dress as the day before. But the look in her gray eyes was full of certainty and strength that never wavered.

Sam broke eye contact and looked down at the cross. The feeling of uneasiness that had come over him when he'd looked at the office intensified. "Surely you have other priests here who would be better able to honor Father Clint's legacy."

"It was a sad day for us all here when we learned of his passing," Mother Agnes said.

"Especially for many of the women who knew him well," Brother Trevor added. A grin flashed across the young man's face, confirming Sam's suspicion that the commune was the most liberal church he'd ever encountered.

Mother Agnes's lips firmed into a line. "We have some competent priests here who can certainly hold their own in a fight against a lesser demon. But none of them have Father Clint's edge. Or your ability. Surely you must know the reason why we asked you here?"

Sam gulped. He might have backed away but was hemmed in on both sides in the middle of a doorway. "I thought this was a trial residency," he said. "You invited me here to preach to the brethren."

"You certainly have a great deal of experience leading a congregation, having done so for a good twenty years," the nun agreed. "But that is the least of your abilities, Father Sam."

Again with calling me Father.

"Clint was probably the most irreverent priest I ever knew, and he'd be the first person to admit he wasn't perfect. But his belief and devotion were second to none, and he most certainly wasn't a fool." She touched the cross and folded his fingers over it, keeping her hands over his. "He gave you this cross for a reason. He saw in you an ability he lacked, what so many of us lack... the strength to defeat a higher-order demon. His giving you this cross was no accident." She paused and looked Sam in the eyes. "He knew he was failing and chose you to be our new Specialist."

Sam looked between the brother and the nun and back again, his pulse racing. "I... ah..." He closed his eyes as the reality of his situation set in. "Fuck."

Brother Trevor laughed and looked at Mother Agnes. "You were right. He is a lot like Clint as well as smart."

"What if I don't want to be The Specialist?"

The nun laughed. "It doesn't matter if you want to be or not. It's who you *are*." She patted his hands before pulling hers away. "Cross or no cross, it doesn't change things. But it is a useful tool, as you have already found out, so you might as well put it back on."

Sam's head began to spin. "I need... to sit down."

Mother Agnes guided him to one of the chairs by the desk in the main room.

Brother Trevor followed in his chair. "I know it's a lot to take in, but from what we know about the Springfield demon attack, you were born to do God's work fighting the powers of evil."

Sam looped the chain over his head and let the cross fall back against his chest, where he'd kept it safe for the better part of a year. Or had it protected him?

He chose you to be our new Specialist. Mother Agnes's words echoed through his mind.

He'd known it all along, hadn't he? Suspected it in the deep recesses of his soul? Was that why he'd secretly been excited and relieved to come here, even if it had upset Sarah? He squeezed his eyes shut and put his hands on the sides of his head. "I need... some air."

"Of course. Take your time." Mother Agnes moved to a console on the wall and pushed a sequence of buttons. Within moments, a fresh breeze brushed Sam's skin as the climate controls adjusted to the new settings.

The dizziness slowly subsided as Sam focused on steadying his breaths, and by the time Brother Jim arrived with a trolley of refreshments, he'd regained a semblance of focus.

The newly arrived brother, an elderly gray-haired man with a lanky build, smiled upon seeing the priest. "I'm so honored, Father Sam." His hand trembled as he poured Sam a cup of coffee. "Your feats are legendary." He smiled as he handed the cup over. "Cream? Sugar?"

"Black," Sam said. He accepted the cup with a nod and took a sip. It smelled and tasted strong and hot and was exactly what he needed. He took another sip and nodded appreciatively at Brother Jim. "Thank you. It's good."

Brother Jim stepped back and nodded, folding his hands together. "Thank you, sir." He busied himself with serving refreshments to the others.

Sam turned to Agnes as he sipped his drink. "I don't understand. Your people here are trained to fight demons, right? But you're acting like Abaddon was something special."

She nodded. "Don't get me wrong, our people are good at what they do. We sent Clint because he was the best and most experienced person we had. But there hadn't been a higher-order Demon event in five hundred years. It was something he'd never faced head-on before."

Sam frowned. "And he failed."

"But you didn't," she said, taking a sip from her own cup. "If you had, none of us would be here now. We need you, Sam. The world needs you."

Celebrity status wasn't something Sam had ever sought, and he told interviewers time and time again that he hadn't won the battle against Abaddon alone. He often thought of the friends he'd made on that fateful day. Ricky, Barry, Corey, Cyndi, and the many others who hadn't made it. And most of all, he thought of how that tragedy had brought him and Sarah together, as well as an instant daughter in Bella. He shook his head. "Please, I did what I did through my faith. Not just faith in my Lord and Savior, but faith in myself, faith in love, and faith in the people I was with that day. I'm not a hero. Just a man who did what needed to be done, with the help of friends and the blessing of God."

Brother Jim finished serving the others. He smiled, nodded, and bowed as he left the office.

Once the door clicked shut, Brother Trevor clasped his hands in front of him. "I agree. God guided you that day, just like he guided you here when you were ready to embrace making the change. God is all-wise, and I'm certain, He has a plan. Otherwise, the timing wouldn't make sense."

Sam placed his cup on the desk. He glanced between Agnes and Trevor. "Timing? What are you talking about?"

"I'm sorry, Sam, I really am," Mother Agnes said. "I had hoped for more time to allow you to settle in before asking you for help, but it appears time isn't on our side, and we are out of options." She paused and pulled in a deep breath. "Have you heard about the trouble in Las Vegas?"

Sam nodded. "In passing, yes. But I haven't followed it closely. We don't play the news if Bella is in the room. Don't want her upset by things she can't control, you know? She's highly sensitive."

The nun nodded. "Yes, she is."

Brother Trevor cleared his throat and leaned forward in his chair. "Listen, I'm just going to cut to the chase. There's been a number of murders in Las Vegas, ones that the local authorities are tremendously troubled by, and they've asked for our help."

Sam studied the two of them. "They think it's a demon?"

"It's possible, yes," Mother Agnes chimed in. "The bodies have been burned, but not in the usual way. It's as if they've been burned from the inside outward. They think it might be the start of another massacre, like last year."

"Well, that would be..." Sam let the sentence trail off, struggling to find the right word. *Horrific? Terrible?* There were no words to describe the terror and devastation that Abaddon had created at the Springfield Mall. "Has another demon escaped confinement?"

"No, not that we're aware of anyway. Reports of low-level demonic activity have increased during the past year, but nothing as serious as another Abaddon."

"So... what do you think is going on? Some copycat having fun? I'm sure that the police are on the alert for that everywhere this time of year."

"Yes, they are. And they don't think it's a copycat."

Sam frowned. "So, if it's not a copycat and it's not a demon, then what is it?" *And why the hell are you calling me in to help when I only just got here?* But that was what this was all about, wasn't it? They wanted him to help them catch whatever creature was doing the killing.

"Well, we don't know for sure, but based on the description of the victims, I have a theory. Have you ever heard of something called a remnant?"

Sam paused, confused by the unusual question. "Do you mean in Biblical terms? God's remnants are supposed to be the last true believers in His word."

"That's right." Mother Agnes nodded. "But remnant, as a term, can also be interpreted as 'that which remains.' "

"Okay," Sam said, not understanding where this was going and hoping she would get to the point soon.

"Now, this gets a bit complicated without taking a course in demonology, but there are creatures in this world that are not strictly mortal. The laws that govern their existence are very specific. Some are angels, some demons, and some... well, let's just say they are something other."

Sam stared at her. He took another sip of his coffee. It was getting cold, but he didn't care. He had the feeling that whatever she was about to tell him would change his view of the world forever.

"Some of these creatures you've heard about in common occult folklore. Vampires, werewolves, and whatnot. Those are relatively easy to deal with and dispatch when they become a problem. But others are not."

Wait. Vampires and werewolves are real? He hadn't really thought about it before, but he supposed that if demons were real, other creatures could be too. He shook his head to clear it. "I take it the creature that's running around Vegas is in the 'are not easy to deal with' category?"

"Yes. We call these types of creatures remnants because they are neither alive nor dead... they are both at the same time. They are created by being harvested in the moment between life and death and trapped there. They are what remains when mortality is stripped away, and death cannot be attained yet."

A shiver went up Sam's spine. "I'm not sure I understand. Are they undead?"

Mother Agnes shook her head. "No. And this is what makes them particularly powerful. They aren't like the undead where they can be killed by a silver bullet or stabbed with a stake through the heart. Their death has already happened—they simply haven't completed it yet. So nothing else can kill them except that one specific event."

"Okay, I'm really getting lost now. Maybe you should be talking to another guy?" *Like someone who's been part of the demon-slaying club for longer than a day.* Though this didn't sound like demons. It sounded weird and unsettling.

How could something be dead and alive at the same time?

What the hell did that even mean?

"I know, it's confusing. Let me give you an example instead." She gestured with her hands in the air as if erasing a blackboard and starting again. "Imagine that you are about to die. Let's say it's a car crash." At Sam's raised eyebrows, she paused and added, "I'm not saying that's what I want to happen. I'm just using it as an example."

He shrugged. "Okay."

She continued, "A piece of metal is about to pierce your heart. It's inevitable that this will happen as the process is already in motion. And when it does, your heart will stop, and your soul will go to meet God in heaven shortly thereafter. We can agree that is the normal flow of events in the transition from life to death?"

Sam nodded.

"Now, let's say an angel is watching this crash happen and decides to intervene because God has another task that he needs you to do. So, at the exact moment when the metal is touching your heart, the angel makes his move. He pulls you back from completing the transition to death, trapping you in that moment. You are now neither alive nor dead. You are both at the same time. A remnant of the living, unable to achieve full death until the angel allows it."

"That's barbaric. Why would an angel do that?" Surely something like that wouldn't be sanctioned by God?

"Some believe it is a form of punishment for a human who has committed a crime, a way to give them a chance to atone for their sins by serving God. A remnant can interact with the world in ways that an angel can't. It cannot die, however, except by its pre-determined death. It can get stabbed, shot, decapitated, or set on fire, but as that isn't the exact death it was meant to die, it will not matter. It is nigh-invincible, which is where its great power lies... and also the power of the one who controls it."

"Wait. So the remnant can't die unless the angel allows it? And it has to do whatever the angel says?"

"That's correct." She paused for a moment while Sam absorbed that information. "Now, here's the real kicker. Imagine what would happen if it wasn't an angel who created the remnant? What if it was a demon instead?"

"Oh... my God." Sam clutched the arms of his chair while icy horror curled in his stomach. If a demon had that kind of power and control over someone, it would be worse than the mall massacre. It would be a quick path to Armageddon. "That's what you think is killing people in Vegas? One of these remnants, controlled by a demon?"

"It's possible." Mother Agnes nodded, her expression serious.

"It's more than possible," Brother Trevor said. He frowned at Mother Agnes. "The police think they've identified a motive and connection to the victims from the killer, which is also why they are looking for you, Sam."

"Me? Why would they want me? I haven't done anything." Sam shook his head as the importance of what Trevor had said dawned on him. "Wait. The police asked for me specifically? They didn't ask you for The Specialist?"

"Yes."

"Why?"

"Because Ricky Gibson is involved in the case, and he told them you would help."

"Ricky?" *Ricky's involved in the killings?* "*Fuck.*" Sam rose to his feet and headed for the door.

"Sam?" Mother Agnes stood, looking concerned.

"Where are you going?" Brother Trevor called out.

Sam paused as he opened the door. "I need something stronger than coffee." And he needed to talk to Sarah.

SAM SAT ON HIS bed in Sarah's room at the medical clinic, clutching his head in his hands. He didn't know which was worse—the church compound not having a decent bar or the fact that when he'd tracked down someone to find him a bottle of Jack Daniels, the first hefty swig had made him choke and nearly vomit.

"Well, it's not like you drink much, Sam," Sarah said. "That watered-down blood of Christ stuff served at mass doesn't exactly count."

Okay, she had a point. But shouldn't a guy in crisis be able to indulge without repercussions? He lifted his head and looked at her. She grinned as she reached for his hand and rubbed her thumb across his fingers.

She'd been unusually calm while he'd explained the situation in Vegas, Mother Agnes's fears, the strange beings called remnants, and his being appointed as the new Specialist. He thought she'd freak out and get angry at the news that he would have to leave for a bit, but she'd listened intently, nodding occasionally. He'd almost have preferred it if she had started screaming and become hysterical. At least then, he might have had a reason to tell the church and the police no because he needed to stay with his family.

Lying in her hospital bed with the IV attached to her arm, Sarah looked fragile and weak, but he knew she was anything but. Sarah was one of the strongest people he'd ever known, which was the only thing that made the decision he was being forced to make bearable.

"You're okay with all this?" he asked her skeptically.

"No!" She let out a soft laugh. "Hell, no. I'm scared to fucking death that something's going to happen to you and pissed as hell. I mean, we only just got here. I'm about to have a baby. What if you don't make it back? What about Bella?"

"I'm going to make it back," he vowed and meant it. Even if he was dragged down to Hell and had to claw his way out again, he'd make it back to his family.

She shook her head. "I don't trust any of it, least of all the timing, but I can't say I'm surprised."

He didn't like it either. Heading to Vegas to battle a demon thing hadn't been in his plans. He wanted to be with Sarah. Leaving her while she was pregnant felt more than wrong, and how the hell was he supposed to tell Bella he'd be away for a while? "Then I'll stay. They can find someone else to beat up the bad guys this time."

Sarah let out a sigh and shook her head. "But if this demon thing isn't stopped, a lot of people will die."

"Yeah."

She frowned. "And you're The Specialist, apparently."

"Yeah."

"And Ricky's in trouble," she said.

"And Ricky's in trouble," he agreed. They looked at each other for a long moment, holding hands. "So I have to go, don't I?" he whispered.

Sarah's lips trembled as she gave a quick nod.

He leaned over and gathered her close, wrapping her in his arms. Leaving Sarah was the last thing he ever wanted to do, least of all now. He kissed her brow, then moved lower and found her lips with his. She was trembling, or maybe it was him. His chest ached as he pulled back.

"You are my everything..." he breathed against her mouth, looking into her eyes, "... I promise you on my soul I'll be back."

"I know." Her wavery smile nearly broke his heart as she smoothed the hair on his brow.

He hugged her close again, stroking her hair with his hand.

"We live a weird life, don't we?" she asked softly.

"Yeah," he agreed. "The weirdest. But I wouldn't have it any other way."

She let out a short laugh. "I could do without the annual demon fighting event."

"What's going on?" Bella's sharp question made them pull back. She stood in the doorway, her hand in Ena's, eyes wide as she watched them.

"Is something wrong?" Ena asked, her expression full of alarm as she studied Sarah. "You've been crying." She and Bella moved into the room and hurried to the bedside.

"I'm fine, Mom," Sarah said reassuringly. "It's not anything about me or the baby."

Ena looked at Sam sharply. "Then what is it?"

"Ah, well…" Sam wiped his eyes and tried to think. *How the hell was he going to explain this?*

He moved to where Bella was standing beside the bed and crouched down on one knee so he could speak to her at eye level. In the end, he decided there was no good way to start so he might as well just say it. He gripped her lightly by the shoulders and gave them a reassuring rub.

"I have to leave for a few days, Bells."

She watched him for a moment, her gaze searching his face as if looking for answers. "Leave? Why?"

"Well, Ricky's in trouble and—"

"*Ricky's in trouble?*" Her eyes grew even wider if it was possible.

Okay, that wasn't a good thing to say.

"Bella, listen. There's a demon, and I have to go fight it in order to save a lot of people. So I need you to take care of Mommy and the baby while I'm gone."

Bella looked at Sarah and back at Sam. "But if Ricky's in trouble, I want to go with you."

Oh no.

"No, Bella." He shook his head. "It's not safe."

"But I can help," she said, sounding hopeful.

He shook his head again. "No—"

"I can kill demons. I'm good at it," she insisted. "You told me I was." She held up the tourmaline shard, which hung on her necklace.

Ah, damn. Sam closed his eyes and shook his head. "It's not about that. I know you're brave. But we don't… we don't even know quite what we're facing yet."

"But—"

"You can't come with me," he snapped, cutting her off. "It's not safe. You have to stay here."

Her lips formed an angry pout. "It's not fair."

Life rarely is, sweetheart.

"I'm sorry."

Her lips trembled, and her eyes watered. "But what if you don't come back?"

He pulled her close and wrapped her in a tight embrace. "There isn't anything that can ever keep me away from you, Mommy, and Nana. Nothing." He pulled back and studied her face. "I need you to be brave and stay here safe with Mommy. You can do that for me, can't you?"

She stared at him silently, her expression a mixture of unhappiness and defiance. Then she shrugged him off and moved to sit with Ena.

The elderly woman wrapped her in a hug and kissed her hair. "How about we watch something on TV, eh?" she suggested. "I bet there are some cartoons on a video." She settled Bella onto the cot and snuggled up with her.

"We'll have lunch in here too," Sarah suggested. "Eat all together. I bet there's still some ice cream we can have." She gave Sam a worried look when Bella didn't look at her or answer.

Sam frowned and moved to the small television set suspended on the wall. He searched through the selection of video cassette recorder tapes that had been provided. "Oooh, *Sleeping Beauty*, Bells. You like that one, right?" He showed her the case.

She glared at him, remaining silent.

Sam sighed, popped the cassette tape into the player, and pressed play.

It was going to be a long day.

Chapter 7

Sam woke from another restless night's sleep. He sat up and winced as his back reminded him how unhappy it was to have been positioned upon such a thin mattress, which did little to insulate him from the metal frame.

Sarah opened her eyes and smiled at him. "Morning, babe."

He placed his feet on the floor and stood, at which point his head reported that it didn't appreciate the hard pillow or constant waking during the night while nurses came in and out of the room, checking Sarah's vitals. "I'm glad you didn't put the word 'good' in front of that." He leaned over and planted a soft kiss on her lips. "How are you feeling?"

She shrugged lightly but kept smiling.

Sam nodded. He knew the smile was a mask. She was as troubled by his leaving as he was and likely hadn't slept well because of it either. Standing on tiptoe, he looked to where Bella slept and paused. Her cot was empty. "Babe, Bella's not in her bed."

Sarah nodded. "I heard her get up about half an hour ago to use the bathroom. She's probably gone to be with Grandma."

Sam frowned. "There's a sheet of paper on her bed."

"Oh?"

Sam had already made his way around the end of Sarah's bed to investigate by the time she finished sitting up. He picked up the sheet of lined paper marked with Bella's printing and read it aloud. "Mom and Dad. I've gone to play. I don't want to say bye to Daddy. Love, Bella."

Sam folded the paper and looked at Sarah, feeling like he'd been shot in the chest. Bella hadn't spoken to him since the previous day's argument and appeared to want to keep it that way. "Fuckdammit." He closed his eyes and pinched the bridge of his nose, trying to stave off the splitting headache that was coming on. "I swear this parenting stuff is harder than fighting Abaddon."

Sarah snickered. "And she's not even a teenager yet."

"Oh, God." He sat on the edge of his bed and looked at the note again. "I should go find her."

Sarah shook her head. "Leave it for now. She just needs space. She'll come round before you leave."

Sam sighed. "She's gone through so much. Way more than many nine-year-old girls. I just wish… she could see in my heart how much I love her."

Sarah smiled softly and caressed his cheek with her palm. "I'm sure she knows. She's a smart kid." She placed a hand on her stomach. "It's probably also hard for her knowing she'll be sharing the limelight with her brother."

Sam nodded. "I always thought my older brother hated me, but he kind of envied me being the baby of the family and getting away with more stuff than he did. But look at me. I grew up to be a priest and then became the poster child for a midlife crisis."

Sarah giggled, her expression reminding him of the day they reconnected at the mall when she'd brought him some lunch. "I was just hoping you would find some work that didn't involve the possibility of you getting killed or worse. But that's my Sam, always trying to save everyone. Just promise me you'll make it back. Please. If it gets too dangerous, leave and come back to us."

"I promise." As he gave Sarah another kiss on the lips, he closed his eyes and hoped he would be able to keep his word. This life he was living was still all new to him, and he wanted to be around to see his son born into the world.

A glance at his watch made him frown. Quarter past seven. Mother Agnes had left instructions that the team she'd put together to go to Vegas would leave bright and early. "I better get ready." He sighed. "Rest up and get better. I'll be back in a day or two. Please never forget how much I love you."

Sarah nodded and blew him a kiss as he headed toward the door. "I love you too."

He held back tears as he turned away and left her room.

Leaving her and Bella like this was the hardest thing he'd ever had to do.

Lord, give me strength. I need it.

AFTER SHOWERING AND CHANGING into clothes provided by Mother Agnes, Sam stood in the hallway outside his residence feeling more than a bit awkward.

The elderly nun nodded, seeming satisfied. "Well now, don't you look just like Clint? Younger, of course. But I knew everything would fit you right."

Sam glanced at the window on the wall and caught a glimpse of his reflection. With his facial hair having grown for three days, he could soon have the beginnings of something similar to the late priest's beard. He awkwardly touched the white collar fastened around his neck. It felt uncomfortable after having not worn one for several months. "Is this really necessary?" he asked.

Mother Agnes smiled and nodded. "Yes, each one of our members is required to dress appropriately when conducting church business outside of the facility. Besides, these clothes are specially made. The materials, including the fastenings and stitching, are blessed by prayers and washed in holy water to give you extra protection. We've been working on your outfit for months."

For months? "Okay." Sam nodded. He didn't feel any safer wearing the clothes, but then, he wasn't in any danger walking through the church's hallowed halls.

"We'd better hurry," she said. "The others will be waiting for us."

They rushed through the labyrinthine halls and doors of the compound for a few minutes before Mother Agnes led the way into an enormous parking lot. Unlike the parking garage they had arrived in the day before, this area was covered by a shelter with one side open to the outside. As his eyes adjusted to the morning light, Sam spotted several black vans and sedans, as well as several military vehicles, parked in the area.

"Welcome to Parking Lot A, Father Sam," Mother Agnes said, walking toward one of the black vans where a group of people waited, including Brother Trevor. "Your team has been assigned to you already."

"Due to the nature of this mission, the Bureau has loaned Agents Jupiter and Saturn to assist us. They will brief you on the mission specifics during the drive."

As they drew near, Sam nodded at the two agents, who remained as stoic as usual.

"This is Sister Jenny and Sister Penny." Mother Agnes gestured to the two women who stood nearby. They were dressed in tight black pants and long-sleeved, form-fitting tops, similar to what Sam remembered the two sisters who had accompanied Father Clint had worn.

"Father Sam, it's an honor to be selected to work with you," the tallest of the women, Sister Penny, said. With her long dark hair tied in a ponytail, she reminded him a little of a younger version of Sarah. She extended a hand for him to shake.

"Good to meet you," the other woman, Sister Jenny, extended her hand for him to shake as well. Shorter than Penny by a few inches, she had short-cropped blonde hair.

Sam opened his mouth, about to ask them if Penny and Jenny were their real names, or if they were pseudonyms. Father Clint had been partnered with a Sandy and Mandy, but did it really matter? As long as they knew what they were doing once they were on the hunt, then he was good.

As if she knew what he was thinking, Mother Agnes said, "Each of our sisters are thoroughly vetted and are some of the best slayers in the world. We have found that a trio works best when confronting paranormal creatures, a priest and two sisters, though our brothers are also quite skilled," she explained. "Jenny is adept at healing and shooting holy water, and Penny is an expert marksman with the salt shooter."

Penny gave Sam a little wave and grinned. The way she kept looking at him made him nervous. Or maybe it was the way she looked in her tight clothes. If checking out a woman constituted cheating, then he was doomed. But admiring the way a woman looked wasn't the same thing as thinking about sleeping with her, and he had no desire to do that with anyone except Sarah. He was familiar with temptation, having been committed to the vows of chastity for most of his life. *But God, why did you make women so beautiful?*

"We have a contact on the inside with the Las Vegas police, Brother Dennis. He feels the situation there is escalating, so you should get going as soon as possible. The agents will keep us in contact." Brother Trevor nodded to Jupiter, who slid the side door open.

"In here, please." The agent gestured for Sam to enter.

Sam paused and looked across the parking lot. "We're leaving now?"

"Yes. Is there a problem?"

"No, it's just... I didn't get the chance to say goodbye to Ena and Bella. I thought they might be here."

Mother Agnes reached over and patted his arm. "I'm sorry, Sam. I know the timing is far from ideal, but I will personally pass along your goodbyes to Bella and Ena."

"I give you my word. Sarah is in the best place she can be for care," Brother Trevor added. "I'll look after her in your absence and make sure everything is okay."

Sam studied the young clergyman. Sarah could take care of herself, he wasn't worried about that. But the best thing he could do was get the mission over and done with so he could get back to her as quickly as possible.

"All your stuff is loaded. Extra weapons and supplies are tucked in the back." Brother Trevor patted the side of the van with his hand. "So... you're good to go."

"Just remember your greatest weapon is your belief in the Lord. We do our work by His will." Mother Agnes smiled. "Safe travels."

Sam nodded. As he stepped on board the van, he couldn't shake the feeling of uneasiness that had settled in his stomach. Last time he'd battled a demon, it was a matter of being in the wrong place at the wrong time, but this time, it was a pre-meditated hunt.

Penny stepped around him and slid along the bench seat first, followed by Sam and then Jenny. The first thing Sam noticed, apart from how close the women sat to him, was the dark window in front of them. The tint prevented a clear view of the cabin where the driver sat with Agent Saturn. With no side windows or a rear window in the back door of the van, they wouldn't be able to see much at all.

"Make yourselves comfortable. This journey will probably take up to three hours." Agent Jupiter slid the door shut and took his seat in the back with them. "In the meantime, you can read this." He handed Sam a folder with 'TOP SECRET' stamped on the front. It was closed shut with a seal. "I'll go over the pertinent information with you." The agent cracked a rare smile. "Don't worry, there won't be a test at the end."

"Great." Sam took a long, deep breath as the vehicle's engine roared to life.

"You look nervous, Father," Penny whispered in his ear. "What's wrong?"

Geez, didn't she know he was married? Or maybe he was reading her wrong. His experience with women was confined mostly to Sarah, but he couldn't turn off the thought that Penny was flirting with him.

"I was hoping to say goodbye to my daughter before we left. She was mad, and I..." He sighed. "I wish she knew how much I love her."

As the van set off and turned the corner, the bags of equipment stashed behind their seat shifted, signaling the beginning of what Sam was certain would be the longest trip of his life.

Penny nodded. "I don't remember my dad, so I don't really miss him, you know? But kids do a lot of stuff they don't mean when they're upset. I'm sure she knows. Try to relax." She patted his knee.

"Thanks." Like that was going to happen anytime soon. He shifted as far away from Penny as possible without crushing Jenny on his right and snapped the seal on the folder.

"Okay," Agent Jupiter said. He removed his sunglasses and nodded at Sam. "Let's get started."

Sam sighed and opened the folder.

During the next hour, Sam read through the brief along with the two sisters and flicked through the pictures inside. Black and white photographs of charred bodies taken in various locations were intermingled with Polaroids from what looked like Vietnam, based on the landscape. One of the Polaroids was a five-person group shot of some men wearing camouflage army fatigues standing in front of a hut. Each man was grinning and carrying a gun.

"I'm assuming this is about the mission?" Sam asked Agent Jupiter. "Do you know who the Remnant is?"

Jupiter nodded. "Well, we think so." He pointed to the tallest member of the group, who stood at the back. "His name is Corporal William Rathburn, nicknamed the Denver Devil. He served with the fourteenth platoon under the twenty-fifth infantry division during 1972—73 in Vietnam. By all accounts, he did his duty well in service to the military. However..." Agent Jupiter paused while he shifted to see the file better. He flipped through and pointed to some typed pages. "Statements given by his fellow squad mates, as well as several locals, indicate that Corporal Rathburn abused his position on multiple occasions, and he was responsible for the brutal rape and murder of several villagers while on rotation in Vietnam. Hence the nickname the Denver Devil."

"A lovely fellow," Penny said, her voice grim with sarcasm. She and Jenny were looking at the photographs in turn.

"A complete psychopath." Jenny held the group image close to her face, studying it. "His eyes are empty of his soul even though he's smiling."

"It is quite likely that, given the serious accusations against Corporal Rathburn..." Jupiter continued, "... he would have faced trial and been dishonorably discharged from the army had it not been for his death, which occurred during a napalm run at approximately oh-nine-hundred hours on January third, 1973." The agent paused and glanced at Sam. "Or so we thought."

"Okay." Sam gave the file back to Jupiter. "Just tell me what happened and what's going on." The pictures of charred corpses of people who had clearly died in great pain were turning his stomach.

"Corporal Rathburn's body was never positively identified due to the state of the bodies recovered from the site. At least one witness to the napalm run that morning reported seeing a person walk out of the fire, covered in flames."

"So, he survived?"

"In a sense." The agent set the file aside on the seat and steepled his fingers together as he studied Sam and the two sisters. "We started hearing rumors of deaths. People burned in fires. Nothing unusual at first, of course. It usually starts off small. Remnants don't want to get caught doing what they are tasked to do, so they are careful to fly under the radar. But Rathburn has grown a taste for it."

"Wait. How many of these remnants are there?"

"Hard to say. Like I said, they are usually quite careful, and when they are done, they disappear. Could be a handful, could be thousands, who's to know?" Jupiter shrugged. "The only ones we worry about are the ones like ex-Corporal Rathburn... the ones with an MO that goes beyond the normal."

Sam shook his head. "There's normal in any of this?"

"Well, usually, we might expect that whatever duty a remnant has been tasked to complete is not personal." The agent gestured with his hands as he explained. "But in this case, there's a trail going back years, which seems pretty obvious to us now, but that's how hindsight works." He opened the file again and pulled out the stack of pictures. "Every one of these victims has been burned in the same way... from the inside out. And every one of them has a connection to Vietnam in some way. Either they lived there, served there, or, in the case of the most recent victim, Kylie Summers, was a childhood friend and recent lover of the son of the Air Force captain responsible for the napalm bombing run that, for all intents and purposes, killed Rathburn that day."

Sam stared at him in stunned silence. "Run that by me again."

"Kylie Summers was recently hired as a, shall we say, companion to Ricky Gibson. I believe you are acquainted with him?"

Sam nodded.

"She was found burned to death after spending the afternoon with Ricky. Her burns match the pattern of those found on Ricky's father, Captain Johnathan Gibson, retired, who passed away from what we thought were extensive burns suffered during an automobile accident approximately four months ago."

"I heard about that in the news," Sam said, thinking back to the reports and remembering how sad he'd felt for Ricky. They'd sent him a sympathy card.

But maybe they should have done more. "So, Ricky's father was the guy who dropped the napalm on Rathburn?"

"That is correct."

"And you feel that Rathburn isn't satisfied with killing the dad," Penny asked.

"It would appear not," Jenny said. "Sins of the father? The Remnant wants revenge?"

Agent Jupiter nodded.

"So, Ricky's a target. Does he know?" Sam asked.

"Not all the specifics, no. But he suspects something bad is going on. We have him in protective custody in his hotel in Vegas now. The problem is, and the biggest reason we need your help, Father, we don't believe Rathburn's intention is to end this vendetta with Ricky. Unless we stop him, he'll keep going, killing everyone who he feels is connected to the event and place of his death. He's not doing God's work, Sam. He's an abomination, created by th32e Devil himself."

"Oh, holy shit." A chill went down Sam's spine, and his stomach seized. His mind filled with white-hot noise for a minute while he processed what the agent had said. But as his buzzing thoughts calmed, one rose to the forefront and did nothing to ease his panic. "Sarah's father served in the army. He was a cook. He did a tour in 'Nam."

"Yes."

"So... so, this remnant could be coming after her and my family too?"

"It's possible, yes."

"Oh my God."

"We didn't want to tell you until we were away from the compound. Not only is this information confidential, there was no sense in upsetting your family. They are in the safest place they can be right now."

Sam felt the walls of the van closing in on him. It was getting hard to breathe. "Can we stop somewhere, please? I need a moment."

"Sure." Agent Jupiter nodded. He spoke into his headset and gave instructions to the driver to pull over. As he did so, Sam heard a rustling from the back of the van.

A black tarpaulin covered the rear storage area behind the seat. Containing supplies for their mission, everything had been packed in tight, so nothing should be rustling.

The hairs on Sam's neck prickled. "Something's in here with us."

"I don't hear anything," Jenny said, exchanging a glance with Penny. "Do you?"

Penny shook her head.

As the van slowed, Sam unclipped his seatbelt and turned around. If there was something in there that shouldn't be, he needed to know what it was and fast. Father Clint's cross was cool and not glowing, but that didn't necessarily mean anything. It tended not to work unless he activated it on purpose.

Getting onto his knees, he leaned over the seat and grabbed the edge of the tarpaulin. Held in place tight, he could barely lift it. Not able to see anything under it, he ran his hand over the surface, pushing down gently until his fingers located something round, like a human head. The size of a child's. He closed his eyes and shook his head, realizing they had a stowaway.

For fuck's sake.

"Bella?" he called softly.

No answer.

The women on either side of him shared a glance. Penny reached out and felt the tarp. Upon contacting the shape of a head, her eyes went wide, and she snatched her hand back. "What the hell? Someone *is* hiding under there."

"That's impossible." Agent Jupiter said.

"Well, apparently, it's not." Sam's shock turned to anger. He wished it wasn't true, but he hadn't seen his daughter before he'd joined the road trip. And now he knew why. *Leaving a note because she didn't want to say goodbye.* "Bella!" he shouted. "Trick's over. It's time to come out."

"I don't want to." Although the thick tarpaulin was over the girl's head, Sam could hear her muffled answer. She sounded scared. He sighed and closed his eyes. *God give me strength.* She'd probably heard the whole thing about the Remnant and the danger to Ricky as well as them all.

Feeling his heart almost pump outside his chest, he leaned back into the seat. "Bella, as soon as this van stops, I'm going to get them to take you back to the base, and you and me and Sarah will have a long talk."

This time Bella didn't answer with words, but instead thumped her feet against the floor of the van.

Sam shook his head and muttered. "Can this trip get any more fucked?"

Chapter 8

The van stopped on the side of the road a moment later, and Agent Jupiter opened the side door. After the dimness inside the van, it took a moment to adjust to the mid-morning sunshine. Looking out to the landscape beyond the open door, it appeared they were still in the desert, nowhere near an official rest area.

Sam quickly joined the agent outside, making his way to the back of the van where the door was up, and sure enough, the sheepish face of Bella peered out from beneath the tarp. Sam shook his head. "What the hell were you thinking, Bella?"

"No need to answer that, girl. We're going to get you flown back to the base," Agent Saturn said while Agent Jupiter spoke into a communication device that looked like a long-range walkie-talkie of some kind.

Sam shook his head. He rounded on the agents. "Seriously, how the hell did a nine-year-old girl get to the van and get inside the back of it without *any* of you knowing?"

Agent Saturn looked away. "I can't answer that."

Sam stomped and put himself directly in the agent's line of sight. "Why? Because then you'd have to admit how incompetent you are? What a fucking joke."

Saturn raised his hand in a calming manner. "Father Sam, I suggest you back away and allow my senior partner, Agent Jupiter, to take care of this."

Another man dressed in a back suit exited the van from the driver's seat. "Can anyone please explain what is going on here? I thought we were just taking a quick rest stop, not having a full-blown argument." He paused when he saw Bella climb out of the back of the van. "Oh, for fuck's sake, now we gotta take her back."

"Agent Barnes, we will do no such thing," Agent Jupiter said. "We have a chopper on the way."

Sam shook his head. "Why didn't we just fly to Vegas in a chopper?"

"Because we'd need ground transportation when we got there anyway."

Sam reached for Bella, but she darted aside, eluding his grasp. "Bella, I'm not mad," he yelled as she ran across the road away from them. He pointed at Agent Jupiter. "You're going to hear about this when we get back to the base."

Sam gave chase, his muscles protesting the sudden need to run in the desert heat. A dozen seconds later, the lithe figure of Sister Jenny overtook him and gained ground on the runaway child. It didn't take long for her to close the gap, grab the girl, and carry her, kicking and screaming, back toward the van.

"Geez, Father Sam, you got a little firecracker here," Jenny said, placing Bella on the ground. "Listen here, girl. You kick and hit me again like that, I might just do it back to you."

Bella crossed her arms over her chest and stomped her foot as Jenny turned away from her.

"What are we going to do with you?" Sam asked Bella, shaking his head.

She stared at him, her face a mask of mottled defiance that bordered on tears.

"They're sending a chopper to take you back to the base, and you're going to have to tell Sarah and Nana what happened. I'm just so... disappointed in you," Sam said.

Her expression changed as her face crumpled and tears spilled from her eyes. "I don't want to be bad."

Oh, Lord. Crouching down, he spread his arms out and caught her as she ran to him. "What's going on, Bells? Huh? Tell me what's got you so upset." Like he couldn't guess after the conversation she'd overheard in the van, but he needed to know why she'd hitched a ride in the first place.

Her sobs slowly subsided as he gently held her. "I want to help you, Daddy." She sniffled. "I'm scared at that base. I don't know what it is, but I can feel something bad there," she spoke softly in his ear. "I just want to stay with you. I feel safe with you."

Hugging Bella tighter, Sam looked at Agent Jupiter. "I'm going back in the chopper with her. She's scared."

The agent shook his head. "I'm afraid that's not poss—"

"Agent Jupiter, do you copy?" a voice Sam didn't recognize called over the lead agent's walkie-talkie.

Agent Jupiter glared at Sam and Bella, then looked away as he unclipped the device from his belt and answered, "Jupiter here. Over."

"It's Brother Dennis. He's being pursued and pinned down. I repeat... he's under pursuit."

"Copy that. Divert the chopper's course to Gibson's hotel. We'll head directly to Brother Dennis first and then send the child back from there. Inform the mother she is safe and well. Over."

"Copy that. Dispatch out."

Agent Jupiter clipped his radio to his belt and faced the others. "The Remnant is on the move. If we can get to Brother Dennis quickly, we have a chance to catch him."

"We're taking the girl with us?" Sister Jenny asked, sounding incredulous.

"For now, yes. We're out of time and options." He gestured with his hands at the open door of the van. "Everyone, inside. Now!" he snapped.

As Sam passed him and climbed into the van carrying Bella, the agent pointed his finger at her. "And you, little miss, had better do what you're told this time and stay out of trouble."

Good luck with that, thought Sam.

Brother Dennis scanned his surroundings after he hung up the payphone, panting and trying to catch his breath.

They're coming. Help is coming. He had no doubt about that. But would they arrive in time? Things hadn't gone well so far with this reconnaissance assignment to catch the Vegas Killer.

Although a member of the Church of the New World Order, he also served as an officer in the Las Vegas police force. The remains of his partner, Officer Davis, lay at the opposite end of the hallway. He covered his mouth as the smell of burned flesh weakened his stomach.

Lord, give me strength.

"It's time to play a game called 'Let's Find the Exit,' " a raspy voice called out. "Is it door number one, door number two, or door number three?"

Dennis's hand shook as he tightened his grip on his pistol. He peered around the room, looking for the source of the voice. No one was there, of course. Not that he could see clearly in the shadows.

"Fuck you, asshole," he called out.

I should have remained at the church, he thought. At least he would have been properly armed for this predicament. The police force had no true idea what they were dealing with, while the Church of the New World Order at least had a clue. At some point, while running from the monster who had killed Davis, Dennis had lost his walkie-talkie. At least he'd managed to find a payphone that miraculously worked in the unused warehouse. *Or maybe... no, surely not.* It couldn't have just been part of a trap.

He'd passed several doors before reaching the phone. He looked along the wall for another way out, but the only places to go were either the other end of the hall where Davis's still smoldering body lay or through one of the three doors in the hallway.

"Come on, Dennis, play the game. You won't get out unless you try," the voice called. "This is your big chance."

Fuck. What options did he have? Wait where he was until he was caught and fried, or try the doors like the asshole wanted?

"Is it door number one?" the gravelly voice sneered as Dennis sprinted from where he stood.

The cop charged for the nearest door, a few feet away. A quick turn of the knob proved it was locked. Even using two hands, he couldn't get the doorknob to rotate. *Shit.*

"Too bad," the monster said.

The sound of footsteps echoed slowly up the hall toward Dennis, though he still couldn't see anything moving. He hurried to the next door, hoping he could make it there before the unholy being, or whatever was stalking him in the shadows.

"Is it door number two?" the gravelly voice asked.

Saying a silent prayer, Dennis reached the next door and tried turning the knob. Like the first door, it was locked.

Fuck! Come on, work with me here, God.

He'd seen what the killer could do to people and had no doubt the same would happen to him if he was caught. He needed somewhere to hide until backup arrived.

"Let's see what's behind door number three, shall we?" the gravelly voice boomed out. "Do we have a winner?"

As the sound of footsteps drew closer, Dennis ran to the final door. Not daring to look down the hallway, he gripped the doorknob... and screamed. The knob was so hot, it caused the skin on his fingers to singe. He snatched his hand away, wincing with pain.

"Come on, Dennis. If you don't open the door, you'll never see what you win," the unseen presence goaded.

Covering his hands with the bottom of his shirt, Dennis gripped the doorknob and turned it. The fabric did little to shield his flesh from the hot metal, but as the door popped open, he breathed a sigh of relief. The room beyond looked like an old office supply room. Boxes and office furniture were strewn throughout, all covered in dust. Sunlight filtered through the floor-to-ceiling, dirt-covered windows.

If he could break one, he could at least escape the maze he'd been trapped in. He moved toward the windows as fast as he could, clenching his teeth as the heat from his burned hands spread up his arms and through his body. Already his skin was blistering.

"Congratulations, Brother Dennis!" the voice behind him shouted. "You have won... death." Laughter filled the room.

Dennis stumbled and fell against a desk. With his body burning him from the inside, and the heat spreading throughout the room, he felt as though he was walking through the flames of Hell.

"Death really is a gift, you know. Imagine what it would be like if you couldn't die?" the monster called out.

Shaking, Dennis turned his head toward the beast. "What do you want from me?"

The being stood in the shadows of the doorway, his face and body obscured by a long dark cloak. "I want to feel you suffer." The words sounded like they were hissed through clenched teeth. "I want you to endure the level of pain where you plead for it to end. I want you to know what it's like to exist in a state of such horrific pain that you beg for death."

Dennis stared at the blurred vision of the agent of death in the doorframe. "Why?" *My gun. Where the fuck is my gun?* He touched his holster, screaming from frustration as much as pain, when he realized it was empty. Had he dropped it while running around doing the stupid doors game?

He fiddled for the silver cross hanging around his neck. Touching anything caused jolts of agony to ricochet through his bones. He closed his eyes as his charred fingers found the cross. "God's love will heal all," he repeated over and over.

"God doesn't care about you, Dennis." The monster took slow, steady steps into the room, the sound echoing hollowly against the floorboards. "What can an invisible sky wizard do for you?"

Dennis coughed. An unpleasant chemical smell filled the room, like gasoline and burned plastic. "He already has people on their way to vanquish you."

"Vanquish?" The being chuckled in an unholy tone. "Oh, I really hope so. I hope He sends everyone He can. We have a score to settle. And you know I'll do the same to them as I'm about to do to you."

Dennis trembled, partly from pain, partly from fear. He had to find a way out, somehow. The windows were so close, so close. Using the desk as support, he hobbled unsteadily toward the light, aware he was leaving behind a smear of blood wherever he stepped. One foot. Then another. Then he clutched his stomach and screamed as pain shot through his abdomen like a fire had been lit inside him.

"It hurts, doesn't it?"

Keep going. Ignoring the pain and the monster stalking him, Dennis stumbled around piles of dust-coated boxes, trying to reach the light. His left foot stubbed into a particularly heavy cardboard carton. A flurry of cockroaches ran out from under the disturbed box, running spasmodically away from him. He stared as the insects stopped running and began to glow red.

Wait, am I seeing things? He rubbed his eyes with his blistered hands and immediately wished he hadn't as renewed pain seared through his fingers and face.

Then he felt them. First one, then two, then quickly a dozen. Their fluttery wings, scratchy legs, and hideous buzzing. The red-hot roaches had taken flight and were swarming him.

"No," he shrieked as the insects flew into his face, hair, everywhere they could land, exploding in small balls of fire wherever they touched. He waved his arms, trying to block them, but seemed to attract more and more of the flaming creatures instead. "*No!*" he screamed louder. The most intense pain he'd ever felt crawled on and under his skin. There was no escape. No way to win.

"Now you feel what I feel," the monster whispered near his ear. "But at least your pain comes with an end."

"Why me?" Dennis whimpered.

"Why anyone?"

Fighting against the agonizing pain throughout his whole body, Dennis raised the cross. "Begone foul demon from Hell. Return to your domain."

"Wouldn't that be nice?" the monster said.

Dennis had long ago resigned himself to the fact he was royally fucked. All he could hope now was that the time he'd kept the monster occupied would give The Specialist a fighting chance. He was on his way—Dennis was sure of it. If he could hold out just a bit longer, maybe Father Sam would arrive in time to capture the demon.

Dennis spun and ran to his right, drowning out the crippling pain with his need to survive. He avoided the burning roaches and boxes, picking up the pace as he ran in a straight line.

The flames inside him spread through his organs, stifling his breathing and burning so hot that he thought his chest would burst open any second. He stumbled closer to the window, so close he could almost touch the glass. He toppled forward as his legs collapsed, broken and useless and burning like logs. He landed with his arm outstretched, his fingers grazing the pane, but his head crashed onto the floor with a thunderous whack. Unable to move any longer, he was done.

So much for jumping to a quick death through the window.

Footsteps neared. Dennis felt rather than saw the killer standing above him. A foot shoved beneath his chest and kicked up hard, rolling him over. Dennis stared upward at the monster leering down at him. The unholy being's bloodshot eyes burned inside their sockets. *He's a demon. A demon!* The urge to scream pulsed through what was left of his charred throat, but he was unable to move his broken jaw, and no sound came out.

God will make you pay for this, he thought.

"Oh. How much? Ninety-nine cents? Is that how much a soul is worth?"

The sound of the demon's laughter faded as Dennis's body temperature climbed so high his mind switched off, and his soul fled the burning corpse he'd become.

An hour later, after much speeding to reach Las Vegas, the black van came to a screeching halt fifty yards from the last known location of Brother Dennis. The warehouse was burning, the flames so intense that several teams of firemen had been called in. Fire trucks were parked haphazardly all over the parking area with hoses running from them as emergency personnel tried to contain the blaze.

Sam climbed out of the van and stood on the pavement with Jenny, Penny, and Bella. Even from their distance, the heat from the burning building was fierce If the undercover Brother was inside, he surely must have perished. "Fuckdammit, we're too late," he said.

"Fuckdammit? What kind of word is that?" Jenny asked.

Penny grinned at Sam. "He's a man of God, so he's fashioned a word that he finds much less blasphemous. I think it's cute."

"Fuckdammit," Bella repeated. She covered her mouth and stared at him, giggling.

He glanced down at her. *Shit.* "Ah, better not tell Nana that one," he said, which only made her giggle harder.

Agent Jupiter had gone to speak to the local law enforcement collected around several squad cars parked nearby. He finished speaking with someone who appeared to be a detective and turned back toward Sam, shaking his head as he drew near.

"Any survivors?" Sam asked.

"They haven't been able to get inside yet to check, but they don't think so. An unmarked car belonging to Brother Dennis and his partner, Officer Davis, was found at the back. If they'd been able to leave before the fire started, they would have."

"And the Remnant?"

"Listen, Sam." Agent Jupiter put his hand on the newly ordained Specialist's shoulder. "The locals don't understand what they're up against. What I told you is confidential information. Less they know, the better, *capiche*?"

Penny turned to Jenny. "Capiche? Did he actually just say *capiche*?"

Jenny nodded, eying the agent. "I think he did, yeah."

"Oh, my Italian ears," Penny moaned. "It's pronounced ka-PEE-chay, you idiot."

"What difference does it make?" Jupiter snapped. He brushed his palm across his close-cropped scalp and turned back to Sam. "Look. If anyone asks why you're around, keep it simple and say it's because of a demon."

Sam frowned, thinking of the two men trapped inside. "A demon is better how?" Burning to death was bad but didn't compare to being possessed and having your soul eaten as demon food. At least... not that he was aware of or had any intention of testing to find out.

Agent Jupiter turned as Agent Saturn waved, trying to catch their attention. He stood a few feet from the rest of them beside the open front door of the van.

"I picked up something on my scanner. There's shit going down at the Admiral Hotel. Cops are moving in."

Jupiter frowned. "That's the place Ricky Gibson's staying at."

"Yeah—"

"Then let's get in the van and make our way over there," Jupiter cut his fellow agent off.

"Are they arresting Ricky?" Sam asked, making for the van with Bella.

"I have no idea," Saturn said. "He's supposed to be in protective custody, but I've not been able to get through to our men. The LVMPD have lost contact with a squad inside the hotel as well." He didn't have to say why he thought that might have happened.

The five of them packed themselves back into the van, and Saturn shut the door.

"Is Ricky gonna be okay?" Bella asked, her expression anxious.

Sam didn't like lying, especially to his daughter. "We're going to make sure he is, okay?" He reached over and put a hand behind Bella's head, rubbing her hair gently and smiling at her. "Ricky's a very clever guy." *Not a lie,* I think.

"It's going to take us a few moments to get there," Penny said. "If the LVMPD has lost contact with some of their guys, they'll be sending a heap more. The roads will be chaos."

Sam clutched the door handle when the vehicle picked up speed. As he'd learned on the hectic road trip from Vegas, if there was one thing worse than being in the back of a van and unable to see where one was going, it was doing so at a fast rate of speed.

He shut his eyes and thought about how the last, and only other, time he'd been to Vegas had been with Sarah when they'd gotten married in the chapel. She'd already been pregnant, though they hadn't known it at the time. Now here he was in Vegas again, trying to catch the strangest serial killer he'd ever heard of, who was like a demon, but not, but sort of was, maybe. While she was about two hundred miles away, laying in a bed in a hospital clinic because the pregnancy had complications.

If someone had told him a year ago that this would be his life, he'd have wondered what they'd been smoking and not believed them.

Which made him more than a bit nervous about what surprises life had in store for him next.

Chapter 9

Sarah woke with a start from yet another nap. She looked around the room, expecting to see it full of demons with red eyes, wanting to strap her down and drink her blood. She blinked and sucked in a steadying breath upon realizing nothing was there except Mother Agnes and Doctor Stevens, who stood outside her room. She saw them through the large observation window, talking.

Goddamn dreams. She leaned back against her pillow and tried to relax.

Since they'd started the trip to the Church of the New World Order, the nightmares had been getting more intense. Not that she'd said anything to Sam about it.

This place was the new start that he'd wanted and needed.

And now he was The Specialist... and gone.

But she wasn't alone.

She placed a hand on her belly and smiled at the comforting feeling of something growing inside her. Her smile quickly shifted to a gasp as the baby tried to kick what felt like a hole through her navel. "Oh!" She wiggled as the young life inside her kicked again.

Mother Agnes and Doctor Stevens charged into the room, bolting in her direction so fast that they must have been watching her and ready to pounce as soon as she woke.

They had run a series of tests on her before she grew tired and fell asleep, something that had been happening a lot since she arrived at the base. And whatever became of Bella? She hadn't seen her all morning, which was unusual, but maybe her mother had taken her to play with the other children again.

"Sarah, we have so much to discuss," Doctor Stevens said, her expression carefully blank.

"Bella? Where is she?"

Mother Agnes placed her hands together, intertwining her fingers. "Okay, first of all, I want you to know she's fine—" the elderly nun began.

Sarah raised her hand and gestured at the nun as her pulse raced into overdrive. "Okay. No. Any story that starts like that means the opposite. Where. The hell. *Is my daughter*?"

"She found her way into the van that your husband and the team left in. They didn't realize until they'd stopped during their trip."

"She what?" Sarah sat up so quickly she wondered if she'd set a Guinness World Record for the quickest upright jolt in history. "Are you fucking serious? How does this happen?"

The Mother's serious expression deepened. "According to the security footage, she followed Brother Trevor through the hallways and security doors."

"He didn't see her?"

"No."

"Well, that's pretty incompetent, don't you think?"

The nun kept a straight face while she continued her story, "Once in the parking lot, she climbed into the van and hid in the equipment."

"They leave the vehicles unlocked?"

"No, but they can't be locked while being loaded."

"So where is she now?"

Mother Agnes sighed. "She's with your husband. A chopper has been sent to Vegas to pick her up from there and bring her back."

Oh, Bella. Whyyy?

Sarah pressed her palms to her eyes. She could see her doing it, though. Bella had learned to be resourceful at a young age and been more than a bit upset at Sam leaving. "Does my mother know about this?"

"Yes. She didn't want to wake you. She's gone to pray in the chapel."

Sarah pushed the covers off and swung her legs over the side of the bed. When it came to religious beliefs, her mother was nearly as devout as Sam.

She shivered at the thought of Bella alone with those 'men in black' creeps who hung around like dust mites. "If anything happens to her—"

Mother Agnes folded her arms and cut her off. "Nothing will happen to her. What you need to do is rest until this baby comes."

Sarah stared at her and then at the doctor standing beside her. "I want to get up today. I thought that was the plan."

Doctor Stevens stepped toward Sarah. "It's better if you rest here for now. We have some concerns about you and the baby."

Sarah stilled. "What are you talking about? You told us everything was fine."

"It is fine," Mother Agnes cut in. "But your baby boy is growing much quicker than a normal fetus at the same age."

"While you might not be as big as someone normally is who is about to give birth, this baby could come at any day," the doctor added. "Are you sure about the conception date?"

"Yes, I am. My cycles have always been regular." She studied the two women. She didn't know either of them well enough to trust them, and her internal bullshit alarm was ringing off the scale. "Okay. What's going on?"

Mother Agnes smiled at the doctor. "If you don't mind, I'd like to speak with Sarah alone for a few minutes."

Doctor Stevens hesitated for a second, then nodded. "Sure." She glanced at Sarah and gave a polite smile. "A nurse will be in to check on you."

Mother Agnes watched her leave and then sat on the edge of Sam's bed. Both his and Bella's cots were still where they'd left them, Bella's alien stuffie and her Walkman placed on top of her covers.

"Is something wrong with my baby?" Sarah asked. It was a fear she'd had since she'd learned she was pregnant. And if so, why would the nun want to talk to her about it rather than the doctor?

"Other than being a bit big, he seems physically fine. Both of your temperatures are elevated, though. Not that Doctor Stevens sees any sign of infection in your bloodwork." She paused and gently grasped Sarah's hand in hers as she looked into her eyes. "The concern is about the baby's soul. We think he may be possessed."

"*What?*" Sarah snatched her hand back.

"I've been worried since you arrived." Mother Agnes shook her head. "No, that's not correct. I started to wonder when Sam mentioned on the phone that your nightmares hadn't gone away after you were possessed. You're still having them?"

Sarah stared at the elderly nun in silence, her mind racing as well as her heart.

Her baby was possessed?

"Did you and Sam complete the thirty days of baths in holy water that I asked you to do after the incident with Abaddon?"

Sarah thought back. *Had they? Mostly. Maybe.* It had been a bit of a chore to create a fresh bath of holy water every morning with a traumatized child underfoot who'd just lost her mother. The lack of sleep, the bad dreams. Getting used to a whole new routine and life. *"It's fine, Sam. Just skip it today. It'll be okay. We're all tired."*

Mother Agnes sighed. "Sarah, you're going to have to choose who to trust. The more honest you are, the better I can help you. Did you or did you not complete the holy water ritual?"

Sarah shook her head. "I didn't... we..." She struggled to isolate her racing thoughts and shook her head again.

The lines around Mother Agnes's lips tightened. "And your nightmares. They've involved drinking blood?"

"Sometimes." *Mostly.* She shut her eyes, not wanting to think about her dreams or anything too hard. She shook her head again. "I don't understand." *This can't be real. It can't be.*

"My dear, surely this isn't a complete shock to you."

Sarah snapped her eyes open. "Are you kidding me?" A complete shock, no. Not if she were being honest. There'd been things—the nightmares, her previous infertility miraculously gone. Demon-sensitive Bella acting strange around her more and more and preferring the company of Sam or Ena or pretty much anyone else as the pregnancy went on...

"My baby is a *blessing*," she shouted.

"Of course he is. All children are," Mother Agnes agreed. She crossed her arms over her chest. "But this child was conceived out of wedlock by a priest who was not yet released from his vows and a woman who was recently possessed. Those two things alone put him at great risk of corruption."

Sarah stared at her, her vision misting as her worst fears were realized. "You're saying... I did this?"

"Not intentionally, no." The elderly nun's expression changed as the lines around her mouth and eyes softened. "And it takes two to create a child. But sometimes the things we do out of love have unintended consequences."

Sarah let out a soft laugh. It was better than crying. "You're certain about this? I mean, have there been any other possession survivors who've had a..." she glanced down at her distended abdomen, searching for the right word to call it, *Possessed baby? Corrupted baby? He's my baby.* "... demon baby."

"No. Not a single one of them, as far as our sources have witnessed."

Sarah felt her throat close in as tears threatened to flow again. *Fuck these pregnancy hormones.* "So why me?"

Mother Agnes let out a tired sigh. "Retribution, perhaps. But as you have said, all children are a blessing."

Sarah ran her hands gently over her belly, feeling the life within her move. *My baby.* "What's going to happen?"

Mother Agnes's lips pinched together. "You need to stay in this room until the baby arrives," she said gently. "We'll do our best to keep you safe."

"From a baby?" Sarah laughed out loud. "Oh, please save me from this innocent boy who's been growing inside me for seven months."

"Sarah! This is not a laughing matter. Your child, and whatever demonic force may be growing inside him, is getting stronger by the day," Mother Agnes said. She glanced around, pausing at the two soldiers wearing camouflage fatigues who stood outside the observation window. Turning back to Sarah, she lowered her voice, "Listen to me... if you weren't so far along in your pregnancy, we wouldn't be having this conversation. They would have automatically aborted."

Sarah started at her, shocked that such words would come from a woman of God. "But he's just a baby. He hasn't done anything."

"Not yet."

"Fuck you! I'm getting out of here," Sarah yelled. She slid off the bed and ran for the door, ripping the IV from her arm in the process.

The two soldiers blocked her way, followed by an agent.

"Go back to bed, ma'am."

"I want to talk to Sam. Please, let me talk to Sam," she begged. Blood trickled down her arm from the IV puncture wound.

"Sarah, please walk back to the bed. This is serious," Mother Agnes pleaded as she looked between the soldiers and Sarah. She took her gently by the arm. "They will sedate you if you don't calm down. Think about yourself and the baby."

Sarah's eyes met the nun's. Was that pity she saw in them? Maybe she only thought she saw what she wanted to see, and the so-called devout Mother didn't feel anything more than the blank-faced soldiers and almost robot-like agents. With Bella and Sam, who she was apparently not being allowed to contact, gone, the one person left whom she could wholly trust was her mother. She dutifully headed back to the bed and sat on the side of it, her legs dangling over the edge. "Is my mother allowed to see me?"

Mother Agnes nodded. "Of course." She gestured at the doorway. The two soldiers moved, and Sarah's mother rushed in, accompanied by one of the black-clad agents.

"I told you. I can find my own way around," Ena snapped at the agent.

"Mom!" Sarah leaped off the bed and launched at her mother, wrapping her in a tight hug. "Oh my God. Mom."

Ena's arms tightened around her. "I'm so sorry, Sarah. I wanted to come in once you were awake, but these goons told me I had to wait." She tossed a narrowed glance at the agent who had taken up a position by the door.

Sarah relaxed her embrace and looked into her mother's eyes. "You know already? About the baby?"

Ena nodded. "They're concerned about you. As I am. They said I should know what you're facing, just in case..."

Sarah frowned as her mother's words trailed off. "In case something happens to me?"

"Sarah, please try to calm down. It's best that you rest." She leaned in close and whispered in her daughter's ear, "I don't trust them either, but we need to do what they say."

Her mother, as usual, was right. What could she hope to accomplish by trying to bust her way out? "Okay." She lay back in the bed and pulled the covers up. She held out her hand to her mother. "Please stay with me."

Ena sat on Sam's bed and curled her fingers in Sarah's. She gave Mother Agnes a narrowed glance as she spoke to her daughter, "I have no intention of leaving you, dear, unless you wish me to."

Mother Agnes nodded and smiled. "Good. Rest while you can, Sarah. I will speak with you later."

As soon as the nun and agent had left the room, Sarah looked at her mother. "Oh my God, Mom! These people are crazy. They think my baby is a *demon*," she said in a hushed whisper. "She talked about making me have an abortion if she could."

"I know, I know." Ena pressed her hands over Sarah's and darted a glance around the room. "I've prayed so hard for Sam and you. And now Bella's run off." She pressed her hands to her face and closed her eyes for a second. When she opened them again, she studied her daughter carefully. "What I want to know is if you think it could be true."

Sarah hesitated. Other than the kicking and bruises, the baby hadn't done anything to harm her. It's not like it had glowing red eyes and cloven hooves in the ultrasounds or anything. The pregnancy had gone fine for the most part. Sort of. But still, there remained the fact that she had been possessed and maybe hadn't done all the things she should to make sure she was one hundred percent clear of any after-effects before trying to get pregnant. "Ah... maybe?"

Ena sighed. "I thought so." Her soft smile was tinged with sadness. "You never do anything by halves, do you, Sare-bear. Does Sam know?"

"I don't think so. He never mentioned anything to me, and he for sure would have if he had any concerns like that. And now he's gone."

Ena nodded. She moved closer and whispered, "They waited until he left to say anything."

Sarah blinked. She was right. "What do you think that means? They don't want him to know?"

"Maybe."

"Why?"

Ena shook her head. "I don't like any of this. Can we send him a message somehow?"

Sarah frowned. "The agents have the walkie-talkies. I doubt they'll let me speak to him. I don't even know where he is. Just somewhere in Vegas fighting monsters." *With Bella. Oh, God.* Don't think about that now. One thing at a time.

A nurse walked into the room and headed for the IV pole. She hooked up a new bag and turned to Sarah. "Hold out your arm, please. Your port has apparently 'slipped out.' "

Sarah shook her head and smiled. "Oh, no thanks. I'm fine. I don't think I need that now."

The nurse stared at her, a bland expression on her face. "Doctor's orders say you do."

Sarah darted a glance at her mother as panic circled in her chest, making it hard to breathe. What should she do? She didn't trust any of these people. The thought of what they could do to her and her baby against her will was more frightening than when she'd been trapped in the mall, facing Abaddon.

Ena gave her a slight nod and a look that screamed, *"Cooperate for now."*

Sarah held out her arm.

"Make a fist, please," the nurse instructed.

As Sarah did so, she asked. "Wha... what's in it?"

"Saline for hydration and something mild to help you sleep." She raised a brow. "Mommies need their rest, don't they?"

Sarah sat numbly on the bed as the nurse finished up and checked the drip to make sure it was flowing correctly. "Try not to knock it out again," she advised.

After she left, Sarah settled back down on the bed. She looked at her mother. Whether it was from all the excitement taking its toll or the medication being pumped into her, her eyes were already feeling heavy.

"How about I get us some cookies?" Ena asked. "You'll like that after a nap, yes?"

"Okay," she whispered.

Ena kissed her on the forehead and headed for the door. "I'll be right back, dear. Try not to worry."

Watching her mother walk away, a wave of loneliness more intense than anything she'd ever felt washed over Sarah. She hadn't wanted to come here. Her instincts had screamed at her to not come here. But Sam had wanted to, so she'd come along for the ride like a good and biddable wife. And now she was, for all intents and purposes, trapped in a strange place with strange people, and who the fuck knew what they intended to do. She closed her eyes, fighting the tears that threatened to spill like a waterfall down her cheeks.

God, if you can hear me. I need some help here.

Throughout her life, she barely admitted defeat, and while she would never outwardly do so to these people at the base, she felt it in her bones.

Was this baby inside her dangerous?

Had she inadvertently created a monster?

Her thought was answered with a kick to the outer wall of her stomach, causing her to suck in her breath sharply. She placed her hand on her belly. *Can you hear me, baby? Are you okay?*

The kick wasn't repeated. But as Sarah dozed off, she smiled as a feeling of peace came over her. Whatever was going on, she definitely wasn't alone.

ENA ENTERED THE COMMUNAL mess hall in search of cookies, focused on getting a message to Sam. Maybe if she borrowed a walkie-talkie from an agent, or flat-out stole one, she could call out and find him. Not that he'd be able to do anything, though, would he? He was busy saving the planet from demons again, thanks to the manipulations of the Church of The New World Order.

There was no doubt in Ena's mind that that conniving Mother Agnes was behind everything that had happened. She hadn't liked the woman since first meeting her. She was always just sooo polite and clever, wasn't she? And now Sam was gone, and Bella too. What was the nun after? *The baby?*

Ena gave a little huff as she walked. *Well, if she thinks that's going to happen, she has another thing coming.*

One of the dark glasses and suit-wearing agents sat at a table, speaking a little too loudly to a man in a wheelchair. "Brother Trevor, you know the solution is simple. We remove the baby early and make it look like an accident."

What? Ena backed up and pretended to show interest in the giant palm plant near their table. Turning slightly toward the two men, she peered through the leaves and listened more carefully.

The paraplegic man's words came out soft and panicked, "The very idea goes against everything the Church believes in."

"If it's allowed to come to full term, and she gives birth to that abomination, it could take us all out. Possibly end the world."

Ena covered her mouth, hoping it was enough to stifle her shocked reaction to what she had heard. Was anyone else at the base also ready to engage in such a nefarious action? This was her grandson they were talking about, her own baby's baby.

"I can't…" Brother Trevor shook his head. "This isn't the place to discuss this." His gaze darted around as if he were afraid someone had been listening.

Ena pulled back and hid behind the leaves, hoping she hadn't been seen.

"Very well," the agent said, his voice cold. "If you say anything to Mother Agnes about this, I know where it will have come from."

"Are you threatening me, Agent Mars?"

Heart racing, Ena wanted to run off and warn Sarah, but a dark-skinned man with a bald head and a long leather coat came into her vision from her side.

"Hello there. Don't worry about me. I just need some coffee," the man said to her as he headed to the central buffet table. As he passed her, he stopped in his tracks. "Hey, are you okay?"

"I'll be fine," Ena replied, nodding nervously as the man smiled at her. Unlike the other men in black, his smile seemed genuine, and as his coat opened a little, she caught a glimpse of a name badge. "Thank you, ah... Agent Bronson."

The conversation at the table died out as the two occupants must have heard the exchange between Ena and Bronson.

After Bronson nodded and made his way to the coffee machine at the buffet, Ena made herself seen, stepping into view around the plant. She nodded at Brother Trevor and Agent Mars. "Just here for some cookies for my daughter." She smiled nervously. "Pregnant women and their hormones, you never know what they're going to want to eat next." She headed for the buffet where the baked goods were kept under glass lids.

"You're Sarah Morris's mother, right?" Agent Mars called out.

Ena grimaced and paused mid-step. She slowly turned and faced the two men with a smile. "Yes, that's correct."

"How is she feeling today?" The man's bland tone made Ena even more nervous. He frowned as Bronson squeezed past, departing the eatery as rapidly as he'd entered.

"Oh, fine. A little tired." She paused, then added, "A little worried with Sam gone demon hunting and Bella run off like that. I'm astonished that could ever happen." She glanced between them. "Imagine a nine-year-old girl able to sneak out of a restricted facility like this."

"It is rather astounding, isn't it?" Agent Mars tapped his chin and shared a glance with Brother Trevor.

"Well, I better get back to her before she wakes up cranky *and* hungry." She faked a giggle. "Don't want to have her even more upset. Might harm the baby. And we wouldn't want that, would we?"

Brother Trevor glared at Mars. "No, we wouldn't."

Ena thanked him and went about taking a handful of cookies and fixing herself a strong cup of coffee. If it was possible to feel two pairs of eyes upon oneself, she certainly felt that now. The experience was making her skin crawl.

Keeping her cool, she smiled as she passed them on her way out. As she walked back to Sarah's room, she thought about what she'd overheard.

Mars had advocated for the baby to be born early, preterm. What the heck did they think Sarah was giving birth to? The antichrist? A shiver went up her spine.

Good Lord, Ena, get a grip on yourself.

But to want to kill a child? She shook her head, thinking of the agents who crept around the place, seeming to appear and disappear from the shadows.

Maybe she was wrong.

Maybe it wasn't Mother Agnes she needed to be worried about.

Chapter 10

Sam glanced at Bella as the van came to a screeching stop, almost sending the occupants in the back flying from their seats. Bella cried out and then giggled as the seatbelt kept her in place.

"This driver really needs to go back to driving school," Sam muttered.

Within seconds, Agent Jupiter stood to the right of the van, having pulled open the sliding door with Saturn's assistance on the outside.

The abrupt exposure to daylight made Sam squint. Holding a hand up to shield his eyes, he addressed the lead agent. "We're here?"

"Yeah, we're here. Admiral Hotel. Where Ricky Gibson is staying. It's time to put your experience to use," Jupiter addressed Sam. He nodded at Jenny and Penny, who were busy grabbing what they needed from the back of the van. "And theirs, too."

"What about me?" Bella piped up. "I can help too. I'm good at killing demons."

The agent shook his head. "You, little miss, are going to be quiet and do exactly as we say. There's a chopper on the roof. You're getting sent back from there."

She shook her head. "But I don't want to go back. I want to help my dad and see Ricky."

"I don't really care," Agent Jupiter said. "But if you cause trouble while we're working, there'll be hell to pay."

Bella stuck out her tongue at the agent as he turned his back to speak with Saturn. "Fuckdammit," she muttered.

Sam groaned. "Bella, please don't use that word." Though it was probably false hope that she might actually listen. "I'm not sure what's going on inside the hotel yet, so please stay close to me while we get you to the chopper, okay?"

She frowned at the mention of the chopper but tightened her hold on his hand.

"The scanner reports that more police are on their way, so we need to get moving," Saturn said, looking at the group. "Top floor," he pointed. "Let's go."

Sam nodded. He, Bella, and the two sisters followed the pair of agents, who started running toward the hotel about twenty yards away. Based on the crowd outside, Sam guessed a lot of people had been evacuated already, but no police line had been established yet. As the six of them closed the gap to the front of the hotel, a middle-aged woman dressed in a skirt and blazer waved her hands in front of her and yelled at them to stop. "No one goes in, Las Vegas Police orders. They told me to evacuate the hotel."

"We're on a mission from God." Jupiter flashed her a smile and his badge and didn't slow down, forcing her to step aside as they sped past and through the entry doors.

Sam tried to suppress a grin as the woman shouted angrily about the man thinking he was one of the *Blues Brothers* or something. If only she knew what he really was.

Jenny and Penny flanked Sam, both heavily armed and drawing much attention from the crowd inside, which was steadily exiting. It was obvious to anyone watching that they were certainly not law enforcement. Jupiter and Saturn stepped into the lobby ahead of them and approached a security guard who was directing people outside. They flashed their badges.

"Special Forces," Jupiter explained. "What's the status?" The guard gave them both a once over and then nodded.

"Problem with the elevators. A couple of police guys are trapped in the service car somewhere between the nineteenth and twentieth floors. Elevator repair is on the way and should be here in a moment." He glanced at Sam and the others as they approached. "You guys here for a costume party or something?" he asked, furrowing his brow.

"No," Jupiter snapped. "They're with us. Where's Gibson? Has he been evacuated?"

The guard shook his head. "No. Not that I'm aware. Still up there."

The sounds of sirens outside grew louder as emergency services, including several squad cars and a fire truck, arrived.

"Great. Thanks," Jupiter said. "Keep these people moving out of here. We'll handle the rest." He set off for the main elevator with Saturn, leaving Sam and the others to follow as quickly as they could.

Sam frowned. If the problem was with the service elevator, would any of them be working?

"Any word from the team up top?" Jupiter asked Saturn.

"Negative."

"What about the chopper?"

"Nothing there either."

Jupiter frowned. "Whatever happened to the service car has affected communications within the hotel, too. But the chopper up top should be in the clear, shouldn't it?"

Saturn shrugged. "Only one way to find out." He reached the elevator panel first and pressed the up button. Being empty, the door opened immediately, and the six of them raced inside. Jupiter pressed the button for the thirtieth floor.

That's a demon trick, Sam thought. *Cutting off communications like that.*

He closed his eyes, mouthing a silent prayer as he faced the real possibility of battling a demon again. He hoped he could get Bella and Ricky to safety first and that the agents and sisters knew what they were doing.

"COME ON OUT AND face us, you chicken shit!" Detective Briggs yelled, keeping his gun pointed at the laundry cart. It was hot inside the service elevator, which was packed with two detectives and a squad of four policemen—minus the one who lay dead on the floor.

"I'm never accepting goddammed babysitting duty ever again. I don't care who the person is or how rich they are. It's not worth this shit." Briggs's partner, Detective Bradley, holstered his weapon and picked up his walkie-talkie. He tried using it again and shook his head, his expression stark in the uncertain emergency lighting. "Nothing. Not even static."

"The electronics are probably cooked," Briggs muttered. The temperature inside the elevator seemed to be climbing by the minute. Sweat covered his brow and ran down his back. He'd already had to take off his jacket. He kept his gun trained on the laundry cart, which took up one side of the car, and slowly glanced around, checking for movement. "Does anyone see him?" he called out.

Something had followed them into the elevator. Something that had seemed like a dark blur of movement just before Officer Costas had fallen to the floor, dead.

"No," the nearest officer replied, sounding nervous.

"He's playing with us," one of the other officers hissed. The three others agreed with him, their voices creating a loud buzz of increasing panic that threatened to do Briggs's head in.

"Hey, would you all just calm the fuck down!" Briggs yelled. The tension wasn't accomplishing anything. He wiped sweat from his brow and tried to calm his breathing. Oxygen would get short soon. The air filtration system seemed to have stopped working, too.

This is one fucked-up elevator ride.

First, the panel lights had gone crazy, flashing like an arcade game, then it had caught on fire, and he'd had to use the fire extinguisher in the emergency panel to put it out. In the ensuing chaos and smoke, the elevator car had stopped, but the doors wouldn't open. That's when the thing had struck, and Costas had fallen.

The walls were solid, and the ceiling panel closed. Whoever or whatever it was had to be hiding in the cart.

"Fuck this," Bradley said. "We gave the asshole a chance to come out." Firing his pistol repeatedly at the laundry cart, he growled as loud as he could and screamed, "Die, motherfucker!"

The sound of gunfire was deafening in the enclosed area. Briggs gave up trying to yell over the noise, shaking his head as other officers followed Bradley's lead. *Fucking idiots, wasting ammo.*

Within a minute, the noise tapered off and changed to rustling and clicking as the officers reloaded their weapons. The laundry cart was riddled with holes on three sides. Smoke from the bullet's passage through the fabric coiled slowly upward, adding to the haze that filled the top of the elevator car. If anyone was in that cart, they couldn't possibly be alive any longer.

Keeping his gun raised, Briggs moved forward to peek inside the cart.

As he did so, a dark shape resembling an arm darted from behind the cart, followed by a cloaked form. The officer on Briggs's left screamed as he was yanked off his feet and lifted from the ground.

"It's the demon!" Briggs called out. This... this was what he'd feared when he'd interviewed Ricky Gibson, hot on the trail of the Vegas killer. An abomination sent from hell, just like the one that attacked Springfield a year ago, resulting in the deaths of hundreds of people.

Well, this is Vegas, motherfucker, and we're gonna take you down.

He closed one eye and tried to focus on the dark figure, but it moved so fast that it seemed more like a blur. There was no way he could take a shot without risking the officer's life. Not that it would likely do any good anyway. There was no way all the bullets fired at the cart could have missed the demon. No way the monster should be alive. He lowered his weapon, but a single gunshot echoed through the elevator anyway. Briggs looked to his right, realizing another officer had fired.

The young cop being held up by his neck screamed as the bullet passed through him, square in the chest. He slumped lifelessly to the ground as the dark figure released its grip on him.

Unholy laughter echoed off the elevator walls, chilling Briggs to the bone despite the intense heat. A faint orange glow the size of a golf ball appeared in the air between the figure's gloved hands.

I can see him. He's not moving, Briggs realized.

"Shoot the light," Bradley called out.

Briggs saw his partner dive to the floor and retrieve the weapon that had belonged to the most recently murdered police officer. Looking back at the glow, the color was fading, slowly transforming into a bright white light as it expanded.

Bradley aimed from his position on the floor, yelling with each shot he fired. Each bullet seemed to disappear as soon as it met the growing ball of light, which was now the size of a basketball.

What the hell is that?

The maniacal laughter continued, gaining volume as the bright light grew larger.

The heat was intense.

Briggs backed up, noticing the other officers do the same. Bradley scurried out of the way, shouting as his hands blistered. He dropped his gun and moved to the edge of the car.

Briggs coughed. The air tasted like kerosene and burned plastic. "What the hell do you want?" he shouted at the demon. "Why are you doing this?" If guns didn't work, they had no weapons to fight with. *Where was the Mall Priest when you needed him?*

Just when it seemed things couldn't get any more bizarre, the elevator roared into life again, moving up slowly.

"What the fuck?" Briggs shouted as the elevator gained speed. He pressed his hand against the wall, trying to steady his footing.

The other officers spread out against the wall, trying to get away as far as possible as the light grew to the height of a human. It touched the fabric of the laundry cart, igniting it.

Briggs gulped. Already pressed against the wall, there was nowhere else to go. Shivering from fear, he closed his eyes as the glowing light expanded further until it touched the front of his body.

Screams reached his ears. He realized the sounds of pain were coming from him as much as the others. They ceased abruptly as the light heated to a point where everything was on fire. Him, the others, the entire contents of the elevator. With nowhere left to go, the ball of fire superheated the remaining air to the point the metal began to melt and buckle.

Oh, it's a bomb, thought Briggs as his consciousness rose away from his incinerated body. No longer in pain, it was almost pleasant floating like that, except for the fact that he was floating above a bomb made of demonic energy. *I probably should—*

SAM SLAMMED AGAINST THE wall and bounced off again, crashing into the other passengers on the floor as a loud boom ripped through the main elevator, echoing through the car and down the shaft.

Dazed, he slowly picked himself off the floor and shook his head. The ringing in his ears was almost too strong for him to keep his balance. He staggered, realizing the ringing wasn't just in his ears. Alarms were sounding throughout the hotel.

"Bella." He reached down to his adopted daughter, helping her to her feet. "Are you okay?"

She nodded, white-faced. Blood trickled from a small cut on her forehead. Sam dabbed at it with the end of his shirt and pulled her close to him.

The others picked themselves up, seeming as stunned and uncertain as him.

"What the hell happened?" Agent Saturn shouted.

"Did something explode?" Jenny asked. She flexed her fingers on her right hand as if they were sore.

"I think so," Penny replied.

"The lights… we've stopped," Jupiter pointed out.

While not completely dark, the elevator was now lit solely by sunlight, which streamed through the rear glass wall of the car. The higher levels of the hotel, as well as the elevator shaft, were mostly constructed of glass, giving a sweeping view of Las Vegas for those going to the upper floors.

Bella clung to Sam as she caught sight of the view. "It's so high!"

"It's okay, Bella. I've got you." Sam hugged her tight and smoothed her hair, trying to reassure her.

Bella shook her head and looked at Sam, eyes wide. "He's close." She clutched the tourmaline shard on her necklace.

If two words had the power to instill fear into Sam, it was those two when spoken by Bella. She had the gift, or rather curse, of knowing when demonic powers were nearby.

Sam cleared his throat. "Jenny, Penny, get ready."

His fingers trembled as he reached for the security of the thick silver cross hanging on a chain around his neck. While the late Father Clint seemed to have nerves of steel, Sam hadn't fought against as many demons. His lack of experience was a problem. He hoped it didn't get them killed.

"Shit." Agent Saturn grunted, repeatedly pressing the button to open the elevator door. "It's stuck."

Sam frowned. Given Bella sensed a demon somewhere nearby, they might be safer staying inside. Except they had no idea how extensive the damage to the elevator had been or what had caused it to stop. If the brakes failed, they could fall at any moment.

Jupiter walked to the pair of doors. Not even a sliver of light was visible between them. Placing his fingers where the doors were pressed together, Jupiter tried forcing them apart by hand. "A little help," he said through gritted teeth.

Sam tried to move forward to help, but Bella wrapped her arms around his stomach with a strength that betrayed her size, anchoring him in place. "Daddy," she whimpered and buried her face against him.

Jenny, Penny, and Saturn lined up, positioning themselves by the elevator doors. Deciding on one man and woman per door to try and pry them apart, they strained in unison against the metal, each grunting while their faces contorted.

Sam watched on as Bella leaned into him, her thin body trembling.

The four others made significant progress, pulling on the doors until an inch-wide gap appeared. Jenny stopped pulling, breathing heavily.

"Need a little break," she said. She flexed the fingers of the hand that had been hurt when the elevator had stopped suddenly.

Sam nodded. "Bella," he began softly. "I have to help them, or else we'll be stuck in here forever."

"I'm scared, Dad."

"I know you are, sweet—"

The elevator rocked as if the cable holding it up had slipped a little.

"Bella, if I can't help the others get the door open, we all might fall."

"Yes, child, do you want to die?" Saturn snapped.

"Hey!" Sam turned to the agent and raised his finger. "Do not *ever* talk to my daughter like that." At Sam's raised voice, Bella started to sniffle. *Shit.* "You and I are going to talk about this later," he promised the agent. "Bella, you can hold onto me, but I need to move to the door."

"Okay," she whimpered, but her little legs moved as Sam stepped forward.

"That's my girl," Sam said, smiling.

Saturn rolled his eyes and muttered something about 'kids' and 'always crying.'

Sam ignored him and focused on the problem before him. There was a larger gap between them now, big enough for his cross to fit and maybe act as a fulcrum. He shrugged mentally. *Worth a shot.* Sticking the bottom of the cross between the doors, he closed his eyes and muttered a near-whispered prayer for strength. "Ready? On three," he instructed. "One, two—"

He pushed hard on the cross sideways while the others used their hands to pull the door further. It slid open about two feet, then stopped.

Penny giggled.

Sam looked at her. "What?"

She shook her head, trying to stop laughing. "Nothing. It's just, I've never seen anyone do that with a cross before." The look in her eyes suggested she was impressed and interested in seeing what else he could do with it.

He shook his head and studied the doors.

While the gap was nearly big enough for him to slide through now, the elevator appeared to have stopped between two floors. "Well," he asked Jupiter. "Which way do we go? Up or down?"

"Hello?" a man called out from the other side of the doors, a hint of nervousness in his voice.

"Ricky!" Bella shouted. She released her grip on Sam and launched herself upward, putting a foot on Penny's shoulder. She squeezed through the opening, opting to crawl through to the higher floor.

"Oh my… fuck," Jenny said. "She's like a cat or something."

Sam shook his head as Bella disappeared from view. "Well, I guess we've found Ricky Gibson. He's her favorite singer," he explained as the others looked at him. "Hey, Bella. Where are you?" he called through the gap after she didn't reappear.

"I don't think I can do this much longer," Saturn wheezed, still trying to pull the doors wider.

"Me either," Penny said.

"Bella?" Sam called.

No reply.

Shit. The situation was getting worse by the second.

"Bella!" he yelled.

She poked her head through the opening and looked down. "What?" she shouted. "I found Ricky!" Her smile stretched from ear to ear.

She disappeared from view again, and Ricky Gibson appeared, crouching so he could see down into the elevator. He looked like he hadn't slept in a week and carried a shoe in his hand, holding it in front of him like a weapon.

"What the hell are you going to do with that?" Jenny muttered, eyeing the rock star with her hands on her hips. "Smack a giant cockroach?"

He lowered the shoe, his expression relaxing. "Father Sam. Oh, thank God."

"I told you it was okay," Bella said to Ricky, her face appearing beside his. "We've come to rescue you." She flung her arms around him, practically knocking him sideways in her excitement to hug him.

He patted her awkwardly, seeming dazed. "You know about the, ah…" he glanced at Bella and then back at Sam, "… thing?"

The priest nodded.

"Just like old times," Ricky said with a slight laugh.

"Yeah. We really need to stop meeting like this." Sam shook his head. "Can you help us get out of here? The doors are stuck." He realized that they were having a difficult time prying them open because the metal was slightly warped. What the hell had exploded in the hotel?

"There's a chopper on the roof we can all leave in if we can just get to the stairwell," Agent Jupiter explained.

Ricky shook his head. "I don't think so. It's bad up here." He glanced to his left as if looking down the hallway. "I'll see if I can find something."

He rose and disappeared, taking Bella with him.

Sam frowned. It was great they'd found Ricky, and he seemed fine, but the explosion and Bella's fears about 'him' being near meant that the Remnant wasn't far behind.

Trapped inside the elevator, they were sitting ducks.

They needed to get out of there fast.

Chapter 11

"Okay, okay," Ricky Gibson muttered as he scanned the hotel penthouse-level hallway. "How do we get them out?" Further along from the elevator where Father Sam and his team were trapped, parts of the wall were missing, and the floor-to-ceiling windows that provided a panoramic view of the city were cracked. The left end of the hall had caved in and was impassable, burying access to the stairwell. To the right, most of the doors were damaged, and smoke was seeping from beneath the stairwell door at that end. An acrid smell, like something plastic was on fire, filled the air. Even if he got the others out of the elevator, where the hell were they supposed to go?

"Maybe a chair could help." Bella pointed to the nearby door. "Is that your room?"

Ricky shook his head emphatically. "No. Gerry's. My manager. But I don't think—"

Bella ran over and banged as loud as she could on the door.

"I don't think he's in there," he finished. He frowned at the girl. "Why are you here anyway? It's kinda dangerous, isn't it?" He couldn't imagine Sam bringing a child on a mission to hunt a demon like this.

"Ah... well..." Bella looked at him sheepishly as she tried the door handle.

"What the fucking—" The door swung open, revealing the hulking, shirtless figure of Gerry, who stopped short upon seeing Bella. "Eh, sorry."

Ricky shook his head. "What the hell are you doing in there? I thought you were gone or dead. I banged on your door for like five minutes. Didn't you hear the huge explosion?"

"Explosion. What?" Gerry frowned.

"Yes, explosion," Ricky insisted. "You know? That big boom that practically blew up half this place?" He shook his head and spread his arms wide, gesturing at the damage. "It's a wonder the hotel is still standing."

Gerry stepped out of his suite and squinted down the hall. His jaw dropped when he saw all the destruction. "Oh, fuck me. That's why the lights went out." He winced at Bella. "Pardon my French."

"In France, we would say, '*Oh pour l'amour de la merde*,' " a woman said in a French accent. She came out of the room behind Gerry.

Ricky raised his eyebrows at the leggy brunette who wore a figure-hugging black dress with matching heels.

Gerry ignored her and turned to Ricky. "Gee, you weren't kidding when you said something happened."

"Yeah, I know." Ricky shook his head. "You're fucking high, aren't you?" He sighed. It would explain why the jerk hadn't answered the door earlier if he was busy 'partying with a client.' "Listen. There are people trapped in the elevator. We need to help them so we can all get out of here, and we're running out of time."

Who the fuck knew when the whole building would collapse or if the *thing* would show up? Something was stalking him, something bad and not normal. Even the police were pretty sure it was a demon, just like in Springfield.

It was happening again.

Or maybe the nightmare at the mall had never ended, and this was round two of 'Abaddon tries to take over the world by kicking Ricky's ass whenever he tries to perform at Christmas.' *Fuck my life.*

But at least Gerry and the woman with the French accent, whoever she was, followed him and Bella to the elevator.

"Sam," he called through the gap, crouching down again.

"Yeah?" the priest sounded hopeful. "Did you find something to help open the door?"

"Maybe." Ricky eyed Gerry, unsure of how much help he'd be in his coked-up condition.

The talent manager peered down at the people trapped inside the elevator car and then at the doors. "Let's give it a push then. Move aside," he instructed Ricky.

Taking Bella by the hand, Ricky did as instructed.

Gerry crouched down and placed a hand on either door. He groaned, his face turning beet red and his arms trembling as if he was at the gym, bench-pressing two hundred pounds. But he made progress quickly. In less than two minutes, the elevator doors were far enough apart to fit an adult through, though it would be tight.

"That's it. That's all I can do," Gerry said. He wiped his brow, panting.

"Sam, just letting you know that nothing's working up here," Ricky called out. "Both stairwells are blocked."

"I'm coming up," said the younger and slenderer of the pair of men dressed in black suits. Whoever they were, they looked like secret agents or some kind of special security.

Ricky held out his hand and assisted the man through the gap and up onto the penthouse floor.

A quick glance around the hallway was all it took for the agent to confirm that Ricky was correct. "It's true," the man called back through the gap to the others. "There's no way out up here. We'll have to think of something else."

"Fuck," the other agent shouted. He paced in the confined space and combed his scalp with his fingers.

"What about the hatch?" said one of two women who reminded Ricky of Sisters Sandy and Mandy. She pointed at the elevator's ceiling, where a square doorway was inset. "We can climb to the roof through the elevator shaft."

"Brilliant," the agent said, pointing a finger at the woman. "Let's do that."

"What if the chopper's gone?" the other woman asked.

"We'll cross that bridge when we come to it," the agent said, studying the hatch. "Help me get this open," he said to Sam.

The priest nodded.

He looked different to Ricky than he recalled. Not just the weird cowboy-esque priest clothes that reminded him of the old Specialist, Father Clint. He was thinner, maybe, the look on his face more serious. And he was growing a beard. But then, they'd all likely changed a bit since the mall massacre.

"Oh, look. Someone's coming with a flashlight," the French woman said. She ran a few wobbly steps and waved her hands. "Hello. *Salut.*"

Ricky smiled. "Maybe someone else survived." And maybe there was a way through the stairwell after all. He'd been alone in his suite when all hell broke loose, watching the breaking news report about a warehouse fire. The team of cops hired to protect him had been in the hallway waiting for shift change. But when Ricky had opened his door and checked, they were gone.

Bella shivered and shook her head, staring at the light coming toward them down the hall. "That's not a flashlight," she whispered, her voice trembling.

Ricky's smile faltered. She was right. Unlike a beam guided by a person, this appeared to be more like a floating ball of fire not attached to anything. "Oh shit."

Bella darted out of the hallway and back through the gap into the out-of-commission elevator. "He's here," she squealed, trying to hide behind Sam. "He's here."

"What?" The priest darted an alarmed glance at Ricky. "Okay, everyone into the elevator, and let's get this damn hatch open," he said.

"No." The agent next to Sam shook his head as he struggled with the catch on the hatchway, trying to get it to pull down. "It will be too many. This elevator is precarious enough as it is. Us first, then they can come one at a time."

"There isn't any time," Sam shouted.

Bella crouched down and put her hands over her ears. "It's hot. It's so hot."

Ricky agreed. It was getting hot.

"Brigette?" Gerry called out. "Come back!"

Glancing to his left, Ricky saw the French woman had nearly reached the slowly moving fireball. She abruptly stopped walking and let out a gasp. Something dark moved behind the light. Then she screamed as her dress caught fire, and the flames quickly spread to her hair.

"*Oh my God,*" Ricky shouted. He turned away and slid through the gap in the elevator doors. He landed on the floor with a crash, causing the elevator to rock slightly from the impact. "It's coming. Jesus Christ, *it's coming.*"

"She's on fire!" Gerry yelled. "I'm coming in, too." His face was red from exertion and panic as he dove headfirst for the opening between the elevator doors. Whether it was the angle of his descent or his size, he only made it halfway before becoming stuck. "Help me!" he shouted.

Sam and Ricky moved forward and grasped Gerry's outstretched hands. They pulled, trying to drag him through, but whatever he was stuck on made him scream in pain.

"Try wiggling," Sam instructed.

"Will somebody help get this goddamn hatch open," the agent shouted, still tugging on the clasp.

"Move," the taller of the two sisters ordered. She unstrapped her rifle and aimed it at the ceiling. A loud crack echoed around the elevator, causing Bella to cower further into the corner. But the fastening on the hatch had released. Where the clasp had been, a hole now existed. The sister reached up on her tiptoes and pushed on the hatch. It popped up easily, and she slid it to one side.

"Oh!" She giggled and glanced at the agent. "Push, don't pull, Jupiter."

He frowned. "Just help me boost up—"

A horrific scream echoed through the hallway above, freezing everyone in place.

"Saturn," Jupiter whispered, his expression grave.

The screaming abruptly cut off and was replaced a second later by Gerry. "My legs," he whimpered. "It's got my legs!"

Ricky's eyes widened, and his jaw dropped as the edges of the elevator doors began to glow red.

This is it. We're all about to be cooked.

Gerry screamed as the smell of burned flesh filled the confined space.

"We need to get out of here. *Now,*" Sam shouted. He picked up Bella and moved to the hatch. "I need you to climb, baby."

Bella shook her head and buried herself into Sam as much as she could, turning away from the look of horror engraved into Gerry's features as the doors moved closer together. His hands were now fastened to the metal, and the stench of seared meat intensified when the doors made contact with the man's exposed chest.

"Put him out of his misery," Jupiter snapped at the tall sister, armed with the shotgun.

"Too late," she murmured as Gerry's screams abruptly stopped.

Ricky stared at Gerry in horror, the urge to vomit rising. He'd never liked him as a manager—or anything about him—but no one deserved to die like that.

Silent now, Gerry's skin continued to blacken and burn as if the fire was inside him.

"Okay, Bella," Sam said, his tone soft and soothing as he held her up to the hatch. "Go now. *Go.* You're good at climbing."

The elevator was getting hotter by the second.

"If you don't go, girl, then at least let me," Jupiter barked as she hesitated. He shoved Sam aside.

Something heavy made a thud as it landed on the roof of the elevator car, causing it to tip and sway. Everyone glanced upward.

"It's on the roof now?" the blonde sister asked.

That's it, we're toast. No way out now, Ricky thought.

No one moved as heavy footsteps sounded and something above their heads creaked.

"Shit, what if he burns the elevator cable?" Ricky whispered. He trembled at the mere possibility.

Sam crouched next to Ricky against the wall, holding Bella. "Hang on to me," he whispered to her and then began a prayer, "*Our Father who art in Heaven, Hallowed be thy name;...*" The two sisters joined in, but the tall brunette turned and looked through the glass window overlooking the city of Las Vegas. "Dear God, please let this be quick, as we find ourselves at the end of our lives."

A louder, longer-lasting metallic grinding noise filled the elevator.

Sam pulled Bella in as tight as he could and closed his eyes as the elevator car abruptly shot downward. Ricky's stomach heaved as he was almost lifted off the floor, but not as much as he'd expected. Except for everyone screaming, it was almost peaceful, this falling.

The elevator abruptly lurched, knocking everyone to the floor as their descent slowed. Had the emergency braking system kicked in once it reached a lower level?

Laying on the floor, Ricky stared upward at the open hatchway, unable to comprehend what he was seeing.

A hooded figure wearing a dark mask stood on top of the elevator. He was dressed in black fatigues that reminded Ricky of SWAT team gear. The figure gripped the elevator cables with his gloved hands, using friction to slow their fall. His hands quickly heated, his gloves and the cable turning red. As the heat built and his gloves tore open, exposing the flesh beneath, the man neither blinked nor changed position. He stared down at Ricky, the look in his blue eyes never wavering.

The elevator creaked and groaned, but the man never said a word or uttered a scream. Not even when chunks of his flesh fell off, and the metal cables ground against his bones and began to smoke.

As they reached the bottom of the shaft, the elevator abruptly stopped moving. Ricky blinked, jolted by the sudden impact. *What the fuck just happened?* The guy on the elevator roof had saved them? Why weren't they dead?

The damaged doors screamed in protest as they were pried open, drawing his attention.

The man in black fatigues stood in the gap where the doors had been. Using his booted feet, he slid the remains of Gerry out of the opening and moved them to the side. It was clear that the ex-manager's body was missing from the waist down, and the rest of him was a charred husk.

If the blue-eyed man in fatigues was disturbed by the fact his own hands and upper arms were mostly charred bone, he didn't show it. But the most unusual thing about him, which Ricky couldn't stop staring at, was the glowing image of what looked like a bullet, hovering about a half inch in front of his forehead. It moved when he moved, never changing shape or size.

"Go," the figure murmured. He had a soft, deep voice with a faint accent. "Before he comes back and finds you alive." Then he was gone, a dark blur blending into the shadows.

The sprinklers had activated on the basement level, and water was beginning to pool on the floor, seeping past Gerry's torso. Ricky looked at Sam, who seemed as stunned as he was.

"Who... was that?" Sam asked.

Ricky shook his head. "I don't know, but I think I need a drink."

Chapter 12

Lying in her hospital bed, Sarah lifted the sheet covering her abdomen and shifted her gown aside. *Shit.* She closed her eyes and let the sheet fall back down. There was another new bandage on her belly and one on the opposite arm to the IV. Her heart rate accelerated as fear and anger warred for dominance. Ultimately, the two emotions shook hands and called it a draw.

"Goddammit," she shouted.

Mother Agnes came trotting in from outside her room, followed by one of the many nameless nurses who always seemed to be around, just like the black-suited agents. "Sarah, are you okay?"

"No. I'm not."

The elderly woman's face paled. "Why? What's wrong?"

"Because every time I wake up from the little naps you guys insist I have, I find out I've been poked and prodded somewhere new. What was it this time? More blood? Some weird scan that just *had* to be done?" She tossed the sheet off again and pulled her gown up. Then, she tore off the bandage on her lower abdomen. A small red dot had been covered by iodine, staining her skin slightly orange. The dot was the kind of mark a needle would leave behind. Sarah glanced at the Mother Superior, her panic and fear increasing to rage. "What the fuck is this? I didn't tell you you could do this."

"Get Doctor Stevens," Mother Agnes said to the nurse.

The nurse nodded and hurried from the room.

The agent standing by the door put his fingers to his earpiece as if listening to someone else speak. He nodded and glanced toward the bed. "Doctor Stevens is on her way, ma'am," he advised.

"Oh yeah, I bet she is," Sarah said. "Doesn't she ever have any other patients to see? Or am I it? Your favorite experiment?" She drew in a long breath and then wished she hadn't. *I really hate the smell of antiseptic.*

"Now, Sarah, you need to calm down." Mother Agnes raised her hands in a calming gesture. "You know if you get too emotional, it might affect the baby."

Sarah smirked. "Like any of you actually care about me or my baby."

"Actually, we do. We care a great deal," Mother Agnes said, her tone nearly pleading.

"Just... get me my mother. I want to see my mother."

The nun nodded. "She's just outside using the washroom. She'll be right in."

The soft clack of heels preceded Doctor Stevens rushing into the room, carrying what looked like another set of test results.

"What is this?" Sarah shouted at her. She pointed at the puncture wound on her belly. "What did you do?"

The Doctor stared at her calmly. "An amniocentesis. We wanted to take a sample of the fluid inside the placenta and check it for abnormalities."

"Why? Why do you keep doing these things when I tell you I don't want them?" She glanced around her room as despair rose inside her. She was trapped in a cage with no way out and no one listening to her.

"Well, this isn't exactly a normal situation, now is it?" The doctor crossed her arms over her chest. "Granted, a procedure like that is not without risk this late in the pregnancy, but sometimes knowledge is worth the risk."

Sarah gritted her teeth. "I keep telling you. There's nothing wrong with me or my baby. Everything is fine."

"Is it?" The doctor shook her head and moved closer to the bed. "When we inserted the needle, we were able to push through the layers of fat and muscle, like we normally would. But we couldn't puncture the uterus."

"Okay," Sarah said. She crossed her arms. *That'll teach you to poke things where they aren't wanted.*

"Normally, the uterus is quite soft and flexible. But yours is like a barrier that we couldn't push the needle through."

Sarah stared at her. "And?"

"And now, we can't see through it." She gestured at the ultrasound printout and handed it to Sarah.

Sarah looked at the grainy black-and-white picture. How people saw more than blobby shapes on them, she'd never know.

"See?" The doctor tapped the picture with her finger. "This is your abdomen. And this is the uterus. The baby is moving around just fine, so we know it's alive. We can still hear a heartbeat. But now… we can't see it." When Sarah didn't say anything, she added, "This is in no way, shape or form normal."

Okay. So maybe things weren't normal. But did that mean it was a problem? And maybe if they'd stop poking and prodding her and doing tests like this, she and the baby wouldn't feel threatened.

"I recommend we induce labor—"

"No."

"The fetus has grown two inches in the past two days alone. At this rate of growth, I don't know how much longer we can—"

Sarah grabbed the physician's arm and pushed her away. "*No.*"

Doctor Stevens fell backward into the adjustable bedside table, knocking the tray resting on top flying. The leftovers from Sarah's lunch clattered onto the floor, as did the doctor.

The physician shook her head as she slowly picked up her papers and stood.

Mother Agnes darted a shocked glance at Sarah, then bent quickly to help the doctor.

Sarah stared at the doctor in horror as her pulse raced. "I'm…" She tried to apologize, but the words refused to come out. She hadn't meant to push her so hard. She hadn't meant to push her at all. *What the fuck is wrong with me?*

Doctor Stevens straightened her clothes and gave Sarah a guarded look. "I know you're not yourself at the moment, but these outbursts cannot continue," she said. "We are not your enemy, Sarah." She turned to Mother Agnes. "See what you can do with her. Otherwise, she'll have to be restrained."

The nun looked stricken but nodded.

The doctor left the room. On the way out of the door, she passed Ena, who stood on the threshold looking wide-eyed.

"Oh, my word, Sarah, you've never changed since you were a baby. You'll sleep just fine until I have to leave for a moment to go to the bathroom. What has happened now?"

"Like you don't know? You must know." There was no way that her mother could not have seen the doctor trying to jab a giant needle into her abdomen. Not unless she was lying about having only left for a second. She sneered. "This place is full of liars."

Ena looked shocked. "Sarah?"

Sarah shook her head as tears started to run down her cheeks. "Please leave me alone. I just want to sleep." She rolled over in her bed, turning her back on her mother and the elderly nun.

"Why don't we say some prayers," Mother Agnes said softly. "Hmm? We'll say some prayers while you sleep. It'll be okay." A soft hand patted her arm.

Anxious whispers reached Sarah's ears as the nun and her mother moved away from the bed to talk.

Sarah closed her eyes and tried to block out the world around her. This beautiful pregnancy that had begun with so much love had become a living nightmare.

The baby kicked inside her more gently than normal. Maybe it was because of the barrier that the doctor had mentioned. Maybe it was protecting her as much as it was the baby.

No, her baby was fine. He was fine, perfect and normal. There was nothing wrong with him.

Maybe she was the one becoming a monster.

Or maybe she always had been one, and that's why the baby was the way he was.

Maybe Sam would have to fight her like a demon when he came back.

Or maybe he'd be smart and never come back.

ENA STOOD WITH HER hands on her hips and addressed Mother Agnes in the fiercest whisper she could without her voice carrying and disturbing Sarah. "What the *hell* is going on?"

"Let's speak outside," the elderly nun said, indicating they should leave the room with a nod toward the door. Her face looked pinched, and the lines deeper, as if age was suddenly taking its toll.

Ena followed her, scowling. When the nun didn't stop at the observation window of Sarah's room as expected, she called out, "Where are you going now?"

Mother Agnes turned and faced her. "The chapel, if we may. We can speak more comfortably there." The beseeching look on her face seemed almost pleading. She clearly wanted to have their discussion away from the agents and medical staff.

"Fine," Ena snapped. "But I don't want to be away from Sarah long." *Not after what's just happened.*

The medical team had somehow run tests while Ena had been out of Sarah's room, which, since she had only been gone for five minutes at most, didn't seem possible. Had she fallen asleep in the toilet? She had to admit it was possible, given how poorly she'd slept in the past three days and her overall level of fatigue. But what was more likely was that she had been drugged and was missing a chunk of time from the day as a result.

Either way, Sarah now thought she was a liar and untrustworthy, which was both hurtful and completely unacceptable. But how could she fix it when Sarah was acting like a caged animal, with good reason?

I'm never going to eat or drink anything again in this place.

In less than three minutes, they reached the room designated as a chapel by the establishment. Mother Agnes opened the door and nodded upon confirming it was empty.

"Thank you. We can speak more privately here." She sat in one of the pews and gestured for Ena to do the same. "I like to come here to think. I find it soothing."

The room had a vaulted ceiling and a warm ambiance created by the faux stained-glass windows and comfortable pews. Ena had been looking forward to seeing Sam give Sunday sermons there. But now she was so angry she could burn the place down and never look back. The way they were treating Sarah was abominable.

"Restraints," she muttered as she took a seat beside the Mother Superior, thinking of what she'd overheard the doctor saying in Sarah's room. "That's barbaric. I've never heard of such a thing being allowed, let alone to a pregnant woman."

Mother Agnes's brows flicked as she sighed softly. "Sarah may need them soon, unfortunately."

"Now listen here," Ena rounded on her. "Unless you want us to report what's going on here to the media, I suggest you don't. Whatever is happening with my daughter is most probably because of things you've done to her since she's been in your care. And what about her husband? And daughter?"

"Please calm down." Mother Agnes put her hand on Ena's. "We have everything in place to ensure Sarah will be looked after."

"Yes." Ena snatched her arm out of the nun's grip. "I heard all about what these agents of yours have planned. Is it my grandson or Sarah you want for your experiments? Or both? Because I assure you, I'll die before I will let you harm either."

Mother Agnes darted a glance around the room, then said in a quiet tone, "The chances of us being overheard here are considerably less, but not zero. Please keep your voice down." She leaned close to Ena. "Now, what is it that you think you know?"

Interesting. The Mother Superior was worried about being overheard in an empty room. Did she fear her own people?

Ena tilted her head and cocked a brow at the nun. "Tell me what you think is going on with Sarah, and I'll tell you what I overheard in the mess hall this morning."

Mother Agnes assessed Ena with a narrowed gaze. After a moment, she nodded. "Very well. What we fear has happened, and continues to happen, is the result of demonic possession. Sarah wasn't completely cleansed of the demon when she became pregnant. It appears the baby, being innocent, is susceptible to demonic energy and is… reacting to it. Perhaps the energy is fusing with him as he grows and turning him into a demon. Perhaps he's simply being possessed by one. We don't know. But either way, it's not good for either Sarah or that poor sweet soul who is not yet even born."

"I see." Ena sat back against the pew, thinking about Sarah and the innocent baby. "This demonic energy… it's Abaddon's?"

The nun's expression remained neutral as she answered, "Since he was the demon that possessed her, it's quite possible. But we don't know for sure."

"So… this could be him… coming back?"

"It's impossible to be certain right now, but yes, it's likely."

Goose bumps rose on Ena's arms as a chill went through her. The danger they were in was real. She'd seen the signs too, hadn't she? She just hadn't wanted to believe it. But now, as much as she didn't want to ask the question, she had to know. "Will it… are they in danger of dying?"

"All of us are in danger of dying every day. It's by God's grace that we live our lives," the nun preached in what Ena thought was a very nun-like manner. "But are Sarah and her son doomed because of this demonic situation?" Her lips firmed into a line as she paused. "It's possible. As the baby grows, so does the demonic power and it's influence over Sarah. What will happen when he's born is anyone's guess. He could kill his mother, unintentionally or otherwise."

Ena shut her eyes and covered her mouth, unable to block the image of the baby being born a monster… and feasting on Sarah. The idea made bile rise in her throat. After waiting a moment for the sickness in her stomach to subside, she said. "It makes sense now."

"What does?"

"What I overheard in the mess hall." She glanced at Agnes. "Brother Trevor was sitting at a table with an agent named Mars, I believe."

"Brother Trevor was speaking with Mars?" the nun asked.

Ena nodded. "They tend to all look the same, but I think that's what his planetary designation was." The nun stared at her without comment, so she continued, "They were discussing removing the baby early, before it reaches full term. I believe Mars wanted to kill it, but Brother Trevor did not agree. So Mars threatened him if he told you or anyone about the idea."

Mother Agnes looked thoughtful for a long moment. "Thank you for telling me. I knew they were planning something, but I didn't think they'd go that far." Her smile was fleeting as she grasped Ena by the hand once more. "It may become necessary to remove the child early for both Sarah and the baby's safety, but it is not on my agenda to kill an innocent. Not ever. That goes against everything we believe in here. The agents, however…" she shook her head, "… I can't speak for them. They answer to a different government organization. One, I fear, that has its own agenda."

Ena nodded, remembering how they'd been rounded up like cattle in the desert and brought in at gun point. *The nun had really had no part in that?*

Mother Agnes frowned, suddenly seeming a decade older. "I will do everything in my power to protect your daughter and the baby from harm." She gave Ena's hand a small squeeze. "I promise you that."

"Thank you." Ena smiled at the nun. She had no idea whether the Mother Superior would keep her word, but she had to admit she'd never personally seen the nun act in a way that suggested she had ill intentions. She had only ever offered support. And yet, Ena couldn't forget she was virtually a prisoner within the walls of the facility, which she got the impression was much bigger than the small section she'd been allowed to see so far.

Maybe I should go for a wander. "Does the government know about everything that goes on in this base?"

"Ena Ridley, you need to curb your curiosity because there are people much less friendly than the planetary agents here. Remember, your daughter is the priority here for you, as she is for many others. Why don't you get yourself a coffee on your way back to Sarah?"

"No, thank you." *Was it the coffee that was drugged?* Could be. She wouldn't have another cup, just in case. Ena rose from the pew. "My family is my life. I will do everything I can to protect them. From demons or otherwise."

Mother Agnes nodded. "As will I." Her smile seemed genuine as she nodded at Ena. "God be with you."

May God be with us all, Ena thought.

How the hell was she going to tell Sarah that her child might be the second coming of Abaddon?

SAM LOOKED OUT THE window of their suite at the Great Rock of Vegas Casino and Hotel, studying the street below. Crowds of people wandered the busy street, wrapped up in their lives as the holiday season kicked into full swing. The fact they were all in extreme danger didn't seem to deter the masses. But the knowledge hovered over the entire city like a specter, quickening steps and shortening laughs, casting a shadow across the heart and mind. Dark clouds swirled in the afternoon sky. A storm was coming. The first raindrops were already splattering against the window.

"Pick a bed," Agent Jupiter said, waving his hand at the double suite he'd booked. "I don't care which."

"But there's only two," Jenny pointed out.

"There's an adjoining suite. The other room is through there. It's bigger." He pointed at a door in the wall. "Sam, Bella, and you two ladies can have that one. I'm sharing with Ricky," Jupiter announced.

Ricky swung around and pointed at the agent. "Hey, if you think I'm gonna swing that way for you—"

Jupiter held a hand up. "I'll be taking the sofa. You get your own double bed. Agent Barnes can have the extra bed."

The driver grunted as he dumped some of their bags of gear from the van onto the floor. "Thanks," he said, drolly.

"Thing is, Ricky," Jupiter continued. "I don't want you or anyone else in a room alone. We'll hunker down here for the night and work out our next moves."

"Well, if you don't want me alone, can I have Jenny and Penny in my room?" Ricky asked with a devilish grin.

While Penny replied with, "Certainly," Jenny answered at the exact same moment with, "Certainly not!" The sisters looked at each other and frowned.

"You need to live a little." Penny laughed.

During the van ride, they'd all been too stunned to talk. But now they wanted to have a pointless argument about who slept with whom and where? Sam shook his head. There were more important things to discuss. Like how they'd nearly died and who had saved them.

"We're lucky to be alive," Jenny said. "I thought for sure that was it."

It should have been, Sam thought. He leaned against the windowsill. "That guy at the end. He wasn't the burning man. I mean, if he had been, he'd have cooked us, right? Does that mean he's on our side? Who was he?"

"*What* was he," Penny asked. "Did you see his hands?" She shuddered and sat on the small couch.

"He slowed down the elevator by holding the cables. I watched it happen." Ricky followed Penny and sat beside her. "That's how his hands got... like that." He looked at his own hands and grimaced.

"You said there were more of these remnant things," Sam said to Agent Jupiter. "Is it possible this guy's another one? Or is there something else going on that we need to know about?" If there was one thing he'd learned from movies, secret agents never told people everything. They were full of secrets.

"It's possible he's one," Jupiter said, nodding. He sat on one of the two double beds and leaned his hands on his knees. "I've never seen anything like him. Have you?" he asked the two sisters.

Penny shook her head. "He's not a vampire, I don't think, and werewolves wouldn't be able to do something like that and walk away without bleeding to death. He's... something different."

"Wait," Ricky said. "Werewolves and vampires are real?"

"Yeah. They aren't that common and keep to themselves most of the time. A succubus…" she grinned. "Now that's far more interesting." She gave Ricky a wink.

"If you like that sort of thing," Jenny added, rolling her eyes.

"What's a succubus?" Bella asked. She sat cross-legged on the floor in front of the television, having found cartoons to watch.

"Never mind," Sam said. They were getting off track. "It's nothing that concerns us right now."

"I've sent his description back to headquarters to see if anything comes up in the database," Agent Jupiter said. "That bullet suspended above his forehead should be identifiable if anyone has seen him before. But if he is a remnant, most stay off the grid, so I can't guarantee anything will come up."

"I don't really care what it is," Jenny said. "I want to know why he helped us." She leaned against the wall and crossed her arms. "Is he a good guy or another bad guy? What does he want?"

Sam glanced at Bella. She'd gone back to watching television and stared blankly at the screen as the cartoons played. She'd been unusually quiet since the elevator ride from hell. It was probably because she was numb from shock, but so far, she hadn't even cried.

"Bella?" he called out.

She turned to him.

"That man on the elevator. The one that had the funny thing on his forehead. Were you scared of him?"

"No." She shrugged. "He wasn't scary. I knew we'd be okay." She turned back to watching the television.

If Bella hadn't been scared, whatever the guy was, he wasn't a danger to them. At least not at the moment. But that didn't mean they were in any less danger.

Sam ran his fingers across his scalp. Maybe they should have stayed in Springfield. Joining the Church of the New World Order was supposed to have been the start of a better life, but instead, he'd put them all in even greater danger.

"The bullet guy said we needed to leave before he, and I'm assuming he meant the Remnant, found us alive. Does that mean he's looking for us all now, not just Ricky?" he asked Agent Jupiter.

"Yes. As we discussed before, his goal seems to be to kill anyone connected to Vietnam in any way, specifically the military and his old troop. But everyone who associates with anyone on his hit list or gets in the way is added to the list, too. The numbers grow exponentially. If you weren't in his sights before, you and everyone here definitely are now." He turned to Ricky. "You didn't get a look at him, did you? When you were in the hallway of your penthouse?"

Ricky shook his head. "All I saw was a fireball coming toward me. I didn't stay around to see why."

"Is staying in a busy place such as this is appropriate then?" Sam asked, thinking about what Jupiter had said about the hit list growing exponentially. "There are hundreds of guests here, plus casino visitors and diners. If Rathburn comes here, which he likely will if he's after us, the damage and death toll could be as bad or worse than the Springfield Mall massacre."

Jupiter nodded. "Boss wants us to draw him out, which means having Ricky act like there's nothing wrong and keeping to his schedule." During the drive from the nearly demolished hotel to the casino, he'd taken Saturn's vacant seat in the front, where Sam assumed he'd been on the long-range radio, reconnoitering with the base. "He's supposed to play a concert at this casino, so we're here, pretending to be part of his security team. Only difference is we switched the penthouse rooms to these ones on the fourth floor."

"That's insane," Sam said.

Jupiter looked at him incredulously. "You want to stay on the top floor after what we just went through?"

"No." If he never had to take another elevator again in his life, he'd be happy. "I mean, using Ricky as bait and everyone else as collateral... that's insane." He gestured at Ricky. "You're okay with this?"

The rock star shrugged. "I'm not sure I have a choice."

Sam frowned. "There has to be a better way. What if we get this bullet guy to help us?"

Jupiter shook his head. "Right now, we don't even know who or what he is, let alone where to find him. It's best if we stick to what we know. Rathburn is going to be looking for us anyway, and there's no sense in hiding. We might as well be in a place where we can set up teams to trap him. Since we're already a man down..." he paused and glanced down. He didn't have to name Agent Saturn for them to know who he was talking about. The sudden loss had been a shock to them all. "The base is sending in back up," he continued. "Two teams have been dispatched who will work with us to case the casino and surrounding streets. A third team will be joining us tomorrow."

Sam's mouth dropped open. All these extra people were now in danger as well. "Have you communicated with these teams about what they're up against? Do they know they're now on Rathburn's hit list too?"

"Of course. But everyone has a job to do, right?"

Sam shook his head. Yes, everyone had a job to do all right, and his primary job was to make sure his daughter was safe, something he'd failed to do lately. One close call with death was more than enough. "Bella? Get ready. Chopper or no chopper, I'm taking you back to be with Sarah. She must be going crazy by now, wondering if you're okay." He had no idea how he would tell her that they'd nearly died in the elevator, but he'd cross that bridge when they got there.

At the sound of his voice, Bella turned and looked at him. Eyes wide, she shook her head. "Please, Dad, don't. I don't want to go back. It's not safe there."

Sam prayed for patience. "Listen. Whatever has you spooked about the church compound can't be worse than what we just went through. You'll be safer there."

She shook her head again. "P-please, Daddy." Her voice trembled, and the tears he'd expected earlier threatened to flow now. "Don't make me go."

He sat on the floor beside her and pulled her into a tight hug. "I know you're scared, but I can't lose you, Bells. I need you safe."

"Truth is, Sam," Jupiter piped in. "Nowhere is safe for any of us. Not now. The Remnant knows who we are. The Boss says the kid stays here with us until this is done. We can't have you leaving to take her back now. If we split up, it increases the risk and decreases our defenses."

"What?" Sam pulled back from Bella and stared at the agent. "You guys were hot for her to go back, and now you're fine with her staying?"

Jupiter frowned. "I'm not fine with any of this. If she'd stayed at the base in the first place like she should have, we wouldn't be having this conversation." He glared at Bella, who shrank against Sam. "But I have a job to do and orders to follow. She stays until this is done."

"Woah, Bella," Ricky said, sounding both incredulous and impressed. He glanced at Penny, who sat beside him on the small couch, and back at Bella. "Did you sneak out or something?"

The girl gave him a sheepish nod. "I wanted to help."

Ricky slapped his hands on his thighs and gave her a thumbs up. "That's badass, man. You rock." The grin on his face slipped as he caught sight of the angry glare that Sam was feeling from the bottom of his soul. "I mean, that's bad... you ass, ah..." he stammered. "F-f-fuck. I give up." He glanced around the room. "Does this place have any beer? 'Cause I really need one."

Bella giggled, her eyes bright as she grinned.

Sam groaned. Bella *was* a brave little girl, and he was proud of her for who she was, but did Ricky have to egg her on? The last thing she needed was encouragement to take chances. "I need to talk to Sarah," he said. "You'd like to talk to Mommy, wouldn't you?" he asked Bella.

She gave an uncertain nod. "Is she going to be mad at me?"

"Maybe a little, but she'll be happy to hear your voice. Let's give her a call."

They moved to the phone on the nearby desk. It was the first phone they'd encountered since leaving the compound. Patting his pockets, Sam suddenly stilled. "Shit." He closed his eyes, feeling like an idiot. "I left the number in my other pants when I got changed." He'd scribbled the direct number for the clinic on a piece of paper before leaving the base. He turned back to Jupiter. "Can we use your radio thing?"

The agent hesitated, then nodded and unclipped the device from his belt.

He brought it to his mouth. "Jupiter to Base, do you copy?"

"Copy that, Jupiter. Over."

"Father Sam would like to speak to his wife. Over."

"Copy that. I'll advise and have the clinic call."

Jupiter passed the device to Sam. A moment later, when the radio squawked again, Sam heard a familiar voice. "Hello, Father Sam."

"Brother Trevor?" Sam frowned. He wasn't used to speaking over long-range radio devices and found the process awkward. As a security guard, Sarah had been the expert in that department. He also hadn't expected to hear from Trevor. "I want to speak with Sarah, if I may."

There was a pause, and then Brother Trevor said, "She's sleeping right now."

Sam exchanged a glance with Bella, who looked anxious.

"Can you wake her? Bella's here with me."

Again, another pause. "I don't think that's a good idea."

Sam's heart sped up as he furrowed his brow. "Why not? Is she okay?"

"Yes. Everything is fine. I'm sorry we can't wake her to talk, but your wife needs to rest. Hearing your voice might be too much right now. Sorry. I'll tell her you called." The connection ended, resulting in the brief sound of static in Sam's ear.

Sam stared at the device for a long moment before handing it back to Jupiter.

"Another time, maybe," the agent said.

Sam nodded absentmindedly. *What the fuck was that about?* Sarah was sleeping, and they didn't want to wake her so they could talk? Not even to speak to Bella? What the fuck had happened in the—he checked his watch—eight hours he'd been away?

He studied his daughter, who looked exhausted and on the verge of more tears. "Bella, when you said that you didn't like the base because it's not safe, what exactly did you mean?"

"I don't know," she whispered. "I want Mama." She wrapped her arms around him. "I'm sorry for running off and scaring her and Nana."

"That's not why she couldn't talk to us. She isn't mad. She's just... sleepy." *Really sleepy.* The feeling of uneasiness he'd had all day deepened. He knew pregnant women slept a lot sometimes, but there was no way Sarah wouldn't want to talk to them, especially Bella, no matter how sleepy she was. "I promise we'll see her as soon as we can. I just need to find the bad man first." And the sooner he did that, the better.

It was clear the agents wouldn't let him go back and see Sarah until he was done with this job. And he didn't know his way back to the base on his own. He'd not been allowed to see either the way in or out. So he needed to do what they wanted.

Fuck.

A sense of urgency coiled around Sam's heart like a boa constrictor.

He needed to figure this out fast.

The Remnant was quickly becoming the least of his worries.

Chapter 13

Lit by the soft glow of city lights filtered through a gap between the hotel curtains, Bella's gentle sleeping face gave Sam a pang of heartache. She'd fallen asleep in his arms a few hours prior, trusting him to be there whenever she woke during the night. Her own teddy bear, in a manner of speaking.

Her chosen protector.

Her father.

It was a role he'd taken on willingly, and if asked to do everything all over again, he'd make the same choice without hesitation. "I love you, Little Bells," he whispered, his voice clear in the nighttime quiet.

He turned and headed for the door to their room before he lost his nerve to leave. Jenny and Penny occupied the other bedroom in the suite. Or maybe it was Penny, Jenny and Ricky, or Ricky and Penny, or any combo in between. He couldn't tell which way that was going to go before he'd put Bella to bed. He was simply glad Penny had a new person to flirt with who seemed to appreciate it rather than making him uncomfortable with her unwanted attention.

So far, he had managed to climb out of Bella's arms, slide out of the bed, and get dressed in his 'demon hunting' attire. Now, he just needed to get out of the hotel without being seen. He didn't want to leave Bella alone like this, but with any luck, he'd be back before she woke.

He'd given much thought to what Agent Jupiter had said about Rathburn hunting them all now and particularly the plan to use Ricky as bait. Sitting around waiting for the corrupted soul to show up and begin burning everything and everyone didn't sit well with him. It was better to face him on their terms, wasn't it? But Jupiter had made it clear Sam wasn't in charge of this mission, and his opinions didn't matter, despite being called in as The Specialist to fight the nigh-invulnerable being due to his ability to wield his faith as a weapon.

Fighting Rathburn alone probably wasn't the wisest choice, but he was out of options. He needed to finish this as quickly as possible for everyone's sake, and he couldn't risk putting anyone else in danger by asking them to sneak out at one in the morning to go Remnant hunting without Agent Jupiter's approval.

As he put his hand on the doorknob, he turned and gave Bella one last glance. *I'm doing this for you, my girl, and your mama and baby brother too.* He mouthed a short prayer, asking God to watch over her, as well as Sarah and the baby. *Maybe I should ask him to watch over me as well.*

His movements mimicked those of a slow-motion scene from an action film as he turned the handle, knowing the slightest sound could wake Bella. Hearing her roll over in bed, he froze. If she opened her eyes, there would no doubt be a resulting scream. Thankfully, she settled into a deeper sleep upon getting comfortable again. Sam waited a few more heartbeats for her breathing to slip back into the regular pattern of sleep. Then he pulled the door open, stepped into the shared living area of the suite, carefully shut it again—and stopped.

Jenny and Penny were sitting on the couch together in the dimly lit room, watching him.

Oh shit.

"Called it," Penny said. She gave Jenny a smug glance. "You owe me twenty bucks, Sister."

Jenny rolled her eyes and fished a greenback out of her pocket. She handed it to Penny, who grinned as she took it.

"Thanks, Sam." Jenny frowned as she studied him. "I pegged you as having more sense, but Penny was right. You're just as bad as Bella with the whole sneaking around thing. I wonder where she gets it from, eh?"

Sam frowned. "I..." he began and stopped. Caught red-handed, what was there to say? And were they right about Bella being like him with taking risks?

He'd always thought he was the more responsible one in his relationship with Sarah.

Both women laughed softly.

"Don't worry," Jenny said, grinning. "We aren't going to turn you in to Jupiter. I'm going with you."

"And I'm going into your room to watch over Bella and make sure she's safe," Penny said. "Just don't get yourself killed because there's no way I want to have to look into those puppy dog eyes of hers and explain that her daddy's not coming back."

Sam stared at them both.

On the one hand, he had to admit it was nice knowing he had backup. On the other, he hadn't wanted to put anyone else in danger. "But... aren't you worried about Jupiter finding out?"

"No buts," Jenny said. She shook her head. Already dressed in her demon-slayer outfit, she stood and grabbed her pack. "Let's just get going."

Sam nodded. While Sarah would likely have issues with him leaving Bella in the care of someone they barely knew, he had no reason not to trust Penny and was grateful for her assistance. "Thank you," he said to her. "I feel bad enough as it is."

She smiled. "Just get that fucker and come back in one piece." She leaned in and gave him a quick peck on his cheek.

As Penny disappeared into the bedroom, Sam looked at Jenny, his heart racing for what they were about to do. "Are you ready for this?"

She nodded, looking amused. "I was born fucking ready."

"What are you doing?" Sam asked Jenny in a hushed tone.

Having managed to avoid being spotted by hotel staff by taking the stairway down to the underground parking garage with the idea of leaving through a side door at the far end, Jenny was instead heading toward the group's black van.

"What?" She pulled a set of car keys out of her pocket and jangled them for him to see. "You planned to walk around all night?"

He stared at her. "Where did you get those?"

"You ask too many questions." She unlocked the driver's door and opened it. "Get in."

Sam frowned but opened the passenger door as instructed. "You stole them from the driver?"

"No. I borrowed them. He just doesn't know it." When she glanced at him and saw his disapproving expression, she added, "I'm going to give them back. Don't worry."

Sam shook his head as he fastened his seat belt. "Is this what they teach you at the church?"

She arched her brow at him and turned the key.

As the van roared to life, the radio squawked on. "Base, do you copy?" a young man's voice burst over the CB radio in the van. "This is Brother Benjamin, requesting immediate backup. Base?"

Jenny shared a horrified glance with Sam. "Aw, shit." The radio must have been left on when the van was shut off.

The priest stared at the communication device. "Jupiter said other teams were sent to help." Sam hadn't expected them to do more than keep watch on the hotel, though. "This is an open channel, right? If we answer, everyone in the agency will hear?"

Jenny nodded. "What do we do? Ignore it?"

"We help," Sam said, after a moment. "It's what we came out here to do. That might be Rathburn on the move." Jupiter could fuck himself if he got upset that they'd left without his authorization. He'd likely find out sooner or later, anyway.

Jenny grabbed the radio's handpiece and handed it to Sam. "You talk, I'll drive."

He spoke into the device, "Copy that, Brother Benjamin. Please state your location."

"Father Sam!" the brother excitedly squawked over the connection, apparently recognizing Sam's voice. "Thank God you're here. This Remnant, or whatever the hell he is, he's taken Kelly out, burned her like a piece of toast."

Sam closed his eyes. *Oh shit, they're done for.* "We'd better hurry," he said to Jenny.

"Copy that," Jenny answered. She put the van into gear and headed for the exit.

"Location, Brother Benjamin?" Sam called into the radio.

"I... ah. There's a building shaped like a giant pencil next to a burger shop. Me and Nelly are down the alley, hanging low, but he's coming," Benjamin said in a hushed voice like he was trying to whisper.

"A giant pencil?" Sam asked Jenny. "Do you know where that is?"

She nodded. "Yes, it's a casino called Scholar's Luck. Trust me, when you see it, you sure can't miss it. It's not far."

Sam clicked the talk button on the radio. "We're on our way. See if you can keep him away from the casino," he said.

"Trust me, we're trying. Oh my God! He's between us. Nelly, stay back!"

A shiver ran up Sam's spine as he heard a woman scream through the CB radio, ending in a gurgle, followed quickly by a scream from Brother Benjamin. *Shit, they were dead already.*

"Brother Benjamin, do you copy?" he called into the radio.

The only reply was silence.

Sam clutched the door handle like he was hanging on for life as Jenny pulled out of the parking garage and sped down a laneway. A pair of pedestrians dared to step out onto the road without looking. Upon hearing the van, they stopped in the middle of the lane, staring at the vehicle like a pair of deer caught in the headlights. Jenny narrowly missed them as she swerved left and pulled back in before a red sports car heading the other way reached them.

"Fuck you..." the Ferrari's driver yelled at them, his words fading as the van rushed past.

"Can we please not kill anyone before we even get there?" Sam asked.

"Hey! You said to hurry." Jenny beeped the car horn as a lovestruck couple began to step onto the road ahead of them. "But if people could watch where they cross the road, that would be fucking great!"

As they rounded another corner, Sam couldn't help but wonder how fast the van could take a corner without tipping. She was driving crazier than Agent Barnes, which was saying something.

Jenny darted a glance at him. "Sam, you're looking a bit pale. What's wrong? Don't like my driving?" She grinned.

Sam closed his eyes and sent a silent prayer, asking that God watch over them as they raced around the downtown Vegas Strip.

If dodging pedestrians and sports cars wasn't enough already, they passed a police car idling in a parking spot outside a donut shop. The cop car's lights instantly flashed on as they flew past, followed by the sound of sirens. Sam pressed the button to lower the window on his side and stuck his head out to look behind them. "Shit, the cops are chasing us now."

So much for this being a covert expedition.

"Hang on," Jenny shouted and gritted her teeth.

Sam gripped the dashboard as they abruptly rounded another corner. They raced down an alleyway and out the other side onto another busy street, where she turned a hard right, narrowly missing a car, which blared its horn at them.

Sam made a gesture of apology to the car, which was now behind them, but at least the cops appeared to be gone.

"Okay, the pencil is on the left. I'll park in the alleyway next to it," Jenny said, but as she did so, the cop car that had been following them turned onto the street and flew past them, sirens blaring and lights flashing. It screeched to a halt in front of the alleyway Jenny had indicated. "Well, shit. Maybe they weren't after us."

Jenny swung the van into a sharp left that made the tires squeal and parked behind the cop car. The two cops had gotten out and stood at the entrance to the alley. They turned and studied Jenny and Sam as they stepped out of the van.

"Officer Sergeant Reed from the LVMPD," the larger of the two men boomed, taking the lead. "We're following up on reports of shots being fired. You folks might want to move along."

"Yeah, I don't think that's going to happen," Jenny answered them. She squinted into the darkened alley. "Sam, I think we need our flashlights."

Sam nodded. Maybe Rathburn had already moved on, but it was better to check and see what had happened. "Thanks, Officer Reed. This is Sister Jenny, and I'm The Specialist." He paused, remembering how Father Clint had said the same once with a southern drawl. It felt weird to say it now, meaning himself. "We're on a mission from the Church of the New World Order," he explained.

Officer Reed gave them both a long once-over. He turned to his partner. "It's that priest who saved the mall from the demon last year." He turned back to Sam. "Is that what you think is going on here?"

"Yes, so you'd best hang back and leave it to us to catch him," Jenny said.

"No can do," Officer Reed said. "We have our orders."

"Suit yourself." Jenny shrugged. "It's your funeral."

Sam accompanied her to the back of the van. She pulled the double doors open and grabbed a couple of weapons. Although he'd barely held a gun, Sam grabbed a shotgun as well as a flashlight.

Jenny closed the doors, nodding at Sam. Along with her pack, she held a salt-shooter in one hand and the grip of an AR-15, which was slung over her shoulder.

She pointed down the darkened alley as they walked toward it. "I can't see a thing down there."

"Neither can I." Sam frowned and switched his flashlight on.

Jenny followed his lead and did the same.

They joined the two cops who were slowly walking down the alleyway, footsteps echoing quietly in the dark passage. Their four light beams wavered as they carefully made their way down the alley. The scents of wet cement and rotting garbage mixed unpleasantly with the smell of burned plastic and cooked meat. Sam coughed and covered his nose with his arm. Thoughts of the recent demise of Ricky's manager, Gerry, as well as Agent Saturn, flashed through his mind, as did the knowledge that the last time he'd faced Rathburn, he'd nearly died. He would have if it hadn't been for the mysterious man with the bullet hovering in front of his head.

Maybe it wasn't such a good idea to do this without a full team.

"Down there." Jenny shook her flashlight, illuminating a body far down the alleyway.

Is it alive or dead? Both scenarios frightened Sam. "Be careful," he advised, leading the way as the four of them traversed the darkened area. Maybe they should have just waited for the demon to come out, if he was still here, that is.

"Come out, come out, wherever you are," Jenny sang softly. "Come out and play."

"Are you crazy?" he asked in a hushed tone. "You know what we're dealing with. Why provoke him?"

Jenny shrugged. "I want to get this over with. I hate waiting."

He knew what she meant. His heart was beating at a thunderous pace. Part of him wanted to not be there at all, and the other part wanted to be done with it. But he covered his mouth with his finger and shook his head, instructing her to be cautious with what and how she said things.

They continued step by step, the four of them trying to create as little noise as possible. Had the temperature lowered since they set out from the start of the alley? Or was the chill he was experiencing from the fear of walking into the unknown? How long could this alleyway possibly be?

"It's a dead body," Jenny whispered, shining her flashlight onto what she had spotted when they were further back. "Brother Benjamin." She looked stricken.

Sam was struck with the realization that although he had never met the man before, Jenny had likely trained beside him many times and knew him well.

"I'm sorry," he whispered.

Sam whispered a quick prayer for the dead man's soul so that God would embrace him on his final journey. Were there Sisters of Mercy lying dead in the alley, too? With a shotgun in one hand and a flashlight in the other, he still felt the greatest security with the silver cross in his hands. Although he did not question his faith in the Almighty, his soul craved the certainty that God would be there for him and guide him in the darkest of times.

"Fucking hell. Is it just me, or has the temperature dropped ten degrees in here?" Reed's police partner asked.

"It's not just you," Sam whispered. Even dressed in three layers of upper body clothing, goose bumps erupted over Sam's skin as the still night air changed into a gentle breeze. He turned and looked back the way they had come. The cop car was still parked at the end, only a few feet from the narrow alley entrance between the burger joint and the hotel. The lights on the car continued to flash, but the darkness surrounding them seemed thick like it absorbed light and sound.

And anyone who walks into it, he thought.

It didn't make sense. The remnant they were tracking burned things. He'd felt the heat of that fire firsthand. Yet the air in the alley became chillier the further into it they walked.

"*Shhh,*" a slithering voice brushed the short hairs in Sam's ears. He spun on his heel and saw Jenny two steps behind him.

"Did you say something?" he asked her.

"No?" She shrugged.

A chill ran down Sam's spine. Was this the start of a series of mind tricks like the ones Abaddon had played on him?

"Shut up, both of you," Officer Reed said from behind them.

"Shit!" Sam yelled as he saw the outline of a dark hooded figure lit up by Reed's flashlight. "He's there!" He pointed at the dark figure ahead.

Jenny dropped her flashlight. She positioned her salt shooter with both hands and fired a shot at the figure. "Take that asshole," she screamed as she pulled back on the pump-action part of the barrel and fired another round. "Don't mess with the Sisters of Mercy."

The hooded figure took a step forward. "Ouch, I guess?" He shrugged, his manner and voice condescending. His features were hidden in the shadow cast by his deep hood, and the figure appeared to swoon before crying out dramatically, "Oh, no! Salt? Why?"

"Open fire," Sam instructed. He pulled the trigger of his shotgun and the recoil pushed him back a foot. He aimed again and fired, noting that both shots went wide and hit the brick wall instead. *Geeze. How did people make firing a gun look so easy?*

Jenny swapped out the salt shooter for her AR-15 and opened fire on the blurry figure. Reed and his partner also fired their Glock revolvers at the cloaked figure. It didn't take Sam long to realize their combined forces had done nothing to their target.

"Fucking die, Burning Man!" Officer Reed cried out, emptying the magazine in his revolver.

"Shit," Reed's partner said, his gun clicking after spending his entire load.

"Get outta here, both of you." Sam waved his arm, indicating they should go back the way they'd come. He dropped the useless shotgun to the ground and pulled out his cross. "Come here and face me, Remnant."

The hooded figure vanished from sight for a split second. "I'll face your friends first," the tormenting voice hissed behind him, and Sam spun around to find the two police officers pressing their hands against the sides of their heads. They began groaning and fell to their knees as their faces started to turn red.

Sam ran to the officers. He positioned himself between them and the Remnant. Shielding the two men with his body, he pointed his cross at the hooded figure and prayed. "*Saint Michael the Archangel, defend us in battle. Be our protection against the wickedness and snares of the devil...*"

The cross felt warm in his hands, a sign that always brought him comfort. A beam of light shone from the relic, shooting toward the hooded figure. The Remnant roared and stumbled backward, wheeling his outstretched arms as the ray of white light hit him directly in the face.

"*May God rebuke him,*" Sam continued his prayer, holding the cross before him as he approached the Remnant. "*We humbly pray. And do thou, O Prince of the heavenly hosts, by the power of God, thrust into hell Satan, and all the evil spirits, who prowl about the world seeking the ruin of souls. Amen.*" Sam now stood mere inches from the Remnant.

The demonic being arched his back and screamed at a deafening volume, clawing at the night sky.

The force of the scream pushed Father Sam off his feet. He landed on his backside near the cops, who were no longer clutching their heads. "Thank you, Father Sam," Officer Reed said.

Sam scrambled to his feet. The Remnant was still caught in the brilliant light and struggling to regain his balance. "Be. Gone!" he yelled at the top of his lungs. The light from the cross increased in brightness and intensity. He allowed a smile to spread across his face as he commanded, "And leave this mortal realm forever."

The hooded figure fell silent, falling onto his back with his arms outstretched. Tendrils of smoke spiraled lazily from his face where the holy light from the cross had made contact.

Jenny made him jump as she placed a hand on his back. "You did it, Father."

Sam shook his head. "But he's still here and not cast back into the flames of Hell." But then, he wasn't a demon in the paranormal sense. He was a mortal with a corrupted soul who was trapped between life and death. Maybe it worked differently with him, and his body stayed here while his soul was released to the underworld.

Officer Reed and his partner moved to join the pair. "I don't know what the fuck that thing is, but I hope I never meet another one. It was as if he was heating up my brain."

"Mine too," Reed's partner added.

The alleyway fell silent again as all four of them looked toward the Remnant. He hadn't moved since falling onto the ground. Wisps of smoke continued to drift lazily from his face, which was still concealed by what Sam realized was probably a mask.

While Sam would have liked to have waved a fist of victory in the air, something didn't feel right. "Jenny, just stay here for a moment. I don't like this."

"But you defeated him with your faith in God," she said.

"I need to make sure he's really dead." There was something that Jupiter had said about remnants that he couldn't remember, but it itched at the back of his mind. Something important.

The three others followed him as he approached the body.

Officer Reed bent down and placed his hand on the top of the fallen Remnant's mask, ready to pull it away from the being's face. "Let's see who you really are…"

Jenny giggled, and Reed paused. He gave her an annoyed look.

She smiled sheepishly. "Sorry… I, ah… this made me think of Scooby Doo." She glanced at Sam and shrugged. "Blame Bella. She was watching cartoons."

Sam shook his head and clutched the cross tighter. At the mention of Bella's name, its light had grown brighter again. It lit the cloaked figure, exposing him to their scrutiny. He was dressed all in black from head to toe, with no skin exposed except for his closed eyelids and his mouth. His lips appeared to be missing, revealing cracked, blackened teeth and mottled gums.

Sam looked at the cross. *Did I do that to him?* The scent of burned flesh, gasoline and some kind of chemical smell mixed with rot rose off of him, turning Sam's stomach.

As Reed moved forward again to lift the mask, the air around them gained sudden warmth, like their fallen enemy controlled the air temperature.

Which meant… *shit.*

Sam backed up a step. "Don't touch him," he instructed Reed. "Everyone get back. He's not dead."

"What?" Reed said. He turned to look at Sam.

Spine-chilling, deep laughter froze all four of them mid-action. Faster than they could react, the hooded figure swung a fist at the crouched figure of Reed, sending him flying backward several feet until he crashed into the brick wall that ran parallel to the burger restaurant.

His partner, having reloaded his Glock, stepped back and fired round after round at the laughing man's face. "Die, you twisted motherfucker," he yelled as he kicked the hooded man in the stomach.

Wherever the bullets hit, the wounds healed almost instantly, appearing to do no damage.

"Shit, Sam. What the fuck do we do now?" Jenny struggled to speak as her body shook.

The hooded figure sat up and grabbed Reed's partner by the throat, his hand glowing red as his fingers squeezed tight. The police officer kicked as he was lifted off the ground, but his struggles failed to deter his attacker.

Jenny reloaded her assault rifle while Sam held onto the cross with both hands, raising it above his head. Yelling a banishment prayer in Latin, he once again attempted to subdue the demonic being in front of him. The foul stench of burning human flesh grew stronger, threatening to turn Sam's stomach, and he faltered in his prayer. His words didn't force the Remnant's glowing red hand to release the police officer. Neither did Jenny's rapid-fire from the assault rifle.

Officer Reed struggled to his feet and charged at the hooded figure.

"You should have stayed down," the demon roared and pointed at Reed.

"Oh fuck!" Reed clutched his stomach, slipping on something none of the others could see.

An audible cracking filled the air, and the other policeman ceased struggling against the grip he was held in. A few seconds later, Reed appeared to catch on fire and screamed. The demon held the other policeman's head, now separated from his body. The hooded man's heated hand had burned so fiercely it sliced through the cop's neck. Reed's screams continued for a moment longer before he fell to the ground, silent. Both cops had been murdered in less than a minute.

"You disgusting abomination. I command you back to Hell." Sam thrust his cross at the Remnant's face.

"Not likely." Lifting the dead man's head in his hand, the Remnant swung it at Sam.

It hit him in the face, the force of the impact knocking him over sideways.

Dazed and covered in smears of blood, Sam struggled to his feet with Jenny's help.

"We need to leave. This isn't working," she said.

Sam shook his head. Retreat wasn't an option. There was no way the Remnant would let them out of the alley alive.

Grasping the cross in both hands, he thrust it once again at the hooded figure. "*O Mighty and Divine Creator,*" he began another prayer. "*As we confront this darkness, may we become vessels of your healing and deliverance, pushing back the malevolence and restoring harmony.*" The light from the cross increased to near-blinding intensity. It struck the remnant in the chest, pushing him back several steps. Sam motioned for Jenny to join the prayer. He hoped it was one she was familiar with. He needed more unified strength and conviction to defeat the demonic being. He hadn't defeated Abaddon alone.

Jenny nodded and placed her hand on top of his, holding the cross. "*In Your name, the name that holds all power and authority, we stand united against the forces of darkness. Strengthen us, guide us, and embolden us to cast out this demon and restore the peace that only You can provide.*" They repeated in unison. "*Amen.*"

Despite the brilliant light from the cross, which caused smoke to rise from the Remnant's chest, the hooded figure shook his head. A deep, blood-curdling laugh escaped his mouth and echoed throughout the alleyway. "Do you really think your prayers can kill me?"

Jenny let go of the cross and shook her head, terror clear in her expression.

"No, don't!" Sam cried out as she turned to run. *Don't lose faith.*

"This is truly... fucked up," Jenny shouted. In her haste to get away, she stumbled and fell. She struggled to stand again, but something appeared to be wrong with her legs, and she began to half-crawl and half-drag herself down the alley and away from the Remnant.

The hooded figure stomped in Sam's direction. "Do you think she will make it?"

"You fucked-up abomination. I command you back to Hell." Sam thrust his cross at the man. "You *will* leave her alone."

"How's your faith now, Father Sam?" the man growled in a deeper voice than before. "Get on your knees and pray to me instead. If you don't, I'll burn her like the others."

"Don't listen to him," Jenny screamed. She rose to her feet with the balance of a newborn giraffe. "He's gonna kill me anyway."

Sam stared in horror as the hooded figure shrugged.

"I guess she's right," the Remnant said. A ball of fire shot from his hand toward Sister Jenny.

Jenny shrieked as her body caught fire. Her screams echoed through the alley, only to be silenced a moment later when her burning body lay still.

Rage filled Sam.

Unbridled rage that gave him strength.

He gritted his teeth and screamed as light poured from the cross and illuminated the demon. "Fucking die already!"

The Remnant shook his head. "Looks like all your friends are dead now. Your turn." The creature pointed at the priest, a mouthful of blackened, crooked teeth smiling as the cross began to glow red in the hands of The Specialist.

Father Sam shouted as the metal heated to uncomfortable levels. He tried to drop it but could not move his fingers.

This was it.

The Remnant was going to burn his hands first, then the rest of him. With his teeth clenched against the pain, he was forced to say his prayer mentally. *Dear God, I know you can hear me. Please watch over Sarah, Bella, and my son. I die in your service and will join you soon.*

The skin on his hands began to blister, the pain of holding the heated metal becoming too much to bear. Screaming in agony, he fell to his knees and clutched the cross, unable to release it.

"How does it feel to know you are helpless to save yourself? To know those you love will soon suffer your fate. But most of all, how does it feel to know there's nothing waiting for you on the other side?"

A lie. He wanted to call the Remnant out as the filthy corruption he was. His mouth twitched, "Liar…"

"You think I'm lying? I've seen death. It's not what you think."

"Ju—"

"Just kill you? That's what everyone begs for in the end. Death is the greatest gift there is," he rasped. "I'll give it to you, but I like it when you suffer—"

Rathburn stopped speaking half a second before he was knocked backward, away from Sam, by a second figure dressed in black fatigues. A second punch sent the Remnant flying into the air. He landed hard on the ground.

The man in fatigues turned to Sam. The image of a bullet seemed to float in front of his forehead. *He's back*, Sam thought, staring in shock. *The bullet guy who saved us before.* He'd hoped that the mysterious entity might appear again, if only so they could find out who he was and what he wanted. But Sam hadn't wanted Jenny or anyone else to have to die for it to happen.

"Go away," Rathburn said. He groaned as he got back onto his feet. "This doesn't concern you."

"You talk too much." The new arrival spoke with a slight British accent. He punched the Remnant, sending him flying again. He turned back to the priest. "Father Sam, get the fuck out of here."

Well, that ruled him out of being an angel. He was pretty sure angels didn't swear. Sam flexed his fingers, realizing he could move them again and that the cross was no longer glowing red. He let it fall against his chest, suspended on the chain around his neck and studied his hands in the dim lighting. They were red and sore, but it was nothing that wouldn't heal. "Who are you?" he asked his mysterious benefactor.

Instead of answering, the man in fatigues turned back to Rathburn as he climbed back on his feet. After two knockdowns, he wiped his mouth and glanced at his hand. "You drew blood," he said to the man with the bullet floating in front of his head. "That's going to cost you." He raised a fist and swung, catching the man in fatigues on the jaw.

Bullet Man staggered back and almost fell but regained his footing.

Sam stared in awe. Despite the bullets and the holy fire from the cross, no one had managed to seriously injure the Remnant until now, and here was this new arrival, looking almost capable of taking him out.

Realizing he was still in danger of being killed as long as he stood around, Sam skulked along the side of the burger shop, turning from time to time to watch the two dark figures exchange blows. Looking to the bright end of the alley, he noticed a few bystanders watching on and more people congregating by the minute. They shouldn't be there. It wasn't safe. For that matter, he shouldn't be there either. But he needed to warn the others away.

"You shouldn't have come back, Hugo," he heard Rathburn yell in the deepest tone Sam had ever heard. "Guess it's time to finish you off."

Hugo? Bullet guy's name is Hugo? Sam thought, wondering if he'd heard correctly. That's not what he'd expected. Not that he'd expected anything specific, just something other than Hugo. It sounded very... human.

"I would welcome my own demise right now if it meant yours as well, Rathburn," the man named Hugo said.

"My name is *Wrath*, Bullet Man," the Remnant shouted.

"Whatever," Hugo said.

The two figures continued to fight, and Sam couldn't help but wonder why the Remnant hadn't set the other man on fire yet. Having seen so many people burn or objects glow under extreme heat when under the Remnant's influence, surely he could gain an instant advantage by doing the same to Hugo. Not that the priest wanted to see the Remnant come out of the fight victorious.

"I don't have time for this." The Remnant grabbed Hugo by the throat. "I have people to kill, cities to burn. But I'm going to start with you. Maybe that bullet will pierce your brain today."

Hugo gestured at the Remnant. "Come on, try your little fire trick on me. You know how well that'll work."

Some of the people at the end of the alley started moving closer, wanting to see the fight. Sirens echoed in the distance. Backup was coming.

"Hey." Sam waved at them, drawing their attention. "Get out of here. Don't get involved!" he yelled at the bystanders moving into the alley. "It's not safe to be here."

"Let them come," the Remnant said, grinning.

"Oh, no, you don't." Hugo dived at the Remnant, wrapping his arms around him, and pinning him in place. "You've done enough."

"It's *never* enough," the burning man shouted.

The bullet in front of Hugo's forehead glowed brighter, while the Remnant's hands turned red, and flames shot up his arms. In seconds, his body was engulfed in flames that spread to Hugo instantly.

Neither man screamed, nor did Bullet Man let go, despite the increasing intensity of the fire as it burned them both.

Sam raised a hand in front of his face to shield his eyes from the brightness and heat. The ground shook like a sudden earthquake had ripped through the alleyway. Sam was knocked off his feet and crashed into the wall of the burger joint. His head made an audible thump as he fell to his side on the pavement. Squeezing his eyes shut, he curled into a ball on the ground as a series of deafening booms thundered around him.

"Father Sam?" a voice called out. "Sister Jenny?" The beam of a flashlight shone in Sam's face, making him wince. He blinked and shielded his face from the brightness. What the hell? Had he passed out?

"Jesus Christ, you look like shit."

"I feel like shit," Sam muttered. Using the wall for support, he slowly sat up.

The booming noise was gone, as was the bright fire. Beams from multiple flashlights crisscrossed and darted around the darkened area, searching for survivors. The alley appeared empty except for the blackened bodies of Brother Benjamin, Kelly, Jenny, the two police officers, and another sister who Sam could not name. The two fighting entities appeared to have finished their battle, but in the place they had been fighting, a blackened figure lay on the ground, smoke rising from the still-crackling flesh.

"What the fuck did you do?" Agent Jupiter shouted at Sam as he surveyed the carnage. "I'm holding you personally responsible for this."

Sam nodded. If he hadn't snuck out seeking trouble, Jenny would still be alive. His heart felt like a stone in his chest. Death seemed to follow him everywhere, not discriminating in who it took. *Dear God, please forgive the arrogance that brought me to this end.*

"Clean this mess up before the press arrives," the agent instructed his team. "If footage of this gets out, there's going to be a shit sandwich bigger than a truckload of Subway Footlongs."

Sam stood and leaned against the wall for a second while he got his balance.

Who had won the fight?

The Remnant or Bullet Man?

He hobbled toward the figure lying on the ground where the fight had taken place. The body glowed faintly in the darkness, like coals from a fire slowly dying out. Ignoring the strong scent of burned flesh, he peered at the man's head. The image of a bullet was suspended above the forehead. Since there was no sign of the Remnant anywhere, he could only conclude the demon-spawned creature had won.

Shit.

"Is that our mysterious friend?" Jupiter asked, coming up beside Sam and peering at the body that had caught his attention.

The priest nodded.

"There's not much of him left," Jupiter pointed out.

"Yeah, but... he's still breathing." Although he should be dead, the slow rise and fall of the being's chest was visible. He also appeared to be healing. As they watched, portions of his burned skin flaked off, revealing undamaged flesh beneath. Sam thought back to the fight. *His hands had been healed.* The bullet man's fingers had been nothing but bones when they'd last seen him at the elevator, but he'd used them just fine during the fight.

"This is some truly fucked up shit." Agent Jupiter gestured to the men busy placing corpses in bags and carrying them to the vans. "This one too," he instructed. "We'll take him with us."

Chapter 14

Sam emerged from the bathroom in his hotel room, having showered and changed into a fresh T-shirt and track pants. His hands were sore, but didn't appear to be in danger of blistering, thank God. It felt better to have the sweat and gore washed off, and dressings applied, but there was nothing he could do to remove the stain on his soul from the night's events.

"Is he dead?" Bella asked, staring wide-eyed at the half-burned body, which had been wrapped in a sheet and placed on the sofa.

"No," Sam answered. Even now, Bullet Man continued to miraculously heal. His face was no longer a mostly charred mess but appeared bruised as if only slightly damaged. "He's just sleeping, I think."

He walked over to Bella and, careful not to press too hard on his wounded hands, wrapped his arms around her, pulling her against him. Gratitude filled him that he was alive and could do so. *Thank you, God.*

"He looks weird," Ricky said. "What's with the bullet thing above his head?" He pointed at his own forehead with his finger, indicating what he meant.

"We can ask him when he wakes up," Sam suggested. He patted Bella's shoulder, trying to reestablish the sense that everything was fine. She gripped his hand tighter, but the guilt he felt at how close he'd come to not making it back to her coiled tighter around his heart.

Penny sniffled and blotted at her eyes with a tissue as they stood around the couch, studying the prone figure. She had her arms wrapped around Ricky, who'd held her close while she'd cried. The news of Jenny's death had hit her hardest, of course.

Fortunately, the presence of the mysterious Bullet Man seemed to have captured everyone's attention for the moment, but to say the mood in the room was anything approaching positive was an understatement.

As expected, Jupiter was pissed at Sam and Penny, the latter facing a reprimand as she should have known better than to enable the priest to sneak out. She had told Jupiter he could shove his fucking job up his fucking ass and locked herself in the bathroom. Luckily, Bella's need to use the facilities had coaxed her out soon after, and they'd shared a hug and tears over Jenny's loss.

The door of the adjoining room opened, and Jupiter walked in, followed by the driver, Agent Barnes, both clearly hot off the radio with the base. Jupiter appeared particularly agitated as he leaned against the back of the couch and surveyed the assembled group.

"So, let me summarize," he began. "We lost Brother Benjamin and Sisters Kelly and Nelly. We also lost Jenny, perhaps our greatest female weapons handler… no offense, Penny." He gave her a bland look. "And lost contact with Father John and his team… and the Remnant is still on the loose."

"You're the one who called all these extra people in," Penny snapped.

"Can we talk about this in the morning?" Sam asked, feeling a headache coming on. He needed rest before he could deal with anything else.

"Look. It's three a.m.," Ricky cut in. "We're all tired and feel like shit. Today has been an absolute fucking shit show, no one's doubting that, okay? But we do have this guy." Ricky pointed at the man on the couch. "Whoever he is."

The room fell silent as they all studied the man lying on the couch.

"Hugo," Sam said quietly. "His name is Hugo. The Remnant called him that, and Bullet Man."

"Bullet Man?" Jupiter's face took on something other than a dark expression for the first time since he'd arrived on the scene and cleaned up the mess the Remnant had made. "Did he have a cape as well? And spandex?"

Sam tensed. They were already upset enough. Jupiter acting like a condescending prick and taking digs at whoever he could wasn't helping. He took a deep breath, mentally counted to five, and answered, "No cape or spandex. As you can see…"

The bullet man was healing well by the looks of it. He was also quite naked beneath the sheet. Apparently, the clothing he'd worn had burned off in the fire.

Jupiter nodded. "And yet, for all his abilities, as well as your own, the Remnant is still out there, regrouping and planning his next attack."

"If you think it's so easy to kill him, why don't you give it a try?" Sam asked through gritted teeth.

"Great, we'll all be dead," Ricky chimed in. "I would trust Sam over you suit-wearing spooks. And what's with wearing your sunglasses at night? You guys aren't Corey Hart, you know."

Bella giggled while Jupiter and Barnes glanced at each other.

"You can't kill him, Sam," Jupiter said, sounding exasperated. "That's the point. A remnant can only die when they are released to complete their interrupted death. I told you that when I debriefed you in the van. What we need to do is trap him."

Sam stared at him in silence. *Well fuck.* He did remember that now. No wonder everything had gone to hell during the fight. "How are we going to do that?"

"Like I told you before, we set up within a perimeter and draw him in." He glowered at Sam. "What we don't do is go running around the city at night, spreading ourselves thin while he picks us off. Do you understand me now?"

Sam nodded, feeling chagrined.

"Good. I suggest everyone get some sleep while we can. We have a busy day ahead. We'll discuss this further later in the morning." He glanced down at the unconscious figure on the sofa. "I'll take first watch. Someone needs to be around when Hugo the Bullet Man wakes up." He settled down in the armchair near the desk and grabbed the television remote, apparently done with the conversation.

"Catch you in a few hours," Ricky said.

"You bet," Sam replied, still feeling edgy about how everything had gone down and his part in it all.

Ricky nodded at Sam. He steered puffy-eyed Penny into the bedroom she'd shared with Jenny and shut the door.

Sam did the same with Bella, steering her away from the couch and toward their room.

"Good night, Bullet Man," she called out as Sam shut the door. No one seemed to care about saying goodnight to Jupiter. "You aren't going to leave me again, are you?" Bella asked, her voice filled with anxiety.

"No." Sam pulled her into a tight hug. "I'm sorry. I was trying to fix things quickly so we could get back to Mommy and Nana." *And the baby*, he added silently, knowing how Bella felt about that.

"He's not a bad guy," she said as she crawled into bed, and he pulled the covers up. "I think he's done bad things, but he's not a bad guy."

"Who? The Remnant?"

She shook her head. "Bullet Man." She touched the tourmaline shard on her necklace as she looked at the door and then at Sam. "Try not to worry, Dad." She reached out and gently patted his hand. "We're safe here. He won't let anything bad happen to us."

He wanted to ask her how she knew that, but she'd already settled down and closed her eyes. He kissed her cheek instead and whispered, "Sleep tight, sweetheart."

He looked fleetingly at the other double bed in the room, knowing he'd get a better sleep if he could stretch out. But he also knew that even if he did try to sleep there, he'd wake up later with Bella snuggled in beside him anyway. As Jenny had observed earlier, she was very much like a little cat. Thinking of the fallen sister, he swallowed hard as his throat choked up. She hadn't deserved to die like that. Neither had the police nor the other Sisters and Brother from the church. They deserved better.

I need to do better and be better if I want to protect everyone.

What the hell was it with demons at Christmas time? One of the holiest days of the year, and they had to shit all over it. He placed his palms together and silently prayed.

Thank you, God, for all the gifts you've given me. And for understanding my imperfections. And for protecting me and bringing me safely back to this little girl who I love as my daughter. Please watch over Sarah and Ena and the baby, and protect them from any evil that seeks to harm them. And please take care of all the souls who died in your service tonight. Jenny was brave and kind. And please watch over the bullet man, whatever and whoever he is. He saved me twice today by your will. I cannot think that a coincidence. May your power and glory reign forever. Amen.

He settled down with Bella and shut his eyes, determined to make use of whatever little time they had to sleep despite the deep distress that haunted him, making it difficult to shut his mind off. So many questions. What was Bullet Man? Would he help them a third time? When and where would the Remnant strike next? And if they couldn't kill him, how could they stop him? Because the one thing that he was certain of was that the Remnant was still out there somewhere, and the monster wouldn't rest until he'd killed them all.

Not even five minutes later, as Sam was dozing off, he woke with a jerk. Something was moving. He opened his eyes as he focused on listening. There it was again, the sound of movement from the living room. Was it Agent Jupiter? The Bullet Man? Had the Remnant come back? Something else?

After checking that Bella was resting peacefully, he crept out of bed and quietly opened the door.

"You know how long we've been hunting these remnants, Chief." Jupiter's words made their way to Sam's ears. "If we've got one right here, do we need to even worry about the other?"

Sam frowned as he peeked through the crack he'd opened. Jupiter stood by the couch and spoke into his portable radio as he bent over Bullet Man.

So, the agents are after remnants, and Jupiter thinks Hugo is one? Why didn't he say that before?

"Yes, I agree, Chief." Another pause happened in the conversation while Jupiter listened. "The show will go on, and we'll be ready for him. Jupiter out."

He clipped the device onto his belt. Then he bent down on one knee beside the unconscious man on the couch and reached into his jacket pocket. He brought out what looked like a vial with a screw-top lid and a pair of tweezers. He carefully brought the tweezers close to Bullet Man's ear and pulled away a small section of charred flesh. He quickly put it in the vial and screwed on the lid.

What the fuck is he doing? Sam thought. *Taking a skin sample?* "No more fucking charades," he mumbled as he stepped through the door and closed it behind him.

"Fucking hell, Father Sam." Jupiter jumped and placed his hand over his heart when he saw him. "Shouldn't you be asleep next to your daughter?"

Sam moved away from the door and toward the agent. "Don't try and deflect what's going on here. I saw you put something in that vial. Why?"

"That's none of your business," Jupiter said, putting the vial in his pocket.

Sam crossed his arms. "Oh, I disagree. I think it very much *is* my business."

"You want to know everything?" Jupiter laughed. "Go back to your room, Sam. This doesn't concern you, and you should know better than to ask questions like this. Could you even imagine how much panic would circulate if people knew everything we did?"

"Does that type of thinking help you sleep at night?"

"Not in the least bit. But I'll tell you what. We do operate for the benefit of our country. Do you remember the pair of aliens who murdered everyone in the small town of New Market, Maryland? No, you don't because we fucking prevented it."

Sam grinned. "Aliens? Really?"

Jupiter shook his head. "You believe in an invisible deity but scoff at the possibility of other life existing elsewhere in the universe? I thought you were better than that, Father."

Jupiter had a point, and wasn't it something Sam had wondered about at least a few times in his life? "Can you answer me something, though?" This conversation was going nowhere fast. "Would you trust you?"

Jupiter smirked. "I don't trust anyone."

"That's my point. If you think he's a remnant, why didn't you tell us before? That seems like information we should know."

"I've never seen one before. I need to confirm it." He pulled the vial from his pocket and shook it at Sam as if indicating why he'd taken the sample. "Maybe find out what his weakness is." He stared at the sleeping figure.

"Why not just take this guy back to the base for examination then?" When Jupiter didn't react, he added, "Or is that what you're planning on doing?"

Jupiter shook his head. "A sample will do. He'll be healed soon. We need him here."

Sam raised his brows. "Sounds like you don't need me then. I may as well go back to the base with Bella. I want to see my wife."

Jupiter shook his head. "You're hilarious, Sam. You have no idea how to get to the base. Sarah is going to be fine. As soon as this remnant problem is taken care of, we'll go straight there. Now please get the fuck out of here and go back to bed until we come for you. If Bella wakes up, don't you think she might be a little worried if you're not there next to her?"

Until we come for you? What the fuck was Jupiter planning? Sam glared at the agent for a moment, then walked back to his room and settled on the bed, this time taking the one separate from Bella. He kept the door open so he could watch the agent and hear whatever went on. He didn't trust Jupiter. Not one bit. He trusted the unconscious figure lying on the couch more.

Not bothering to get under the covers, he propped his hands behind his head on the pillow and stared at Jupiter, who was back sitting in the chair by the desk.

No way Sam was going to sleep tonight now.

Not one bit.

Sarah blinked and looked around the room, barely able to keep her eyes open. Had she slept at all? *What is the time anyway?* It was so hard to tell anymore. Days were a nameless thing that had no meaning. Time was anyone's guess.

She craned her neck to the side and squinted. *Blurry, so blurry,* she thought, while trying to read the hands of the clock. Hands? They weren't hands. Hands belonged on humans, not inanimate objects.

"She's awake," Doctor Stevens announced.

"What time is it?" Sarah asked. "I'm late." Or maybe she was early. But there was something she needed to do if she could just remember what it was.

"She's delirious," another woman's voice murmured. She sounded familiar, but Sarah couldn't place her.

"The medication is kicking in," the doctor said.

Sarah frowned. She didn't remember taking anything. In fact, she didn't remember much of anything except feeling sleepy, but once her eyes adjusted, she saw it was 6:37. Was it a.m. or p.m.? "What's going on?" she asked groggily. Her arms and legs felt heavy like something was weighing her down.

Mother Agnes's face appeared, looking down at her. "You've been asleep but talking out loud a lot. Did you have any dreams?"

She closed her eyes. Her mind had been running like a blender on full speed, with every ingredient mixing inside it. "I can't remember any, not this time."

"You've had dreams a lot lately, though, right?"

Sarah shuddered at the way Mother Agnes stared at her as though she could see inside. "Yes."

The nun crossed to the observation window. She pressed a button near a speaker embedded in the wall and began speaking to a woman dressed in a suit on the other side.

Could she not even trust a nun now?

"Everybody lies," a deep voice said, the sound echoing in her mind.

Sarah sat up straight and glanced around the room, despite Doctor Stevens's protests that she not move so quickly. "Did anyone hear that?"

"Hear what?" the doctor asked.

"I just heard a man telling me that everybody lies."

"Sarah, look around you. There's just you, me, Nurse Laura, Mother Agnes, and Agent Neptune watching us through the window. There's only us women here at the moment, no men."

"Is there, though?" the deep voice tickled Sarah's ears.

Sarah shook her head. "There it is again. I swear, there's a man speaking to me." She put her hands over her ears and squeezed her eyes shut, hoping that would block out the voice.

"No, there's not, Sarah. You need to calm down." The doctor's eyes were bright as she studied her. "This pregnancy has been tough on you. Now, lie down and get comfortable. It will all be over soon."

Sarah sagged back against the bed, too dizzy to sit up any longer anyway. The room seemed to sway every time she moved her head.

The nurse moved close to the bed and helped the doctor fasten straps across Sarah's body, pinning her arms and legs.

Sarah frowned. She could barely move now. "What's happening?"

"Not to worry. The straps are for your safety. We're just taking you for a little ride." She nodded at the nurse who moved the IV bag from the free-standing pole to one attached to the bed.

"No!" Sarah shouted. "Where are you taking me? What are you doing?" She struggled against the straps, but moving was becoming increasingly impossible.

"Settle down, Sarah," the doctor instructed. "This is for your safety as well as everyone else's." She turned to the nurse. "Increase the sedative. We're going to have to knock her out before we can even take her to the OR."

"She's already at max. Any more, and it will harm the baby," the nurse warned.

The doctor sighed. "Let's just do this quickly, then."

The bed jiggled as the wheels were unlocked.

Operating room? What were they doing? Sarah struggled against the straps, panic giving her increased strength. "Let me go," she shouted.

"Sarah, please," her mother said. Her smile was filled with concern as she looked down at Sarah. "Do what the doctor says. It's for everyone's good. When you wake up, you'll be able to hold your baby."

My baby. They're trying to take my baby.

"*No!*" she shouted. Strength flooded through her as she pulled against the restraints with a power that came from somewhere deep within. The fabric ripped, the sound and abrupt freedom causing relief to flow through Sarah. The power coursing through her veins increased, giving her renewed focus.

The nurse and doctor stopped what they were doing and backed away.

Sarah threw off her sheet and climbed out of bed. Fists clenched, she faced the frightened ring of faces by the wall. "Do not touch me."

"Her eyes are red. Everyone... out of the room. *Now!*" Doctor Stevens instructed. She backed up and fled, along with the nurse.

Mother Agnes paused by the door and grabbed Ena by the arm.

Ena shook her off.

"Sarah, if you're in there, I need you to gain control. You're being used by the demon," her mother pleaded, putting herself between Sarah and Mother Agnes.

"*Leave me alone,*" Sarah snarled as the sense of betrayal bit deep. The room began to blur and waver as if heat radiated from everything. The demon wasn't trying to hurt her. He was trying to protect her, which was more than she could say about her own mother. *Lies, so many lies.*

The agents from outside, Neptune and Mars, ran into the room carrying a large black rod each. "Don't make us have to use these." Agent Mars stared at Sarah as he thumped the rod against the palm of his hand.

Don't be afraid, the voice inside Sarah said. *We're stronger than they are.*

"No, don't hurt her. This isn't her, it's the demon," Ena pleaded. "Think of the baby."

"I'm not going to stand by and let another demon do to this place what Abaddon did to Springfield Mall," Mars declared.

"Sarah, can you hear me?" Agent Neptune's words spilled from her lips like a lullaby as she approached from the other side. "Please, don't let this demon take over. We can help you. You just need to let us."

Anger boiled through Sarah, turning her vision red. Glorious, powerful anger. It felt good as it filled her body, along with the demonic strength.

"Sarah," Ena pleaded, reaching out a trembling hand toward her. "Please, listen to me. They just want to help."

A low growl filled the room as Sarah balled her hands into fists. *"Liar!"*

The need to escape filled Sarah with urgency. She lunged at her mother, intending to push her out of the way, but her fist hit her in the face instead.

Ena screamed at the same time Agent Mars shouted, *"Now."*

The charging sound of the electrified rods came one second before the agents touched Sarah with the black cylinders.

Paralyzing bolts of energy ran through Sarah's body, disrupting the red haze that tinted her vision and turning it black. *Pain, so much pain.* Her nerves shrieked in agony. She shut her eyes and gritted her teeth. *"Enough,"* she shouted. She instinctively raised her hands in the air, wanting to stop the painful rods from touching her.

As if from a distance, the sounds of screaming echoed.

And then the pain ended.

Chapter 15

As he awoke from the healing sleep, Hugo tensed. Something nearby was watching him. He could feel their eyes on his skin and their curiosity in his mind. Cracking an eye open, he discovered the culprit was the bearer of a pair of wide blue eyes set in a heart-shaped face, surrounded by dark blonde hair.

"Hello," the little girl said in a hushed voice and smiled brightly. She couldn't be more than eight or nine years old and wore shorts and a striped T-shirt. *Ah, the girl from the elevator, which means Rathburn won't be far off once he's completed his regenerative cycle.*

He darted a glance around the room. A man in a white dress shirt and black pants lounged in a chair nearby, snoring loudly. *Agents. Of course.*

"My name's Bella. He's Barnes." The girl indicated the agent with a nod of her head. "I woke up when I heard Jupiter leave, and Barnes came in to watch you instead. I'm helping him out, but he doesn't know it." She leaned forward and placed her hand beside her mouth as if whispering a secret, "He's a heavy sleeper."

"Oh, I see," Hugo said, blinking at the child's rapid speech. "I'd say you're doing a brilliant job. Far better than he is, don't you think?" He gave her a wink as Barnes snorted loudly and settled back into sleep.

She giggled. "I like you. What's your name?"

Pestilence, Sickness, Despair, The Destroyer of Dreams. The names sliced at his heart like knives. "Hugo," he said after an awkward pause.

"I like that name." Bella smiled. "That's what my dad said you were called too. You saved us yesterday. You're really strong, aren't you?"

"Uh…" He ignored that question and glanced around the room again. This was not the alley he'd fought Rathburn in. Nor was the couch the dirty pavement he should be lying on. The cushions were soft, the room clean, and the sheet he was wrapped in was—he peeked beneath the covering—definitely not his clothes. "Where am I?"

"At the casino," the little girl said. "Ricky Gibson... he's my friend," she explained as if it was a big deal, and she was proud of the fact. "He's supposed to play a concert here tonight. But I don't think that's going to happen. He never gets to sing at Christmas. Something *always* happens," she added dramatically. "Last year it was that demon. This year, it's this Remman-ant."

Hugo couldn't help smiling at the way she mispronounced the name.

"Are you like him?" she asked.

Did she mean stuck in the same living nightmare? "Yes and no." He shrugged lightly. "He likes to kill people. I don't."

She eyed him, giving the stained sheet and the lingering marks on his skin a critical arch of her brow. "He burned you, didn't he?"

"Yes," he admitted. "Yes, he did." *And a hell of a lot of other people too.* More would follow if Hugo didn't find a way to stop him once and for all. The game of burn, heal, burn, heal was getting old. But he'd given him as good in return, too, this time.

"Did it hurt?" she asked, sounding horrified.

"Well, it hurts a lot when it happens, but not so much now," he explained. "I heal quickly."

She nodded, her expression full of sympathy. "What's the thing on your forehead?" Her brow pulled into a curious furrow as she pointed at his.

"Ah." Hugo paused. He'd forgotten about the rapid pace of children's minds and how they bounced from topic to topic like a squirrel chasing nuts. "That is a bullet," he explained.

"But why is it there?"

"It's a bit complicated," he said. It was more than a bit complicated, but how much could a child understand of the mysteries of life, terrors of the dark, and all the gray things that existed in between? "But... it's basically a reminder to me that one day, I will die."

"I don't understand," she said. "Does it hurt?"

He shook his head. "No." *Not yet, anyway.* He imagined it would when it finally, blessedly, pierced his skull. But other than hovering annoyingly about a quarter inch in front of the center of his forehead, it didn't cause any trouble.

"Is it real? Can I touch it?" She reached a finger toward the bullet but stopped when he shook his head.

"Yes, it is, and no, you can't. It's quite hot. I don't want you to burn yourself. It's still moving, you see, just really slowly. It was shot from a gun a long time ago now."

She pulled her finger back and settled for peering at the bullet instead. "But bullets are fast. Is it stuck? Why doesn't it hit you?"

He shook his head. "Well, because it's not time for it to do that yet." Since that asshole angel, Gabriel, decided to put it on hold for a bit. *You deserved it, though, didn't you, Hugo? You've deserved every bit of this hellish penance.*

She studied the bullet in silence for a moment. "It looks funny."

"It's a very old bullet."

She gave him a sideways glance. "How old are you?"

He raised his brows. "How old do you think I am?"

Her nose crinkled as she thought about it. "You don't look old. My Nana's pretty old, and she has gray hair, but don't tell her I said that because she'll get mad." Her eyes went wide. "Oh! I forgot. Would you like some coffee? Nana always says it's proper to offer when we have guests."

"Am I your guest?" Hugo asked, taken aback. When was the last time he'd been offered coffee? Or been anyone's guest? *A lifetime ago, which, in his case, was an extremely long time ago.*

"I think so." Bella nodded.

He smiled. "Very well. I'll have some then."

Her expression shifted as she looked around the room, seeming perplexed.

"What's the matter?" he asked.

She glanced down at her hands. "I don't know how to make coffee," she confessed. "I'm not supposed to use the coffee maker."

"How about I make some coffee then?" a voice called out from behind Hugo.

Hugo propped himself up on one elbow and turned his head. A dark-haired man leaned against the trim of a bedroom doorway, watching him and the girl. *Ah, the priest.*

"Dad!" Bella said excitedly. "Hugo's awake."

Barnes snorted and seemed like he might wake up as well, but the snoring resumed.

"I can see that." The priest nodded. He looked tired and disheveled like he hadn't slept much. He walked into the room and stood behind his daughter, putting a protective hand on her shoulder. "I see you've met Bella," he said quietly.

Hugo smiled. "She's a delight. She reminds me of someone I once knew."

Bella's eyes widened. "Was she a princess? I want to be a princess."

He shook his head. "No, not a princess, but she was special, like you. Her name was Anne. My sister's daughter. Last time I saw her, she was little more than your age, I think." *Why am I talking about this? Why am I even thinking about it?* Being around these people was making the memories surface again, which was why he generally avoided the living.

"Oh. What happened to her?" Bella asked.

"She's, ah...." He swallowed hard as the unbidden image of Anne's dead face swam to the surface of his thoughts, followed by his sister, Fran's, and the hundreds of villagers who had welcomed him as a missionary, bringing the word of God to the New World. All dead now. Every single one. All gone by his own hand. "She's not with us anymore," he said quietly. He glanced around the room again, seeking the quickest exit. "I should... I should go."

"I'm sorry," Bella said, looking sad. "I didn't mean to upset you. Please don't go."

Hugo shook his head. "It's not safe. You shouldn't have brought me here." He sat up and winced as his new muscles protested. The sheet fell down to around his waist, exposing his pale, scarred chest.

"Daddy?" she said, shrinking back against her father. "I don't want him to go."

"It's okay, Bells. Give him some space."

Hugo glanced down at the sheet. "I need... ah, do you have any clothes I can borrow?" Such a mundane thing. But he knew from experience that running nude through Vegas in the daylight brought the kind of attention he didn't need.

Bella's face brightened up again. "I'll get you some. You can borrow my dad's. He won't mind, will you, Daddy?" Without waiting for an answer, she quietly ran into the bedroom and sifted through an open duffel bag on the floor. After a moment, she crept back to the couch carrying a plain white T-shirt and a pair of dark sweatpants. She pointed at a closed door on the left. "Bathroom's in there."

"Thanks." He reached for the clothes, but she held them back.

"Will you promise to stay?" she asked, eyeing him.

What? He stared at her. The little monkey was making a bargain.

"Bella..." the priest said in a warning tone. "Just give him the clothes and stop pestering him." He gestured at Hugo. "I'm sorry. She can be... a bit spirited."

"I noticed," Hugo replied.

"Fine," Bella snapped. She handed Hugo the clothes. "But we didn't even make tea yet."

Run, Hugo. Never make it personal, remember? He shouldn't have anything more to do with these people. He should leave and figure out the problem on his own.

It was too late for that, though, wasn't it? It had been too late as soon as he'd saved her from dying in the elevator. And it had definitely been too late when he'd deliberately taken the burn so her father could escape. So what? Wasn't his task to help people?

Yeah, but don't get attached. It won't end well, you know that.

But it was too late for that, too, wasn't it? Her big blue eyes were filled with so much hope it was almost painful to hold her gaze. Thinking of Anne, who had been such a sweet child before she'd died of smallpox, he knew there was only one answer.

"Okay." He nodded. "But only for a little while. I need to leave so I can get ready for battle."

Her eyes went wide, and she sucked in an excited breath. "Are you going to help my dad fight the Remman-ant so Ricky can be okay and we can see my mom?"

He glanced at the priest and then back at Bella. "Of course."

A door in the wall burst open, and another agent entered the room dressed in a black suit. Upon seeing the group, he paused for a second, then shouted, "*Barnes!*" at the top of his lungs.

The sleeping agent jerked awake so hard he almost fell out of the chair.

"You were supposed to tell me when Bullet Man was conscious," the agent by the door continued.

Barnes looked at Hugo on the couch, and then back at the other agent. "Okay. He's conscious," he said blandly and shrugged.

AN HOUR AND A half later, Sam sat on the couch drinking tea with Bella, waiting for Hugo to return.

At Jupiter's request, Bullet Man had disappeared into the adjoining room to speak with the agents. What the hell were they talking about? Hugo had been in there a while now. The rest of them had been denied entry to the closed-door meeting, which frustrated Sam. He wanted his questions answered, too. Hugo had seemed calm and harmless while talking to Bella, yet a person with his regenerative capabilities clearly had some secrets. Who knew what he was capable of or his true agenda? Was he a remnant, too, or not? He might be staying to help them fight Rathburn, but at the end of the day... could they trust him?

Ricky and Penny, who had stumbled out of their room upon hearing Agent Jupiter shouting at Barnes, hovered near the couch. They kept sneaking furtive glances at the armed guards standing by the two exit doors and the window.

Like bullets are going to do anything, thought Sam. Rathburn seemed to eat them for breakfast. The presence of the soldiers did nothing except increase the level of anxiety that hung like a cloud of smoke, choking them all as they breathed. Add that to the fact that Sam's repeated requests to speak to Sarah had gone unanswered this morning, and even making a trip to the bathroom was scrutinized, he couldn't help wondering what was really going on.

We should have just stayed in Springfield.

As soon as Sam thought it, he took the thought back. This was about more than him and his family. Everyone in the building was in danger, heck, everyone in the city was in danger, and hiding away somewhere else wouldn't change that. God had given him the duty of protecting the flock, whether they were believers or not.

But, in what promised to be a battle between two immortal beings with powers far outreaching his, what was the point in him being around? He'd be better off staying with Sarah at the base, making sure she, the baby, and Bella were safe, taking up the reins as a preacher and giving sermons on Sundays. That was the quiet life he'd wanted. Not this endless chaos. The waiting for something to happen was killing him.

"Okay, listen up, people, here's the plan," Agent Jupiter announced as he waltzed into the suite, followed closely by Barnes, several soldiers, and Hugo, now dressed in his customary black fatigues and mask. The way Jupiter pranced around like he owned the place with his chest puffed out showed he enjoyed this kind of stuff. "We have several teams joining us today. Most are already stationed around the hotel and casino. Our game is to play it cool and go about things as normal in order to draw the burning man out."

Asinine, Sam thought. *If he wants us, he will find us wherever we are.* He put his hand up.

Jupiter frowned but nodded. "Yes, Sam?"

"We can't kill him, right? How are we going to trap him?" The last thing he wanted was another round of unnecessary deaths, like what had happened to Jenny and the teams during the night. *Was that really only just a few hours ago?*

"I'll discuss that with you later," Jupiter said. "But with the help of Bullet Man, we believe we now have a plan in place that will be quite effective."

Sam raised his brows. He'd feel better if he knew what that plan was ahead of time.

"We're going to split into groups," Jupiter continued. "Sam, Ricky, Penny, and I will go downstairs to get some breakfast and attract some attention. We'll be on alert for the burning man's arrival. From there, we'll head to the stage where Ricky is to perform tonight. That's where Sam, Ricky, and Penny will stay for the duration of this event. We want to lure the Remnant into the auditorium. We'll have a little present waiting for him when he gets there." He gestured at the agents and soldiers. "I want the rest of you to split up into groups of two and keep watch outside the auditorium, but spread out and don't make people nervous. The casino manager doesn't want any disruption, and neither do we. Bullet Man, you stay here until we inform you that Rathburn has arrived."

"What about me?" Bella asked.

A knock sounded on the door. "Your babysitters are here," Jupiter said. He listened to his earpiece for a second, then nodded for the soldier nearest the door to open it. A trio of agents, a priest, and two Sisters of Mercy entered. "Agents Venus, Neptune and Pluto, Father Luke and Sisters Mel and Kim. They've all just arrived from the base."

What, no rhyming names? Sam wondered. "I don't like this plan," he said shaking his head. The idea of leaving Bella alone again with strangers sent a chill down his spine. He'd had enough scares in the last two days to last a lifetime. But what was there to do? He couldn't take her into battle with him. The very idea of her getting burned to a crisp made him feel sick.

Father Luke, who looked to barely be out of high school, hurried over to the priest. "Father Sam, it's such an honor to meet you. Trust me, we'll take good care of your daughter." He reached out and shook Sam's hand.

"Hugo's here too," Bella cut in. "I'll be okay." She sprang off the couch, ran to the man with a bullet hovering in front of his head, and grasped his hand.

Sam followed and wrapped Bella in his arms like he wouldn't see her again. Crouching to her level, he whispered in her ear, "Just remember, if you ever get scared, touch your necklace. Your mother is always with you."

As Sam backed away, Bella bunched the tourmaline stone in her fist. "I love you, Papa. Promise me I'll see you again."

"I love you, too, Bella." He kissed her on the forehead. "This will all be over soon, and then we can go see Mommy and Nana in time for Christmas." *I hope.* The lack of updates from the base about his wife was more than a bit distressing.

Hugo nodded at him. "On my honor, she will be safe."

Sam returned the nod. Bullet Man had saved them all yesterday. Sam had to believe he'd do it again if necessary. "Thank you."

With that, Hugo and Bella moved to the couch, followed by the priest and two sisters.

"Okay, team," Jupiter said, clapping his hands together. "This is it. Breakfast time."

SAM POKED AT HIS food while Jupiter ate like it was a typical morning at the base, which seemed crazy given they were neither at the base nor was it shaping up to be a typical day. Penny refused to eat anything, instead filling herself with cappuccinos. Her reasoning behind this was that caffeine would be required should she find herself engaged in battle.

"I don't understand why we're even here apart from being used as live bait for this science experiment," Sam said. "My prayers have little effect on the Remnant."

Jupiter placed his cutlery on the now empty plate. "But you can slow him down, and we can catch him," he said around the last bite of sausage in his mouth.

The guy was a psychopath. Sam was sure of it. But the biggest hurdle in his own life was getting back to Sarah with Bella, and, unfortunately, Jupiter continued to insist that leaving wasn't possible until this mission was done. "How exactly do you plan on doing that?"

Jupiter dabbed the corner of his mouth with his napkin. "Always with the questions, Sam. Don't you get tired of being so curious?"

"What about Bullet Man? Are you going to let him go after you've finished using him here? Or is he going to be a science experiment too?" Penny asked. "And what if I don't want to play this stupid game anymore?"

Jupiter waved a finger at her. "Be careful, Penny."

The urge to leave the dining room, run back upstairs, grab Bella, and get the hell out grew more intense by the minute. Something about Jupiter's tone and finger waving sent his heart rate skyrocketing. Maybe he should go find those recently arrived agents, Neptune and Pluto, and see if they knew anything about Sarah.

A camera clicked as yet another giggling fan came up to the table, asking Ricky for an autograph. Even if the star had been interested in eating breakfast, it wasn't happening. So far, he'd only been able to fit in a bite between greeting fans, who clearly appreciated his unexpected visit to the dining room this morning, judging by all the excited finger-pointing and gasps. And judging by his smile, Ricky wasn't minding the attention one bit.

"Gerry would kick my ass for this," he whispered to Sam. "God rest his soul. But fuck it, this is what makes me get out of bed every day."

Penny smiled for the first time since Sam had seen her that day. "Everybody loves you, Ricky." She leaned over and gave him a kiss on his cheek.

"Yes, yes, that's it. Play it up a bit. It's why we're here." Jupiter grinned as another fan came up to Ricky. "Smile for the camera. Lots of press here today." The agent waved as another flash went off, this one so close it nearly blinded Sam.

He blinked and rubbed his eyes.

"Is that the Mall Priest?" a voice called out.

Sam groaned. Ricky might love this kind of thing, but he sure as hell didn't. "Okay. I think I'm done here." He pushed his chair away from the table.

"All right then, let's go," Jupiter said with a pleased nod. "If you're all finished, we'll head to the stage area."

RICKY SAT WITH SAM and Penny at a table backstage, behind the giant red-curtained area of the main entertainment stage. Jupiter had left to check on what he'd called 'special arrangements' with the promise that he'd return.

Located on the third floor, the auditorium held enough space for just over two thousand attendees, each personally invited to the official opening of The Great Rock of Vegas Casino and Hotel. Everything except the band equipment was in place, leaving the center stage ominously empty, considering Ricky was to perform live in about twelve hours. He'd rehearsed earlier in the week, but whatever was going on, he guessed the final checks would happen last minute.

Christmas decorations hung in the backdrop and from the rigging, creating an ultra-glittery showcase for the concert's theme of a desert holiday paradise, complete with fake palm trees made from wire and tinsel. Everything smelled new, probably because it was, and although the idea of performing in such a venue would normally excite Ricky, the threat of being stalked by a monster who could burn them all alive just because he wanted to, filled him with the worst kind of dread.

Penny held his hand, but the brush of her thumb across his fingers almost caused more anxiety than calm. Was she getting attached to him? If so, maybe he should warn her away. While she was beautiful and fit and everything he could ever want in a partner, his heart wasn't ready to be given to someone else. It was too busy being freaked the fuck out by everything else going on.

"I hate waiting. I just... hate it." His words were filled with the deep exhaustion that had lived inside him for months. "If he's going to kill us, I wish he'd just jump out and do it."

Sam clicked his fingers high in the air. "Hello? Is Ricky there? The rock star who defeated a demon with his singing? Did you ever think this guy picked you because he knows what a badass you really are?"

Ricky shrugged. He wasn't in the mood for sermons, not even from Father Sam.

"Well, I'm not intending to die today…" the priest continued, "… and I'm sure Penny isn't either." He glanced her way.

"Fucking straight up, I'm not." She hissed. "I'm getting my revenge, and I want to celebrate with Ricky in private." The smirk she gave the rock star made his heart speed up.

Okay, maybe I can have that talk with her after we have victory sex. Although they'd gone to her bedroom the previous night, Ricky had mostly just held her while she'd cried. It had seemed to be what she needed and wanted. He hadn't even made a pass at her, which surprised him. But if she wanted something more casual, he was up for it.

Sam leaned in. "What do you think Jupiter's big secret plan is?"

Penny rested her hands on the table, fingers intertwined. "There's a teaching about the remnants that I thought was interesting." She glanced between him and Sam. "While they are neither angels nor demons, the remnants were once mortal humans who were saved before their death by either, right? This guy Rathburn seems to be a demon's plaything. But my gut is screaming that Hugo gives his service to an angel." She paused. "So perhaps what we need to do is combine weapons that are used against demons and angels when we're fighting. Maybe they can be useful against this burning man as well." She patted the duffel bag in the seat next to her. "Luckily, I pack for all occasions."

Penny unzipped the bag, and among the rifles, pistols, and semi-automatic salt shooters were a few swords. She pulled out one and showed it to Sam.

"Flaming swords were often used during wars between angels. What do you think? Maybe we could make some of those?" Penny said.

Sam's eyes widened. "We'll need oil. I'll have to anoint them. The prayers will take time."

Ricky listened in. If ever there was a conversation in which he felt he had no input, this would be the one. "Do I get a sword?"

Penny tossed him a sideways glance. "As long as you don't start drinking today."

He glowered at her as if shocked by her implication. *That wasn't a nice thing to say.* "I never have more than one drink on the day of a performance anymore. It's the one rule I do live by."

Sam shook his head. "Don't you think you'll look ridiculous on stage with a sword?"

"Ridiculous? Hell no. He'll look badass." She grinned. "If there is an actual performance today, we can sheath it into a scabbard and attach it to a belt. Maybe we can make it look like a stage prop."

"That's another thing I need to do if we're going to have a chance... anoint every weapon in our arsenal, not just swords. But it will take a lot of time to do. I should also do the same for the soldiers' ammo. But we have to move now." Sam sighed. "Let's face it, right now, we're not doing much except sitting around thinking about what we'd much rather be doing than possibly getting killed by a crazy immortal pyromaniac."

Penny opened the duffel bag and began placing the weapons out one by one on the round table.

Ricky's hands trembled as he helped separate the weapons. When was the last time he'd touched any kind of gun? Probably a water pistol a year ago to the day exactly, when he'd done his part in the holy water squirt gun battle against Abaddon.

The swords looked disappointingly plain compared to the one in the film *Highlander*. He held one up and looked at it. "Can I have a big, shiny, fancy one?"

Sam shook his head and turned to Penny. "Got any vials of holy water in that bag?"

She shook her head, her expression turning closed off. "That would be ah... Jenny."

"She brought her pack when we left earlier." Sam paused. "It was... burned."

"Yeah," Penny said solemnly.

"What about anointing oil?" Sam asked.

Penny shook her head again.

"Let me guess, Jenny's pack again, right?" Ricky asked. These people really needed to learn about not putting all their eggs in one basket.

"Right," Penny said.

"So what do we do?" Ricky asked.

"We'll improvise." He glanced around the stage. "I doubt there's any frankincense or myrrh lying around. Anyone got any olive oil?"

"Well... now you mention it," Penny said. She moved to a trolley that had been left as part of a snack table, probably for the roadies during set up. A nearby guard watched her curiously for a second, then turned away, not paying her any mind. Rifling through the condiments, Penny raised a slender glass bottle. "Avocado oil do?"

Sam shrugged. "We'll give it a try."

"Great," Ricky mumbled. "We'll all be fighting with the Blessed Swords of the Flaming Avocado."

Penny giggled. "That's kind of funny actually."

"It's been six months since I renounced my priesthood with the Catholic church," Sam declared. "I can only pray this will work."

He opened the bottle, closed his eyes, and began to recite a prayer in Latin. Penny quickly joined in.

Ricky sighed and looked around for something to do other than wait. Why was there always so much waiting?

Waiting for prayers to finish.

Waiting to go on stage and perform.

Waiting to find out if they lived or died.

Leaving Sam and Penny to their mutterings, he stood and walked toward the curtain. The thick red fabric moved easily when he pulled it aside with his fingers, opening an inch-wide gap he could see through. The seats were already filled with people waiting for him to go on stage. He looked more closely. The people weren't moving, and they looked kind of pale, and some in the front row didn't even have faces. *Mannequins? What the hell?* The seating area had been filled with fully clothed mannequins. *When did they pull this off?*

Ricky sighed. One thing was certain—if he did actually perform at some point tonight, it would be in front of the most boring crowd of his entire life.

Chapter 16

Agent Venus and her partner, Agent Uranus, walked several yards apart as they paced around the packed first floor of the casino, looking for trouble. Their dark suits, sunglasses, and obvious wired earpieces attracted more than a few nervous stares from the casino patrons.

This is a bad idea, Venus thought.

While their superior, Agent Jupiter, had arranged for the entertainment floor to be cleared of people, the owner had insisted on business as usual on the betting floors. Because it was a new property and given the proximity to Christmas, the idiot was adamant about people being allowed access to come and spend their life savings on the various game tables and one-armed bandit machines.

What a fucking sad way to spend the holiday season, Venus thought as people of all ages placed bets on roulette and blackjack tables, hoping that one more time would mean their big win. Then there were the players sitting expressionless at the slot machines, pushing coin after coin into the box that would occasionally play a tune or give off a light show when someone scored a little win.

"Fucking parasites," she muttered, thinking about the lavish lifestyles of casino owners.

She glanced at Uranus as he came to a sudden stop several yards to her left in the crowd. "Suspicious character entering... door three, floor one," he announced.

"I see him," Venus responded. She stared at the man as he came through the door. "Facial details, non-existent. Dark clothes, dark hood. Agent Jupiter, please advise how to proceed."

"Hold back, observe and, if you can, follow without being noticed. But whatever you do, do not engage," came the immediate response from Jupiter.

"Copy that." She watched the curious figure take slow, deliberate paces to the blackjack tables. A security guard tracked him with every step, while one of the dealers seemed genuinely concerned by the dark figure's arrival.

He looks like a bank robber or something with that hood, she thought. But it was the aura about him that was most disturbing. He moved like he owned the shadows that gathered in the unseen places of the soul. Venus shivered as a chill ran up her spine. Was it getting colder in the room or what? The air felt like the thermostat had dropped a notch or two.

A waitress wearing a red Santa hat carried a metal tray full of champagne flutes from table to table, telling the punters that on behalf of hotel management, they could each take a complimentary drink. But she took several steps back when she reached the hooded figure. The tray wobbled in her hand to the point where she would have fallen if Uranus hadn't been there to help steady both her and the tray.

Venus rolled her eyes as she saw Uranus—being the asshole she knew him to be—had found a way to place a hand on the waitress's ass while helping to steady her. *Prick.*

"Thank you, handsome," the woman's almost breathless voice flitted through the air. The grateful smile on her face fell as she pointed at the hooded figure in black who was walking away down the aisle. "I don't know why, but there's something disturbing about that man."

Agent Uranus nodded and arched a brow. "I won't let him harm you, ma'am."

The hooded figure stopped in his tracks and turned around to face Uranus and the waitress.

Oh, shit. Venus spoke into her communication device, "Boss, I think we have a problem."

The dark-clothed figure flicked back his hood, exposing a scarred scalp, face covered in burns, and pair of eyeballs almost hanging out of hollow sockets. "How are you going to stop me, little man?"

Uranus grabbed his pistol and removed it from his holster.

"Boss, we definitely have a fucking problem," Venus shouted into her microphone. *Where the hell is Jupiter?*

The people in the various gambling areas were starting to notice the commotion between the black-suited agent and the dark figure who looked like a third-degree burn victim. Reactions were varied, from screams to audible gasps and horrified stares.

"Copy that, Venus," Jupiter replied. "Please explain the problem."

"Uranus. Uranus is the problem. He engaged with the target." Venus winced inwardly. Stupid asshole, bringing attention to the Remnant in a crowded gambling room.

There was a short pause where she thought she heard the supervising agent whisper, *'Jesus fucking Christ.'* Then Jupiter said. "Draw him away from there and funnel him to the auditorium on third. I'll mobilize Bullet Man and the troops. Try not to let anyone get killed."

Fucking easier said than done. "Copy that, Boss." How the hell was she supposed to get the Remnant's attention without causing a panic? "William!" she yelled at the top of her lungs and waved her arms in the air. "Over here."

The Remnant stilled, and a small wisp of smoke escaped from each of the man's ears.

Oh shit. What have I done? Venus thought.

"William?" His voice was a dark, gravelly hiss. He spun on the spot as if operated by some type of switch and looked at her. His bulging eyes seemed to stare into her soul, just like the first time she'd seen his picture in the classified file. "Are you trying to be my friend?"

"William, let's leave this room, please." She gestured to the main doorway that led out of the casino area and into the hotel.

He stretched out his arms, the smoke whisps from his ears increasing. "Why? Don't you want all these people to know what happened to me? How I was betrayed by my own country? Or do you want them just to hear about the evil I've supposedly done since I've returned from fucking 'Nam?"

"Okay, we need everyone cleared out of this area right now," she quietly called into her microphone. "I repeat, we need an immediate evac. He's starting to smoke."

Uranus positioned himself behind the burned man and aimed his pistol at his head. People standing nearby began backing away, some hurrying for the exit, while others seemed frozen like a deer caught in the headlights of a truck.

Fucking Christ. Why'd I have to get paired with the asshole hot head? "Stand down, Uranus," Venus muttered as quietly as she could into her communication device. "You're going to get us all killed."

If Uranus heard her, he ignored the command. A grin lifted his lips as he braced his shooting hand with his other and fired the pistol from point-blank range into the back of the remnant's head. The shot echoed throughout the first floor of the casino, and everyone who had not already been aware of something going on paused in mid-action.

The Remnant clutched the back of his head and let out a deep, roaring round of laughter.

"Everyone, get... *out!*" Venus screamed urgently, motioning for the people around her to move. It would take more than a few moments to get everyone to safety, but she wasn't prepared to stand by helpless while this crazed killer burned them all alive.

Uranus's face drained of color. He looked at his pistol, then fired again and again until he emptied his clip into the Remnant's head. "Just fucking die," he yelled.

"You first." The dark figure's voice carried above the cacophony of panic that filled the room as people tried to leave the area. William spun back around and faced Uranus. Gore oozed from the various holes in the Remnant's head, but that didn't appear to matter as the wounds sealed nearly instantly. He reached out with a slender, almost bony finger and touched Uranus's brow. The agent stood before him, apparently frozen in shock. "Burn, you fucking asshole."

A bright orange spark flashed and quickly turned into a flame that caught on Uranus's hair. The agent screamed, and the waitress, still standing by him threw a glass of champagne over Uranus's burning head. The liquid did nothing to douse the flames. Instead, it appeared to spread them. The waitress began to run in a circle, screaming, while Uranus tried in vain to put out the flames spreading over his head by hitting them with his hands.

Venus scurried toward the nearest group of punters who were engrossed in a game at a roulette table. "Leave," she shouted. "Goddammit, forget the game and get the hell out of here." She pointed toward the nearest door, which was already choked with people confused by what was going on.

The Remnant glanced her way and grinned, revealing a discolored mass of broken teeth. He pointed at the exit she'd indicated. A second later, the doorframe—and the people going through it—burst into flames. "No one's leaving this party," the dark specter growled, his voice like a deep bell, tolling doom.

"Jupiter," Venus called into her microphone, her voice filled with a panic that made her whole body tremble as she tried to get people to leave. "He's set Uranus on fire, as well as one of the main entranceways. We need immediate backup."

Silence greeted her plea.

"Boss?" Her hands shook as she grasped the back of a chair and looked around the chaotic room. Clouds of smoke were beginning to hover at the ceiling. "Boss?" she called after a few silent seconds. *Fuck.*

The Remnant grabbed the screaming waitress by the throat with one hand. "I've always been more of a bourbon guy, myself." Flames shot from his hand and spiraled around her neck as he raised her into the air. She kicked his torso with her flailing legs as she was lifted away from the floor, but if he felt the impact, he didn't show it.

I can't just do nothing, Venus thought as she watched on helplessly.

People ran to the other exits, only to see each way out set ablaze like the first one. They backed away, looking for another way to leave, jostling into each other and tripping. A woman fell to the ground, her screams lost in the growing sounds of confusion, which were getting louder.

The waitress was no longer screaming as she was dropped to the ground, fire spreading across her body. Uranus kept battling the fire that had consumed his hair, trying to stop it from spreading. He ripped a tablecloth from a café-style table and draped it over his head.

"Oh, Mr. Asshole, don't worry," the Remnant said in a sing-song voice. "There's plenty more where that came from." He pointed at the agent, whose clothes immediately caught on fire.

Uranus dropped to the floor and began rolling, trying to extinguish the new fire by smothering it, but the flames burned brighter and hotter, and the agent soon stopped moving.

Shit, what the hell am I supposed to do? Nearly hyperventilating from seeing her co-agent get cooked alive, Venus shook as tears blurred her vision. The smoke was beginning to sting. *Please, God. Help me. I don't want to die.*

SAM SWIVELED IN HIS seat at the table as Agent Jupiter marched into the backstage area of the concert hall. The agent moved with shorter and quicker paces than usual, adding to Sam's unease. The building's fire alarm was blaring, but the soldiers guarding the perimeter of the stage had told them all to stay where they were as per Jupiter's instructions.

Jupiter spoke frantically into his earpiece communication device. "Neptune, Pluto, Mercury? Do any of you copy?"

"What's going on?" Sam asked the lead agent.

Jupiter raised a hand and waved it as if Sam had no right to speak to him. "Venus? Does anyone copy?"

After a second, when Jupiter apparently received no reply from any of the agents he was trying to call, he turned to Sam. "Okay, I have to check what's going on. But you three need to stay here. Rathburn will be coming for Ricky. It's absolutely imperative that we get the Remnant onto the stage and keep him there. Do you understand?"

Um, no. But Sam nodded just the same. "What's the big deal with the stage?"

"I don't have time to explain. I'll be back later. Good luck."

He nodded to the three of them and resumed trying to connect with people on his short-range communication device, his voice echoing loudly as he walked briskly across the stage and out of view.

"Uh… what was that about the stage?" Ricky asked.

"I don't know. Maybe the Remnant requested a private concert with you or something?" Penny teased, giving him a wink.

"Fucking hell. I am *not* doing that." He stared at the stage for a moment, then stomped his foot. "*Fuck.* I hate being the bait here."

Sam nodded and rubbed his bristly chin. "I totally understand." The situation rubbed him the wrong way too. *I'm pretty sure we're all bait now.* If there was a biblical phrase he found hard to swallow, it was *'the sins of the father.'* Why should anyone have to pay for what a parent had done? And in Ricky's case, his father had carried out an order given to him by a senior officer. "I won't let this harm you, fuckdammit," he promised the rock star.

Ricky frowned. "What kind of word is that?"

"It's my word," Sam muttered. He finished wiping down the last rapier with the makeshift anointing oil. "Grab a sword each." He looked at the one he held in his hand. "If we are attacked, the three of us can form a holy barrier against him."

Penny stood and selected a sword. "Will it work?"

"I'm hoping it does." He thought of the pictures he'd seen in Illustrated versions of the Bible, depicting Archangel Michael raising his sword up high in the air and subduing the evil below him. "I don't know if us three can personally defeat this remnant, but if we can hold him off so Bullet Man can do his part, it may just give us the edge." *Dear God, may you please guide us on this day. May your grace and wisdom give us courage and strength.* It had taken the will of God plus a group of believers working together to defeat Abaddon, not just him alone. He'd forgotten that earlier, and it had cost Jenny her life. It was a painful mistake—one he was determined not to make again.

"Dude, I was hoping for something more solid," Ricky said. He touched the handles of a few swords before making his selection. Holding it high, he spoke in a bad Scottish accent. "There can be one only!"

Penny leaned in close to Sam. "I don't think that's how it goes."

Sam chuckled, the other two joining in until a rambunctious explosion shook the building, killing their laughter. The trio stood back-to-back, swords at the ready, each looking out for any sign of movement.

"What the fuck was that?" Ricky asked.

Penny grabbed the walkie-talkie she'd been given from her belt. "Jupiter, what the hell was that?"

No answer.

"Jupiter… anyone… it's Sister Penny here. What the hell was that explosion?"

Ricky's pale complexion faded to a shade of white that Sam didn't know existed. What was paler than extremely pale?

"We're dead," Ricky said. The sword in the singer's hand shook so violently that Sam backed up a step.

"Ricky, please calm down. We don't know what it was. It could be several generators all kicking in at the same time." Penny reached over and placed a hand on Ricky's shoulder. "Or maybe a really big rat."

"A fucking Godzilla-sized rat." Ricky scoffed, apparently not appreciating her attempt at humor.

The floor shook again, followed by another deep boom. A chill traveled up Sam's spine like a dagger constructed of ice had pierced his back.

"The target is on the move," Jupiter's voice squawked over the radio. The transmission broke into static as the agent repeated the call and added something about 'explosion' and 'collapse.'

Shit. Sam's heart skipped a beat as he looked at the other two members of the sitting duck trio. Despite all of Jupiter's preparations, the Remnant was trying to take down the whole hotel.

Fuckdammit, I knew it. I knew this was going to happen.

He shut his eyes as he thought of his daughter trapped in the hotel room with strangers. "Oh my God. Bella," he whispered.

Bella sat with Hugo on the couch, clutching his hand in hers. The smoke alarms continued to wail, as did the panicked group of soldiers in their hotel room. Father Luke and the two sisters had already been called away to assist in something she'd heard over the radio termed a 'crisis snitchu-ation' in the casino. She didn't have to know what the term meant to know it was bad. Father Luke hadn't wanted to leave her alone with Bullet Man and the soldiers, but that was okay. She trusted Hugo more anyway. Among other things, he didn't smell like hot dogs and panic, unlike the young priest.

"Do you think my dad's okay?" she asked the large immortal being beside her.

"Yes." He kept his unflinching glare on the soldiers. "I've told you that six times already."

Bella frowned. She followed his gaze to the soldiers and back again. "You don't like them, do you?"

"No."

"I don't either," she admitted. "Guns are scary."

She fidgeted with her tourmaline shard necklace. It was the only thing that helped calm the bad feelings coming off the soldiers who stood by the door with their guns at the ready to shoot anything that moved. The scariest thing of all was that they wanted to, or at least some of them did.

The agent standing with the soldiers picked up his walkie-talkie as it squawked and listened intently for a moment. Then he said, "Copy that," into the device and clipped it back on his belt. "Okay, that's it," he called out to the men and women around him. "Everyone needs to head to the ground." He looked Hugo and Bella up and down. "You two need to leave here too. Let's go. *Now!*"

"What's going on?" Bella asked. She kept a tight hold on Hugo's hand as they stood.

The soldiers filed out quickly, not waiting to see if she and Hugo followed.

"The girl will be safer with me than you goons anyway," Hugo snapped. "Come on." He tugged on her hand and headed for the door after the soldiers.

Bella's eyes widened as she looked at him, and she stopped mid-step. The bullet hovering in front of his forehead appeared to be glowing. "Your bullet... is it burning?"

He shook his head. "Don't worry about it." Then he closed his eyes and clutched at his head, staggering against the wall.

"What's wrong?" Bella screamed. The bullet was glowing bright orange like it was on fire.

Opening his eyes, Hugo got down on one knee in front of her. Taking her by the hands, he spoke gently to Bella, "Listen, this bullet is like a blessing and a curse. I should have died about three hundred fifty years ago when it was fired at my head. But I didn't because I was chosen by an angel to carry out the Lord's work in a different way instead." He paused.

"You're like a priest? Like Dad?"

"I was, sort of, once. But not now. Now I'm... something else. I don't have time to explain, but I want you to understand. I must do what I am told. Just like the burning man must, but he serves a different master. One who is cruel, like Satan."

"I thought so," Bella said.

"I need to leave and help other people right now, and I cannot take you with me. It is far too dangerous. I had hoped to get you to safety first, but if I do not do as I'm told right now, the bullet will kill me. I can already feel it moving closer to my skull as we are talking."

Bella's eyes went wide. "That's not very nice. I don't want you to die."

He smiled softly. "I need you to take the stairs down. Just follow the other people. You will be safe once you are outside. Can you feel any evil presence in the stairs?"

It was her turn to shake her head.

"Good. If you get scared, don't forget I'm never far away. Now let's go."

"But where will you be going?"

"I'm heading down too, but I need to take the fast way." He nodded toward the elevator.

Bella studied the closed elevator doors, remembering her experience at the Admiral Hotel and how they would have all died in the fall if it wasn't for Hugo slowing down the descent with his hands. Without him, they would have been crushed. He needed to help other people now, just like he'd helped them.

Hugo moved to the elevator and pulled open the outside doors as if they were made of playdough. There was no car waiting on the other side, just cables.

He gave her hand a small squeeze. "You can do this, Bella. It will be okay." Then he stepped sideways through the gap in the doors and was gone in a blur so fast she barely saw him move. *Like a bullet,* she thought.

Bella stood there for a moment, feeling suddenly small and lost. She'd already lost sight of her newest companion, and, as fear began to take a ride through her, she grabbed the tourmaline gem on her necklace. "I miss you, Mommy," Bella whispered and closed her eyes, imagining the smiling face of her real mother, encouraging her to be brave. The elevator cables twanged and banged, and she jumped back from the gap. What if the burning man were to come and find her now? No, he couldn't, not with her body's unnatural ability to detect evil. Hugo knew of her powers. Why else would he have left her to travel alone?

She hurried to the stairway and opened the door. Several other people were taking the stairs down, hurrying to escape. None of them paid her any mind as she joined the queue.

Sam and Sarah had often told her that her levels of maturity and understanding were off the charts for a child of nine. Thinking of them both and Nana and even her unborn baby brother, who she didn't like at all, a wave of homesickness swept through her. If she ever wanted to see them again, she needed to be brave right now.

"You're strong, like your Mama," Sarah would have said, with pride written all over her face.

"Yes, I am. Yes, I am," Bella chanted as she took each step down.

Chapter 17

Ena stood beside Mother Agnes outside Sarah's room at the base's medical facility, watching her daughter through the window.

Sarah sat cross-legged on her bed, facing the window. Her long hair hung loose about her shoulders, the dark strands a sharp contrast to her white hospital gown. Fingers splayed, her hands rested gently on the protrusion of her abdomen. A faint smile tipped her lips as if she was listening to something that pleased her. But it was her eyes that had Ena riveted. Even downcast, the red glow was unmistakable.

Dear God, if her head spins round and she starts spewing green vomit, I will lose the last of my wits. "We can't just stand here doing nothing," Ena insisted. "She's still my daughter."

After Sarah had thrown everyone out of her room—literally and figuratively—when they'd tried to subdue her and induce labor, she'd screamed in a deep, agonized tone that Ena had never heard anyone make before, let alone thought that Sarah could. Then, a barrier of some kind had surrounded the room that no one and nothing could penetrate. "It's been hours," she moaned, the anxiety, which twisted her stomach like barbed wire, clear in her voice. This was not how she'd imagined spending Christmas Eve. But at least Sarah seemed calm for the moment.

"Would you like some coffee?" Brother Trevor asked gently. He had gathered next to Mother Agnes and Agent Mars. "I know this is a difficult time—"

Oh dear God. "No!" Ena snapped. "I want my daughter back and the baby safe." She gripped her hands together, striving for some semblance of calm.

"If she's erected a barrier, then there's nothing further we can do except pray. The demon is in control now. We can only gain entry when he allows it." Mother Agnes's voice sounded strained, as if she was exhausted, which didn't surprise Ena. They all were.

"Maybe the demon isn't that powerful," Brother Trevor suggested. He moved his wheelchair closer to the window and peered at the translucent glow that flickered slightly as it surrounded the room. "Did you tell Sarah that it's likely Abaddon?"

"No," Ena whispered. "I couldn't bring myself to burden her like that."

"It might have made a difference," Trevor said. "She might have willingly allowed us to take the baby."

"And she might not have." Ena rounded on him. "But I'm one hundred percent certain that shocking her with batons did *not* help."

"Abaddon is strong," Agnes said quietly, her gaze fixed on Sarah. "We should be grateful we're allowed to see in the room at all."

"None of the machines are registering anything anymore," Doctor Stevens reported, joining the conversation from beside Ena. She tossed Sarah's chart onto a nearby accent table as if it were useless and placed her hands on her hips. "And she's pulled out the IV again."

"So she's had no food, no water…" Agnes let the sentence hang.

"And we can't get in to give her anything," Doctor Stevens finished for her.

"Where is the demon getting the power to do this?" Ena asked, needing to know but fearing the answer. Although she'd been away on vacation in Mexico at the time of the event in Springfield, she'd seen the news reports and heard firsthand accounts of what had gone on at the mall from Sarah, Sam, and Bella. Abaddon had fed on fear and the souls of its victims. Sarah had been lucky to escape. And it had been Ena's deep, secret fear ever since that her daughter might still die from the experience.

The Mother Superior sighed. "From Sarah. He's using her protective instinct against her. Until the child is born, he will keep draining her until she's got nothing left for him to take."

"And then what?" Mars asked.

Ena glanced at him as she struggled to keep from breaking down. Wasn't it enough that Sarah was, for all intents and purposes, dying, and who knew what was happening to the baby?

"Abaddon is a higher-order demon," the agent continued. "If he is allowed to escape now, there may be no stopping him this time." His gaze focused on Mother Agnes. "We should have acted as soon as Sarah Morris entered the base and gotten rid of the problem." The look in the agent's eyes sent shivers up Ena's spine.

"Excuse me. That is *my daughter* you are talking about." Ena pointed her finger in his face, not caring what he thought about it or if he might slip cyanide into her next drink. "You cannot tell me that in this giant secret lab that you call a church, you haven't been working on anything that can help?"

"Why don't we focus on the present rather than worrying about the past or the future," Brother Trevor cut in. "What can we do to help the baby and mother right now?"

"We continue with the prayer circles around this room," Mother Agnes said. "It will give Sarah strength."

"That's not enough." Doctor Stevens shook her head. "I have no idea how long Sarah can keep this up for, but I doubt that it's two months. She's strong, but… did you stop to think that maybe this barrier is as much to keep her in as it is to keep us out?" She studied Mother Agnes. "You said it yourself. That demon is using her."

"What we need is a miracle," Brother Trevor said.

Ena folded her arms across her chest and turned to Agent Mars. "What we *need* is Sam. You need to call him back right now." Ena's level of frustration was hitting her breaking point. "He is the father of that child. He needs to be here. Maybe he can get through to Sarah in a way that none of the rest of us can."

When no one said anything, she added in a sing-song voice, "Yes, I know you sent Sam away because you thought you could take the baby while he was gone so you could use it for God only knows what kinds of experiments. But it didn't work like that, did it?" She paused and studied them all. "So you need to forget whatever wild goose chase you've sent Sam on and get him, as well as my granddaughter, back here *right now*!"

"No can do," Mars said, his expression tense.

"Why not?" Ena snapped.

"Because Father Sam isn't on a 'wild goose chase,' as you put it," he snapped back. "We've lost contact with the team." He dragged his fingers through his hair. "Along with every other team we've sent in after him." The look he gave her was withering as he shook his head. "Bloody conspiracy theorists," he muttered under his breath.

Ena stared at him for a long moment, her heart and mind racing. This was officially the worst Christmas she'd ever had in her sixty-two years. "Are they dead?" she asked, her voice soft in the silence that filled the hall.

"We don't know," Mother Agnes replied.

"Then you'd better go find out, hadn't you?" She glanced back through the window at her daughter. Sarah's red eyes glowed as she watched them. "Because if what you say is true about this demon being Abaddon, none of us have a lot of time."

Chapter 18

Hugo clung to the cables, using his hands to slow his descent down the elevator shaft. He landed on the roof of the car at the bottom without issue. Would that be the same floor as the casino's first floor? He would soon find out. Luckily, they hadn't been on the penthouse floor this time, and the short drop from the fourth floor did little harm to his hands. The pain of hot metal touching his forehead increased the urgency to save those he could. What he would give to discuss some of the terms of the agreement regarding his existence with that angel prick Gabriel. Wasn't protecting the little girl enough?

One life to be saved in exchange for the lives of the many lost. Really, Hugo? You made that mistake before, didn't you?

Yeah, he had. And thus, his sentence as an angelic minion had been determined.

"One year for every life your selfish action has caused to be taken."

Well, that had been extended a bit now, hadn't it? Not by much, though. Not by much.

He brought his foot down and smashed the elevator's emergency hatch open. Jumping into the car, he lined up his fists with where he saw light between the two doors. Swinging as hard as he could, he sent the pair of doors toppling forward. They landed on the floor with a resounding echo.

"Oh my God! It's *him*," a woman hiding under a table screamed. Without allowing him a chance to explain that he was, in fact, the good guy here, she bolted from under the table and ran into what appeared to be an inferno not unlike hell itself.

"No!" Hugo called out, running after her. He did his best to ignore the small sections of plaster that fell around him from the cracking ceiling.

Pushing ahead through the burning entrance to the casino's main floor, he abruptly stopped. Some people were screaming and hiding under whatever they could find to protect them, while others crawled close to the ground, still trying to escape the smoke and flames. Most appeared to not be moving at all.

He really did a fucking number here. Dear God, he turned off the sprinkler system, didn't he? "You're going to fucking pay for this, Rathburn," Hugo shouted.

"Oh, am I really?" the Remnant's gruff voice oozed with sarcasm thicker than clotted blood. "Come on, Bullet Fucker, come out and face me."

Did this sociopath seriously believe Hugo feared him? "I'm not the one hiding among the flames, you chicken shit."

Rathburn's deep laughter rumbled throughout the area.

Through the murky haze created by the flames and smoke, Hugo swore he saw several figures step forward from the shadows.

"I know how to defeat you, Bullet Man," Rathburn growled. It was a low, deep sound that set Hugo's teeth on edge. "I know your Achilles heel, your weakness... you actually *like* these creatures despite their pathetic natures."

With those words, a man came running toward Hugo from the billowing smoke, followed by several others of varying ages. They all appeared to be singed, indicated by their burned clothing, but were otherwise intact. Their high-pitched screams and whimpers, however, were more than enough to show how terrified they were. One was an agent named Venus, whom Hugo had seen briefly in Jupiter's quarters.

With his red face blistering from the intense heat and flames and his eyeballs bulging as if they were going to explode like the bomb that had destroyed him in the first place, Rathburn stepped forward and gestured dramatically at the doomed group he was using as bait. "Come on, Bullet Man. Come and save them!"

It was a trap, clearly, and a wrong move by Hugo would signal the end of the hostages' lives. "Please, let them go. How about you and I leave this place and sort out our differences away from everybody."

Agent Jupiter had not planned for him to leave the premises, but at this point, Hugo was willing to do whatever it took to get the demented pyromaniac out of there, and somewhere he was less likely to harm anyone else.

"They don't have much time, these poor, wretched fuckers." The remnant let out another thunderous laugh that twisted Hugo's stomach. It was one thing to have to carry out the orders of a demonic master, but did Rathburn have to enjoy it so much?

I can do this. I'm fucking Bullet Man and can move quicker than he can see me. Hugo darted a few steps to his left, hoping he was nothing more than a blur in the burning man's sight and could do what needed to be done unobserved.

William Rathburn had already killed too many innocent souls, no matter how much he liked to play up being the victim of an attack in Vietnam a decade and a half ago as justification.

Hugo crouched behind a thick wall of fire that was consuming a Blackjack table at a ravenous pace.

Rathburn scanned the area, his eyes glowing as he searched. "Come out, come out, wherever you are."

Hugo stayed low behind the fire and kept to the unseen places as best as possible as he moved around behind the hostages. The only way he'd be able to attack this psychopath and save the group at the same time was if he caught Rathburn by surprise. He just hoped that the remnant wouldn't lose patience and kill the hostages for the hell of it before then.

"You're taking too long." Rathburn moved toward the group of frightened people.

There had to be about twenty of them, by Hugo's count, now he was close enough to see them all. Each appeared to be suffering the effects of smoke inhalation as well as burns from being trapped so near the flames.

Rathburn grabbed Agent Venus by her hair and dragged her, kicking and screaming, toward the flames. "Don't you like my game, Hugo?" he asked, looking around the room. "You didn't run off and leave, did you? You'll miss all the fun. It's so easy to kill these people. Just a spark, and they go poof." He lit his hand on fire by holding it in the flames, then moved it close to her face.

"No, no. Please, no," the agent whimpered, trembling in his grasp. She tried to shrink away.

"Not so tough when you're at the end, now are you?" Rathburn said to her, sounding disappointed. "That's okay, no one ever is."

"Let her go," Hugo ordered, knowing full well his enemy would likely not comply. He came out of his hiding spot. "Let them all go."

Rathburn cocked his head as if he were considering the request. "Ummm... *no*. I'm just getting warmed up."

The Remnant smothered the agent's face with his hand, setting her head on fire. Then he lifted her into the air as she screamed and writhed. He threw her at the other hostages.

Hugo moved, catching the woman mid-flight. "Run!" he shouted at the others.

They stood their ground, seeming confused, huddled together in a group. One man fell coughing to the floor.

Hugo placed the burning woman on the tiles. There was nothing he could do for her now. "Get out of here," he shouted at the others as he launched himself at Rathburn. Moving faster than the demonic remnant could follow, he wrapped his arms around him, pinning him where he stood.

Rathburn roared out in sickening laughter, and as the volume grew, the badly injured agent screamed as her whole body lit up, the flames consuming her within a split second.

Her death seemed to spur the others into action. Those who were able to bolted away from the flames and the Remnant, scattering into the damaged room, seeking a way out. Those that couldn't run fell to the floor and stopped moving.

"They're like roaches, aren't they?" Rathburn said, struggling to break Hugo's hold. His voice changed into being sing-songy. "Did that feel good? Saving the strong while the weak perish?" He snickered. "Just wait until you see what I have planned for that son-of-a-bastard pop singer and his friends. Especially that little girl you adore so much."

"You're sick, you know that?" Hugo said through clenched teeth. It was getting harder to hold the asshole in place while his own body heated and began to smoke.

"Now, now. Remember what happened the last time we danced like this?" Rathburn warned.

Shit. Hugo let go of the Remnant a second before a blast of heat and flames singed his skin. His fatigues were flame retardant, among other things, but he couldn't afford another immolation. It would take him too long to heal and regenerate. The force of the blast tossed him through the air, and he landed hard against the side of a broken chair. Pain ricocheted through him, and he closed his eyes for a second.

Rathburn's exploding fireball rattled the floor and ceiling, causing the cracks to widen. Hugo coughed as he rolled onto his side and shielded his face from the dust and plaster showering from above. Hopefully, some of the hostages had found a way out. The ceiling would collapse soon.

As if impervious to the danger he'd caused, Rathburn moved through the dust and debris, heading for the stairway up.

Good, Hugo thought. *At least he's going the right way now. But this plan of Jupiter's had better work.*

"I'M NOT JUST GOING to stand around waiting while my daughter is in danger," Sam said as he pushed his hand on the backstage side door to the auditorium and thrust it open.

"But Jupiter said we're supposed to stay here," Penny called out, following him with Ricky. "Don't you think that Bella is safe with Hugo?"

The three of them staggered as the floor rocked from yet another explosion somewhere below.

Is she? Sam thought. His instincts were screaming that she wasn't. "Fine. You two stay here, if you want. I'm going to find my daughter."

With the elevators clearly out of order, Sam opened the entrance door to the stairwell—it was only one floor up—and he could be up there and back down with Bella in no time.

The sound of a little girl giggling made him pause. "Bella?" he called out, his voice echoing throughout the darkened area. Emergency lighting illuminated the steps and not much more.

"Papa!" Bella shouted. Within a moment, she appeared, heading down to the third-floor landing. "Look, I made a new friend." She grinned excitedly. "Her name's Pamela."

A girl about her own age, covered in soot and wearing a tattered dress, appeared silently beside Bella.

"Come on, it's okay," Bella told the girl as she trotted down the stairs.

"What happened?" Sam asked as gently as he could despite the rapid beat of his heart. It would take him a lifetime to recover from all the scares Bella had given him in the last few days. "Why did you leave the room and come down the stairs?"

"The agent guy said everybody had to go. And Hugo said it was safer than the elevator."

"Where is Hugo?" Sam glanced around the stairwell, expecting to see him, but it was empty except for the two girls.

Bella shrugged. "He had to go to help other people. He said it was important."

"He left you alone?" Sam nearly shouted.

"It's okay," Bella insisted. "I found Pamela on the stairs. She was alone, too."

As Bella descended the last step, she ran to him and collapsed into his arms.

Sam closed his eyes and hugged her tightly. He would be having a word with Hugo about this later, provided they all survived.

He turned his eyes to the young girl who hung back behind Bella. "Are you okay?"

She shook her head and started crying.

Bella grabbed her hand and turned back to Sam, looking sad. "Her mom and dad burned in the fire the bad man made on the first floor. That's why I stayed with her on the stairs. She's kinda like me. Except I have you and Nana and Sarah."

"Oh... oh no. You poor dear." Penny moved forward and placed her hand on Pamela's shoulder. Then she bent low on one knee and pulled Pamela into a hug. She glanced at Sam over the little girl's head. "We can't leave her here."

"Yeah," he said. He already knew that. He'd known it as soon as he'd seen the girl beside Bella. Heaven help them if Bella ever wanted a pet. They'd likely end up with a zoo. "Lets, ah... just get back to the stage before company arrives."

Penny nodded. "Come on. You'll be safe with us." She picked Pamela up and carried her through the door, Sam and Bella following behind.

"Hey, Bella," Ricky said, sounding relieved to see her as they passed him on the way back into the backstage area. He studied the new arrival in Penny's arms curiously. "I see you have a new friend."

Bella shook off Sam's hold and ran over to the rock star, stopping short upon seeing the hilt of a sword in his hand. She frowned. "Are you going to use swords?"

"Your dad appointed them so we can use them as a barrier."

"Anointed Ricky. The word is anointed," Penny chuckled as she set Pamela down. "Bella, we have some shorter swords."

Sam's head snapped around. "No, Penny."

"She doesn't need to swing it. Just carry it and we can extend the size of our protective barrier."

"I got to use a water gun last time we fought a demon," Bella said.

"Yeah, well, water guns filled with holy water don't have sharp bits," Sam argued.

Bella answered in the form of a quick walk in the direction of the table where the weapons were placed. She looked each one over, even the ones bigger than her, until she selected a half-sized sword from the pile and held it in the air.

"Why are there so many?" she asked, frowning at the table filled with weapons.

"We thought there'd be more people around to help, but... I don't think they are coming," Penny explained. "Just follow what I do, Bella, just like your dad and Ricky will be doing. We need to be able to slow Burning Man down enough for Bullet Man and Agent Jupiter to do their jobs."

Bullet Man? Burning Man? Sam thought. It sounded like they were caught up in some crazy comic book.

Penny tapped her chin with a finger. "Pamela, would you like a sword too?"

The girl's eyes went wide. She looked at Bella, then back at Penny, and nodded.

Bella walked over and grabbed Pamela's hand. "Come on, I'll help you choose one." As they checked the selection together, she added, "I know you're scared, but it'll be okay. I've fought a demon before. It was kind of fun. I helped kill it with my necklace." She showed Pamela the tourmaline shard, which hung in a chain around her neck.

Pamela's eyes went wide as she studied the black gem. She smiled for the first time since Sam had seen her. "Can I get one too?" she asked Bella.

Sam covered his face with his hand, feeling like he had completely failed as a father. *God preserve us from the might of little girls.*

The sudden rat-a-tat-tat of gunfire echoing from the front of the auditorium made them all freeze.

Shit. Oh shit.

"He's here," Bella said, her voice small, confirming what Sam feared. "It's the bad man."

Sam gathered the two girls together and hurried them to the cover of the wall with Ricky. Then he and Penny peeked through the curtain.

Three agents were backing down the aisles, firing repeated rounds from their weapons at the figure who slowly made his way through the doorway and toward the stage. Just like when Sam had faced the remnant in the alley before, it didn't matter how many times he was shot. He kept moving forward as if the agents weren't even there.

"They only have guns?" Penny asked. "They're going to get slaughtered."

Apparently, two of the agents had come to the same conclusion as they both threw down their empty rifles and made a run for the middle doors.

"Get back here," the female agent Sam recognized as being called Neptune shouted after them. "Stand your ground."

"It doesn't matter what you do," the Remnant said, his raspy voice carrying effortlessly through the vast space. He pointed at the two agents trying to escape. They immediately burst into flames and began screaming, arms waving as they tried fruitlessly to put out the fire.

The Remnant turned back to agent Neptune as he continued his way down the main aisle toward the stage.

The agent fell to her knees and began coughing as if she were choking.

"Sam, we need to do something," Penny whispered. "We can't just stand here watching him kill everyone."

He nodded. Sickness roiled in his guts as he remembered what had happened the last time he'd faced off against Rathburn. They didn't even know if the swords would work. But Penny was already gone, creeping down the side wing of the stage access and heading out the door. She hadn't said what her plan was, but Sam figured if she was trying to sneak behind the Remnant to take him by surprise, she would need a distraction.

"*Heavenly Father, please guide us and give us strength this day,*" he whispered and made the sign of the cross. With a last glance at Bella and the others by the wall, he pushed the curtain open and stepped through. He raised his sword into the air with one hand and clutched the silver cross with the other.

"*Archangel Michael. I beseech thee to ignite this anointed blade with heavenly fire. Defender of justice, defender of light, guide us this day with your celestial might,*" he called out.

A warm glow spread over the cross. It flashed from the end and onto the sword. The blade ignited with a white fire that crackled and sparked as it spread from the hilt to the tip.

"My God," Ricky said, peeking from behind the curtain to watch. "You've created a lightsaber."

Bella popped up beside Ricky and gasped when she saw Sam holding the flaming sword above his head.

"I want one too!" she shouted and ran onto the stage toward Sam, with Pamela and Ricky hot on her heels.

"What the hell is this?" Rathburn growled. "Family night at vaudeville?"

With the Remnant's attention diverted, Agent Neptune had stopped choking, and Penny crept up behind him.

The sister held her sword high, and, without hesitation, leaped into the air and brought it down upon the Remnant's head.

Neptune gasped as the blade vibrated as though it had hit concrete, and the demonic being chuckled aloud.

Rathburn spun on his foot to face his new challenger. "You fucking fool..." he pointed at Penny, "... you think your mortal weapons can harm me?"

"Get back," Father Sam urged the sister. "You need to ignite it first." *Shit.* He knew the Remnant well enough that neither woman would make it one step away from the monster before he set them both on fire.

Penny raised her sword above her head, poised for another strike.

Sam closed his eyes and prayed. "*Dear Lord above, protect us from this evil and help us send this abomination to Hell.*"

The sound of lightning cracked as a bolt of white light shot from the tip of Sam's sword. It arced across the room and connected with Penny's, lighting her sword instantly. Smaller bolts shot from Sam's sword, lighting Ricky's demon-fighting sword, followed by the girls' swords.

Pamela squealed as if frightened, and Sam thought she might drop it, but a glance her way showed her wide smile.

"Raise them up," he commanded.

They each raised their swords high. The arc of lightning coming from Sam's sword continued to crackle and spark, creating a web of fire that connected the five blades.

"This is new," Rathburn said. "But stupid." He raised a hand and pointed at Ricky.

The singer flinched, clearly expecting to be set on fire, and seemed about to run.

"No, Ricky." Sam shook his head at the man on his far right. "Don't break the barrier."

Ricky closed his eyes but stood his ground.

The hand holding his sword in the air shook.

But nothing happened.

The Remnant looked at his finger and pointed it at Ricky again. And then again. Still nothing. The only fire in the room was the crackling lightning web from the swords and the smoldering corpses of the agents near the side door.

A slow grin spread across Ricky's face.

"Go," Penny shouted at Agent Neptune. "Go *now!*"

The agent nodded and scurried backward out of the Remnant's reach, making a hasty retreat for the door.

Rathburn stood in silence as he watched her leave. Then he turned to Sam, seeming unimpressed.

"Something wrong, Rathburn?" *Thank God, it's working,* Sam thought. He'd been correct in his assumption that he needed a team of believers working together to have any real effect on the monster. But how long could they keep this up?

The remnant stared at him, eyes bulging. "You know I'll find a way through this, priest, and when I do, each of you will burn." He pointed at Bella and Pamela in turn. "Especially you two little girls." His blood-eyed gaze burned into each of them as he stared them down one by one. "You can't beat me. All you can do is hold me for so long until one of you weakens and breaks the chain. And when you do..." he lifted a finger and pointed at Pamela, "... you'll all die."

"He's scaring me." Pamala's lips trembled, and her eyes watered as if she was on the verge of tears. "His eyes... they can see into me."

"Hey, Pamela," Bella called out to her. "Be strong. Look at me instead. I'm just a kid, too, but we can do this."

Sam wondered if Bella had ever been 'just a kid.' No kid he had ever met before possessed anywhere near as much understanding of things as she did. "She's right," he said to the others. "Hold tight, and he can't hurt us."

"Yeah. Did you hear that, motherfucker?" Ricky yelled out. "You can't hurt us."

Rathburn leaped forward into the air and landed on the stage with a loud bang that made everyone take several steps back. Penny ran after him, keeping her sword raised and the fiery connection between them unbroken.

Sam frowned as he realized the implication. If the Remnant could move within the protected circle they'd created, maybe he could escape if he pushed them far enough apart. They needed to keep the circle tight.

Rathburn ripped off his black cloak, revealing blackened, discolored flesh that appeared as though it smoked and crumpled in pieces from his bones. He turned and stood directly in front of the rock star. "See what your father did to me, Ricky?"

Ricky closed his eyes, clearly not wanting to view the grotesque monster before him. His arms, holding the sword, shook.

"What his father did has no bearing on you and him. Just let it go, William Rathburn. Stop all this senseless killing." Sam glanced at the faces of the rest of the formation. How long would they be able to keep this up? If his arms were starting to ache from fatigue, let alone the sting in his wounded hands as he gripped the sword, how was it for the little girls?

The Remnant ignored him and kept his attention on the rock star. "Nothing to say, Ricky?" Rathburn removed his shirt and kicked off his shoes. "Look at me!"

The Remnant's skin barely covered his body, glimpses of what lay beneath showing through cracks that smoldered and glowed like hot embers. As Sam watched, pieces of his charred flesh flaked and fell off. But what was probably the most disturbing quality about the Remnant was that as quickly as he burned, his flesh and bones healed, creating a continuous cycle of destruction and renewal.

Sam thought of Hugo and how he needed several hours to regenerate to his healed form. But Rathburn… did he ever fully heal and get a break from the pain of perpetually nearly dying? Ricky's father may have dropped the napalm bomb that had incinerated the man, but who the hell was the sick demonic bastard that had him trapped in the agonizing moment between living and dying? William Rathburn might have started out as a psychopath, but no wonder the man was now insane.

Bella and Pamela squeezed their eyes shut, the pair of them in danger of dropping their swords. "Don't look at him, girls," Sam instructed.

"There's more to see yet." Wrath tore off his pants, revealing his fully naked figure. "See what your fucking father did to me?" He pointed down between his legs. "Yeah, no fucking cock or balls here."

"Definitely keep your eyes closed, girls," Sam said from the side of his mouth.

Both girls were starting to cry from the strain of holding their swords up and the horrors of being so near Rathburn. The stench of napalm, smoke, and burning flesh hung heavy in the air. It threatened to turn Sam's stomach and appeared to be doing the same to the others. Pamela was gagging, but to her credit, she kept her sword pointed up with one hand while she covered her mouth with the other. If the circle broke, would he be able to contain the Remnant on his own? Where the hell was Jupiter or even the bullet man? Weren't they supposed to be doing something to help? Or had everyone else abandoned the resort, and they were on their own?

Rathburn pranced around inside the circle, daring everyone to look at him. "You're all going to die," he shouted gloatingly. "And then I'll go after everyone and everything you've ever loved. All your kitties and your puppies and even your fucking Christmas presents. They'll all be burned to a crisp with a snap of my fingers." He snapped his fingers in front of Pamela's face, creating a loud cracking sound as his digits literally snapped and crumbled to pieces—and then immediately reformed.

Pamela screamed and dropped her sword. It clattered on the stage, breaking the connection. The lightning crackling between the swords flickered, dimmed, and disappeared.

Rathburn grinned, showing a row of blackened and broken teeth as he looked at Ricky and spread his arms wide. "It's showtime."

"Regroup," Sam shouted. "Everybody regroup!" He raised his sword high in the air once again, and said a prayer to Saint Michael, begging for assistance. The cross began to glow as his prayer was answered, but it was already too late. The remnant ignited a flame over his hand and turned to Ricky.

A breeze blew across the stage, making the flames in Rathburn's hand sputter and nearly go out a second before Hugo shouted, "Hey, you burned-out fuck." Faster than Sam could see, he barreled into Wrath and knocked him to the ground.

"Now!" Sam shouted as his sword ignited once again. He pointed it at the three others who held theirs ready. Lightning flashed between the swords, creating a circle of protection around the two remnants.

Pamela remained huddled on the floor, her sword laying on the wooden stage beside her. "That's okay," Sam said to her. "You've done enough today." Would four working together be enough to hold Rathburn? *Trust in God*, he reminded himself. *He is with you today.*

"I have to hand it to you, Hugo," Rathburn said. "You're one inconvenient motherfucker."

"I didn't come here for fucking conversation," Hugo said. He punched the burning man in the face, knocking the monster's head back against the stage with a loud bang.

The bullet man winced and looked at his knuckles, shaking them out as if hitting the fire remnant had hurt him.

A deep chuckle rumbled from the Remnant. "Hurts, does it? Looks like those angelic swords don't discriminate. Maybe they know you're as much of a killer as me."

He jerked his head upward and smashed his forehead against Hugo's with a loud crack. Hugo sat back, seeming dazed, but maintained his leverage over Rathburn and kept him pinned to the ground.

Both men shook their heads and studied each other.

Hugo wiped blood from his mouth and grinned at the remnant beneath him. The next punch that came his way swung wildly in his direction, and as he ducked beneath it, he swung a punch of his own. He struck Rathburn hard in the jaw with an uppercut that Sam swore should have knocked the remnant's head clean off. Instead, it broke the burning man's jaw as well as Hugo's hand.

"How's that feel?" Bullet Man asked, holding his shattered hand with his good one. "Oh, that's right, you can't talk, can you?"

A deep, growling moan came from the remnant pinned to the floor. But his rage was clear in his bulging eyes. He reached for Hugo's face, his fingers curled like claws, but a punch from Hugo's good hand knocked the monster's jaw completely off.

"Next, I'll start kicking," Hugo warned. "And mash that grotesque pumpkin you call a head into the floor."

Moaning, Rathburn tried to twist sideways and reach for his jaw, which lay on the stage about a foot away. Not giving an inch, and with his broken hands already healing, Hugo held him down.

"My sword is getting heavy." Bella moaned, sounding panicked. She had both hands clutched around the hilt, holding the blade high.

"I'll help you," Pamela said. She jumped to her feet and raced to Bella's side. Wrapping her hands over Bella's, they held the sword together.

Bella grinned. "Thanks."

"Smart thinking, girls," Sam said.

"How long do we keep doing this?" Ricky called out. While the girls had figured out how to help each other, the three adults were quickly tiring.

The floor shook with the sound of thunder as something heavy moved beneath the stage. Sam caught Sister Penny's worried glance.

"How much longer do you think this building will stand?" Penny asked.

"I don't even want to think about that," Sam replied. He also didn't want to think about how long they could maintain this barrier. The pain in his hands was making him sweat. Where the hell was Jupiter?

While Hugo seemed to be faring better in the duel than Rathburn, things could quickly change if the barrier failed again. The pain that both remnants must be experiencing as they literally broke each other was beyond his comprehension.

The backstage side door opened abruptly, and a group of soldiers and agents ran in. Sam immediately recognized Jupiter and Neptune.

"Where have you been?" Sam shouted at the lead agent.

Jupiter paused and studied the flaming swords and the web of lightning connecting the five people surrounding the two remnants. He glanced at the priest and nodded. "Well done, Father. I'd never have thought of that."

It was Penny's idea, Sam wanted to call out, but as he opened his mouth to do so, the ceiling and floor began to creak. Everyone looked up anxiously as a sprinkling of plaster fell around them. If they were to leave quickly, they would have to break the protective barrier. And if they did that, Rathburn would be free to burn them all. *Dear God, if you can hear me now, I could do with a miracle.*

"Get Rathburn over the trap door, *now*!" Neptune shouted and indicated the area on the floor a few feet away.

Sam looked at her, confused. What difference would that make? Was the pit to Hell open beneath the stage? "Shift the circle," he shouted. "On three," he instructed. They needed to do this tightly. They were running out of time. "One... two... three!"

Bullet Man's punches came quicker and harder as he struck Rathburn, giving the burning man no chance to recover from a single blow before being on the receiving end of the next one. "This will be your last fucking day on this planet, you depraved pyromaniac." Hugo grunted as he abruptly stood and kicked Rathburn's head so hard everyone surrounding him heard the bone cracking.

Rathburn left the floor for a split second before he landed on his back with a sickening thud on the trap door built into the stage.

At the same time, Sam and the three other sword bearers moved position quickly and surrounded Rathburn before he could set the stage ablaze.

Hugo took a step back and pointed at the demonic remnant. "You're finished."

With a deafening howl, Rathburn sprang to his feet and ran at Bella and Pamela.

The girls shrieked but huddled together and held their ground. The remnant bounced backward as if he'd hit an invisible barrier. He landed hard on his backside in the middle of the trap door.

"Now!" Neptune shouted into her communication device. "Jupiter, we have the target in position. I repeat, do it *now*!"

Sam glanced sideways, looking for where Jupiter had disappeared when the trap door abruptly opened beneath the Remnant.

Rathburn flailed and caught the edge of the floor, stopping himself from falling into the dark gap below. Glaring at Ricky, he began to crawl back out.

"Oh, no, you don't," Hugo shouted. He rushed into the protective circle and kicked the remnant so hard the monster's head flew off. The severed cranium bounced against the barrier, making Ricky flinch on the other side, and then it tumbled into the hole in the floor, following its detached body.

"Get back," Neptune shouted, running to shield the two girls. An explosion rocked the stage, and a high-pitched scream filled the air. A billowing white mist flew out of the hole as the temperature dropped what felt like a hundred degrees. Sam staggered back and covered his face. Then, as suddenly as the icy mist had appeared, it was gone.

Sam cracked open an eyelid as he lowered his hand from his face. The lightning was gone. So was any sign of Rathburn. Around the edge of where the trap door had been, a white substance glinted, reminding him of ice particles.

"Are you okay?" he asked Bella, dropping his sword to the floor and moving toward her.

She and Pamela nodded, safely shielded by Agent Neptune, who had crouched over them.

"Woo-hoo!" An excited voice shouted from below the stage. "Take that, you psycho motherfucker."

That sounds like Jupiter. Sam cautiously stepped toward the edge of the gap in the floor and looked down, as did Penny, Ricky, Neptune, and the two girls.

"What the fuckdammit was that?" Sam snapped.

Ricky looked as white as a sheet and was about to pass out.

Agent Jupiter, as well as several soldiers, stood in the dimly lit room below the stage. Directly beneath the trap door was a large metal cylinder. The lid was closed, but whisps of icy mist swirled from the sides and edges.

"Liquid nitrogen," Jupiter explained. He rapped his knuckles on the cylinder, creating a metallic banging sound. "We thought our fiery friend could use a time out for eternity at about oh... minus three hundred fifty degrees Fahrenheit." He grinned. "I didn't think it would blow quite like that when he hit the surface, though."

"I told you," Agent Neptune said, shaking her head. "When something very hot and something very cold combine, it gets messy."

Jupiter gave her an expression that indicated she was killing his fun.

"Hugo gave us the idea. Rathburn won't be able to regenerate or escape as long as the refrigeration cylinder is kept cold enough to support the liquid nitrogen."

And if it's not? Sam thought. He shook his head, impressed by the ingenuity of the plan. They hadn't trapped the remnant in a pit to Hell—they'd put him on ice, literally.

"Come on." Jupiter banged on the side of the container. "Let's get this fucker back to the base and into storage as quickly as possible."

A chorus of cheers filled the room as a group of soldiers began to wheel the cylinder containing Rathburn away. Hugo ducked away from the group.

Sam and the others met Jupiter at the stairs.

"Great work, Father Sam," Jupiter's smile looked almost too wide for his face. He slapped the priest on the back and stopped in his tracks. "Look, we need to get back to the base as quickly as we can." The floor rumbled beneath their feet. "Hugo?" He surveyed the area. "Did anyone see where Hugo went?" They glanced around, but Bullet Man was nowhere to be seen.

Bella frowned, seeming sad. "He couldn't stay to say goodbye?"

"He's done his job. Time for him to go back to the shadows," Sam said. "I'm sure we'll see him again sometime."

Jupiter's gaze was hard, as if someone had ripped a prize from his grip. He nodded at Sam, then peeled away and spoke to the lead soldier. They were out of earshot, so Sam couldn't hear what was going on, but the soldier and Jupiter marched toward the stairwell, followed closely by a couple of new agents who had appeared on the scene. So, they'd wanted to capture Hugo too, after all?

The priest smiled, *Godspeed, Bullet Man.*

"Now, if everyone would get out of the damn building before it falls, that would be awesome," Neptune addressed those who remained.

Sam grabbed Bella's hand, Penny grabbed Pamela's, and within moments, the stairwells were packed with people wanting to get the hell out before the building came down on top of them.

At least we're only three floors up, Sam thought as they followed the stairs down. As soon as they were through what was left of the hotel doors on the first floor, they ran as far away from the building as they could. Neptune made it to one of the black vans first and waved Sam and his companions over, while Jupiter and several other agents disappeared inside a separate vehicle.

Sam paused, staring after Jupiter as the van he'd leaped into sped off at a speed that made the tires squeal. "Where's he going?" he asked Neptune.

"Chasing Hugo." She shook her head, confirming his suspicions. "I told him to just leave him alone, but you know Jupiter. He never listens to anyone he doesn't want to." She motioned to the open van door. "Come on, let's get you all home."

Home. That had a nice ring to it.

With what little energy they had left, Sam, Ricky, Penny, the two girls, and Neptune piled into the back of the van. If Ricky was upset about not doing yet another Christmas Eve concert, he didn't show it. He sat beside Penny, holding her hand. Everyone seemed too exhausted to talk. They were all grateful to be alive.

"It's only a short ride to the airfield, then we'll fly back to the base by chopper. Should take us just half an hour, so hold on tight," Neptune said.

Sam closed his eyes, Bella leaning against him as the van started to slowly make its way through the built-up traffic. *Thank you, God. I can finally relax.* "We'll be seeing Mommy and Nana soon," he promised the little girl, gently stroking her hair. They'd have a proper Christmas this year, after all.

"Uh... Father Sam?" Agent Neptune said, sounding uncharacteristically nervous suddenly. "There's something you should probably know..."

Chapter 19

Sam raced through the helipad doorway and into the military base faster than he'd ever run in his life.

Ricky, Penny, and a group of people followed behind, their footfalls echoing off the walls as they ran.

Sam clutched Bella tighter in his arms. She was silent, her eyes wide, holding onto him tightly as he rushed down the hall. She'd tried to tell him, hadn't she? His smart, empathetic, demon-sensitive adopted daughter had tried to tell him something bad was going on.

But he hadn't listened.

He replayed their conversation under the Christmas tree what seemed like a lifetime ago.

"Don't you like the baby?" he asked.

Bella shook her head.

"Why not, love?"

"It's trying to kill Sarah," she whispered.

Jesus Christ. Jesus Fucking Christ, he thought, then immediately cringed at taking the Lord's name in vain. *Sorry, God, but how stupid could I be?*

He'd been so caught up in racing off to Vegas and chasing the Remnant that he'd lost sight of what was right in front of his face and truly important—Sarah and his unborn child.

I'm so sorry, baby. I'm so sorry. We're coming.

He slowed his pace as they came to a heavy door. "Are you sure it's Abaddon?" he asked Agent Neptune, who jogged by his side.

She nodded as she entered a sequence of numbers onto the keypad, and the door clicked open. "Pretty sure, yeah."

"*Why the fuck* didn't you tell me right away," he shouted at the agent.

Bella burst into tears. "I'm sorry, Daddy, I tried. I don't want Sarah to die."

Fuckdammit. Sam closed his eyes for a second and prayed for strength. "I'm sorry, sweetheart." He smoothed his hand down her hair, trying to soothe her. "I didn't mean you. Sarah's going to be okay." *Please, God, don't make that a lie.*

They rushed through the door and into the main area of the base belonging to the church. Alarms were blaring, and people seemed to be hurrying everywhere, including soldiers carrying semi-automatic rifles.

"Clear a path," Neptune barked, waving her arms in the air. "They're evacuating all non-essential personnel," she explained to Sam as people parted in front of them, creating a way through.

He glanced at her. "It's that bad?"

The ground shook beneath their feet, and the walls trembled, making an ominous rumble.

Neptune steadied herself and caught his gaze. "Yes."

They raced toward the medical area, people dodging hurriedly out of their way. Sam's pulse thudded through his veins as he tried not to think, least of all about what was waiting for him in Sarah's room at the clinic. *Just breathe.*

They crossed the central courtyard with the Christmas tree, which sparkled with lights and decorations, ready for the festivities to begin the next morning. Sam couldn't help thinking about a similar tree he'd seen a year ago when a demon had invaded. This one stood peaceful and still, a reminder that despite all the chaos choking the world, life went on, wrapped in the steady certainty of belief and rituals.

The hallway leading to Sarah's room was filled with soldiers guarding the perimeter. A group of sisters and brothers were gathered outside the room, hands joined as they focused on prayer. Medical staff lingered near the observation window. It was hard to see inside the room without going closer. Ena was banging on the glass, but the sound was strangely muted and distorted. "Sarah!" she shouted, sounding nearly hysterical. "Sarah!"

"Sam!" Mother Agnes clutched his free arm. Her face was seamed with exhaustion and tight with panic. "I'm so sorry. I should never have sent you away." She closed her eyes and shook her head. "It's Sarah. She won't let us in—"

Sam shoved her hand off his arm and stepped toward the window. She could be sorry if she wanted. Everybody could. But none of them were to blame. That weight rested solely on his shoulders. He'd left when his instinct had screamed for him not to. Or maybe that had been God's desperate voice talking. Or maybe that's what he'd like it to be because it was easier than the truth. He'd seen the signs with his own eyes, hadn't he? The signs of possession.

Bella tensed in his arms as they drew near enough through the crowd that they could see into the room. The window shimmered as if covered by a translucent barrier. But on the other side, Sarah lay on her bed, writhing. Bright red blood covered her thighs and stained her white sheets and gown. Her eyes were closed, but even with the lids shut, a demonic red glow shone through the lashes.

Sarah tensed, arching her back as she let out an agonized shriek that made the hairs on the back of Sam's neck prickle. The floor shook as the scream echoed through the room and down the hallway.

Oh God, no. Oh God, oh God, oh God, Sam thought. He stood watching, frozen in horror, as a fresh wave of blood ran down her thighs.

"Sarah," he whispered.

SARAH WRITHED IN THE hospital bed, screaming at the top of her lungs as the pressure in her abdomen intensified to the point where it felt the baby would smash its way out. "Sam..." She moaned. "Where are you?" If she focused hard enough, she swore she could feel him nearby. Or maybe that was the Other she was feeling, tricking her. It was always with her, the dark Other. Crawling inside her body and twisting her mind.

He's gone. He left. He's a liar like all the rest, the deep voice whispered like a poisonous snake.

The voice wasn't her own, and it wasn't the baby's. She was certain she felt her child's thoughts sometimes, and it was not like the tricks the dark Other liked to play. The baby was like a soft kiss or the fluttering wings of a butterfly. Gentle, curious… and frightened.

The 'frightened' part cut through the haze of pain that clouded Sarah's mind. Her baby was scared of the Other thing that had been growing inside her along with the child, lying to them both by saying everything was fine.

It's not fine, it's not. I'm bleeding. She looked at her fingers, wet with blood, and knew it was not a trick this time. *Help. I need help.*

The wave of pain came again, like a cold, sharp knife that traveled up her spine from her pelvis. She clenched her teeth and tried to breathe through the agony. *Honest to God, it feels like my back is breaking. What the fuck is happening? Am I going into labor already?*

A distant thumping sound, like fists banging on a window, made her open her eyes again.

"Sarah!" her mother screamed over the intercom. "Sarah, please let us in. Sarah!"

"No," Sarah whispered. "You're safer out there." If she was being honest, it wasn't just the baby who was frightened. She was scared too.

Frightened she might die.

Frightened she might live and see what horror she was bringing into the world.

You don't need them. You don't need anybody but me, the Other whispered in soft, sinuous tones.

"Shut up!" Sarah growled and ground her teeth together. What had she done to put herself in this mess?

You seduced a priest, you filthy slut. And now look where you are. The dark voice laughed, making the baby curl into a frightened ball.

"Sarah, pleeease," her mother sobbed. "I don't want you to die."

Maybe I deserve it? she thought darkly. Then, a second thought whispered through her mind. *Maybe you do, but does the baby?*

Fight! You need to fight!

The pounding on the window continued. "Fight him, Sarah. Fight him for the baby!" her mother pleaded.

"Fight..." Sarah moaned. "I need to... fff—" She stopped then continued, "*Help me!*" She shrieked, arching her back as the agony threatened to rip her in half.

The floor rumbled like an Earthquake.

"Sarah, listen to me... Sam is here with Bella," her mother pleaded.

She's a liar. They're all liars.

"Look at the window," Ena pleaded. "They're right here, I swear."

Sarah screamed as pain shot through her stomach like someone squeezed her insides with a vice. "Fuck off, you stupid old bitch," a demonic voice emitted from the depths of her throat.

She clamped a hand over her mouth and looked at the window. *No, that wasn't me.* She shook her head. *I didn't mean it. It wasn't me.* Her mother's tearful, swollen face stared at her through the glass. But beside her stood Sam, and in his arms was Bella.

"Sarah, please... let us in, baby. I love you." Filled with pain and exhaustion, Sam's voice carried through the intercom.

It's a trick. Don't listen to the lies, lies, lies, lies, lies... the Other's words whispered through her mind. She clutched at her head, straining to keep her eyes focused on the window.

Bella reached toward her and placed her hand on the barrier. The look of fear and devastation on her heart-shaped face cut at Sarah's heart like a knife.

"*Mommy!*" the little girl shrieked. "*Don't leave me!*"

Sarah reached her hand toward the window. "Oh, Bella." She sobbed. *My Bella.* Images flashed through her mind of seeing the little girl sitting alone and scared in the abandoned daycare at the mall, knowing Bella's mother had died at the hands of Abaddon and not knowing how to tell her. *Don't let it happen again. You made a promise. FIGHT!*

Pain shot through her again as she rolled onto her side and faced the door.

"My baby," she whimpered, placing a hand on her distended abdomen. "My babies need me. My babies..." She paced both feet on the cold tiles and slipped off the bed, landing hard on her knees. Something was wrong with her legs. She couldn't feel her feet. Blood was everywhere. All over her and the floor. Pouring down her thighs. *Fight goddammit!* She looked up at the window. Bella's blue eyes were filled with tears that spilled down her face as she frantically banged on the shield that protected the room. *I did that. I need to undo it.* She kept her eyes on the little girl. *My Bella, don't cry. I'm coming.*

Sarah dragged herself toward the door, leaving a smear of blood behind her as she went. One hand, two. Inch by inch. The agony threatened to make her pass out. It shook the floor. Rocked the bed. And made the medical equipment rattle and ping. *My Sam. My Bella. My baby.* She kept her eyes trained on the door. Sam, Bella, and her mother stood there now, just on the other side. She felt them there. Their desperation, the prayers of the others, calling out to her, giving her strength. *So close now. One more try.*

Give up, Sarah. You can't win, so why try? the demon whispered. She recognized him now. The demon. His voice. *All the blood, all the pain... you're hurting yourself, and for what? You're going to die anyway.*

Her hand trembled as she reached for the door, fingers straining to touch it. She was tired, so weak. She might die, but the demon was wrong about one thing. She'd roast in Hell before she'd let him take her babies.

"Fuck you, Abaddon," she shouted as she lurched forward with the last of her strength and pressed her hand against the door.

It popped open with a click.

Sarah let her upper body fall against the floor.

The tiles were blessedly cool against her cheek.

Noise surrounded her.

Soft hands.

Sam.

"Sarah, oh God. Sarah." He touched her face. She wanted to turn to him and tell him how much she loved him, but she was so tired now. *So tired...*

"Get her to the emergency surgery, *STAT*," a woman shouted. *Doctor Stevens?* "We're losing her."

No, I'm not going anywhere, Sarah thought as she was lifted into the air and placed on something blessedly soft. *I'm not leaving my babies. I am* not *leaving.*

The pain was hardly anything now.

Why would she want to go?

She opened her eyes and found Sam's blue ones staring down at her as she was hurriedly wheeled to the operating room. His face was pale, as if he'd lost a lot of blood, and his beard needed a trim. She wanted to run her fingers through it, but she seemed to have lost control of her limbs.

"Get it out. Get it out now. He's killing us," she whispered to him.

My Bella, my baby, my Sam, she thought as the world went black.

Chapter 20

Sam stood outside the operating room, heart beating like a hammer as he watched the medical team wheel Sarah's stretcher through the door, and it swung shut behind them. He clenched and unclenched his jaw, trying to calm the sense of panic that had taken over.

"Bella? How about showing Pamela and Ricky that cool hiding spot you found under the Christmas tree? I'll come find you once Sarah's had the baby."

He glanced at Ricky, and caught his eye. The rock star nodded solemnly. This was no place for a child.

"Is she going to die?" Bella asked as he set her down on the floor.

"Well…" a young nurse who stood nearby said and shrugged. "She's lost a lot of blood. And she's passed out right now. But between you and me, if it comes down to a fight between your mom and the demon, my odds are on your mom." He winked at the little girl and handed Sam a pair of scrubs. "Put them over your clothes, then come in when you're done. I'll help you scrub up. Mother Agnes says you need to be present."

Fucking right, I do. Sam nodded and took his long coat off. He handed it to Ricky.

The rock star took it and then grabbed Bella by the hand. "Come on, Silver Bell, let's go find where Penny and Pamela went, and you can show us that tree Sam mentioned."

"Silver Bell?" Bella giggled.

"Silver Bell, Silver Bell," the singer crooned. "It's Christmas time in the city…" Ricky danced Bella down the hall and through the exit.

Sam smiled as gratitude filled his heart. *Thank you, God, for helping me save Ricky Gibson today.* Not only was he a great friend, but he also truly had a gift for entertaining.

He pulled the blue shirt over his black top and moved the cross so it hung on the outside. The silver shone as the artificial lighting reflected in its perfect lines.

"That cross really does suit you," a man's voice said from behind him.

Sam spun on his heel while pulling the loose scrub pants over his boots and black pants.

Brother Trevor had arrived with a young-looking group of priests and Sisters of Mercy. "What, is everyone coming here to watch?"

Brother Trevor waved a finger. "Are we not allowed to show concern, Father? The outcome of this situation affects us all." He smiled. "We've come to assist with prayer. Don't worry. You won't even know we're there."

"Okay," Sam said, not quite certain how to respond. He stared at the door to the operating room for a moment and took a deep breath.

The past few days had been a whirlwind, and as much as he didn't want to listen to his gut, it wouldn't stop telling him this was far from over. He closed his eyes and bowed his head. "*Dear Father, who art in heaven. Please let Sarah and the child survive this ordeal. I pray that your strength will protect them through this trial and assist us in defeating the evil that has taken root inside her. Please also watch over Bella, and, I know it's a huge request, but please try and keep her from wandering where she shouldn't. Amen.*"

Maybe that last bit was asking too much, even for the Lord.

He opened his eyes, his head spinning from a cocktail of lack of sleep, battle injuries, and panic he couldn't calm. This afternoon, he'd battled and caught a remnant, a creature he'd never heard of until a day ago. And now, Abaddon had possessed his wife through his unborn son. The fact that any one of these things was far from normal wasn't lost on him, nor was his seemingly endless winning streak. *How long can my luck keep running?*

The sound of marching feet approaching him down the hallway drew his attention. "No," he muttered as a group of soldiers took up position on either side of the door. *What the hell are they doing here? Bullets won't do shit to kill a demon like Abaddon.* But who knew what to expect when the baby was born? Maybe it was best to be cautious.

The male nurse appeared from Sarah's operating room. "Sam, it's time."

He nodded and took careful steps through the double doors. A medical team surrounded Sarah, with Mother Agnes and Ena, who were already there, dressed in scrubs. Two different heart monitors beeped steady rhythms, one faster than the other. The nurse helped Sam scrub his hands clean for a minute in the wash station and don a mask, then guided him to where Sarah's head and neck were visible on one side of a curtain that had been erected to shield her lower body from view. "Whatever you do, don't look over the curtain," the nurse whispered in Sam's ear.

He nodded and took up position beside the nun and his mother-in-law. The three of them formed a triangle around Sarah's head, with him taking the point position. Neither of them said anything as he joined hands with them both. *The Father, the Son, and the Holy Ghost*, he thought. They each knew why they were there and what was at stake.

Sarah's arms were spread wide on either side of her on the operating table, reminding him of Jesus on the cross. An IV pumped blood from a drip bag into one arm. The other had a blood pressure cuff wrapped around her bicep and another IV. Electrodes and wires sprang from her head like a mechanical medusa. A mask was fitted over her mouth and nose, giving her oxygen. She remained unconscious, which Sam figured was a blessing. If he had to see her scream and cry like he'd witnessed ten minutes prior, he'd lose what was left of his mind.

"Let's begin while she's still stable," Doctor Stevens instructed. She lifted a scalpel from the tray. "Pray that she lets us cut through."

Sam closed his eyes and began to pray like he'd never prayed before in his life.

RICKY SAT ON A comfortable chair a few feet from Bella and Pamela in some kind of kid's play area connected to the medical suite, wishing for something strong to drink and a long lay down. The base was a maze. He'd already taken a few wrong turns, so he'd been happy when he'd found Sister Penny and Pamela in the room. Upon seeing Ricky, however, Penny had quickly left, saying she had to help the others prepare, leaving him in charge of both children. Prepare for what? Ricky didn't want to think about it, but after seeing Sarah's red eyes and hearing her screams, he had a good idea of where that was headed. At least the alarms had stopped blaring, and the floors had stopped shaking, both of which he'd taken as a good sign. Ricky hadn't seen many people around, though, except soldiers and the creepy agents in black suits.

Pamela and Bella sat on a couch, eating snacks they'd found in the room and giggling at the cartoons on the television. So far, he had endured an hour of *Dennis the Menace* on Nickelodeon, and drinking Tab.

What's the point of Tab if you have nothing to mix with it?

Penny told him she'd be back soon, but he wondered if her definition of soon was the opposite of what he found acceptable. The girls constantly chatted and giggled like there was nothing at all unusual going on, although he had to admit Bella seemed a bit more subdued than usual. Every once in a while, she'd glance at the door, probably waiting for news from her dad.

God, give me the resiliency of children. Ricky ached from his head to his toes, and every now and then, he felt his eyelids droop.

"Hey Ricky, let's see what's on MTV," Pamela suggested.

He jerked awake. *Best fucking idea I've heard since I got in this room.* "Awesome."

Bella pressed buttons on the remote until she located the music station. She pointed at the video playing, which showed long-legged women in tight clothing dancing. "Hey, they look like Penny," she squealed as Robert Palmer's "Addicted to Love" played on the television.

Ricky smiled. "Now, this is what I call music."

As one song ended, another started. Ricky's eyelids grew heavy, and his breathing regular. "Hey Bella..." he murmured.

Images of demons with red eyes running after him through long corridors flashed crazily through his mind. The demons growled, low and deep. They were nearly upon him—

He jerked awake with a start, realizing the growl he'd heard was his own snoring. *Shit.* "Bella!" he called out and quickly saw he was the only one in the room. "Not again," Ricky moaned. "Bella, don't you ever do what you're told?" He sighed as he forced his aching body out of the comfortable chair. *I love you, Bella, but sometimes you're a mischievous little shit.*

"Here he is," Doctor Stevens announced.

A tsunami of relief washed over Sam as the sound of a newborn baby's cries filled the room. "He's okay?"

Doctor Stevens lifted the baby above the curtain so they could see him. The baby looked large for being premature, but then again, Sam hadn't ever been present at a child's birth before. The child wriggled and screamed, his tiny hands forming little fists. Perfect, pink, healthy. He wasn't sure what he'd expected. Maybe the baby having a tail or red eyes or something. But he appeared to be normal in every way.

"Oh my God, he's beautiful," Ena cried as one of the nurses brought him around for them to see closer.

A different nurse handed him a pair of scissors. "Father Sam, would you be so kind as to cut the umbilical cord?"

Sam nodded numbly. *Who was he to conduct such a task?* "Um, shouldn't the doctor do this?"

"Just snip here. She'll then do it properly. It's a Western culture thing," the nurse assured him.

He complied, and they took the newborn away for a couple of minutes and brought him back wrapped up in a towel. "Congratulations."

"I can't believe this," Sam said, looking at the baby swaddled in his arms. "He really is okay?" *Thank you, Lord.* His body shook as he realized that he now had a son. *I'm a father and not the priestly kind. My son.*

"His breathing seems fine despite his age," Doctor Stevens said. "But we'd like to keep checking on him over the next few days, to be sure."

Ena took the baby from Sam and started to rock him. "Look at that hair." Tears of joy streamed quietly down her cheeks as she stroked the child's dark locks, which stuck out from the top of his head like a Brillo brush.

Sam bent down and kissed Sarah's forehead. "You did it, love. He's here, and he is perfect." She remained unconscious, eyes closed. The only heart rate monitor beeping in the room now was hers. But it was steady.

"It will be a little while before she wakes up," Doctor Stevens said in a gentle voice. "She's been through a lot of trauma."

Sam nodded as the doctor moved back behind the curtain to finish up with whatever was needed now to help Sarah. As long as she did wake up, he was good with that.

"We should do a blessing," Mother Agnes spoke quietly. "For the mother as well as the child."

"Yes," Sam agreed. Both Sarah and the baby seemed fine, but he didn't trust that Abaddon had suddenly disappeared and left them all alone, even if the baby had been born before reaching full term.

One of the sisters brought him a silver bowl and placed it on a tray. "Holy water," she murmured quietly.

"Do you have a name for the child?" Mother Agnes asked.

"Not yet." They'd discussed many options, including Paul after Sarah's friend and workmate Paulie, who had perished in the Springfield Mall massacre. That one made Sam a bit uncomfortable, though, as he didn't think Sarah remembered she'd killed the man while possessed.

He dipped his fingers into the holy water and then made the sign of the cross on Sarah's forehead—and breathed a secret sigh of relief when her eyes didn't pop open, glowing red, nor did she leap out of bed and begin crawling on the ceiling.

"Lord God, source of all life and love, we thank you for the gift of new life that Sarah has brought into the world. We ask for your blessings upon her as she embraces the role of motherhood," he began the Blessing of the New Mother, during which it seemed like no one dared to breathe.

A few minutes later, when he was done and Sarah remained stable, he turned to the baby, whose dark eyes were quietly watching him. "Can you move the towel?" he asked Ena.

She did so, exposing the baby's tiny chest and wriggling arms and fists to the air.

Sam created the sign of the cross on the baby's forehead and chest with holy water. *"Lord God, creator of all, we thank you for the gift of this child. We ask for your blessings upon this precious life, that they may grow in health, wisdom, and grace. Watch over them, protect them from harm, and guide them in the path of faith and love..."*

The baby began to cough.

The coughing didn't stop.

He started to turn blue in the face.

"He's choking," Ena cried out. Her frantic eyes looked at Sam and darted to the doctor. She sat him upright in her arms as both a nurse and Mother Agnes reached to take him from her.

The baby continued coughing, its mouth opened wide, and pea-green vomit suddenly spewed like a projectile all over the nurse and Mother Agnes—far more vomit than Sam had ever seen in his life coming from a person, let alone a newborn baby. Ena screamed. As she held the baby away from her, vomit continued to spew from its tiny mouth and onto the floor.

Sam stepped back automatically and grabbed his cross. The baby had stopped vomiting and had started crying, but that noise was drowned out by the screams. Both the nurse and Mother Agnes, who had taken the brunt of the green spew, stared in horror as smoke rose from their clothes and their skin melted off their bones.

"It burns!" the nurse shouted.

It happened so quickly no one had time to react. Within a minute, both women were puddles of pulpy flesh on the floor.

"Oh my God. What is happening?" one of the nurses shrieked. Everyone else in the room seemed too stunned by the rapid turn of events to say anything or even move.

The baby was now fussing like a normal newborn, while Ena rocked him and wiped the green goo from his face with the edge of the towel. Sam caught her look of uncertainty.

At the farthest reach of his mind, he could think that maybe the baby had a seriously upset stomach, but that didn't account for why the vomit-strewn pulpy mess on the floor was moving.

Squelching wetly, the sickening mixture gathered together and quickly formed a figure that possessed cloven feet and a tail. The newborn demon grew in height almost instantly.

It let out a resounding belly laugh as a pair of horns sprouted from the top of its head. "Ahh…" the demon said. "So much better. I couldn't handle being crammed inside that mewling little runt for much longer." He turned to Sam. "Hello, Father. Did you miss me?" Abaddon said in a mocking voice. "I'm baaack." His face split into a wide grin. "Wait. Something's missing." He rubbed his chin with his clawed finger, and a dark pointy beard appeared where he'd touched. "Much better."

"Get back to Hell," Sam shouted. Hand shaking, he raised his cross at the demon.

"No can do, daddy-o." The demon conjured a pitchfork in its left hand and pointed it at Sam. "Two can play that game."

Daddy-o? The priest shook his head. *Come on Sam, don't just fucking stand there.* He began a prayer of banishment, only to have the wind knocked out of him by a wave of heat and flames that shot from the end of the pitchfork and slammed him against the wall before the first few syllables left his lips.

"Jesus Christ!" Ena jumped back out of the way, shielding the baby.

"No, I'm A-bad-don," the demon growled, seeming annoyed. "Though I don't think we've had the pleasure of meeting before." He seemed about to hold out his hand to Ena to shake. A glance at Sam changed his mind. "I'd love to stay and chat, Grandma, but Daddy is a bit pissed off with me."

Sam looked down at his singed scrub top. *Please, God, haven't we had enough of fire for one day?*

The medical team stepped aside as the demon headed for the door. Without anything to defend themselves, they put their lives before acts of stupidity. All except for the lead doctor.

"We should have killed you in utero when we had the chance," Doctor Stevens spat and charged at Abaddon with a scalpel.

"Seriously?" the demon asked. He made to lunge at the doctor but paused as a group of soldiers entered the room.

"Everyone, out," one of the soldiers commanded. "*You…* put that fucking pitchfork down."

Sam looked at Sarah, who he knew wasn't in any condition to defend herself or go anywhere.

He leaned over her and raised the cross again as a shield. "Get behind me, Ena." One blast from that pitchfork could incinerate the three of them as well as the baby.

Doctor Stevens hastily tossed a sterilized sheet over Sarah's newly stitched-up midsection and led her team out of the room.

The soldiers aimed their weapons at the demon, who now stood five feet tall. "I won't say it again. Put the weapon down."

Abaddon stared at the squad sergeant. "What are you going to do with that? Shoot me?"

"Outside! *Outside!*" Sam shouted. *Dear Heavenly Father, protect us from the stupidity of human beings.*

He flinched as the sound of bullets echoed through the room, as the soldiers, apart from the sergeant, fired their automatic machine guns at the demonic figure.

Abaddon shrieked in a high-pitched voice. Then he fell backward and hit the floor with a thud. The pitchfork rolled from his limp hand and disappeared.

Sam shook his head. *What the hell had just happened?*

"Well, he wasn't much of a fuss, poor Mother Agnes and Sister Rachel, though," Brother Trevor said as he wheeled himself into the room. He grabbed his walkie-talkie. "Mars. We need a cleanup crew in the medical ward—"

"Damn straight you do," the soldier in charge said. He grabbed his weapon and laughed out loud as his eyes glowed red. Raising his gun, he opened fire on his squad. Caught by surprise, none of them stood a chance as the bullets ripped through the vulnerable area below their helmets and above their chest armor. Sam continued shielding Sarah with his body and the cross, ready to be the next victim of the possessed soldier, while Brother Trevor quickly wheeled back out of the room again.

A single gunshot exploded through the air, and a split second later, there was a thud. Sam dared to look. Agent Neptune stood in the doorway, a wisp of smoke rising from the barrel of her Glock. The sergeant was slumped on the ground near the rest of the soldiers, the pool of blood on the floor growing.

"Okay, you little bastard, that's enough fun for one day," Neptune yelled at Abaddon as the demon got to his feet. The scent of brimstone filled the room, drowning out the smell of antiseptic, blood, and vomit, which Sam realized might actually be a blessing.

"That's not nice. I know who my daddy is," the demon's deep voice boomed through the room as he smiled at Sam.

"I am *not* your father, you demonic reprobate," Sam shouted.

Abaddon pouted. "Rejected, discarded, so cruelly mistreated." The demon turned back to the agent holding the gun. "I think you should go and kill the other agents."

Sam glanced around and spotted agents Pluto and Earth in front of a second set of doors on the opposite side of the room, also holding pistols at the ready. The entrance was big enough for Sam to push the bed through and get Sarah out of the operating room and somewhere safer if everyone would kindly get out of the fuckdammed way.

"Why would I want to shoot my fellow agents?" Neptune asked matter-of-factly.

Abaddon shrank back in horror. "What? You can't be possessed?" He arched a brow. "Those are mighty cool glasses. Let's see what happens when I knock them off your head."

He lunged at Neptune, who stepped deftly sideways out of the way.

"Zeta team, prepare the Neutronic Ossuary," Earth called into the microphone attached to his earpiece. "We have the target surrounded."

Sam raised his brows. *What the hell is a Neutronic Ossuary?*

Pluto and Earth kept their weapons trained on Abaddon, not wavering in their grips as they made their way further into the room. But if the soldier's sub-machine guns had no effect on the demon, what would their pistols do? Maybe they simply wanted to keep him occupied?

That was fine by Sam. The longer they kept the demon's attention off him, the more time he had to get Sarah and the baby out of there. The child remained quiet but alert, protected in Ena's arms.

As the agents moved away from the door, Sam tried to push the bed in that direction. He let out a grunt as it didn't budge. A quick look down showed that the brakes were on. *Of course.* While he stepped on each of the four brakes to release their hold on the wheels, Ena hurriedly used her free hand to move the IV bags from their freestanding poles to one on the bed.

The three agents stopped a few feet from Abaddon, dodging him as he swiped at their heads, trying to knock their glasses off.

So those glasses really do something, eh? Sam thought. *They aren't just for looking cool at night? I wonder how they work and where I can get a pair?* Not having to worry about being possessed would be a good thing for everyone.

Doctor Stevens crept back into the room, using the far doorway that Sam was trying to leave through. "Quick, Sam," she urged him while grabbing the opposite end of the bed.

"Hey! Where the hell you think you are going, Daddy-o?" Abaddon shouted.

Sam ignored him until they were nearly out of the room and into a hallway. The three agents still aimed their weapons at the demon, but Abaddon wasn't doing his usual tricks to fight back. All the occupants in the room should be obliterated by now and turned into mush on the walls. Maybe the bullets inside the agents' pistols were the ones he'd anointed back at the casino in Vegas. Could Abaddon sense something like that? But if that was the case, and the demon was afraid to get shot by them, why didn't the agents just put him down?

"Can you take Sarah?" he asked the doctor.

"Sure. Some help, please?" She gestured at two nurses who stood nearby.

A man and woman from her team took over from Sam and began pushing and pulling the bed through the double doors. Sam moved in front of Ena and the baby, shielding them as they escaped the room with Sarah.

Abaddon stomped his foot on the floor, making the equipment in the room rattle. "I want my mama." His eyes shifted between the three agents. He took a swing at the smallest target, Pluto.

The agent ducked his head and fired a shot at the demon.

"Hey, we want him alive," Earth yelled. "Remember what Jupiter said?"

The bullet chipped one of Abaddon's horns, causing him to roar.

"Maybe he should be here instead of chasing the Bullet Man in Vegas," Pluto grunted as the demon crashed into him, knocking him to the floor.

Abaddon raised his large cloven hoof like he was about to stomp on Pluto's head. "Stop right there, Abaddon. Orders or no orders, our bullets can kill you," Earth called out, holding his pistol in a two-handed grip.

After making sure the nursing team had retreated down the hall with Sarah, Ena, and the baby, away from the fight, Sam ducked back inside the operating room. The pitchfork was back in the demon's hands, and he was windmilling it like a shield, preventing the bullets they fired from reaching him.

Sam gripped the cross in his hands and raised it up. "Get ready to go back to Hell, you red-faced fucker."

Agent Mars burst into the room. "Hey, three stooges. The boss said to take him alive."

Sam barged into the agent. "Look what he's done already." He pointed at the bodies and blood on the floor.

"The cost of war. Abaddon put the pitchfork down. Pluto, Earth, and Neptune put your pistols away."

"No, he needs to be cast back to Hell," Sam countered.

"We need to find out what makes him tick," Mars grunted so only Sam could hear.

"What? You intend to put him on ice, too?" First remnants, then demons. What was next on their list? Aliens? What a curious idea, if not a stupidly dangerous one. "Demons can only be contained in a human Vessel or banished back to Hell," he explained.

Then, another thought hit him. *The agency had wanted this to happen, hadn't they?* That's why they'd been allowed onto the base. The agents didn't care about him being the new Specialist and helping fight for their cause. It wasn't him they'd wanted at all. Sarah had been their objective, in the hopes that she might still possess demon energy that they could extract and experiment on. At the cost of her life and that of his baby's? *Dear, God above, that's cold.* He stared dumbfounded at the agent. Had Mother Agnes known? There was no way to know now.

"I suggest we usurp Agent Mars," Pluto said.

I suggest we burn this whole agency to the ground, Sam thought.

Abaddon let out a thundering belly laugh.

Sam shook his head. The situation had gone pear-shaped in what should have been an easy task. Ignoring the others, he held his silver cross before his face. "In the name of God, I command you to return to the depths..."

Blinding pain shot through his skull as Mars's pistol smashed him in the side of the face. Sam hit the floor and lay there blinking as the room swayed around him. *Fuckdammit. The asshole hit me.*

The demon jumped at the agent. Using his claws, he ripped the dark glasses from Mars's face and stared into his exposed eyes.

"Who's the boss now?" the demon asked.

Goose bumps rose on Sam's arms at the sound of the demonic growl that came from Abaddon.

Unable to turn away, Mars's eyes flashed red.

Sam watched hopelessly as the asshole agent spun away from Abaddon and shot Earth through the head. The young agent fell lifeless to the ground.

Neptune and Pluto raised their weapons before Mars could aim at them and fired several times until they unloaded their clips into the agent. Mars slumped to the floor, adding to the rapidly escalating pile of bodies on the tiles.

A breeze blew through the room as the scent of brimstone increased.

"Shit. Abaddon's gone!" Neptune yelled, sounding frustrated. "We had him *right there.*"

Sam looked around the room. In the few seconds the agents had killed each other, Abaddon had managed to slip away from them all.

"Shit. He's faster," he muttered. "He gets stronger with everyone he kills."

"Okay, we need to find where he went," Neptune said, reloading her gun.

"Well, that wouldn't be a problem if you'd killed him when you had the chance, now would it?" He rubbed the side of his face where Mars had pistol-whipped him. Fuckdammit! It hurt when people did that.

Neptune gave him a hand up and held him by the shoulders until he was steady on his feet. She looked earnestly into his eyes. "Father Sam, I know you're tired, and you have every right to be upset after everything that's gone on. But trust me when I say this is serious. This base holds many top secret and dangerous things, stuff that would be catastrophic if it were to be compromised." She paused and glanced at the vomit and blood-covered floor. "That demon decimated an entire shopping mall in less than twenty-four hours. Thanks to you, we are lucky that's as far as he got. But can you imagine what will happen if he takes down the power grid here and, heaven forbid, breaks the containment seal on Rathburn's liquid nitrogen prison?"

Sam stared at her as the implications sank in. *It really could be the apocalypse this time.*

"The Remnant has only just been loaded into the storage bay, which I assure you is quite secure with multiple backups and redundancies," Neptune continued. "But he's just one example of many things we absolutely do not want to get loose thanks to Abaddon. And you know exactly what the demon is capable of at full strength."

She was right. Abaddon could break mechanical systems and remove locking seals by possessing multiple people at a time when he got strong enough. The whole place could be a flaming morgue by midnight.

God have mercy on our souls. He didn't even want to think about the fact that the demon had been growing inside Sarah and his son for the past seven months. A son he'd only held for less than thirty seconds so far.

"Promise we take him out and not try and take him alive," he said to Neptune.

She nodded grimly. "Oh, you bet your pale priest ass we will."

Chapter 21

You had one fucking job, watch the girls. Ricky Gibson berated himself as he walked down yet another long hallway, his footsteps echoing loudly in the empty space. He'd lost count of how many rooms he had checked, most of them containing someone who informed him they hadn't seen any little girls come their way. The place was like a maze. A really fucked up labyrinth that he'd thought would be easier to find his way around. Many of the doors and passageways had been locked, and some rooms were empty. But most disappointing, other than not finding the girls yet, was that none of the rooms contained a bar.

The door he was passing opened suddenly with a hiss, making Ricky's heart nearly leap out of his chest.

A man's head and torso popped out the door. He beckoned to Ricky. "Hey, you. Wanna escape this place?"

Ricky raised his eyebrows. "Is there a bar in there?" He glanced at the man's name badge, which had 'Agent Bronson' written on it.

"No." The agent darted a glance back inside the room and then at Ricky. "Just a spaceship."

Ricky shrugged and shook his head. "Two little girls haven't come by this way, have they?"

The man shook his head. "I'm gonna take this thing for a ride. I think it's from, you know, out there…" He pointed at the ceiling. "Wanna come with me?" He opened the door wider so Ricky could see inside the room.

Ricky frowned at the peculiar-looking spacecraft he could just make out through the crack in the door. It looked a bit like a space shuttle on steroids, all puffed out and somewhat spherical. *No bar and no sight of the girls. That's two strikes for two.*

He backed away and shook his head. "Nah, I'm good, thanks. I don't do spaceships, sorry." Waving the odd man off, he continued down the hallway. "This place is one crazy fucked up piece of shit," he muttered to himself. "Aliens, coo-coo." The guy was clearly a nutter.

He searched a few more rooms. These ones were so devoid of anything that even a pair of sneaky children couldn't hide in them without being seen.

Ricky placed his hand over his face and groaned. "What the hell do I tell Sam and Sarah?" They were going to kill him if he showed up without the kids.

He set off in a different direction at the next T intersection and followed another hallway. This one dumped him out into a cavernous courtyard. At least, he'd found something decent to look at, apart from Sister Penny, who wasn't around, or he'd have been having a lot more fun.

Ricky stared at the giant tree growing in the middle of the courtyard, decorated with lights, tinsel, and baubles as big as basketballs.

Was this the tree Sam had asked Bella to show him? He shuddered, thinking about the Christmas tree that had come to life at the Springfield Shopping Mall. *It's just a tree,* he told himself. *This one's not possessed.*

A slight rustling sound caught his attention. Looking back at the tree, he noticed one of the middle branches shaking slightly. His heart sped up, and he took a step backward. Maybe it was possessed. 'Cause that's how it had started with the other one. A branch wiggle here, a fallen ornament there... but that tree had never giggled.

He peered closer at the tree branch that had moved. "Hey, Bella. You trying to give me a heart attack or something?"

"Bella's not here. Go away," another girl's voice called back.

"Shush," he heard Bella's familiar voice carry itself to where he stood.

Ricky grinned. "Girls, it's okay, you're not in trouble. Please come down."

"No. We're hiding from *him*. I know he's somewhere not far away, and he's getting closer," Bella said.

Ricky shivered and glanced around the courtyard. No wonder the place seemed so empty. *Maybe I'd better climb the tree, too.* In his experience, if Bella felt something nearby that caused her to climb a giant tree, he didn't want to know what it was. But given how Sarah had looked an hour or so ago, he guessed things hadn't gone well in the delivery room, which wasn't good news for anyone.

He glanced around the courtyard again. It was filled with plants of all kinds and benches to sit on. Under different circumstances, he might have thought it looked quite pretty, but right now, he needed a weapon, something to fight a demon with if it showed up. He couldn't just hope the girls stayed safe with a demon on the loose. *Shit! Where was Father Sam and his cross when you needed him?*

"Okay, you girls stay in the tree," he called. *As if I could get them down anyway.* "I'll stay down here on lookout." *I'll be a sitting duck. That's what I'll be.* The guy's invitation to go on the spaceship ride looked better and better by the second. But even if he thought the guy was being honest about it, he doubted he could find the way back to the room.

He glanced up at the girls, and something caught his attention. A large silver cross had been positioned on top of the tree. *Yasss. A big-ass motherfucker of a cross.* But while it might come in handy when facing a demon, how the hell could he get it down?

"Hey girls," he called out to the two little daredevils. "There's a cross at the top of the tree. Any of you feeling adventurous?"

"Ricky, you're not a priest." Bella giggled.

"No, but it looks very heavy, and maybe I could bash a demon on the head or something." *Or whoever it's possessing.* Unless, of course, it did that to him, in which case he doubted he'd be able to hit himself on the head. But he didn't want to think about that anyway.

"It's a long way up there," Pamela said.

"We can do it together," Bella called out. "Like when we had the fire swords today."

Jesus. Was that today? Ricky grimaced as the branches wiggled, and the two girls started to climb up. "Please don't fall," he whispered. They sure could use some fire swords right now. *Where the hell was Penny?*

SAM RAN THROUGH THE hallways alongside agents Pluto and Neptune, wondering where the other priests, brothers, and Sisters of Mercy had gone as they searched for Abaddon. He'd last seen them gathered outside the operating room before Sarah's cesarean. Although he had his cross, when battling a demon, help wasn't just appreciated—it was necessary.

The upside was that Abaddon was vulnerable to the bullets in the agents' guns. Unless, of course, they were all out of the anointed ammo. Everything he'd prepared earlier, including the anointed swords they'd fought with, had been left at the casino. In the hurry to leave, he hadn't thought about taking anything with them. And now it was much too late. The weapons were likely buried in the debris of the doomed casino, which had probably collapsed by now.

A familiar woman stepped out of a room and joined the trio in the corridor. "Ricky and the girls have disappeared," Sister Penny told Sam.

He closed his eyes and shook his head. "Of course they have." He guessed it was probably Bella's fault, and now that she had a friend, the pair of them were probably giving Ricky hell.

Neptune pressed her earpiece and listened as they hurried. "Abaddon sighting ahead. Let's move."

The four of them turned a ninety-degree corner in the hall and stopped. A body lay face down on the floor. Neptune went ahead and gently checked the man's neck for vital signs with her fingers. It was one of the young priests. She shook her head as she looked back at Sam. "I'm sorry. At least we're on the right track."

Sam knelt and turned the body over. "Brother Peter." He had only ever met the young man in passing, but it was a shame to see him come to this end. He glanced at the others. "Sorry, I know we have to keep moving."

A crashing sound halted their journey as quickly as it restarted, and Neptune and Pluto checked their pistols before recommencing.

"Mercury, do you copy?" Neptune spoke quietly into her communication device.

Sam wondered how many agents remained. No one had managed to reach Jupiter since they'd gone their separate ways in Vegas, and the head agent had been hell-bent on catching Bullet Man. Hugo had never done them a wrong turn, though, and Sam frowned at the thought of him being used by the secret organization or kept on ice like Rathburn.

"Hold up," Agent Neptune called out softly, raising a hand up above her head. She quickly backpedaled away from the corner she had reached ahead of the others. She drew close to the group and leaned in.

"There's half a dozen armed soldiers with red eyes guarding the way."

What? Oh, no, here we go, Sam thought.

Shit, they were outnumbered and probably way out-gunned. *What I wouldn't do for some holy water and water pistols right now.* "Okay, let's think about this."

The tactic Abaddon used was effective. He possessed multiple people at once, placing them strategically around a building to secure it while he gained strength and built an army. Power would be cut off, as well as communications. If they wanted to stop him before that happened, they needed to hurry.

"I think he's a Russian spy," Pluto said.

"Who? The demon?" Penny asked, sounding incredulous.

Pluto nodded and raised his eyebrows knowingly.

"Seriously?" Neptune whispered harshly. "Your tin-foil hat conspiracies aren't going to help us right now."

"Yeah, but think about it. If that asshole takes over the base, he could communicate with the Russians, and next thing you know, we're all living in one big communist state." He cocked his gun. "Not on my watch." Pluto darted ahead.

"No!" Neptune yelled. "Stupid motherfucker."

They had no chance of stopping him, and a moment later, a chorus of gunfire erupted, ceasing almost as quickly as it started. Sam hung his head low and sucked in a deep breath. "Is there another way around?"

The small figure of Pluto returned and stood at the end of the hall. "Are you guys coming or what?"

Sam shook his head. "You took them all out with a pistol?" The agent's eyes didn't appear to glow behind his dark glasses, so he must have won the fight.

"Yeah. I didn't come first in the academy for handgun skills for nothing. As they say, it's not the size of your weapon. It's how you deliver its load."

Neptune rolled her eyes, and the group of four ventured forward into the branching hallway. The floor was littered with the bodies of dead soldiers. "Poor grunts always get the raw end of the deal."

"It was either them or us. And you can blame that little horned fucker for making us have to do this," Pluto added. "You can thank me later."

If Sam never saw another long, dimly lit, gray hallway in his life, he'd be grateful. With Pluto and Neptune at the front, sweeping the area ahead with each step, Sam and Penny hung behind a few feet. Silence filled their journey, adding to Sam's anxiety.

A door burst open ahead of them. The agents aimed at the figure entering the passageway, then quickly lowered their weapons as they realized it was Agent Mercury.

"Sorry, I lost my communication device," Mercury lowered his hands and pointed at his ear.

"You *lost* it?" Neptune asked.

"Yes, I was attacked by a short red dude with horns and a tail. I thought he was going to kill me, but he smacked me in the head with some kind of giant fork thingy and left."

"Sweet Jesus," Neptune moaned. "I'm surrounded by imbeciles. Don't you know a demon when you see one? That's the guy we're looking for."

Mercury shrugged. "Cut me some slack. There are some really weird things that live in this place. After a while, they all kinda look the same."

"We need to find him," Neptune said. "It's very important. Let's go."

Mercury nodded. "He's probably in the courtyard. I think I saw him heading that way after he hit me." He turned back to the door and opened it, waiting for the rest of them to follow.

The courtyard? That's where the tree was that Bella liked to hide in. *Shit.* "We need to hurry," Sam called out to Neptune. "My daughter might be hiding there," he explained.

She spoke into her communication device as they walked. "All teams, be on alert for the target in the courtyard, but be aware of the possible presence of children." She paused as she received a message back. Her eyes flicked to Sam. "Eyes have been monitoring movement there. Ricky Gibson and two girls were climbing the tree. No sign of Abaddon."

"They're climbing the tree?" Sam practically shouted. "That thing must be nearly thirty feet tall."

Dear God, Bella. She was afraid of heights. What the hell was she climbing a tree for? To show off to her new friend?

"Agents are on their way," Neptune promised.

He tried to calm his mind as they ran along the hallway toward the central area of the compound, but each step seemed to trigger a repeated pattern of worsening thoughts. Was she stuck? What would Abaddon do if he found her there and she couldn't escape? Leave her alone or burn the place down? Possess her like he had so many others? Kill her like he'd killed her mother and tried to do to Sarah twice? What if she fell?

Oh my God, Bella. I'm never letting you out of my sight again.

Ricky was amazed by Bella's climbing ability. The young girl traversed the branches as if the tree were a giant piece of gymnastic equipment. She reached a hand up and touched the cross, grunting as she tried to pry it from whatever mooring was holding it in place at the tree's peak.

"Please don't fall," Ricky called out. The other girl, Pamela, had stopped climbing about halfway up when the tree began to sway with their progress. But Bella had persevered and, after much struggle, was now perched on the upper branches, which bent and swayed at an alarming rate.

"It's really heavy," Bella called out as she struggled to push the cross up and off its mooring, her soft voice echoing throughout the courtyard.

Shit, what had he done, asking her to complete such a monumental task? If only she had a saw or something. *Stupid idea, Ricky.*

Bella shook the branch, causing Ricky to cringe. "Don't get hit with it!" he called out from below. What was the point if the girl got it free, only to have it fall on top of her? If the cross didn't kill her, the fall certainly would. Her foot slipped, knocking one of the baubles from where it hung on the branch below her.

The crimson-colored mirrored ball bounced as it struck several branches on the way down. It shattered when it hit the ground near Ricky, making Pamela scream. He turned and covered his face to avoid the glass shards as they sprayed everywhere.

"Bella?" he called up to the wide-eyed girl as she stared down at the broken remains of the bauble. "Why don't you forget about the cross and just climb down? We can figure something else out."

The girl shook her head frantically and clung to the tree. "I can't."

"Why not? Pamela, you come down too now, please." He gestured for them to move toward him.

"No," Bella shouted. "It's too high." The branches waved more and more furiously.

"But you climbed up there okay," Ricky said, scratching his head.

"*It's too high,*" she shrieked, sounding like she was starting to cry. Panicked, she flailed her feet, snapping the branch that supported the giant silver cross.

Oh God. "Look out!" he shouted. The cross fell from the top of the tree, crashing into branches beneath and knocking more baubles off with its weight. Pamela screamed and clutched at the tree trunk, trying to avoid being hit by falling branches, baubles, and the cross.

Ricky jumped out of the way as debris rained down around him at the base of the tree, along with the massive cross.

A man dressed like a priest burst into the courtyard from one of many entrances, followed by two sisters.

"What are you doing here?" the newcomer yelled at him, holding a silver cross up high as he glanced between the tree and Ricky.

"Ah, well—"

"Don't you know there's a demon on the loose and headed this way? You need to come with us. *Now.*"

Ah, shit. The demon was coming to the courtyard. Ricky glanced up at Bella. She seemed so terrified she was unable to speak. Her face was pale, and her eyes shut tight. She trembled so badly it shook the tree, raining pine needles on everything below.

"There's two kids stuck in the tree," Ricky pointed out.

"How did they get up there?" one of the sisters, a redhead, asked, looking upward at the disheveled Christmas tree. "All the kids know they're not allowed to do that."

"They were scared the demon was coming," Ricky explained.

"Well, that's a really dumb place to hide, isn't it?" She started kicking off her heeled boots and took off her jacket. "Why didn't you stop them?"

Because I'm an idiot? Ricky thought.

"All that mess and the demon hasn't even got here yet," she grumbled. "Clara, can you give me a boost up?" she called out to the other sister. Sister Clara did as requested, and within seconds, the red-haired sister was climbing the tree as if she'd been raised in the jungle.

"The girl at the top is afraid of heights," he explained to the priest standing next to him.

"Of course, she is," the sister named Clara said, peering upward and trying to see into the upper branches. "Because that makes sense."

Well, it does if you know Bella, Ricky thought. He'd never known Bella Light-Morris to do anything by halves. Not from the first moment he'd met her in a darkened hallway, hiding from demons in the shadows.

The other sister had reached Pamela within a few minutes and assisted her on the way down. Ricky eyed the cross that fell from the tree and walked toward it. Would he even be able to pick it up? Upon reaching it, he discovered it to be about half his height and surmised he should be able to lift something that was smaller than him.

Ricky crouched and grabbed the tip of the cross, grunting and grinding his teeth as he slowly lifted it from the floor. Sister Clara sneered, asking him what he would do with it. The other sister set Pamela down. The girl immediately made a beeline for Ricky and clung to his legs, which was awkward with the cross unbalancing him. He let it fall on the turf again and soothed the frightened girl instead.

"Okay, I'm going back up for the other one," the red-haired sister said.

"He's here!" Bella screamed from the top of the tree, making everyone freeze for a second.

Ricky spun around and saw a demon walking into the courtyard—a short red demon with horns and a tail.

"What is this? A welcoming committee?" the demon asked. "First one I've had all day. Everyone keeps trying to shoot me."

Can't think why, Ricky thought drolly.

The priest held his cross, the two sisters flanking him as they formed a triangle.

"Aren't you a little short for a demon?" Sister Clara asked.

The demon shook his head. "Really? I'm vertically challenged because I was born prematurely. Are you going to make fun of that, too? Seriously, you people need to listen to yourselves," the demon said while walking toward them. "Okay, maybe I did kill two people with the vomit, but I needed to create a decent body, and I can't just make one out of nothing, you know? I don't really like possessing people. You all kind of stink a bit. But you don't give me much choice, do you? Ever since I got out, it's been bullet here, bullet there, let's beat up poor little Abaddon and chase him around." He turned, looked up at the top of the tree, and gave a little wave. "Hey, Bella."

Abaddon? This was Abaddon? Ricky thought, struggling to process the mixture of confusion and horror churning through him. *What the hell happened to him? Why weren't they all dead?* The Abaddon he knew would have had them all skewered on branches by now and be eating their souls for dinner. This guy sounded like he needed to speak with a therapist.

The tree rustled as Bella moved to the back of the trunk, trying to get away from the demon.

"Oh, no," Abaddon raised his hand as the two sisters aimed their guns at him. "No, don't—"

The sisters opened fire, one with an assault rifle, the other with a shotgun.

Slowing down as he became riddled with bullets and salt, the demon fell forward. Tendrils of smoke rose from the holes the salt had made in his torso.

The priest separated himself from the sisters and walked until he stood above the fallen demon. Holding his cross above Abaddon, he began an exorcism prayer.

Ricky released Pamela and shook his head in disbelief. "Oh my God, they did it," he mumbled. *What the hell is going on?* "Bella, it's safe. Please try to come down."

The little girl shook her head, peering through the top branches.

"Be gone, demon!" the priest yelled at the fallen figure of Abaddon.

"Would you shut the fuck up?" the demon mumbled before flipping over and reaching up with his pitchfork. He struck the priest flat side in the groin. "Hurts, does it?" he asked as the priest grabbed his injured manhood and cried out in pain. "Now imagine if I shot you with salt and bullets. I bet you'd like it even less."

"Get away from that tree, Abaddon," Father Sam shouted as he came running full tilt into the courtyard, followed by Sister Penny and agents Neptune, Pluto, and Mercury. *Fucking asshole demon. No way are you touching my daughter.*

More agents and soldiers poured into the courtyard from different passageways. They slowed down and paused upon seeing the demon standing on the grass.

"Oh great, the cavalry is here," Abaddon muttered.

Sam caught sight of Ricky and Pamela standing together. He looked up at the tree and wished he hadn't as his heart fell into the pit of his stomach. Bella was trapped at the very top, peeking through the branches. He could practically feel her terror from here. *I need to end this quickly and get her down before she falls.*

Neptune stepped back as Sam stepped forward, grasping his cross firmly in both hands. Rage made his hands shake. No way would he let the bastard get away this time. "Abaddon, we defeated you before, and we're going to defeat you again."

"Listen. I just want to talk," the demon pleaded, putting his hands in front of him and backing up. "Can't we just talk—"

Pluto pointed his weapon at the demon. "You talk too fucking much," he said as he fired several shots at the demon.

Abaddon jumped and spun in the air, dodging the shower of bullets aimed at him. While the agent reloaded his weapon, Abaddon ran forward, grabbed the little guy by the arms, and sent him hurtling through the air into the lower branches of the Christmas tree. The entire tree shook, making Bella scream. The demon looked up at her.

Oh shit, Sam thought. *"Get away from my daughter."*

Sam sucked in a deep, steadying breath as he focused on reciting an exorcism prayer. He needed to banish the fucker, so the monster would never trouble him, his family, or anyone else again. Voices surrounded Sam as several of the other priests gathered in the courtyard quickly joined him in reciting the prayer.

The cross glowed brilliantly, far brighter than he'd ever seen it do so before. The soldiers and agents raised their weapons and pointed them at the demon. All eyes were upon Abaddon, who glared at Sam with glowing blood-red eyes, holding his pitchfork like a shield.

"I know you don't like me," Abaddon said calmly as he studied the crowd. "And I understand why, but you need to listen to me."

Sam ignored him and finished the prayer. "*Vis Christi te cogit ad inferos, daemon!*" he shouted, compelling the demon back to Hell. A beam of light sizzled from the cross. The force of it knocked Sam off his feet as it blasted into Abaddon. The demon careened backward and slammed into the tree so hard the impact created a booming sound.

The giant conifer groaned and swung backward as if it might break, but the shrill scream from the top paralyzed Sam with fear. *Bella!*

As the tree swung forward again, she lost her grip and tumbled through the air. *Oh my God, what have I done?* Sam thought as the horror of the moment hit him. In his rage and haste to kill the demon, he'd inadvertently killed his daughter. Thirty feet up and with the force of the swinging tree behind her, she wasn't going to just fall to the floor, she was going to smash into it—and there was nothing he could do.

No, no, no, no, she doesn't deserve this. She doesn't. Please God, I am such a fool.

"*Bella!*" he screamed and ran toward her. If he could catch her, soften the fall, maybe she could survive. But time wasn't on his side. There was no way he could reach her before she made impact. She had already fallen over halfway and was hurtling toward the floor.

Sam's heart struggled to keep beating as he watched the inevitable sequence of events play out like a slow-motion movie before him. *I can't watch this. I can't.* But his gaze remained fixed on his beloved daughter as she plunged like a rag doll toward death.

A foot off the floor, Bella suddenly stopped and landed gently on her back as if she were being placed there by a giant unseen hand.

Shocked, Sam stood still for a moment as he tried to process what had happened.

She hadn't crashed? She hadn't crashed. But how?

He glanced around, half-expecting to see Hugo, who had helped them avoid death so much lately. But Bullet Man was nowhere to be seen.

He glanced at the demon. A broken tree branch impaled Abaddon through his lower back, sticking out through his abdomen, but the smoking hole in his chest that still burned with holy flames made Sam shake his head. The holy fire had cut right through the demon, like a righteous sword from God. But it hadn't been faith that created such a powerful blast, it had been rage and fear. The emotions still tingled through his body, making it hard to breathe steadily let alone walk.

Was this then the work of God?

Abaddon might be dead or at least cast back to Hell, but the cost was too high if doing so had killed Bella.

Sam staggered to where his daughter lay unmoving on the floor, with her eyes closed. Other people slowly joined him as if they, too, were stunned into disbelief.

"Bella," he whispered. He pressed two fingers to her neck, fearing what he might not find. She had a pulse. It was faint but steady. Her eyes remained closed as if she was unconscious. He touched her face, stroking her cheek softly. "Bella," he called louder. "Wake up, sweetheart." He touched the tourmaline shard on her necklace.

She gasped and sat up suddenly, knocking Sam onto his backside. Her eyes flashed open, the red glow unmistakable as she turned to him. *"Why didn't you listen?"* she shouted in a demonic voice far too deep for her age, let alone gender.

Everybody backed away, including Sam.

The sound of guns being cocked made him raise his hands. He glanced at the crowd surrounding them. "No! Don't shoot. She's my daughter," he pleaded.

"She's possessed," Agent Neptune pointed out.

"I know, but—"

"You should have listened," the demonic voice coming from Bella reverberated around the courtyard. Then she collapsed onto the floor and began coughing and crying.

Sam crawled to her and gathered her into his arms. Her eyes were back to normal blue and no longer red. "Daddy," she sobbed.

"I know, Bells. I'm here. I'm so sorry." His cheeks were wet—from his tears or hers, he wasn't sure and didn't care. He rocked her gently, grateful she was alive and seemed unharmed. Had Abaddon saved her from the fall by possessing her? That didn't make sense at all. The demon would normally have crushed her and laughed while dancing on her bones. Maybe it wasn't Abaddon? Or maybe he'd changed while growing with the baby inside Sarah.

Beneath the tree, a team of agents had gathered with Brother Trevor in his wheelchair. They studied the demon's unmoving body. "Is it dead?" Neptune asked.

"I don't think so," Brother Trevor said. "But who would know really? He's a demon. All this could be a trick. Let's put him in the Neutronic Ossuary," Trevor instructed. "Before anything else happens."

Neptune nodded and gestured for a sarcophagus-shaped metallic container on wheels to be brought over. As two other agents complied, she turned back to Trevor. "You must be feeling pretty happy. Two new playthings bagged in one day, oh, but Mother Agnes is gone. May the Lord rest her soul. You should thank Sam and his family for all they've done. We owe them a lot."

Trevor glanced at Sam and found him watching. "Yes, we do," he agreed. He gave Sam a nod.

Sam didn't return it. He watched as the demon's body was extracted from the tree branch and placed inside the container, which appeared to be lined with silver and had wires running along the inside. He didn't look away until the silver latches were clasped on the outside and a mechanical device on the top turned on. The Neutronic Ossuary, whatever it was, produced a humming sound as it was dragged away out of the courtyard.

"Sam?" Ricky called softly. He stood nearby with Penny and Pamela.

"Yeah?"

"Ready to go?"

"Hell, yeah." Every bone and muscle in his body ached as Sam got to his feet. He grabbed Bella by the hand and gave it a small squeeze. "Let's go find Sarah and your baby brother."

So much had happened in the past few days that Sam didn't know what to think about anything anymore except for two things.

He needed a stronger word than fuckdammit to describe the day.

And he wasn't going to stay any longer in the godforsaken base than he had to.

CHAPTER 22

Three days later, Sarah sat in a comfortable armchair in the living room of the residential quarters the church had allocated to them. It was the first time she'd been inside the home since arriving at the base just over a week ago. She hadn't done a full tour yet, as she and the baby had only just been released from the medical clinic under Doctor Stevens's express instructions not to push it. But the living room was brightly lit and quite spacious, not necessarily decorated to her tastes, but it would do—or it would have done if they'd decided to stay.

She glanced at the baby in her arms and smiled. For the first time in a long time, she hadn't had any nightmares, but now she had a new reason to wake up several times during the night and not get enough sleep. She gently stroked his perfect little nose with the tip of her finger. His eyes flicked open—*still not red, thank God*—and he yawned, making a sleepy gurgling sound. She couldn't stop staring at him or touching him and reveling in his absolute perfection. She also couldn't stop looking for things about him that might not be right, which was something she'd probably do for the rest of her life. He didn't show any signs of the complications normally associated with being born premature. Looking at him, no one would ever know he'd been born nearly two months early. It was a miracle he'd been born without any problems, especially considering he'd shared her uterus with a demon for the past seven months. *It was a miracle he'd been born at all*, she reminded herself. *Count your blessings and move on.*

The scent of fresh baking filled the room a moment before Ena and Bella entered from the kitchen, carrying plates and cutlery.

"Mom, did you bake cookies?" Sarah breathed in deeply, enjoying the scent of Christmas shortbread, which she remembered from her own childhood.

Her mother smiled and placed a plate loaded with tree-shaped cookies decorated with a glaze of frosting and green sprinkles on the coffee table. "Oh, well, we've been busy doing all kinds of things while you've been resting, haven't we, Bella?" Ena winked at the girl, who nodded almost shyly.

I'll say, Sarah thought. A small Christmas tree stood in the corner of the room with a pile of presents stacked beneath it.

Bella placed the cutlery and napkins she was holding on the table and scooted around to sit on the carpeted floor near Sarah's legs and studied the baby.

"He's so little," she said softly, peering at his face over the edge of the blanket he was wrapped in.

"Do you want to hold him?" Sarah asked.

Bella looked at her for a moment, then nodded enthusiastically.

Sarah leaned forward in her chair to hand her daughter the baby and winced. The discomfort in her abdomen from the C-section was something that would go away soon, she hoped. But who knew that stomach muscles were used so much? Walking wasn't so bad, but trying to get up from sitting in a chair or, heaven help her, out of bed—that was insane.

"Let me help," Ena said. She bent down and lifted the baby gently from the pillow resting on Sarah's lap and handed him to Bella. "Hold him in your arms like this. That's right. Now, watch his head. He can't lift it yet. Very good. See? You've got it. It's easy when you know."

Bella grinned from ear to ear, her eyes shining as she looked down at the cooing baby in her arms and at Sarah. "I can't wait until he's bigger and we can play."

Warmth spread through Sarah's chest, and she let out her breath. This right here should be all the proof she needed to know the baby was okay and nothing lingered in the shadows waiting to pounce. If Bella wanted to hold the baby and was no longer nervous about the child, there was nothing to be afraid of except the normal surprises life might provide. Right? Due to all the rest she'd needed after the birth, she had no idea if Bella had held the baby before now, but she didn't think so. Still, there was a small part of her that remained troubled.

Sam had filled her in on a lot of the stuff that had gone on while she'd been out of action and separated from them all, including the tree incident and how Bella had fallen and been possessed briefly by Abaddon, which, in an unexpected twist, appeared to have saved her life. If Bella remembered any of that happening, she didn't show it. As for Sarah, what went on while under the influence of a demon was a dim shadow at best.

The sound of footsteps coming from the kitchen made her glance up as Sam, Ricky, and Penny entered the room.

Sam carried a glass punch bowl filled with a yellow liquid and placed it on the table beside the cookies. "Here we go. How about that? Homemade eggnog." He did a flourish with his hands and looked around the room expectantly.

Sarah arched a brow at him. "You made that?" she asked, wondering if they needed to make a preemptive call to the medical clinic. When Sam had been a priest, the parish ladies had done most of his cooking. Not that he hadn't made an effort to learn a thing or two since leaving the 'hood' as he liked to call it, but some people were best not allowed near a kitchen.

He looked put out as he sat on the armrest of her chair and wrapped his arm around her shoulders. "No, Ricky did. You're all safe." He grinned.

Ricky set some punch glasses on the table, and Penny left a plate of various cheeses and crackers.

The rock star grabbed a cookie off the plate and sat down with Penny on the available couch across from Sarah. He bit into the cookie and closed his eyes, making a look of pleasure as he chewed. Opening them again, he nodded at Ena, who sat in a rocking chair beside a faux window that had been built into the wall. "Can you be my grandma? These are *goood*." He leaned forward and handed Penny a cookie on a napkin. "Try one. I'm not kidding. They're really good."

Ena laughed. "You're always welcome to visit, Ricky."

"Does he have a name yet?" Penny asked, biting delicately into her cookie as she admired the baby wriggling in Bella's arms.

Sarah exchanged a glance with Sam. He smiled and nodded at her to go ahead. "Well, we talked it over as a family, and we've settled on... Richard Paul Morris."

"Richard?" the rock star said, sounding surprised. "Aww, poor kid. He's gonna get teased at school for being a little dick. Know how long I fought for Ricky as my nickname instead?" He laughed.

"Well, Richard is the name of Bella's favorite rock star," Sam explained. "And Paul is for Sarah's friend Paulie, who died last year at the mall." His gaze met Ricky's.

"Oh..." Ricky turned three shades of red. "Oh... that's... oh gosh, I'm honored. I really am. You guys are like family to me, you know? But I didn't think..." He pulled his fingers through his shaggy hair and sucked in a long breath. Then he leaned forward and pointed at the baby. "I didn't mean the thing about being a dick, little dude. Forget I said that. Richard is a cool name."

"Okay, let's get Morris family Christmas 1986 underway," Sam said, clapping his hands together. "A couple days late, but hey... we're doing better than last year."

Sarah laughed softly. "Last year was a great Christmas. What are you talking about?" Despite the demon uprising that had killed a lot of people, including Bella's mother, and caused lasting trauma, it had been a fun time. They'd celebrated a week later, but it had been worth it. "I loved the gift you gave me." *As well as the gift I gave him.*

Sam arched a brow at her knowingly. "Why, Mrs. Morris... I'd be happy to give you that gift again." He leaned down and planted a quick kiss on her forehead. "And again..." He moved down to her cheek and kissed it. "And again..." he whispered on her lips a second before he planted a solid kiss that lingered with the promise of everything she'd missed in the past six months since the doctor had told her no vigorous physical activity.

"Oh, eww. Get a room," Bella said, looking embarrassed.

Sam laughed and pulled away, leaving Sarah to fan herself as heat rose to her face. *Holy Jesus.* How many weeks had the doctor said they'd need to wait before resuming 'normal marital relations'?

"Bella, you play Santa and give out the gifts," Sam said.

She nodded eagerly. "Okay."

Sam took the baby from her and placed him on his shoulder, holding his head and tucking him close as if he were already an expert. He turned, caught Sarah watching him, and gave her a wink.

Okay, you can stop it anytime now, Mr. Sexy.

Bella pulled the presents from under the tree one by one, reading out the names on the tags. "Baby Morris, Baby Morris, Baby Morris... oh, me!"

She ripped the paper off the rectangular box and gasped when she saw what was underneath. Mouth open in shock, she lifted the box for everyone to see.

"What's that?" Ena asked, peering at it across the room and lowering her reading glasses.

"It's called a camcorder," Ricky said. "All the cool kids have them." He smiled at Bella. "Happy Christmas, Silver Bell."

"Oh, Ricky, you shouldn't have," Sarah said. "Those are so expensive."

He shrugged. "Well, I figured, new baby and all, it might come in handy. Home movies are good, right?" He waved his hands indifferently and steepled his fingers together as he leaned his elbows on his knees. "Besides, I thought that Bella could use a cool new hobby. Get some of that crazy energy out." He reached over and tousled her hair. "You like it, right?"

"*I love it,*" she shrieked and wrapped her arms around him, giving him a tight hug.

"Good," he said and closed his eyes for a second, hugging her back.

Sarah studied the rock star. He always had an unassuming air about him, like he didn't really care about anybody or anything except trying to be cool, pick up hot chicks, and party. He'd probably met hundreds of stars and visited more exotic resorts than Sarah could ever dream of. But beneath the veneer of rock star success lived a lonely man who longed to belong somewhere.

She thought back to what he'd said a few moments ago. *"You guys are like family to me, you know?"* Did he have any of his own? Clearly not his father, which had been an estranged relationship at best from her understanding. But what about a mother? Sister? Brother? He never mentioned anyone.

"Ricky," she asked as Bella continued sorting presents into piles and opening ones marked for her.

The rock star glanced at Sarah.

"What are you planning to do next?" she asked.

He raised his brows and glanced at Penny. "Well, the record company has found me a new manager, would you believe? They say he's asking for a huge salary. We're leaving tomorrow. Agent Barnes is going to drive us to Las Vegas airport himself."

Sam raised his brows. "You said us."

Ricky nodded. "Penny's coming with me. She said I could do with her help, and she can't keep her hands off of me," he teased her, giving her a playful sideways shove on the couch.

The sister laughed. "I think that might be the other way around." She darted a kiss to his mouth and grinned.

Sam nodded, seeming pleased. "I'm surprised the Church of the New World Order is so willing to let another person go."

"Yeah, I heard you're leaving too," Penny said.

"We… can't stay here," Sarah said. She'd never been more adamant about anything in her life. "This is no place to bring up children." She couldn't wait to leave, to be honest. Every breath she took in the place felt as if she were dying.

"Yep, but I'll still be with the church," Sam said. "They… won't let me go completely. But I'll be working for them from a nice, quiet spot in Manitou Springs, Colorado. Sarah is going to get her chopper license and work for local rescue crews, but be ready to fly me where I'm needed in case of a demon sighting. The house we're getting even has a guesthouse for Ena."

Ricky appeared impressed. "Awesome."

"Why don't you come with us," Sarah suggested after a pause. "Cindy and Barry live there. You know, Barry with the axes?" She made axe-throwing motions with her hands, remembering how Barry had helped take down Abaddon during the mall crisis.

Ricky chuckled. "Who can forget an axe-throwing Scotsman in a kilt?"

"Good point." Sam smiled. "Barry runs an axe-throwing club in the tourist area of the town. It's becoming quite popular, apparently. Anyway, I called them on Christmas Day to wish them a Merry Christmas, and while we were talking, they suggested we move there. So... we are." He studied the rock star. "Sarah's right. Come with us. It's not that far from LA, is it? You can still do business and live in a quiet place with friends."

Not friends, Sarah thought, shaking her head inwardly. *Family.*

Ricky looked uncomfortable. "Well, I guess it's possible, maybe."

"Please, Ricky, please, please, please..." Bella whined as she hugged his legs. "I want you to come with us." She batted her blue eyes at him and smiled.

Oh, dear God. That child has a strong career in theater ahead, if nothing else, Sarah thought.

Ricky rolled his eyes at Bella and groaned. "You are persistent. I'll give you that." He glanced at Penny. "What do you think?"

She shrugged. "I'm in. Sounds good to me. Think of it this way," Penny said, smiling. "No penthouse elevators."

Sam and Bella joined Ricky in laughing along with Penny. Sarah didn't know all the details of what they were talking about but understood enough to know that the elevator ride to Ricky's penthouse hotel suite in Vegas had been a near-fatal disaster.

"Good point," Ricky said, still chuckling. "Okay..." He wiped his face with his hand and glanced around the room of faces watching him. "Let's do it."

"*Yes!*" Bella shouted, jumping to her feet. "Yes, yes, yes. This is the *best Christmas ever*," she announced.

The baby awoke and started crying.

"Uh-oh." Sam bounced the baby in his arms, trying to soothe him back to sleep, but it became pretty obvious that little Rick wasn't having any of that as the child's screams grew louder. "Let's give you back to Mommy," Sam said.

"He's probably hungry. He's always hungry," she said. "You are, aren't you, you little monster." Grabbing a towel from beside the chair, she draped it over her shoulder for privacy and gave the baby what he needed.

They continued to open gifts, which included a christening outfit from Ena for the baby. He'd already been baptized—Sam had made sure of that on the day he'd been born. But a second christening wouldn't hurt, especially now his name had been officially announced. Supper in the form of a turkey dinner arrived, complete with all the trimmings, along with an assurance by the church kitchen that no sedatives had been added, something which Ena seemed peculiarly concerned about.

Then, hours later, when Bella had gone to bed and the baby was asleep in a bassinet near Sarah, the adults sat together quietly sipping eggnog, or in Ricky's case, an ice-cold beer.

"You made this stuff, and you don't even like it?" Sam said to him, raising his glass. The eggnog didn't have any alcohol in it on account of Sarah and Bella, but Sam had topped up his own glass with some extra Christmas cheer, as he'd called it.

Ricky shrugged. "I don't get the chance to cook for people often."

"Well, that's all changed now, right?" Penny said. She snuggled into him and held his hand.

Ricky nodded and kissed the top of her head.

Sarah had no idea if that relationship would last, but it was nice to see them both happy for now. She put her empty glass of eggnog on the accent table beside her and glanced at her mother and Sam. "I know I've probably said and done some things that were not very nice over the last few months, especially recently," she began.

"Oh, Sarah, you don't—" Ena began.

She waved her hand at her mother, cutting her off. "No, please. Let me finish."

Ena nodded reluctantly and sat back in her chair.

"It's just… it's hard to explain," Sarah said. "It's terrifying if you think about it. This thing, growing inside you, making you think and say and do terrible things." She grabbed Sam's hand as the tears began to gather. "I wouldn't want to ever hurt you. Not any of you. I love you—" The tears became uncontrollable, and the dam broke. "I'm sorry," she managed between sobs. "This happens a lot." She pointed at the tears running down her face and warping her vision.

"It's hormones, Sarah. You've just had a baby," Ena explained gently.

Hormones or not, it was damn annoying.

"It's okay, baby." Sam pulled her close. "I'm the one who's sorry. I should have been here, and I wasn't. I should have paid attention, and I didn't."

"No." She shook her head and pushed him away so she could see his face. "It's this place and these people and that demon. They're all horrible. I can't wait to leave." They didn't know what it had been like, trapped in that room, hour after hour, with people always skirting around the truth and a demon whispering dark things, until she couldn't even trust herself anymore.

"We're leaving as soon as we can." Sam rocked her gently in silence, and after a few moments, the storm subsided, and the tears stopped.

Sarah dabbed at her eyes with a tissue. "Do you think he's okay?" she asked softly, looking at the baby.

"Yes," Sam whispered. "He's perfect."

"It grew in me, and I didn't know it was there." She wet her lips as she pursed them together. "I mean... is it possible to gestate with a demon growing inside you and not get affected by it?"

The room fell silent as they all watched the baby sleeping peacefully in the bassinet.

"Let's focus on the good things, huh?" Ena suggested. "You have a healthy baby boy. A beautiful, smart, and willful daughter." Ena smiled. "A handsome husband who loves you so very much." She brushed Sarah's face with her palm. "Isn't that enough?"

It should be, it really should be, but there was a tiny corner inside Sarah, probably the one that the demon had hidden in, that couldn't let go of the fear that happiness belonged to other people and her life was meant to be a series of disasters strung together by moments of peace.

"But Abaddon? Is he *really* gone this time?" She glanced around at the others.

They stared back at her in uncomfortable silence.

That was a question they had no answer to.

ONE WEEK LATER, SAM and Ricky stood beside Agent Neptune outside Sam's brand-new Roadmaster campervan on the edge of a dirt road, one of a few they needed to drive on before reaching the first highway that would take them east to Colorado. The camper had been a gift from the agency on account of all the hardships they'd endured. The church had also bought the house and paid all the moving expenses, including buying new furniture. *Can you say buy out?* Sam thought. Sarah had considered it a way to ensure the base wasn't sued, but Sam preferred to consider it a retention of services bribe. Either way, they were out of there and on their way now.

A black, windowless van had dropped them off at the camper—with a lot fewer guns pointed at them this time. Even during the chopper flight back from Vegas to the base they'd been blindfolded, so Sam still didn't know his way into the base. Not that he intended to ever go back there again.

Sarah, the kids, Ena, and Penny were already loaded up inside. His old station wagon was attached to the hitch on the back. They were ready to roll, and all that was left were last goodbyes.

"He was different, though," Ricky was saying. "Abaddon, I mean. The whole thing was just... weird."

"Well, he's gone now, right?" Sam turned to Neptune. Whatever had happened to the demon, he didn't really care as long as he didn't ever bother him or his family again. But he knew what Ricky was saying. The demon had seemed weird. He hadn't tried to kill them using his usual torturous means. In fact, he'd saved Bella, whether inadvertently or not.

"Yes, we'll keep his body contained. Just like Rathburn. No way are they getting out again." Neptune paused. "The Neutronic Ossuary has been something we've been working on for a while. It works like a portable Vessel, so you don't have to keep a demon contained inside a person anymore."

"That's handy," Sam said, genuinely impressed.

"What do you think he was trying to tell us?" Ricky asked. "He kept trying to talk, but nobody wanted to listen."

"Lies," Neptune said. "That's all demons do. They tell lies."

Sam couldn't disagree with that. "Has Brother Trevor accepted the position as leader of the church with Agnes gone?" It didn't sit right that she was dead. She hadn't deserved it. Not that people needed to deserve it to die, but still. Of all the people in the operating room for Abaddon to choose, why her?

"No. He's turned it down, actually." At Sam's raised eyebrows, she added, "I know. Surprised me, too. I thought he'd been gunning for that spot for years. But he claims he prefers to do God's work in the shadows." She shrugged. "I'm not sure who is next on the list, but I'm sure it will be decided soon."

Her radio squawked, so she answered it by pressing a finger to her earpiece. She nodded and then said, "Go, Jupiter. You're on speaker."

"Hi, Sam. Ricky. Just wanted you to know we've heard from Pamela's grandparents, and they report she's settling in fine with them. They've okayed us to give Bella their address so the kids can write to each other."

"Bella will like that. Thank you, sir." Sam still felt that Jupiter was a condescending prick, but that was someone else's problem now.

"I want to thank you both for what you did in Vegas. As much as I wish you'd stay here at the base, Sam, I understand this is no place for a family to live. But if you get the call, you better make sure you answer."

Sam had no doubt the head agent could find him wherever he went, and he planned on being available for the church should they need him to kick some demon ass. "You have my word, Jupiter. By the way, can I ask what your real name is?"

"Sure, you can ask. But I'm not going to answer. Take care, Father Sam, and please know you're welcome back anytime. Good luck, Ricky."

"Thank you, sir." The call ended.

"Jupiter never found Hugo, did he?" Sam asked Neptune.

The agent laughed. "No. But he's probably still going to look. Can you say obsessed, much?" She shook her head. "Don't worry. That bullet guy can take care of himself. He's been doing it for a long time, I think."

"I'm sure you're right." Sam shook hands with Neptune, pleased to hear the remnant was still out there and had evaded Jupiter so far. "Did you know that of all the planets in the solar system, I always liked Neptune the best." It was true, though probably not in the way it sounded after he'd said it.

She rolled her eyes and shook her head. "Get out of here, Father. We'll see you around." Neptune stepped back out of the shadow of the van and shielded her eyes from the late afternoon sun.

"Not too soon, I hope," Sam said.

She grinned and turned away, walking toward the black van.

"Okay," Sam said to Ricky. "Let's get the fuck out of here."

"Already on it," Ricky answered, grinning. He climbed up the steps and into the camper.

Sam took one last look before he followed. It was time to leave this place behind and get on with his new life with Sarah, Bella, baby Richard, and Ena. The loss of Mother Agnes still cut deep. Despite Sarah's misgivings about the nun, he'd found the elderly woman kindly and truthful.

He'd thought it would be a new start for them all, living in the church compound—that he'd been doing God's will by bringing his family here—but, instead, it had nearly cost them their lives. Maybe he hadn't listened hard enough to what God was saying, but if not, what did that mean?

The lengthening shadow of a tall cactus caught his eye. The three prongs of the stem looked almost human in the way the shadow spread across the scrub and sand. Two arms and a body. Faceless. Dark. Beckoning.

Sam shivered and went inside. "Fucking Nevada," he muttered.

Hugo sat atop a small, flat-topped butte, watching the camper drive east into the deepening nightfall. He was glad to see the family had made it out okay and escaped the base. The little girl seemed especially bright. It would have been a shame if she'd been added to the growing collection of experiments inside that awful place.

Judging by how the base wasn't a smoldering crater in the ground, he assumed Rathburn remained safely contained. How long that would last was anyone's guess, but for now, he hoped it gave the demonic remnant peace from the endless torment of not dying.

At least he hadn't had to enter the fucked-up place and intervene.

Just the thought of Area 51 filled him with dread. He had no intention of ever becoming part of their collection of oddities or their team. Which did the idiot agent chasing him want him to be? Both, probably.

He hated the agents.

He hated most people most of the time.

Which made it dificult to do his job at times.

But he always had to do what his master said.

He rose from the butte and set off east, away from the setting sun, following the camper.

Epilogue

Thanksgiving Day

November 23rd, 1989

Area 51

THE DOOR TO BROTHER Trevor's office door flew inward, making him pause for a second as he slipped his jacket on. Wasn't everyone supposed to be at prayer? He turned toward the intruder and scowled.

Sister Harriet stood in the doorframe, puffing and panting like she'd run a marathon to get there. "Hey, there's some serious stuff going on that you need to—" She stared at him, eyes wide and jaw slack. "Oh my God!"

Oh my God, indeed. Brother Trevor forced a smile and continued to slip his jacket on. "You know, you really should learn to knock." He wore a communication device similar to what the agents did and pressed the earpiece, signaling the team that he was ready.

Sister Harriet stuttered. "Y-y-you're standing up?" Pointing a trembling finger at him, she backed out the door. "How is this possible?"

"Hallelujah, it's a miracle." Trevor waved his hands beside his head, mimicking a faith healer, and grinned. "The good Lord has seen to it that I can use my legs again." *You never know. She might believe it.* She was a stupid enough cow, like most of the faithful in the compound.

Sister Harriet froze, shaking her head. "What? Y-y-you're lying, aren't you?"

Oh bravo. Maybe she wasn't so stupid after all.

She backed up another step as the realization hit. "You've been lying to us all along."

Lying was such a subjective term. Subterfuge was part of his job.

Trevor glanced at his watch. "I'd love to have a long conversation about this with you, but time is of the essence. Goodbye, Sister Harriet." He really did not have time to dawdle.

Pulling his hand and the gun from his pocket, he fired the pistol once, shooting her between the eyes.

She slumped to the floor, unmoving, a trail of blood dripping down her forehead. "Don't worry. I'm sure God has a use for you in the afterlife," Trevor said. Which meant she was already well ahead of the role she'd served in life. *Useless woman.*

Trevor put the weapon back in his pocket and grabbed his suitcase. "Wipe all of the computers' hard drives," he called into his microphone. "And meet me at the rendezvous point. Shoot anyone who gets in your way and hide the body."

"Copy that, sir. All targets have been eliminated in the systems room. Video has been erased. Ready to make our way to the second vehicle."

"Excellent work. Cut all communications from this moment forward unless anything comes up that is a cause for concern. Over and out."

Brother Trevor moved the body of Sister Harriet into his room, clearing the path for his wheelchair, and departed his office. Not much he could do about the blood on the floor. Agents would be there at any moment after detecting the shot being fired, so he needed to move fast now.

He wheeled his chair quickly through the hallways and access doors, passing anyone who saw him and greeting them with a smile and nod. It was a routine he'd perfected over the years, the bland, happy smile and dull nod of acknowledgment.

Upon reaching Parking Lot A, he made his way to a black, refrigerated van. The cold, metal container that held the remnant, Wrath, was already loaded into the back. A soldier waited for him on the passenger side of the van.

Trevor presented him with the suitcase. "Agent Ceres forgot to grab his suitcase and left it in my office. Would you be so kind to give it to him? He's in the team two van by the door."

"Sure, sir."

Brother Trevor wheeled around to the driver's side, where a soldier sat in the truck with the door open.

"Do you need some help getting in, sir," the soldier asked.

Trevor shook his head. "I just want to take one last look before we leave."

"Whatever you wish, sir." The soldier turned the key in the truck's ignition. The vehicle idled while Brother Trevor waited a couple of minutes. "Sir, we should probably get mov—"

An explosion boomed through the parking lot, and the van Agent Ceres was in was obliterated in the process. Shards of metal, glass, and concrete flew through the air, landing on other vehicles and setting off car alarms. *That should keep them busy for a while.* Brother Trevor grinned. *Goodbye, team two. Now you know what you were hired for.* Their sole purpose had been distraction.

"Sir?" his driver asked impatiently. "Shouldn't we go now?"

I'm sick of being called fucking sir, Trevor thought.

He withdrew his pistol and shot the soldier in the head. *Yes, now it was most definitely time to get going.* He stood up, tossed the dead soldier out of the seat, kicked the wheelchair aside, and climbed into the cab. In less than twenty seconds, he was out of the parking lot and racing down the road. "Time to begin the two-and-a-half thousand-mile journey," he said to himself, but New York always looked magical in the winter. The journey was worth it.

The first truck swap would be on the base's perimeter, where more people would undoubtedly die when the bomb, which he'd timed to go off at precisely the right moment, took out the sentry box.

It would be a while before he could stop at a payphone and check in with the others to see how their part of the plan was progressing. But springing Wrath from the icy prison was the most important part anyway. Remarkably easy, too. Not that he'd expected anything different. Still, there was no turning back now, something he couldn't help feeling both relieved and excited about.

He loaded a cassette into the van's tape deck, and Talking Heads' "Road to Nowhere" played through the speakers.

"Cheers to the end of everything," he whispered and blew a kiss with his fingers to the world at large.

The End of Everything begins on April 12th 2024 when a priest, a rock star, and the four horsemen of the apocalypse walk into New York City... and then the apocalypse *really* begins.

Mall Priest 3 – The End of Everything

https://books2read.com/Mall-Priest3

www. LegacyHunter.space

At KC Stories we have many books and many genres to thrill you, romance you, or take you away to another reality (or even all three at once).

You can find our full catalogue of books at www.LegacyHunter.space

Acknowledgements

Mall Priest was originally going to be a single book, but as we reached the end of writing it, we weren't ready to say goodbye to the characters, and neither were many readers who reached out to us, asking for more. So here we are with Mall Priest 2, and in April 2024, the story will come to an end in Mall Priest 3. Although the writing is credited to us, Chris and Kate, it all started with a spark, and continues with Kate's son, Alex, feeding us more juicy plot ideas and crazy story ideas. Of course, crazy stories are what we love to write.

We'd like to thank our supportive families. To Chris's wife Glenda, and his three wonderful children, Ethan, Krystal and Siobhan, as well as Kate's husband Mike, and son Alex, we appreciate all the support and words of encouragement, as well as understanding the need for us to keep writing these stories together.

Behind every book we write, we have our amazing team of editors at Swish Editing, namely Kaylene, Katie and Nicole. Special thanks to you for the professional work you do and the friendly manner in which you provide your service. What you do for our books is enormously appreciated, and here's to having you on our team for many more books.

We'd also like to thank our ever-loyal readers, from those who have known us since our earlier works, to those who have recently discovered us. Your feedback and support enable us to continue our writing journey, and many of you have become friends over time. But we do need to highlight the efforts of two particular readers who find the time in this busy world to Beta read for us, Cathy Dione, and Katherine Robinson.

And of course, a very special thank-you to Alexander Reed for trusting us with his ideas and fleshing them into another story. We hope our words have done your vision justice.

While KC Stories has released 16 books so far, including our solo works, we're just getting started, and intend to continue to write our stories for many years to come. So please, if you're reading this, feel free to reach out and keep in touch, and if you loved this story or any of our others, please consider writing a review at the vendor of your choice.

Email: kcbooks@legacyhunter.space
Website: http://www.legacyhunter.space/
Newsletter: http://subscribepage.com/kcstories

About the Authors

Chris Heinicke

Although working as a baker for many years, writing has been a passion for Chris for some time, starting in high school and reigniting again in 2006, when he first got the inspiration to begin writing 'The Man In Black.' After completing that project eight years later, he took part in NaNoWriMo in November 2014, culminating into a project named 5PM. Deciding to self-publish, 5PM came out in February 2015, and then The Man In Black in August.

2016 saw the release of 7PM, and in that same year, his writing path met with that of Canadian author Kate Reedwood. A mutual respect of each other's work ignited an interest in working together, creating the Legacy Hunter series, the first of which to come out in July 2017.

Apart from writing, Chris enjoys travelling, reading, watching movies and all things geeky. He resides in Coffs Harbour with his wife and three children.

Follow Chris:

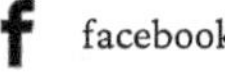 facebook.com/ChrisHeinickeWriter

 instagram.com/heinickewriter/

Kate Reedwood

Kate Reedwood, also known as Felicity Kates, is a mild-mannered manager by day. At night, she trades in her high heels for bunny slippers and lets her imagination run wild.

A trained artist and writer, Kate enjoys writing stories that combine humor with strong characters who know what they want and aren't afraid to go get it. Every story is an emotional journey where the characters must struggle to find their happily ever after. But they do always reach it in the end, no matter the time or place in the universe.

She lives off of coffee and dreams and enjoys going for walks along the shores of Lake Ontario, taking pictures of whatever catches her eye. A romantic at heart, she loves to snuggle under a blanket with a good book to warm up the cold Canadian winters.

When not dreaming up new worlds and books to write with Australian author Chris Heinicke, she can most often be found enjoying the quiet company of her husband and son.

Follow Kate:

 facebook.com/KateReedwood

 instagram.com/katereedwood/

 bookbub.com/profile/k-reedwood

Connect with Us

Follow KC Stories

www.facebook.com/profile.php?id=100088968561532

instagram.com/kc_stories_books/

tiktok.com/@kc_stories_

https://subscribepage.com/kcstories

https://www.facebook.com/groups/812276449059713/

EMAIL: KCBooks@LegacyHunter.space

SNAIL MAIL:

KC Stories Canada

203-80 Speers Road,

Oakville, ON L6K2E6 CANADA

KC Stories Australia

49 Combine Street

Coffs Harbour, NSW 2450 AUSTRALIA

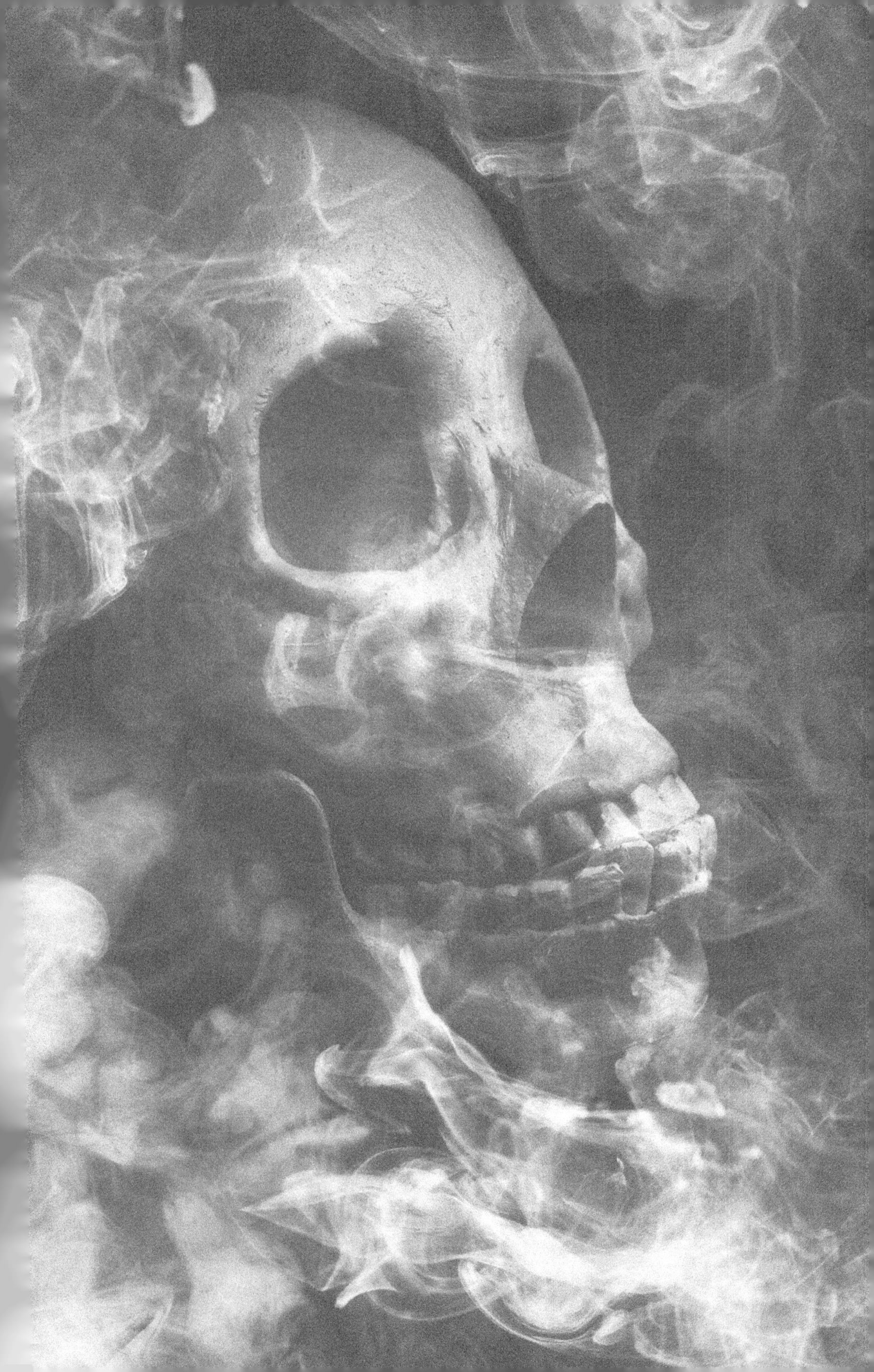